STEPHEN LEIGH

A FADING SUN

Book One of *The Sunpath Cycle*

DAW BOOKS, INC.

DONALD A. WOLLHEIM, FOUNDER

375 Hudson Street, New York, NY 10014

ELIZABETH R. WOLLHEIM
SHEILA E. GILBERT
PUBLISHERS

www.dawbooks.com

First printing, July 2017
1   2   3   4   5   6   7   8   9

DAW TRADEMARK REGISTERED
U.S. PAT. AND TM. OFF. AND FOREIGN COUNTRIES
—MARCA REGISTRADA
HECHO EN U.S.A.

PRINTED IN THE U.S.A.

This book is dedicated to Sharon Leigh, whose fierce dedication to the care of our mother speaks volumes about her dedication to family.

And, as always and ever, to Denise, whose support is what makes all of my books possible.

Table of Contents

Part Three: Albann Deas

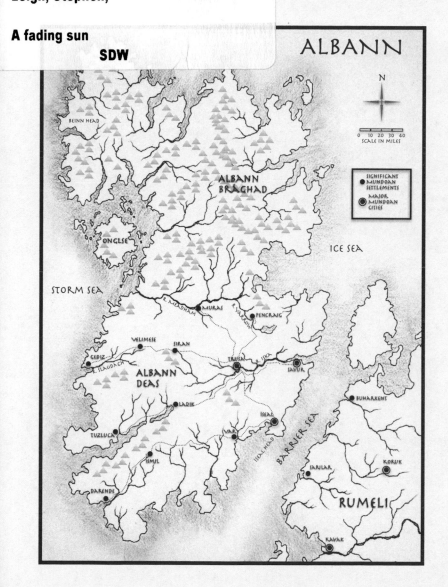

ALBANN

N

0 10 20 30 40
SCALE IN MILES

SIGNIFICANT
MUNDOAN
SETTLEMENTS
MAJOR
MUNDOAN
CITIES

BEINN HEAD

ALBANN
BRAGHAD

ONGLSE

ICE SEA

STORM SEA

R. MEADHAM   MURAI   R. YARGIN   PENCRAIG

VELIMESE   SIRAN

GEDIZ
R. TLAUDACH   ALBANN   TRUEA   R. ITKA
DEAS   SAVUR

LADIK   BUHARKENT

ISEAE

TUZLUCA   VAR
ITEAL HEAD   BARRIER SEA

ISMIL

DARENDE   SANLAR   KORUK

RUMELI

KAVAK

The Ghost's Opening Soliloquy

WE KNEW OUR NAMES ONCE. We were called . . . We were called . . .

No, those names are hard to catch and hold, like a school of silver minnows fleeing through the shallows of the river. Even that of The Strongest and Oldest, who lives in the deepest part of us. A school of silver minnows. . . . Strange—we can still remember seeing that, our bare feet visible for a moment through the clear, frigid water before they were wrapped in the streamers of mud stirred from the pebbled bottom, and through it all the metallic flash of the minnows' scales as they evaded our scooping bucket.

So long ago.

We remember that, and we remember other times and other lives as well, but our names, things that are so much a part of us that we should hold on to them forever . . .

They are lost. As we are. We've been too long away.

We hear so many thoughts, so many voices inside, and they can't all be ours, can they? We see the world only as through a sheer cloth, with everything obscured and blurred. We set out searching when the last of us died. We were pulled here.

Now we see you, and we see your mouth moving as if you are talking to us, but your voice is buried amongst all the others in our head, and we don't know what you're saying to us. We can't hear you.

All we know is that we shouldn't be *here*. In this place. Not if we want to remember. Not if we want you to become part of us.

You shouldn't be here either.

We should be *there*. All of us. *There*.

PART ONE

PENCRAIG

1

The Wraith in the Shadows

THE PROBLEM WITH GHOSTS is that they don't quite realize they're dead.

Voada entered the Temple of Pashtuk, glaring at the muddy tracks of feet on the stone flags, and it was then that she realized she wasn't alone. The ceramic bust of Emperor Pashtuk was illuminated by the sun slanting down from the open roof above the altar in the middle of the room. The pair of east-facing open windows also allowed in shafts of dust-speckled light, creating heavy shadows around the remainder of the circular room.

Once, the temple had been dedicated not to Emperor Pashtuk but to Elia.

Voada noticed the ghost—what her own people, the Cateni, would call a *taibhse*—as a shimmering, nearly transparent presence in the shadows; when it passed through sunlight, the apparition vanished entirely. It paced the room's perimeter, as if it could not bear to keep still. But this one . . . it was entirely unlike any taibhse Voada had ever seen before. Voada first thought the wraith a woman, though the face shifted and changed in the light and sometimes seemed male. All the ghosts she'd seen before had looked like the people whose bodies they'd inhabited before death. But this one . . . It seemed to be not one soul but many.

And before, Voada had always been able to hear the taibhse's voice as well, but not with this one. Its eyes were always on Voada, and its mouth moved as if it were trying to speak to her. Voada almost imagined that she could hear sibilant words, but that might have been the wind that tossed the leaves outside the temple. Voada set down the heavy wooden bucket of water and rags with a grateful sigh as water sloshed over the leather of her boots. She rubbed at her back to ease the kink there, the ache that had been present ever since the birth of her second child, her son, a decade ago now.

When the ghost passed near her, Voada reached out to it and felt a winter cold as her hand passed through its body. The ghost stared at her, its features dim and difficult to read. "Who are you?" Voada asked the ghost. "I've helped others trapped like you before. How can I help you?"

The creature only gave a doleful shake of its head and continued pacing the room.

The temple had been built by Cateni two centuries ago for Elia, the goddess whose visage was the sun. Voada's great-grandparents and their family had served Elia as *draoi*: those who could wield the magic of Elia and the sun-paths that coalesced here in the building, if the old tales could be believed. They'd also been *menach*, the clerics of Elia. The sun-paths were still marked on the floor: pale tiles set against the darker marble in two diagonal lines that crossed where the altar sat and ended at the four great windows that framed the solstice suns at dawn and sunset.

But those days were dust and legend since the arrival of the Mundoa, and the statue of Elia that had once graced the altar had been hidden by Voada's grandparents because they knew that the Mundoa would simply smash the figure and melt down its golden crown. Voada knew where Elia's statue was buried; her grandparents had told her mother, and she had told Voada.

To Voada, this was still as much Elia's temple as Pashtuk's, despite Emperor Pashtuk's dour and serious image replacing that of

Elia. Voada had to admit that the Mundoan sculptors were superior to those of the Cateni. One could almost imagine Pashtuk's eyes blinking or his mouth opening, but for now he only stared blindly at Voada and the ghost.

"I can show you the sun-path," Voada said to the taibhse, pitching her voice so that it echoed in the round chamber, shimmering as the words rebounded from the curve of the roof. "You can still find it. I've shown others."

The ghost seemed to wail silently at that, its mouth open in an "O" that mimicked the central opening in the temple's roof, and Voada saw its head shake violently. It pointed emphatically northward, not to the solstice windows or the sun-paths that led to the plane of the Cateni gods when this had been Elia's place of worship.

The absent gods, now. The forgotten gods, for most. The forbidden gods.

"I don't know what you want if you won't follow the sun-path," Voada said. "I wish I could talk to you. I wish you could hear me. Perhaps my *seanmhair* Ailis could have done that. She knew the spells . . ."

In answer, the ghost pointed northward again, imperiously, then continued its pacing. Voada watched it, then sighed. She knelt down alongside the bucket of water and wrung out one of the rags. She began scrubbing the stone flags around the altar, marveling at the hollows worn into the golden-brown stones by generations of feet. The ghost watched her, still restless.

When Voada had finished her task a few candle-stripes later, she put the rags back in the twice-refilled bucket and stood, groaning and rubbing at her knees. The ghost had stopped and was standing directly in front of her. Voada could see the temple doors through its body, as if she were peering through a thin morning fog. The features hovering in front of her remained indistinct and genderless. "I'm leaving now," she told it. "I'm sorry. I wish you would let me help you."

Once more, the ghost lifted a pale arm and pointed northward. Voada hefted the bucket; as she did so, she saw movement at the door, blurred by the ghost. "Voada?" a deep voice called.

8   STEPHEN LEIGH

"Meir," she answered. "Sorry. I was just getting ready to leave." She took a step toward her husband, shivering as she passed near the ghost's frigid presence. Older than she was by decades, Meir's hair was now largely silver-white with his scalp gleaming through the thin strands at the top and back of his head. His breathing after climbing the hill to the temple was harsh and loud, as it was too often lately whenever he exerted himself. Even a short walk seemed to exhaust him now.

Meir wore Mundoan clothing: loose pantaloons and a vest dyed the rich blue of an administrator, as befitted his role as the Hand of Pencraig, with a simple white linen tunic underneath. Voada noticed that the servants hadn't properly polished his boots that morning—there were still traces of mud from yesterday's rain. Voada was wearing clothing that her grandparents would have found familiar, in the style of the Cateni who were both her and Meir's people—a *chiton* (which the Mundoa scoffingly called a "bog dress") and a woolen wrap in brown-and-ivory plaid, embroidered with elegant, brightly colored knot work around the neck and hem, belted and pinned around her body. Her long, reddish-brown hair was wound into intricate braids, the end of each held by a small gilded ball.

The thought of how they looked together, so vastly different, amused Voada suddenly. She gave Meir a smile, then peered back into the room toward the ghost.

"Thank you for cleaning the temple for tomorrow," Meir said. He was still breathing heavily, leaning over and bracing himself against the railing around the altar. In the heavily shadowed temple, his blue eyes seemed more gray to Voada. "I'll send Orla up to the Voice's estate. That way, Voice-wife Dilara will know she can have her slaves bring in the flowers and decorations for Emperor Pashtuk's birthday celebration tomorrow. Since we're also celebrating his twentieth year on the throne, it'll be a special ceremony. You did well."

Voada shook her head slightly at her husband's misunderstanding. She watched the ghost, which had resumed pacing: glinting in the shadows, lost in the sun . . . "I didn't do it to impress

Voice-wife Dilara," she said. "I only thought Elia deserved a clean home, and the temple was getting filthy. The Voice-wife doesn't have her people take care of this place as she should."

"This isn't Elia's temple," he reminded her. "It hasn't been now for three generations."

"Really?" Voada answered gently. It was an old argument between them, their lines as deeply worn as a rutted road so that they didn't even have to speak them now. Instead, she watched the ghost moving in and out of the light.

"What are you looking at?" Meir asked, still leaning on the railing. "Is there . . . ?"

"Yes," she told him.

"I don't see anything."

"I know. But that doesn't mean it's not there. I can see it."

"Can you make this one go away like the others?"

"I tried to show it the sun-path, but it ignored me."

Meir gave a grunt as he pushed himself upright, and Voada knew that meant the conversation was over. She hefted the bucket and turned. "Come on," she said to Meir, taking his arm. "Let's go home."

The temple stood at the summit of a hill: Pencraig Bluff. Voada and Meir could see the town spreading out below them, looking as if it had mushroomed from the lush greenery. Pencraig, the village, stretched out along the shallow slope, overlooking the River Yarrow and a small dock extending out into the shallow brown water. A few boats were tied up there, and Voada could see the bustling of workers offloading supplies into the warehouses on the bank and others loading sheep, timber, and produce— Pencraig's usual exports—onto the barges for transport to larger towns and cities upriver. Smears of thin gray smoke from hearth fires drifted above several of the buildings, pushed sideways in the breeze and bringing the smell of burning wood and peat to Voada and Meir. To either side, in the pastures, they could see sheep grazing and hear their bleating calls. The percussive, rhythmic ring of a hammer on hot metal came from the blacksmith's shop, halfway down the hill.

The lowest and poorest houses, just past the river dock, bordered a fast and cold stream that led down into the marshes at the meandering river's edges, while a single lane of increasingly larger dwellings ascended the slope to the temple. The houses were a mixture of round, thatch-roofed, Cateni-style buildings—usually farther down the slope—and the newer rectilinear and distinctive Mundoan style faced with polished, gleaming stone.

The latter were poised high above the valley and just below the temple so that anyone looking up from the river or the road the Mundoa had built would see them: resplendent, polished jewels glistening in the sun and nestled in the verdant landscape. Those estates, with few exceptions, were occupied by those of Mundoan blood who had come to settle on Cateni land, almost all of whom were connected with the Mundoan administration or military.

The lane here was stone-paved, though Voada remembered that in her childhood it had been only packed and rutted dirt; in the Spring rains, it would send muddy rivulets rushing down the hill to pool against the raised stone thresholds of the houses lower down or join the water thrashing against the rocks of Pencraig Stream. The Mundoa seemed to have an aversion to muddy feet and the earth. Voada had heard tales that on the mainland across the Barrier Sea, the main roads leading to the Mundoan capital were decorated with brightly colored tiles and were so smoothly paved, straight, and flat that one could roll a ball down each and it wouldn't stop until it reached the far ocean.

She dismissed those tales as stories meant mostly to impress the listener with the teller's wide travels and importance. The roads the Mundoa built here were, she would admit, a modest improvement over Pencraig's lanes of her youth. But her mother and grandmother had told her about the roads of the northern Cateni sun-paths, which—at least according to them—had once been superior to even those mythical Mundoan roads.

"Hand Paorach," she heard someone call as they walked slowly down the hill, Voada holding Meir's arm. They both turned to see Voice-wife Dilara standing at the gated entrance to the Voice's estate, the courtyard green and cool behind her with simply clad Cateni slaves washing the flagstones and pruning the garden around the fountain. "Hand-wife," she said, with a bare nod toward Voada before turning back to Meir. "You were just at the temple?"

"Yes," Meir answered, "and Voada has cleaned it for the ceremony tomorrow. We were going to send our daughter to let you know." Voada noticed that Meir carefully said nothing about the ghost she'd seen there. It wouldn't do to remind the Voice-wife of Cateni superstitions, especially when they weren't visible to her.

Dilara lifted her chin. She was a dour woman, thin as a marsh reed and as brittle. Birthing nine children had left her haggard and gray-haired, despite the numerous slaves the Voice owned to run the household and care for their brood. Both Voice Maki Kadir and Voice-wife Dilara were Mundoan, speaking with the nasal accent of the mainland. Dilara was dressed in Mundoan finery, a long dress dyed a blue so intense it made Voada's eyes burn, richly embroidered with golden threads at the hem and neckline, with a stole of expensive white linen over it. Gold-set jewels gleamed at her throat and in her hair, and her fingers were adorned with rings.

"You did that drudgery yourself, Hand-wife?" she asked, her eyes narrowing as heavy lines creased the corners. Her eyes were the dark brown of sweetnut shells, and she glanced at the bucket and rags Voada was carrying. "That's servants' work. Why, I was intending to send some of household slaves to the temple later today."

"I wanted to do it myself, Voice-wife," Voada answered. "Our temple deserves the touch of someone who honors its history, not just someone who's following her mistress' command."

Dilara's eyes narrowed further, as if she were turning over Voada's words to see if there was something unpleasant buried in them. "Then I must thank you, Hand-wife," she said finally. "It's good that at least some of the Cateni understand their roles, as do you and Hand Paorach." She glanced back into the courtyard, where her slaves were working. "You!" she shouted at one. "Look at the mess you're making. Be more careful, or you'll find yourself cleaning the midden." With that, Dilara turned back to them. "We'll see you tomorrow at the ceremony?"

"Of course," Meir answered her. "We're looking forward to it. Aren't we, Voada?"

Voada forced a smile onto reluctant lips and nodded to the Voice-wife. "We certainly are."

Dilara's sour expression didn't change. "We'll see you then. The Voice and Hand must show the rabble the importance of the emperor and how we're proud and united behind him. Without Emperor Pashtuk and us Mundoa, the island of Albann would still be nothing but an uncivilized wilderness."

With that, Dilara took her leave, going back into the courtyard to scold those working there, and Voada and Meir continued walking down the lane. "I'm sorry," Meir said when they were out of earshot of the Voice's estate. "She doesn't think about who might be hurt by what she says. I've known other Mundoa in other cities; not all of them think as she does."

"It's fine," Voada answered. "The Voice-wife is only saying what she's been taught." Still, part of her wanted to rage and rant. *Uncivilized wilderness? We Cateni had cities and temples everywhere in Albann before the Mundoa ever came here. We had our own ways, and they were good. Why, the tales my grandmother told me before she died . . .* But no, saying any of that would only start the old arguments again. Meir might not like the Mundoa, but as the Hand, he was simply another one of the overlords to most of the Cateni.

And therefore, as his wife, so was Voada.

The Hand's residence was of Mundoan style, about halfway down the temple path, balanced between the old and the new parts of the town. As Hand of Pencraig, Meir was responsible for collecting taxes and tribute for the Mundoan administration centered in Trusa, their capital city well to the south, once just a small village that the Cateni had called Iskameath. Meir reported to Voice Kadir in most things. Recruiting locals to help run the government was one of the ways the Mundoa kept the people they conquered in check. They were integrated into the bureaucracy, living in houses like those on the mainland, speaking the language of the Mundoa instead of their own as generation by generation their history and culture slowly vanished. They became nominally Mundoan themselves.

Voada knew that for the fallacy it was.

Their servants met them in the courtyard. Like the Voice's servants, they were all Cateni; there were no slaves of Mundoan origin in Albann. Hurrying forward, they took the bucket from Voada's hands and slipped the cloaks from their shoulders. "Here, Hand-wife. Sit here, and let me take your boots to be cleaned. Look, here are your house sandals. Would you like some wine, Hand Paorach? You seem tired from your walk. The cook has stewed a rabbit; I can bring the two of you a fresh bowl with some bread . . ." The chatter went on around them. Meir was breathing heavily as he sat in his chair. He waved the servants away, and they vanished into the house, leaving him alone with Voada in the well-shaded courtyard, surrounded by the delicate fragrance of the trumpet flowers blooming on the trellises.

"You know we have to keep appearances, no matter what you believe yourself," Meir said. His eyes were half closed; he spoke to the air.

"When have I ever *not* done that?" she answered him.

"I know. You have." She heard him sigh deeply, and he sat up and looked at her. "This ghost, this taibhse . . . It will be there tomorrow." He said it without the rising question at the end—a simple statement.

"I expect so," she told him.

"You rid the temple of the other ones."

"I know. This one, though—it won't listen to me or can't hear me, and I can't hear its voice."

"Maybe it's not someone's soul. Maybe it's something else."

That comment, Voada thought, was a sign of their long marriage. He spoke exactly what had been in her mind as well since they'd left the temple, and though he couldn't see the ghosts as she could, he had never questioned her insistence that they were really there. She said they were and that she'd been seeing them since she was a young girl; he was still Cateni enough to accept that. In their lore, the souls of the departed sometimes had to be guided to the sun-paths. Her forbearers had done that in the very same temple, so it was unsurprising that Voada had inherited that gift and continued the tradition, even if the temple was now occupied by a travesty.

"In that case, my husband, there's nothing we can do about it. You couldn't see it; I doubt anyone else will either. There's no sense in worrying ourselves over it."

His chin lifted and fell again, a faint nod accompanied by an equally faint smile. She returned the smile.

She wondered if he felt the gesture's emptiness or if he'd heard the lie in her words. If today's ghost wasn't another wandering soul looking for release, then she didn't know what it was or what its portent might be.

The apparition would be in her thoughts the rest of the day and through the night.

2

The Blessing of Pashtuk

THE GHOST *WAS* STILL THERE in the temple. Voada could
see it restlessly prowling the open space near the altar, watching her and gesturing as if trying to call her. Voada did her best to
ignore the taibhse.

She stood with her family on the western side of the altar: Meir
closest to the altar as Hand, then Voada as Hand-wife. Beside
them were their two children: Orla, their fourteen-year-old daughter, at Voada's side; their son, Hakan, ten, next to Meir. It had
taken her a long time to become pregnant again after Orla's birth,
and since giving birth to Hakan, Voada had been pregnant four
more times, but each time the pregnancies had ended in blood
and pain after only a few moons. Since the last failed pregnancy,
she'd been unable to conceive at all despite the fact that Meir still
came to her occasionally. Her moon-time bleedings had become
erratic, no longer predictable.

At thirty years old, she was nearly at the age when she would
be considered an "older woman," when she might reasonably expect grandchildren in the next few years. It seemed her childbearing days had already passed. Despite that, she still prayed to Elia
at the solstices for the blessing of another child, but so far Elia
hadn't chosen to answer those prayers.

At the eastern side of the altar were the Voice and Voice-wife, and clustered around them were six children of the nine Dilara had carried to term, the other three having died of illnesses in infancy.

All around them, the temple was packed with people come to celebrate Emperor Pashtuk's birthday, the crowd ringing the altar at a few paces' distance. A squadron of Pencraig's garrison of Mundoan soldiers, under the command of Sub-Commander Bakir, were stationed prominently behind the altar and at the temple doors. A choral group of Mundoan singers chanted verses praising Emperor Pashtuk's great accomplishments, their mingled voices echoing from the stones. Incense burned in twin braziers on either side of Pashtuk's bust, filling the air with pungent smoke that drifted toward the eastern windows and up to the open sky above the altar. The acrid scent made Voada's nose wrinkle and filled her with a desire to sneeze, and she heard Orla sniff loudly next to her. Voada put an arm around her daughter and shook her head.

"No," she whispered. "Not here." Voada saw her daughter's eyes—grass-green like Voada's own eyes—narrow and focus on something in the shadows behind the altar.

"There's a taibhse, Mother," Orla said, a little too loudly even over the chanters, and Voada saw Dilara's frowning gaze swivel to rest on them.

Voada put a finger to her lips, then bent down to Orla as if she were chastising her. "You see it? Have you seen others, too, before this?"

A nod answered her. "We'll need to talk about that," she breathed into Orla's ear, "but that will have to wait until afterward. Does seeing it scare you?"

Orla screwed up her nose. "The ghost doesn't bother me, but the incense stinks."

Voada smiled at that. "It does, but the Voice-wife's breath will be worse if she comes over to scold us for talking."

She heard the giggle that Orla barely suppressed as the chanters finished their paean and pressed her own lips together in a false serious frown as she straightened up again, holding Orla's hand. She shrugged to Dilara in apology.

Voice Kadir nodded to Meir as the last reverberation of the chant faded, and Voice and Hand now approached the altar, each carrying a silver plate heaped with small copper coins adorned with Pashtuk's profile. They placed the trays in front of the bust. The coins, representing the tribute due to the emperor, would remain there, guarded by the soldiers of the garrison until they mysteriously vanished in a moment during the night, as if Pashtuk himself had accepted the offering. Only the empty silver plates would be there in the morning to greet the first worshipper. That was the ritual, repeated every year. Voada knew that it would be Sub-Commander Bakir who would gather up the coins in the darkness and return them to the Voice.

Meir stepped back while the Voice pivoted slowly to face the audience. Voice Kadir had the sagging posture and figure of a bureaucrat and the same long and thin nose that adorned Pashtuk's bust. Weak-eyed, he squinted constantly, and he had a habit of running his fingers through his close-cut and thinning dark hair.

As the Voice turned to the onlookers, Voada saw that he had moved directly into the path of the ghost, fading out of existence as it moved into sunlight before reappearing again in the shadow cast by the altar and the sculpture of Emperor Pashtuk. No one else in the audience saw it or responded to the taibhse's restless pacing of the temple.

Voice Kadir cleared his throat. "Today," he said, "we celebrate the birth of our great Emperor Pashtuk, blessed by our gods and sent as their emissary to this world, and beloved by all the people he rules as we mark the twentieth year of his glorious reign." Maki Kadir might have been Voice for the village, but his own voice was small and muffled, as if he were too lazy to fully open his mouth. Voada doubted that anyone not directly in front of the man could hear what he said, though no one dared to complain. "Today, we come together to praise Emperor Pashtuk ourselves, as he so rightly deserves."

The ghost was next to the Voice, and as he finished that last statement, it seemed to Voada's eyes that he and the taibhse merged together. Voice Kadir visibly shivered, as if it were full winter and the air were touched with ice. His voice faltered mid-sentence, his eyes widened, and his body went stiff. His head turned ponderously until his gaze met Voada's. "We shouldn't be here," he said then, clearly and loudly, as if someone's else's voice had stolen his own. His words echoed unnaturally throughout the temple. "And neither should you. We belong *there*." With the last word, he pointed northward. "In Albann Bràghad."

There was an audible gasp from the onlookers at that name: the northland, where the unconquered tribal remnants of the Cateni still lived. *Albann Bràghad.* The River Meadham was the dividing line between Albann Bràghad, the northern portion of the greater island Albann, and its southern portion, Albann Deas, which the Mundoa ruled. Sub-Commander Bakir's bristling eyebrows low-ered as he stared at Voice Kadir.

Then Voice Kadir shivered again, and his hand dropped as Voada saw the shadowed outline of the ghost step away from the Voice, its hand still pointing imperiously to the north. Voada wordlessly tightened her grip on her daughter's hand. *The taibhse wants me to go to Albann Bràghad? Why?* The apparition stepped into the sunlight pouring down through the open roof and was gone in the assault of its radiance.

The Voice was sputtering and blinking, his knees seemingly weak underneath him. His gaze swept around the room as the crowd gawked at him and a susurration of whispered comments filled the silence. Dilara stepped forward into the confusion, touching her husband's shoulder, though she—and Meir and Bakir as well—kept glancing toward Voada. "What the Voice means," Dilara declared, "is that Emperor Pashtuk has heard our praises and blesses us all. He wishes us well as we return to our homes, for that is where we should go now. This year, in his lar-gesse, the emperor wishes us to take these coins as tokens of his blessing and leave him."

Dilara tugged at her husband's sleeve. She nodded her head to the plates of copper coins on the altar. Voice Kadir seemed to shake himself awake. "Yes," he said, and it was his own voice again. "Accept the blessings of our emperor." With that, he grabbed a small handful of the copper coins and tossed them into the crowd. A moment later, as the Voice scattered a second handful, Meir joined in with the coins from his own plate of offerings. Children shrieked in glee, diving for the coins as they clattered on the marble flags; the adults laughed, many of them also crouching down to gather the money. Bakir's soldiers watched restlessly, glancing uneasily at their commanding officer over the chaos of what was supposed to be a solemn, dignified occasion.

"Our ceremony is ended," Dilara shrilled over the clamor as both Meir and the Voice tossed a third handful of the coins into the crowds. "All of you should return to your houses and thank Emperor Pashtuk in your prayers this evening."

Dilara nodded to Sub-Commander Bakir, who shouted an order. The soldiers clashed the butts of their spears against the tiled floor and slowly began to move forward, herding the worshippers toward the doors, though they passed around the Voice, the Hand, and their families. Voada could feel Meir staring at her. She kept her gaze on him as something familiar and supportive, not wanting to see the expressions that might be contorting the faces of Dilara or her husband.

She could see the ghost again, lurking in the nearby shadows: still pacing, still speaking wordlessly, still watching her. Always watching her.

"Mother, you're hurting me," she heard Orla cry out. Voada realized that she was still holding her daughter's hand, that she was squeezing it far too tightly. She let go of the hand, putting her arm around Orla's shoulders instead and kissing the top of her head. She did the same to Hakan, who stood next to Orla looking like a small version of his father, with the same yellow-brown hair Meir had once had—though Hakan's gaze was fastened on a copper coin at his feet, not the adults. "I'm sorry, darling," she said. "I'm very sorry." She looked back quickly to Meir. "Should we go, husband?" she asked as Hakan stooped to pick up the coin. "The children are tired." Her eyes pleaded with him. He nodded to her, looking tired and older than his age. The Voice's children were rushing about, picking up the scattered coins and laughing. Voada doubted that either of their parents found anything amusing in the morning's fiasco.

"You go on," Meir told her. "I'll stay here and help the Voice and Voice-wife put the temple back to rights. And why don't you take the Voice's children with you? I'm sure Voice-wife Dilara would appreciate that."

"Certainly," Voada told him. She nodded quickly to Dilara, who looked as if she'd just bitten into a rotten berry, then gestured to the children. "I'll see you at home, then."

Gathering the children together, she hurried from the temple.

When she returned to the house, Voada sent Orla and Hakan away with Una, the house servant in charge of the children: a large-boned, plain-faced Cateni woman, her features worn with the lines of age, her hair thin and white. She had other servants bring retted flax straw, a wooden knife, and a wooden scutching stand to her in the courtyard. "I'll work here," she told them. "Leave me for now."

She began to work the flax, placing a bundle of the straw into the v-shaped notch in the scutching stand so it hung down, then running the blade of the wooden knife down the fibers. It was laborious, tedious work, scraping away the woody, clinging bark from the flax fiber so the resulting bast could later be heckled and combed into flaxen strands and spun with a distaff and spinning wheel into linen threads. The retted straw stank of decomposition and resisted her efforts to free the flax from its wooden sheaths.

It was exactly what she needed. She could concentrate on the work, take out her worry and fear on the flax, and not think about the taibhse or what had happened at the temple. At least not until she could talk to Meir.

Voada glanced up as Meir entered the courtyard some time later. His face was red, and she didn't know whether that was from the exertion of walking down from the temple or from having to deal with the aftermath of the ceremony with Voice Kadir and Dilara. He allowed the servant who scurried forward from the house to take his cloak, gratefully accepted a cup from another, and sat down in the shade next to Voada. She said nothing, only put down the scutching knife and placed her hand over his on the armrest of his chair. From inside the house, they could hear the high laughter of Hakan and the more solemn tones of Orla. Meir's elderly hunting dog, Fermac, came shuffling into the courtyard from where he'd been sleeping in a sunny patch of the portico and nuzzled at Meir's other hand. Voada watched Meir ruffle Fermac's ears absently.

"Was it the ghost?" Meir said, staring past Fermac to a nearby trellis and the trumpet flowers blooming there.

"Yes," she told him. "I'm afraid it was. I saw it walk into Voice Kadir—and I mean walk *into*, not just pass through him, as I've seen other ghosts do. Somehow, the taibhse was speaking through the Voice. I've never seen one do that before. Ever." She decided not to mention that Orla had also seen the ghost.

Meir inhaled long and loudly through his nose. "Was it trying to speak to you? Was it telling *you* to go to Albann Bràghad?"

Voada pressed her lips together, then finally nodded. She picked up the knife again and began scraping at the straw once more. "Yes. I think so. Did . . . did the Voice realize that?"

"The Voice doesn't seem to remember doing anything at all. Voice-wife Dilara, though . . ." His voice trailed off.

"You don't have to tell me. If her stare could have poisoned me, I'd be dead already. What did she say?"

Fermac had settled around Meir's feet, lying with his muzzle on top of Meir's sandals. Meir took another long breath, sitting up in the chair. His pale eyes, pouched with grayish skin underneath, found Voada's own as she paused, scutching knife in hand, woody scraps on her dress and piled on the ground beneath the stand.

"Dilara said very little, actually. Mostly she was complaining about how much the botched ceremony had cost them, having to throw the coins to distract the crowd. She was angry with

Maki . . ." He stopped at the impoliteness of using the Voice's common name here in public, where one of the servants might overhear, and corrected himself. "I mean *Voice Kadir* for not being able to remember what happened or explain to her what he was saying or who he was saying it to. But . . ."

". . . she knows who he was looking at when he spoke," Voada finished for him. She set down the wooden knife on the arm of her chair harder than she intended. It clattered loudly, and they both looked at it. Fermac lifted his head and dropped it down again.

Meir's lips tightened. "Yes." Then, after a moment: "Do *you* know why the ghost was telling you this?"

Voada shook her head mutely. That seemed to mollify him. She didn't tell him what she was thinking: *He said I belong in Albann Bràghad; in the north is where the free clans still roam. It must have to do with our people there, with the Cateni the Mundoa haven't yet conquered . . .*

"I think," Meir continued, "that you should stay away from the temple for a few days. There's no sense in reminding either the Voice or the Voice-wife about this day when the gossip around the town will do that all too well."

"And the ghost?"

"No one else can see it," he answered. "So as far as they're concerned, it's not there."

Orla saw it. But again she didn't mention that to Meir. "This hasn't put you in danger, has it?" Voada asked him. "Would Maki—Voice Kadir—name someone else as Hand because of this?"

"I don't know, but I doubt it. He'd have to make a report about the incident to the Great-Voice in Trusa, and that would reflect badly on him. He might find himself replaced too. As for replacing me, well . . ." Voada saw Meir glance around the courtyard again to make sure no one was within earshot, but he lowered his voice anyway. "Voice Kadir's reputation—and especially the Voice-wife's—might make it difficult for him to find another good Hand from the Cateni community. I think we're safe enough as long as none of this gets back to the ear of the Great-Voice." Meir bestirred himself, disturbing Fermac as he rose from the chair and kissed the top of Voada's head. "I need to rest."

"Then go inside and lie down," she told him. "I have to finish this, and then I'll come in. Tell the house servants not to let the children disturb you."

"Come on, then, Fermac," Meir said, patting his thigh. Voada watched Meir and the dog shuffle toward the portico and enter the shadows of the house. Picking up the scutching knife, she attacked the flax straw once more as vigorously as if she were cutting away this day from her memory.

3

Faring at the Market

TWO DAYS LATER WAS MARKET DAY.

The market square of Pencraig was near the river, where crops could be brought in either by flatboat or along the Yarrow Road that roughly followed the river's course. The stalls were mostly temporary: open-sided tents or rudely erected shelters with sagging wooden planks set on logs serving as tables for the produce.

For Voada, market days were always busy, noisy, and full of wondrous scents. Vendors called out their wares and bargained loudly with customers over their prices; neighbors chatted and gossiped as they walked the square. Freshly slaughtered chickens, ducks, and geese hung by their legs; the smell of roasting meat, freshly baked breads, and exotic spices wafted through the air; the nearby taverns were kept busy providing ale and wine. Bolts of brightly dyed woolen and linen fabrics burdened the tables of a cloth merchant next to a stall featuring painted and carved wooden toys and utensils.

Market Day. It was as much a regular social gathering as a time for shopping.

Voada had sent the kitchen staff down to purchase what they needed. She and Meir often came to market themselves just to stroll the narrow lanes between the stands, talk to their neighbors, and see if there was anything unusual being offered. Theirs had been a slow walk down Pencraig Bluff with Orla and Hakan in the wake of the kitchen staff and Una. Meir was obviously still not feeling well but had insisted on accompanying Voada despite her protestations that he should stay home. Even now, as they strolled down the lanes, Voada could see sweat beading along his hairline despite the fact that the day was cool and the sun hidden. She kept her arm linked with his, not for companionship but because she could sometimes feel him lean his weight on her.

"We don't need to be here, my love," she whispered to him as they stopped at one stall to look at their display of tic beans and vetch. "You should be resting at home. You should take a carriage back up the hill."

Meir only smiled at the farmer's wife, who was watching them from the other side of their stall. "It's market day. The people should see their Hand," he answered Voada softly. "Look, there's the Voice and Voice-wife." He nodded down the crowded lane, where Voada could see Kadir and Dilara conversing near a stand for leather goods, dressed in bright Mundoan finery as if the Great-Voice might pay a surprise visit. Meir started toward them; Voada had little choice but to follow him.

It had been two days since the ceremony for Emperor Pashtuk. Voada had heard nothing from either the Voice or Voice-wife, but she had caught the whispers of the servants and the people she passed in the village. Everyone was talking about the Voice's strange words and behavior at the temple, and some had noticed that his attention seemed to have been on Voada. Some even intimated, cautiously and with much circumspection, that despite the odd message he'd spoken, the Voice had been addressing Voada because he and the Hand-wife were lovers.

No one mentioned the ghost, the taibhse. No one had seen what she had seen, what her daughter had also seen. That, at least, was some small comfort.

"Voice Kadir," Meir said loudly. He waved to the couple as both Kadir and Dilara glanced their way, then said quietly to Voada,

"No sense in trying to avoid them." He smiled and, putting his arm around Voada, began walking toward the two, threading their way through the people between them. Voada tried to match Meir's nonchalance and his smile, feeling that she failed at both.

Voice Kadir returned Meir's smile, if somewhat tentatively. Dilara's mouth remained set in a tight-lipped frown. "Hand, Handwife," Kadir said as they approached. The tanner, who had come to their side of the booth to talk to the Voice as he admired one of the man's hides, slid away discreetly, busying himself in the back of the booth and rearranging the piles of finished hides on the table there. "It's a fine day for the market, I think. How have you been feeling, Hand Meir? Still suffering from lack-breath?"

"I'm afraid that's always with me anymore, Voice. It's the burden the gods have given me to bear."

Kadir frowned. "Let me send you my archiater. She can mix a potion from her herbs that would help, I'm certain. She did wonders for Dilara when she was having trouble with headaches last year, didn't she, dearest? I'll have her come to see you this evening."

"That's very kind of you, Voice Kadir."

Voada was silent during the exchange, trying to keep the smile on her face and nodding at the Voice's offer. She tried not to meet Dilara's gaze, pretending instead to examine the tanner's wares, though she could feel the woman's dark stare on her. The sour scent of imperfectly cured hides hung around them; Voada thought it a fitting accompaniment.

"Think nothing of it," Kadir continued. "Why, just yesterday the archiater gave me a potion so that I wouldn't have another of those, well, *episodes*." He placed a finger against his long nose. "You know what I mean. She believes I inhaled a passing evil vapor in the temple, which now can no longer touch me."

Voada shivered at the words, so close to the actual truth.

"I believe you suffered from a deliberate curse, my husband," Dilara interjected. "An evil spell that some jealous enemy cast on you."

That brought Voada's head around, and she found Dilara's gaze directly on her. The Voice-wife's fingers were stroking the long golden links around her neck, set with small jewels that flashed in the sun. The woman's kohl-enhanced eyebrows were raised, daring Voada to contradict her.

"Who would wish to harm our esteemed Voice or his reputation?" Voada asked Dilara as sweetly as possible.

"Indeed, that's the question," Dilara answered quickly. Her head tilted slightly. "One of those mad northern *sihirki* perhaps. Why, weren't *your* family once sihirki, Hand-wife?"

The words dripped sweet venom. Voada smiled as if she didn't notice. "They were, Voice-wife. Though they called themselves *draoi*; 'sihirki' is a Mundoan word. But that was in my great-grandmother's time and before."

Dilara gave a laugh through her nose. "You would know, I suppose. Still, you have to admit that there are Cateni who consider us to be nothing more than invaders, even when we've brought all the gifts of the Empire to Bhreatain and brought you—" She stopped and smiled without showing teeth. "I mean 'them,' of course. Brought *them* out of the dirt in which they wallowed."

"I'm sure most Cateni below the River Meadham are grateful for what the Mundoa have done for us," Meir told her before Voada could form an answer. "Anyway, I'm certain that the emperor's soldiers will soon subdue the tribes beyond the river so they may enjoy the same gifts."

"Let us pray for that outcome," Kadir agreed. He glanced at the tanner watching them from the other side of his stall. "Well, we're blocking this poor man's customers from getting to him. Hand Paorach, care to walk with us down toward the fishmongers?"

"I'm afraid we've already been, Voice Kadir," Meir told him. "We were walking the other way."

"Ah." Kadir shrugged and took Dilara's arm. "Then enjoy the rest of your day. We should talk soon, Hand. The Great-Voice has sent me a message suggesting that we raise the tribute here given the continued unrest in the north, and I'd like to discuss how we can accomplish that."

"Certainly, Voice Kadir. Enjoy the market day, and I won't

forget your kindness with your archiater. Voice, Voice-wife." Meir gently tapped his chest in salute to Kadir and bowed his head to Dilara; Voada gave a quick courtesy to the two as they moved into the throngs between the stalls, the shoppers shifting aside to give them room.

"You lied," Voada said quietly to Meir.

"I did. Did you mind?"

"Not at all. Come, I smell bread baking, and it's making me hungry. And there's a silversmith near the edge of the market whose work you should see."

Voada took Meir's hand. They moved up the hill, pursuing the scent of bread.

"I've bought some fresh-baked bread, new cheese, and ripe apples from the market," Voada said to Orla. Una and the children had returned to the house from the market well before Voada and Meir. "There's wine from the mainland as well." She set the tray down near the chair where Orla was sitting. She noticed Orla staring at her neck.

"That's pretty," Orla said.

"This?" Voada lifted the silver pendant on a necklace of leather: a single silver oak leaf wrought in miniature. "Your father bought this for me today from the silversmith. Do you like it?" Orla nodded, and Voada laughed. "Good," she said, and handed Orla a small linen pouch that was sitting next to the plate of cheese on the tray. "This is for you. Go on, open it."

Orla stared at the pouch for a moment, then unknotted the string at the top and poured the contents into her palm. A string of soft leather, capped at the ends with a silver hook and eye, pooled around an oak leaf identical to Voada's own. "Oh, Mother . . ." she breathed.

"You're old enough to have such things now," Voada told her. "Here, I'll help you put it on." She took the leather from Orla's hand and let the pendant slide heavily to the middle of the necklace. She stepped behind her daughter, putting the hook through the eye, then came around in front of her again as Orla stroked the pendant with a forefinger. She nodded in satisfaction. "It looks beautiful on you."

"Thank you."

"You should thank your father when you see him. It was his idea, too."

"Did you get something for Hakan? He'll feel left out."

Voada smiled. She crouched down in front of Orla's chair and tucked an errant strand of Orla's sun-golden hair back behind her ear. "It's good of you to think of your brother. Your father bought him a wooden sword and shield, just like the soldiers carry."

That caused Orla to sigh. "And he'll be attacking me with them."

"If he does, take one of your father's walking staffs and remind him why the Cateni prefer the reach of a spear to a short sword."

Orla grinned at the comment, still stroking the silver leaf at her throat, but the smile dissolved and the corners of her mouth tightened. "Father looks so tired lately, and he spends a lot of time lying down."

"It's the lack-breath, dear one," Voada told her. "It's just bothering him more lately. Don't worry. Why, Voice Kadir said that he'd send his archiater to your father, and she'll brew up a potion for him."

"Good," Orla said. She lifted the pendant so she could see it. "I love this. Thank you again."

"It's to remind you of your heritage," Voada told her. "You can see the ghosts, as I do and as your ancestors did."

"Does Father see them also? I know Hakan can't; he wouldn't have been able to keep quiet about it in the temple if he could."

"No," Voada told her. "Your father knows that I see them, but he can't see them himself."

Orla nodded slowly, as if thinking that over. "Una says that the draoi can cast spells. She said she's seen them do it."

"That's what Una is telling you, is it?" Orla nodded again, and Voada resolved to talk to Una about filling the children's heads with tales.

"Can you cast spells too, Mother?" Before Voada could answer, there was a knock at the courtyard door, and Voada saw Una hurrying to answer it.

"We can talk about this later," Voada said to Orla. "I think the archiater might be here."

She was. Una returned to the courtyard escorting an old woman, who bowed her head as she approached Voada. "Hand-wife, this is the Voice's archiater, Boann." Boann lingered behind Una in the shadow of a trellis. Voada could see rheumy, wrinkle-snared, pale eyes regarding her from under the hood of a plain mud-brown bog dress. A long scarf in red and blue plaid was knotted around the archiater's neck. A well-worn leather bag was draped over one stooped shoulder, and as Boann stepped forward into what was left of the sunlight in the courtyard, Voada saw a long-fingered and thin hand atop the gnarled head of a crude wooden staff. The archiater moved slowly, deliberately, and there was a scent hanging around the woman: must, ash, and herbs. As she passed Una, the servant bowed to Voada again and left, shaking her head.

Boann made no courtesy toward Voada; she only stared, one eyebrow lifted higher than the other.

"Archiater," Voada said, "it was good of you to come."

The woman sniffed. "Voice Kadir gave me little choice." Her gaze traveled from Voada's head to her feet; she leaned forward, her nose wrinkling as if she were sniffing the air around Voada. "You're Cateni. Could the Hand not find a Mundoan woman willing to accept him as husband?"

Voada heard Orla, behind her, give a breathy gasp at the comment. Boann heard it too, and a low chuckle emerged from deep in her throat. "Oh, come now, silly girl," Boann said to Orla. "That's just the way things are in our world, and you should get used to it. A Cateni as high up as the Hand might have managed to marry the disposable third or fourth daughter of a Mundoan noble. Now you... A Cateni woman can never marry a highborn Mundoan man—the best you could hope for is a soldier who's willing because there are so few Mundoan women to choose from, and you're at least comely enough."

"Archiater Boann," Voada began warningly, "I don't think—"

"You don't have to *think*," Boann snapped, interrupting her. "All you have to do is *know*. As I know that you're draoi, even if you've never been properly taught. I can smell it on you, and on your daughter as well." Boann tapped the end of her walking stick on stone flags of the courtyard into Voada's silence. "Where's my patient?" The archiater grunted. "My feet hurt."

"Why don't you fix your feet, then?" Orla asked. Voada turned her head to see Orla giving the old woman a defiant stare, her fingers scissoring over the silver oak leaf on its leather thong. Boann gave her a gap-toothed grin.

"There are some things can't be fixed," she answered. "Like our being Cateni, and you being draoi. Now, where's the Hand?"

"I'll take you in," Voada told her. "Orla, find Una and tell her to go ahead and serve you and your brother supper in the south room. Go on now." Orla gave Boann a last glare and walked away into the house. "We'll go this way, Archiater," Voada said, leading her toward the northern wing.

Voada (and the dog, Fermac) watched Boann's slow, silent examination: dangling a hawk's feather tied to a leather thong over Meir's mouth as he breathed; pushing on his stomach as he exhaled; having him spit into her hand, then smearing the sputum across her palm with a claw-like forefinger while she peered at it. She wiped the mess uncaringly on the hip of her bog dress.

Meir looked at Voada with his eyebrows raised. Behind the archiater's back, Voada shrugged.

Boann grunted as she stepped away from Meir's bed. As soon as the woman moved, Fermac jumped back on the bed, circled twice, and lay down next to Meir, who patted the dog's head. "Well?" Meir and Voada asked, nearly simultaneously. Boann didn't answer; instead, she rummaged through her leather bag, which she had placed on a nearby table.

"You have lack-breath, Hand Paorach," she said finally, pulling several packets from the bag and sniffing at each of them.

"We knew that much," Voada said. "Can you help him?"

Boann gathered together a handful of the packets. "Here," she said. "Have your cook steep these herbs in hot water until the water turns brown and she can't see the bottom of the pot. She should strain the liquid into a cup and bring it to the Hand. Hand Paorach, you must drink the potion while it's still warm; once it's cold, it will lose all effect."

"Thank you, Archiater." Meir sat up in his bed, pulling his day robe around himself and disturbing Fermac, who lifted a mournful head. "I appreciate your help, and tell the Voice that I'm grateful to him for sending you. Hand-wife Voada will give you your payment on the way out."

Boann lifted her chin. "I don't make Cateni pay me," she said. "Especially when one of them is a draoi." She stuffed the remaining packets back into her bag and placed the strap over her thin shoulder again.

"Consider the money a gift, then," Voada told her. "I assume even the archiater has to eat."

"As you wish." Boann took her staff from where it was leaning against the foot of the bed. "You should rest for now until you take the potion, Hand. Walk with me, Hand-wife."

"Certainly. Would you care for some refreshment, Archiater? I could have the cook prepare a supper for you before you go . . ."

"No." The archiater hefted her pouch again and started for the bedroom door. Voada followed Boann from the bedroom and out into the atrium. One of the house servants hurried over to escort the old woman, but Voada waved her away. Boann said nothing more until they finally came to the outer courtyard, her staff tapping along the tiles. Then she stopped, abruptly, and turned to face Voada, looking up at her face. "Your husband doesn't have lack-breath," she said.

"You said—"

"I told him what he wanted to hear and what he wanted to believe. To you, I'll speak the truth. His problem is here." She tapped Voada's chest with a forefinger. "His extremities are cold; his color is pale. His blood doesn't warm him. Inside, his humors are broken, and they are becoming worse."

"Will the herbs you gave him help?"

"They will help his breathing some for now." She shook her head. "Beyond that, no. I can do nothing for him."

"Is he going to . . ." Voada stopped, not wanting to say the final word.

"We all die," Boann told her. "It's only the timing of it that's in the hands of the gods." Her cataract-pale eyes regarded Voada. "In another age, you would have been a menach as well as a draoi. You've guided some of the Cateni dead along the way afterward, haven't you?"

Voada quashed the denial that immediately rose in her throat, resisting the urge to look away from the woman's face, wrinkled like an old apple. "Yes," she said finally. "I have."

That earned her only the barest nod. "Then you should enjoy your husband's company while you can. A good evening to you, Hand-wife," Boann said.

With that, she turned and made her way through the courtyard's open doors, staff tapping on stone.

4

The Ghost's Return

"IS FATHER GOING TO be all right?"

Orla's voice interrupted Voada's reverie as she sat on a stone bench in the atrium of the house, staring up to where the failing sun shrouded itself in rags of clouds. She'd had the cook prepare the potion as Boann had ordered, had watched Meir drink it, and had stayed with him until he fell asleep with Fermac alongside him. Now her supper cooled beside her on the bench, and her thoughts were dark, all of them involving Meir.

"Come here, Orla," Voada said. She shoved aside the tray of food and patted the polished stone of the bench. "Sit with me."

"That woman's gone?" Orla asked as she sat.

"The archiater? Yes. She left a few stripes of the candle ago."

"You haven't eaten anything."

Voada glanced at the tray. "I found I wasn't hungry."

She could feel Orla's gaze searching her face. "Is Father going to be all right?" she asked again.

Voada smiled at her daughter. She stretched out a hand and stroked her cheek and hair. "I hope so," she told her. Orla trapped Voada's hand between her head and shoulder, and the tentative return smile told her that Orla hadn't heard the lie.

"Good," Orla said. "Then tell me more about being draoi. Is it true what that old woman said—you're one, and so am I?"

Voada lifted one shoulder. "I don't know, dear. It's more complicated than you might think. There are draoi—those who can create spells—but there are also menach, the priests who maintained the temples of Elia and conducted the services. They can see taibhse too, though they can't do spells unless they're also draoi. In another time, yes, you and I would have at least been menach and perhaps draoi, but now we're *not* draoi. There aren't draoi left south of the Meadham, and neither you nor I has the training a true draoi would have been given on the island Onglse in Albann Bràghad, in the north." Her own words made her pause. *In the north. The taibhse—it said we belonged there, in the north . . . Does it want me to go to Onglse?*

The thought was interrupted by Orla. "Seanmhair Ina—your mother—was draoi, then?"

Voada shook her head. "No more than you or I, if that, but *her* mother, my seanmhair Ailis, always told me that she was supposed to have been sent to Onglse for draoi training when she was about your age. She might have become draoi; at least, that's what Mother always said. But then the Mundoa came not long after Ailis' first bleedings, and it simply wasn't safe to teach someone to be draoi any longer. I think your seanmhair Ina saw the ghosts too, but she would never admit it to me, and if she knew more about the draoi, about their spells and such, she never told me any of it. She made certain that my seanmhair Ailis didn't tell me either while she was still alive." Orla's head lifted, and Voada stroked her hair again, relishing the silky feel of it. "It's best not to talk about such things where others can hear. Do you understand that, dear one?"

Orla nodded solemnly. "Is the taibhse still up there in the temple?"

Voada shrugged. "Possibly. I don't know. The spirits of the dead have their own ways."

Voada heard Orla's intake of breath, as if she were about to say something, but she said nothing. She saw her daughter's gaze travel to the central opening of the atrium, to where the temple could be seen on its crag in the distance. Voada remembered being Orla's age, not long after she'd had her first moon-time bleeding, when she'd first begun to see the ghosts, and how she would sneak away from their house at night to go looking for them.

So many nights after one of the Cateni died in the village, I went up there to the temple to see if the spirit had come there, and sometimes it had, and sometimes it even spoke to me . . .

"We could go see," she whispered to Orla, and Orla's head whipped around eagerly, her eyes bright under her hair. "There's still a stripe's worth of sun left to the day and a full moon tonight for the walk back. But you can't talk about this. If someone asks, we are going only to do some cleaning after the ceremony. So go get a bucket and cleaning cloths from the kitchen and bring them back here. I'm going to see how your father's resting, then I'll come back."

Orla hurried away, grinning. Voada watched her go. Then she went to their bedroom, opening the door quietly. Meir was sleeping, long gold-green shafts of the late sun falling over the sheets that covered him. She watched him, listening to his breathing. She thought that it seemed somewhat easier, but that might have been only her hope.

We all die. The old woman's words lingered in the air, as if they were unable to be unsaid. Voada pressed her lips together. Going to the bed, she kissed Meir gently on the forehead. His eyes flickered open at the touch. "Sorry, my love," she told him. "I was just looking in on you. Are you feeling better?"

He nodded. "Yes. I think the potion has helped."

"Good." She leaned down and kissed him again, this time on the lips. There was a sour taste to his breath. "Sleep, then, and let the potion work. I'll come back in a bit. Orla and I are going to take a walk."

Another nod. His eyes closed. She waited until she heard his breathing deepen again, then left the room.

The ghost stirred in the shadows as Voada and Orla entered the temple, which still reeked of incense and sweat from the ceremony the day before. The bust of Pashtuk glowered in the last rays of the sun, still visible here at the highest point of Pencraig Bluff. The taibhse, moving around the room's perimeter as before, stepped into daylight and vanished, appearing again once it was in shadow. Voada could see its mouth moving, as if calling out to them, and it flung its arm out, its index finger pointing northward. The gesture was strong and almost violent, as if the specter were becoming increasingly agitated.

The temple was silent, though, except for the rustling wings of doves settling into their evening roosts among the timbers holding up the temple's roof. Through the roof's central opening over Pashtuk's head, Voada could see the sky already darkening toward night.

"Why does it look so angry? Why does it seem to have so many faces?" Orla asked as she set their bucket down on the tiles with a scrape that seemed impossibly loud in the hush.

"I don't know," Voada told her. "Sometimes the taibhsean are upset because they know they need to follow the sun-path, but they can't seem to find it. When I've shown them, they've understood and become calm. They walk the path and go away. This one . . ." Voada sighed. "I've tried to show it the sun-path, but it doesn't seem to want that. And none of the others ever looked like this one. They always had only the face of a single dead person."

"How did you talk to the other ghosts?" Orla asked. "The ones you helped."

Voada took a slow breath. "I could hear them in my head. And I spoke to them the same way. It . . . well, the way to talk to them just came to me, as I'm sure it will to you as well."

The ghost was moving toward them, and Orla took a step to meet it. Suddenly uneasy, Voada caught her shoulder. "No," she said. "Don't let this one get too close. Remember what happened to Voice Kadir. You can try to touch it with your hand if you want, just to feel how cold it is, but don't let it come closer."

Orla nodded. As the ghost approached, she put her hand out

toward it, and Voada kept her own hand on Orla's shoulder to pull her back if need be. Voada felt Orla shiver as her hand passed through the apparition. She saw the ghost's multiple, shifting faces look from her to Orla, and there was something eager and hungry in its look that made Voada uneasy. She quickly pulled her daughter backward into her arms. The ghost continued to walk forward, following them. Voada continued to retreat, holding tight to Orla. The ghost pointed its finger to Voada, then to the north, the import impossible to miss.

"No," Voada told it loudly, shaking her head. "No."

The taibhse seemed to shrug. It pointed then at Orla and started toward her. "No!" Voada shouted again. "You stay away from her! Stay away!"

The taibhse glared at them both and slowly moved past, still speaking silently and pointing northward as it continued its restless pacing.

"When I touched it, it was freezing," Orla said in wonder as they watched its movements. "How can it bear that, Mother?"

"The taibhsean don't feel the cold where they are," Voada told her. "I can remember Seanmhair Ailis telling me once, when she thought my mother wasn't listening, that the dead exist in another world, and the cold we feel around them is the wall between us and them. I suppose that's as good an explanation as any." Voada turned to watch the ghost circle behind the bust of Pashtuk once more, and she kept Orla tucked tightly in her arms. Something about the taibhse and the way it had stared at Orla when Voada had refused it frightened her. *Into the shadows, out of them . . .* "Your seanmhair Ina *was* listening, though—that's when she told my seanmhair Ailis that she couldn't speak to me anymore about the draoi and the old beliefs. I remember being so frightened of how angry they were with each other and how loud the argument became that I went and hid in the cow barn and didn't come out until they both came looking for me that night."

The ghost had made most of a circuit of the altar and was coming around toward them again. "Whose ghost is this?" Orla asked.

"I don't know," Voada admitted. "As I said, it's not like any of

the others. The ones that have come here, that I've seen . . . well,
I *knew* them. They were those who had died in Pencraig—those
who still had some belief in the old ways rather than that of the
Mundoa. And I could *hear* those souls; the whisper of their voices
came through, and they could hear me when I told them to follow
the sun-path so they could join with the goddess Elia. This
one . . ." Voada stared at the ghost as it drifted through the growing darkness of the temple. She shivered as if she had touched it
again. "This one is something different. I'm not sure what kind of
portent it might be, and I'm not sure it's safe. Seanmhair Ailis
might have understood. I don't."

"Is it just going to stay here forever?"

"I don't know, Orla." She hugged the girl as they both watched
the specter gliding along the edge of the temple. The moon was
already high in the sky, bright now that the sun had slipped below
the horizon, and in the lunar glow, the ghost seemed to shimmer
as if lit from within by frozen flame. "Maybe. I wish I had the answer to that, because I don't like it here. After what happened
with Voice Kadir, I'm worried that it will affect more people the
same way because they can't see it or move away from it as we
can." She tightened her arm around her daughter. "I think we
should both stay away from here for now and pray to Elia that
She'll take the ghost away from us. I especially want you to stay
away from it. Do you promise me that?"

Orla nodded solemnly. The taibhse was coming nearer to them
again, its pale face staring directly at the two of them. Its mouth
opened again as it tried to speak, and its hands pointed to both of
them in turn, then again gestured northward. Toward Albann
Bràghad. Under her arm, Voada felt Orla tremble as they backed
away from the approaching vision. It followed them this time,
arms open as if to embrace them, but its movement was slow.

"We should leave," Voada told Orla. "Go on, grab the bucket
and we'll go home."

Orla offered no protest at all. Giving the ghost a final glance,
Orla half ran to the bucket in front of the bust of Pashtuk and
grabbed it, going quickly to the temple door. "Mother?"

Voada was still watching the ghost. *Why are you here?* she asked silently, mouthing the words as if that would help the apparition hear her thoughts. *Why have you come? What is keeping you captive?*

There was no answer. The ghost's face was turned toward her and its mouth was moving, but Voada could hear nothing. A dozen different faces seemed to flicker over the ghost's features.

"Mother?" Orla said again, and this time Voada shook her head.

"I'm coming," she said. "Let's go home and see how your father's doing."

Meir was still asleep when Voada and Orla returned to the house, though Fermac padded over to greet them. Voada checked on Hakan, who was playing in the courtyard with Una and resisting her attempts to get him to go to his bedroom. After helping Una bundle Hakan into bed and tucking Orla into her own, she returned to her and Meir's bedroom, Fermac following her. She watched her husband sleep for several minutes while stroking Fermac's head, then finally undressed and got into the bed alongside him. Fermac lay near their feet.

Sleep came only after a long struggle. The taibhse haunted her dreams, its cold hand reaching for her. Reaching for Orla.

The next morning, waking early, Voada supervised the kitchen staff preparing another of Boann's potions and took it back to the bedroom herself. She found Meir awake, dressed, and grinning at her as she entered; Fermac was still nested in the blankets. "You slept a long time," she said. "How are you feeling, my love?"

"*Much* better," he told her. He thumped his chest. "My breathing is easier. Boann's herbs did wonders, even if the potion tastes like ashes and dirt."

Voada had to agree; the odor wafting from the cup on her tray was worse than an uncleaned midden. She sat on the lid of the chest at the foot of their bed. "Well, here's your morning serving," she told him, then shook her head at his budding protest. "No, you're drinking it, since you've just told me how much it helped, and Boann said you have to drink it while it's hot, if you remember. Here." She lifted the cup to him.

Meir made a face. "You're worse than Una with the children," he said, but he took the cup from her. He sniffed it, his nose wrinkling above the silver rim.

"*Drink* it," Voada said sternly. "Pinch your nose if you must, but get it down. All of it. Now."

Meir scowled at her, but he tipped the cup and swallowed what was there. "By Elia, that's awful," he complained as he set the cup down.

"Too bad. The archiater left four more packets for you and told me to come get more when they're finished, so you'd better get used to the taste," Voada said unsympathetically, but she smiled.

"You're a worse tyrant than the emperor."

"I'm your wife, and I intend to stay that," she answered. Then: "We need to talk about Orla."

Meir made a face as if still tasting the potion, then walked across the room to sit in a chair near the curtained window. Voada watched him, listened to his breathing as he sat; it *was* better, but she could still hear the slight wheeze as he settled into the cushions. "Orla? I know she's had her first bleeding, but I thought that we were going to talk about possible marriages after the next solstice. I've heard that Sub-Commander Bakir is looking for a wife."

Voada drew in an involuntary gasp at that. "That cold fish of a man? He'd sell his mother if the Voice told him to do it. Meir, how can you suggest that? Why, I'd sooner—"

Meir was grinning; Voada stopped, glaring at him. "You're not at all funny," she told him.

"You should have seen your face," he told her. "Mind you, I agree entirely about Bakir. However, in all seriousness, I've heard that the Hand over in Savur has a son he'd like to see married, and he has connections into Rumeli, which would be good."

Voada interrupted him, brushing aside the curtains and sitting on the wide sill of the window. "It's not marriage for Orla that concerns me, though we do need to worry about that soon as well. Meir, Orla saw the taibhse in the temple too."

Meir's head drew back on the cushions. His mouth opened slightly; she could hear the airy whistling of his exhalation. "Like you."

A nod. "Like me. She could have been menach or even draoi, as I could have been."

"There are no draoi left here."

The ghost, always pointing north . . . "There are," she told him, "across the River Meadham."

Meir laughed. "In the wilderness, with the wild tribes? They won't be there for long. General Savas and the emperor's army will crush them soon enough, as they did the armies of the tribes in the south when they first came. It'll just take time to pull the tribes out of their mountains and from that damned draoi fastness Onglse."

"You sound like a Mundoan, husband."

"I sound like a realist, wife," he answered. "And it will happen soon."

"Oh?" Voada asked. "Have you heard something?"

Meir nodded. "From both Voice Kadir and Sub-Commander Bakir. The Great-Voice has apparently given orders to Commander Savas to take the army north. But you can't say anything; we don't want wild rumors flying around." He sighed and reached over to pat her hand on the sill. "I'm sorry. Surely you're not seriously suggesting we send Orla to Albann Bràghad to live with the tribes just so she can practice the old religion? Elia hasn't sat on the altar in the southern temples for almost three generations, Voada."

Voada thought of the statue of Elia buried near the temple. "I know. It's just—"

"Teach Orla what you know, if you must," Meir said over her objection. "Tell her about Elia and the other gods. Tell her about the solstice celebrations. Show her how to send the dead along the sun-paths. Voada, I don't want her—or Hakan, either—to forget our Cateni background. But they both have to live in *this* world and in this reality. They need to be *happy* in this world. We are, after all. Aren't we? Happy?"

His voice held a naked vulnerability that tore at Voada. "Yes, my love. We are." *It's mostly the truth, after all,* she told herself.

She could see relief flood his face, relaxing the lines around his eyes and forehead as he slumped back in his chair. "Good," he said with an exhalation. "And later this year, we'll find someone who will make Orla happy too."

"If she doesn't find someone on her own," Voada said. "I've seen Doruk making sure he always finds Orla when we go to market, and she seems to enjoy talking to him."

"The procurator's son? I suppose that wouldn't be a *terrible* match, but . . ."

"We found each other without the intervention of our parents. Do you regret that?"

The lines returned to his face. "No, of course not. But I thought . . ."

"I know. That's not the Mundoan way. I don't care which way things are done as long as Orla finds the same happiness we found." She leaned down and kissed the top of his head. "That's all I want for her." She got up from the sill and bent down to hug Meir. "That's all I'll ever want, for us and for our children. Now, it's time for you to get up. Voice Kadir was asking after you, and you should go see him after being in your bed all day yesterday."

Meir looked up at her and grinned. "I thought you wanted me to be happy."

"And you will be, especially after you leave the Voice." She made her way across the room. "I'll have the kitchen send us food out in the courtyard to break our fast; it's a lovely day, and warm. I'll be waiting for you there."

5

An Army's March

"**M**OTHER! FATHER! COME LOOK!" Hakan shouted as he ran into the courtyard, pointing out toward the temple road. Fermac followed him, barking at the excitement in the boy's voice.

It had been two days since Voada had taken Orla up to the temple to see the ghost; she hadn't been there since. She'd watched Meir instead—after a day of marked improvement in his breathing, he was slowly returning to his previous state, where any physical exertion left him breathless and exhausted. Voada had decided to seek out the archiater again to see if the potion she'd given him could be strengthened, but today was laundry day, and the courtyard was half awash in tubs of warm, soapy water as Voada and Orla helped the house servants with the task.

Voada turned from wringing out the linen sheets in her tub. Hands dripping, she brushed sweat and hair away from her eyes with a forearm and handed a twisted sheet to Una to hang. "Hakan, please be quiet; your father's napping. Here—you can help Orla with hanging your clothes."

"Mother . . ." Hakan heaved a dramatic and loud sigh. "The soldiers . . . You must come see." He half turned, gesturing toward the open archway of the courtyard. "You must, Mother," he repeated.

44

Now it was Voada's turn to sigh. "I'll be right back," she told Orla and the servants. Hakan had run forward to take her hand, tugging her toward the temple road. She followed him and Fermac out of the courtyard to the paved stones curving gently back and forth up the slope of Pencraig Bluff. Letting go of Voada's hand, Hakan pointed urgently down toward the river.

She saw it then.

From their vantage point halfway up Pencraig Bluff, the fields across the river were full of movement, like a plague of ants over-running spilled grain. Sudden mushrooms of white tents dotted the greenery, with banners of varying colors fluttering in the breeze and planted at the intersections of the "streets" formed by the tents. The sun glinted off the segmented iron-and-bronze armor of the thousands of soldiers scurrying about the encampment. The River Yarrow was clogged with boats on both banks, and there was more bustling and hurrying around the docks of Pencraig. Even from this distance, Voada could hear faint calls and the clatter of barrels, chests, and livestock being loaded.

But that was less compelling a sight than the small squadron ascending toward them, replete with standard-bearers and two war chariots, each carrying two officers wearing fitted bronze-and-steel plate armor over their chests and plumed ceremonial helmets. They were quickly approaching Voada and Hakan, the drivers guiding the chariots stolidly between the crowds of curious onlookers who were quickly lining the road. Fermac was barking madly.

"Hold the dog or take him inside," Voada told Hakan, who took hold of Fermac's rope collar. As the soldiers came abreast of Voada and Hakan—now joined by Orla and most of the household staff, who had abandoned the laundry at the growing clamor—the lead officer raised his hand. The driver of his chariot pulled up his horses, and the squadron came to a halt as Voada and the others bowed, as was proper. He looked from Voada to the insignia of the Hand on the gate; his eyes were somber and as dark as his hair. She could see the white line of an old scar puckering his left cheek. She wasn't certain how old the man was; his face was weathered and lined, but the nut-brown eyes and the set of his mouth seemed much younger.

"This is the Hand's dwelling?" the man asked in Mundoan, and Voada lifted her head. The man's voice was a pleasant, low baritone, the accent distinctly that of the southern mainland, not of Albann.

"It is," she told him. "I am Voada, Hand-wife."

The man smiled briefly; the expression didn't appear entirely comfortable on his face and evaporated quickly. "Greetings to you, Hand-wife," he said. "And the estate of Voice Kadir?"

"The last on the left before you reach the Temple of the Emperor," she told him.

A nod of acknowledgment. "Good. Then perhaps I will see you this evening. Tell your husband to come to the Voice's estate as soon as possible; I will meet with him and Voice Kadir there."

"I will . . ." Voada let her voice trail off deliberately, and the man took her cue with a soft laugh.

"Pardon my rudeness, Hand-wife. I am Commander Altan Savas." Turning in the car of the chariot, he waved back down the hills toward the sprawling encampment across the river. For the first time, she saw the triple-star insignia on his shoulder, glinting gold and silver. "It's my honor to lead Emperor Pashtuk's army in Albann."

Voada's breath caught in her throat; she heard Una and some of the other servants gasp. Orla came over to stand next to her, and Hakan pressed close against her side. *Commander Savas . . .* She knew the name well enough; any Cateni would. It was Savas who had rescued the Mundoan capital city of Trusa two hands and one years ago, when the northern tribes had managed to consolidate their forces under a single leader, Tamar One-Eye. Tamar's army had crossed the River Meadham and laid siege to the capital. Savas, then a young leader of one of the legions, had disobeyed his then-commander and led his troops from their fort on the western reaches of the Meadham to come to the succor of Trusa, slamming into the Cateni forces from behind and capturing Tamar in the resulting battle. Tamar and his family had been taken away in chains to be presented to the Emperor Pashtuk. The Cateni

army had dissolved without Tamar's leadership, the tribes' warriors slinking back across the Meadham and into their old fast-
nesses in the hills.

Commander Savas . . . The Cateni hated him, hated his name,
hated what he represented. And here he was in front of her, polite
and standing easily in his chariot as if talking to an acquaintance.
Here he was, with what seemed to be every legion in the land, on
the march northward toward the Cateni tribal lands. Voada had
little doubt about what that army intended to do there.

He must know she was Cateni, as the Hands of the towns and
villages were invariably selected from the Cateni population. That
was the Mundoan style: let the subject people be taxed by their
own. She was certain that he would just as easily draw his sword
and kill her if he thought her a threat.

"Hand-wife?" Savas said now, his head cocked toward her quiz-
zically. Voada shook herself from her reverie, forcing a smile and
bowing to him again.

"I'm sorry, Commander Savas," she said. She put her arms around
her children. "This is my son, Hakan, and my daughter, Orla."

The commander inclined his head toward her children.
"Hakan, Orla. My pleasure to meet the both of you. You should be
proud of them, Hand-wife."

"I am, Commander, and I will let the Hand know that he's expected."

The commander nodded at that. "Until later, then, Hand-wife,"
he said, and gestured to his driver. "Take us on, Lucian." The
driver slapped the reins down on the backs of the horses in the
traces. The group continued up the road, the horses shod with
strap-on, iron-bottomed "hipposandals" that sounded loud on the
flagstones, as did the iron-shod wheels of the chariots.

"He's handsome," Orla said. "But he looks dangerous."

"He is both," Voada agreed.

"I want to be a soldier like him," Hakan said, still holding Fermac's collar. "I already know how to use a sword."

"There's time enough for that when you're older," Voada told
him. She watched the dust rising from the horses and the booted

men as they continued to ascend the road. "Right now, I need to go wake your father and help him to get ready. Una, please take the children. The rest of you, the laundry still needs to be done. You've seen all you need to see here."

She gestured, and the servants hurried back into the courtyard, Una, Hakan, and Orla following behind. Voada cast a last glance at Commander Savas' escort and, wiping her hands on her skirt, went to give Meir the news.

The Voice had been drinking heavily both before and during the banquet for Commander Savas. To Voada, it showed in Maki Kadir's slurred speech, his slouched posture, and the heaviness of the man's eyelids.

"The real problem we have is the damned sihirki, the ones the Cateni call 'draoi,'" Voice Kadir declared. He was using his public voice, high-pitched and shrill. His golden band of office sat askew across his forehead. "It's their damned magic and spells and the filthy gods they worship. Crush them, and you crush all the Cateni, because their so-called warriors haven't the discipline or skill of our own brave soldiers."

They were sitting at a long table in the great dining hall of the Voice's estate, decorated with new-cut flowers woven into garlands of young grapevines. Goldfish swam in crystal bowls on the table, and musicians were playing Mundoan songs at one end of the hall.

To Voice Kadir's left was Voice-wife Dilara, then Sub-Commander Bakir of Pencraig Garrison, then Meir and Voada. Commander Savas and a hand of his officers were placed to the Voice's right. Two double hands of other prominent citizens of Pencraig made up the rest of the guests. Servants stood against the walls or hovered like bees about the hall, waiting to fill wine goblets or offer new dishes from the kitchen.

Voice Kadir, at the conclusion of his statement, reached for his wine goblet, sloshing some of the red liquid over the silver rim as he did so, and lifted it in Commander Savas' direction. "That's what I would wish if I were the emperor. We look to you to perform that task, Commander for the Great-Voice," Maki intoned. "Lead your troops on to that despicable island Onglse in Albann Bràghad, where their cowardly draoi hide, and smash the Cateni resistance finally and for all time."

It was obvious to Voada that Maki expected an immediate and enthusiastic reply to his speech—Meir had told her that Voice Kadir was certain that the army's destination was the island of Onglse, though the commander had carefully not verified that in their meeting. Instead, the man had concerned himself entirely with what supplies Pencraig could provide for the army and whether there were boats they could commandeer that would be large enough to accommodate troops so they wouldn't have to continue overland to Muras before taking ship. *"He's one-minded and close-mouthed, this commander,"* Meir had told Voada. *"I suspect the Voice is right about the commander's orders, but Maki would be wise not to offend the man. I certainly don't want to be the one to do so."*

Now Commander Savas glanced past the Voice and Voice-wife to where Meir—wearing his own band of office on his head, made of silver rather than gold—and Voada sat. His gaze was surprisingly sympathetic and lingering before he turned again to Voice Kadir. "Not all Cateni are our enemies, and in my own experience I've found them as a rule to be neither stupid nor cowardly, Voice Kadir. We shouldn't speak so strongly against them. I would prefer to have the Cateni as allies where possible. After all, there are two such sitting here at your table."

The Voice's goblet was still lifted in salute. Neither the commander nor any of his officers had touched theirs to return the sentiments, though the locals down the table had in anticipation. Savas stared blandly at the Voice, who slowly brought his goblet back down. Voada could see his hand shaking. Voice-wife Dilara's lips pursed as if she'd swallowed rotten fruit.

"Yes, well, ahem . . ." Voice Kadir began, clearing his throat. "Certainly the Hand and Hand-wife understand my meaning and agree with me." He glanced at Meir. "Don't you, Hand Paorach?"

Voada pressed Meir's hand under the table in alarm, but Commander Savas broke in before Meir could form any sort of answer. "I'm sure that the Hand of Pencraig has taken no offense, Voice Kadir, and I'm certain that he, at least, is entirely trustworthy. I have no issue with the Hand or Hand-wife at all. I only hope you can be as certain that none of your Cateni servants and slaves might whisper what you believe are our Emperor Pashtuk's intentions to the wrong ears."

Voada saw the servants stiffen at their posts along the walls. Both Voice Kadir and Sub-Commander Bakir glanced at them in sudden alarm. The song the musicians—also Cateni—were playing crashed to an uneven halt. "Why, Commander, that's not possible," Voice Kadir stated into the silence. "I would personally put anyone who betrayed us to the sword, as would Sub-Commander Bakir." He glared at the servants, as if daring any of them to move or speak.

"And if the whisper of the emperor's plans had originally come from your own lips, because you spoke of them here, in public, with slaves, servants, and guests to hear you?" Savas' arms spread wide, to include the dinner guests as well as the servants. On his right side, his officers were grim-faced, and their hands were below the table, the food in front of them untouched on their silver plates. "Would you then fall on your own sword, Voice Kadir, or would you prefer to blame the wine?" Savas' voice had gone cold, and the lines of his face were stern. Voada tightened her fingers around Meir's hand; she could see the military officer now, not the smooth and polite mask of a diplomat that he'd been wearing until now.

This was a man who could kill without remorse and without a second thought.

She wondered which was the real man.

Did the taibhse somehow know of these plans? Is this what the ghost has been trying to tell me?

Dilara clutched at her husband's arm, her fingers bunching the cloth of his sleeve. Voice Kadir was trembling visibly, his eyes wide and his mouth working, though only strangled sounds emerged. Finally he seemed to find his voice. "Commander Savas,

I . . . I certainly meant no harm. Yes, the wine . . ." He stopped, looking around as if for support. He spread his hands wide. "Commander, you must know . . ." Again his words trailed off. "If I've offended you in the slightest . . ."

Savas gave the Voice a smile that failed to thaw the lines of his face. Instead, the movement of his lips only made them more prominent and caused the long scar on his cheek to go white. "Then perhaps you should apologize, Voice Kadir."

"Certainly," the Voice said hurriedly. "Commander Savas, I'm sorry that I spoke so . . . so freely here. I should not have done that."

From his seat, Savas gave Voice Kadir the shadow of a bow in response. "And your Hand, Voice Kadir? I think he deserves to hear from you as well."

The Voice's eyes narrowed, and the glance he gave Meir was poisonous. Voada felt Meir's hand release her own as he lifted it above the table, both palms up. "Commander Savas, there's no need . . . for Voice Kadir to apologize to me," he said. Meir's wheeze had returned; Voada could hear it in Meir's initial inhalation, in the fact that completing the sentence required a second breath midway through.

"Ah, but I believe there is, Hand Paorach," Savas persisted. "You're a loyal subject of the emperor, and you've been beyond reproach performing your duties as Hand. That you're of Cateni ancestry means nothing, but Voice Kadir has implied that *all* Cateni are suspect simply by virtue of their ancestry." He looked again at Kadir. "Voice Kadir, have you nothing to say to Hand Paorach?"

Dilara's arm tightened around Maki's sleeve again, tugging hard. Savas watched, impassive. A breath later, the Voice turned to Meir again. "Hand Paorach . . . my good friend Meir . . . I'm sorry if I offended you in any way. I certainly didn't intend that." The words fell bitter from his mouth and were not matched by his expression. With Savas still watching, Meir bowed once to the Voice.

"Good," Savas said. "Now, Voice Kadir, your servants wait to hear from you as well."

"My *servants* . . ." The Voice nearly shouted the words, starting to rise, and Sub-Commander Bakir rose along with the Voice he was pledged to protect, his hand dangerously near the hilt of his belt-knife but not touching it. Dilara dragged Maki back down into his seat as Voada heard the scrape of Savas' officers' chairs against the marble tiles pushing back from the table. Commander Savas himself sat placidly in his seat, his hands folded before him.

"Yes, your servants and your slaves deserve your apology, since you've threatened them with death when it was *you* who spoke without thinking while they remained silent. Why, even your garrison sub-commander would agree with that, I think. Or would you prefer that I treat you as you would treat them, Voice Kadir? I assure you, the Great-Voice in Trusa as well as Emperor Pashtuk himself would understand and even approve of my actions if I did that."

Both Voada and Meir gasped at that, but a shrill "No!" sliced the air, the objection coming from Dilara. She held on to Maki as if her grip alone could keep him safe. Sub-Commander Bakir seated himself again, but Voada felt the man glaring at her and Meir as if they were somehow responsible.

Savas' expression softened then, if slightly. "Voice-wife," he said, "you needn't be frightened. This is a simple enough matter. All your husband has to do is tell your servants that he apologizes for the insult he has given them."

Dilara shook Maki's arm desperately. "Just say it," she said. "Say it!"

Maki started to speak. Stopped. Then began again, looking down at the plate in front of him rather than at the servants around the hall. His whisper was barely audible, even in the hush. "I apologize," he said, "to all Cateni here, regardless of rank. I was . . . thoughtless."

"Excellent," Savas said, clapping once loudly. "Then all is forgiven and done. Musicians, why have you stopped playing? And we could all use more of this lovely wine . . ."

The musicians lurched back into the tune they'd been playing; the servants hurried from their places to refill wine goblets. The guests began chattering amongst themselves, pretending, at least, that nothing of import had happened. Voada's hand found Meir's again, on top of the table this time. She tightened her interlaced fingers around his; he did the same.

Neither of them dared to look at Maki or Dilara.

And as soon as it was politely possible, the guests began to take their leave.

Altan Savas endured the strained and ruined shreds of the banquet, waiting until several of the other guests had made their rather hurried leave, each of them politely thanking Voice Kadir and Voice-wife Dilara for a lovely evening before scurrying away as if fleeing from a rising flood. He chuckled to himself, imagining the gossip that would spread through the town the next morning. When the Hand and Hand-wife finally rose to take their leave, Altan gestured to one of the servants to bring his cloak and those of his officers.

His officers in tow, Altan hurried out to the courtyard after thanking a still openly terrified Voice Kadir and a glowering but subservient Sub-Commander Bakir, who seemed torn between his loyalty to the Voice as the head of the local garrison and his subordinate position to Altan. The commander could see Hand Paorach and Hand-wife Voada making their way through the torch-lit garden toward the gates that opened onto the temple road. The Hand-wife's arm was linked through her husband's, but he noted that it was for more than simple affection; she was supporting the Hand, helping him. He could hear the Hand's labored breathing even from this distance. He'd noticed the man's ill health at the meeting between himself, the Voice, and the Hand prior to the banquet. He'd also quickly realized that Hand Paorach was the only competent person among the town officials.

Altan made a small gesture with his hand; his officers wordlessly stopped as he continued walking. "Hand Paorach, a moment, if you would . . ." he called out. The Hand and Hand-wife stopped and turned toward him as he approached. Even in the dim light of the torches, he could see that the Hand's face was pale and that his chest rose and fell too quickly. The man's breath was loud, whistling as it left him.

Hand-wife Voada was obviously concerned about her husband's health. Her gaze kept moving from Altan to the Hand, and her arm gripped his tightly under his cloak. The firelight coaxed the red from her long, plaited hair. She had more of the mark of the Cateni about her than her husband: the blood-touched color of her hair, the less angular lines of her face, the nose more broad than those of home, with the Cateni's light-colored and too-round eyes. Her skin was moon-pale and not the brown of well-steeped tea, like that of most Mundoa. She wasn't unattractive to Altan's eyes—or perhaps he'd been here so long that the Cateni no longer looked so foreign and odd to him. He'd noted that she was younger than the Hand, though probably past her child-bearing years, but it seemed theirs was a marriage of love. He wondered what that might be like. His own wife, back on the mainland, was more than half a stranger to him, a marriage arranged by his parents. She was compliant enough to perform her wifely duties on the rare occasions he was home, but he couldn't help but wonder if all of their five children were actually his, and as for love . . . Well, that was not an emotion either of them shared, nor was her gender the one that Altan preferred. They performed their duties and obligations as husband and wife, that was all.

There were no bastard children of his here on this island. While in the field, Altan found comfort and solace in his driver, Lucian, who was more "married" to Altan than his wife. Between the two of *them* there was love, if not one they could openly share.

Altan found himself strangely jealous of this couple. "There's something I want to make certain you understand," he told them, his gaze going from husband to wife. "I didn't take any pleasure in scolding Voice Kadir. In fact, I would have preferred an evening with nothing more than pleasantries and good conversation. But . . ." He lifted his hands. "The man gave me little choice. He's both vain and incompetent, and I will be relaying that opinion to the Great-Voice in my report."

"Commander," Meir began, but a shake of Altan's head cut him off.

"No, Hand Paorach. You needn't defend the man. It's apparent to me from our meeting today that you're quite the opposite of Pencraig's Voice, and I look forward to working with you over the next few days to get my troops resupplied and ready. I'll need your help and will be grateful to have it. Ah, there are our chariots . . ." He nodded to the military drivers who had brought the two war chariots, each decorated with the insignia of the First Legion and pulled by two horses, to the courtyard gate. Lucian was there in the first chariot, and Altan nodded to him. "Let me offer you transport back to your house. The Hand and his wife shouldn't have to walk alone on such a long and dark night."

"It's no trouble, Commander," the Hand protested, but Altan saw the hopeful look in the woman's eyes, though she said nothing. "It's not far at all."

"Lucian, my driver, will take the two of you and myself; my officers can take the other chariot down to the river. There's room enough for a short trip. We can talk while we ride. Please, Hand. It's no trouble at all."

A look passed between husband and wife, a silent communication that Altan knew. That was something he and Lucian had as well. *I can say nothing in the midst of battle, and he knows where I want him to go. And at night, as well. He knows me as no one else . . .*

"Thank you, Commander," the Hand said finally. "I appreciate the offer and your company."

"Good," Altan said. He gestured to Lucian, standing with the horse's reins in his hand, and Lucian walked the chariot forward. Altan watched as Hand-wife Voada escorted her husband. She shook her head as Altan moved toward her, stepping easily into the chariot, then reaching down to Hand Paorach to help her husband up into the two-wheeled open car. She stayed with him until he had a firm grasp on the iron rail before she moved to the other side of the car. Altan climbed in after them, and Lucian, his muscular, lithe body dressed in plain soldier's linen, leaped up onto the traces with the reins still in his hand. Standing easily on the knotted webbing there, he flicked the reins against the backs of the twin warhorses; they started forward, the chariot bouncing softly over the wide cobbles of the road.

Altan looked toward the Hand as they moved slowly down the hill. From this vantage point, he could see the lamplights of the village and the torches along the quay, as well as the fires of the encampment across the river. "We've learned much about chariots from your people," he said. "The way you hang the axle, the leather suspension, the knots you use to attach the car, the harness to yoke the horses, the iron rims for the wheels—quite honestly, those are all improvements over the old Mundoan war chariots that I first used. Much better for riding over rough terrain. Easier on the joints, and on the teeth as well." He laughed; the Hand smiled in return, though the Hand-wife didn't join him.

"Do you always learn so much from your enemies?" Voada asked him. Her tone held a challenge but stopped short of open insult. Even the first time he'd heard her speak, when he'd passed the Hand's house early in the day, he'd found her voice lower than he'd expected, throaty and strong, her Mundoan touched more heavily with the Cateni inflection than that of her husband, who spoke Mundoan with very little accent. He remembered that before the banquet, Voice-wife Dilara had disparagingly whispered to him that Hand-wife Voada was "half sow and half draoi, dragging down the Hand."

Instead, he thought that Voada supported the Hand well. Both literally and figuratively. "An officer who doesn't appreciate the skill of his enemy is nothing more than a fool, Hand-wife, and usually dies quickly," Altan answered Voada now. "To be honest, I admire the Cateni quite a bit, and I would never underestimate their abilities."

"But you'll kill . . ." She paused momentarily and gave heavy emphasis to the next word. " . . . *them* while admiring them." Altan wondered if the word she'd intended to use was "us."

"An officer who doesn't obey his emperor's wishes is even more a fool." He lowered his voice to a whisper that the sound of the wheels against the cobbles nearly obscured. "And even more quickly dead." Then, more loudly: "I'm a soldier, Hand-wife, a mere weapon in the emperor's hand. Nothing more. I do as I'm asked by my superiors to the best of my ability. That's my honor-bound duty." Lucian pulled the horses to the middle of the road as they approached the Hand's dwelling. "But I also don't consider all Cateni to be my enemies, regardless of the Voice's implication. Even a soldier might prefer peace to war. *Especially* a soldier."

They were both silent at that. He let the silence endure until they were at the gates of the Hand's estate, where Lucian pulled the horses to a halt. He saw servants with lanterns hurrying toward them from the courtyard as his officers in the other chariot halted behind them. Hand-wife Voada jumped down easily from the car. He noticed that she extended no obvious hand to her husband but stood solidly beside the chariot as he eased himself down, his hand on her shoulder.

"Thank you, Commander," the Hand said. "I hope you have a good night, and I'll meet you in the morning to make arrangements for supplies and ships."

Altan nodded. He inclined his head toward Lucian. "I'll send Lucian here to pick you up three turns of the glass after dawn so we can begin."

"You needn't take the trouble. I'll walk down to the quay and have someone ferry me over."

"No," Altan answered, then realized he sounded like he was snapping an order to one of his men. "The Hand of Pencraig shouldn't have to exert himself when he's doing me such a great favor with his help. I insist."

Again that look passed between Hand and Hand-wife as their servant opened the gates for them. An old dog wandered out of the estate's gate and sat at the Hand's feet, and he absently ruffled the animal's ears. "Then I'll await Lucian in the morning."

"Excellent. Hand, Hand-wife, I wish you a good rest, and I thank you for the evening." Altan gave them a brief salute as they both bowed, then nodded—with a quick smile—to Lucian.

Iron clashing against stone, they rode on toward the glimmering fires across the river.

6

Passage

FOUR DAYS LATER, the encampment across the river vanished, leaving behind trampled grass, mud, and ruts in its place. The bulk of the army, according to the rumors coming back to Pencraig, was proceeding northward to the bridge over the River Meadham at Muras and into Albann Bràghad, but Commander Savas had commandeered several fishing vessels as troop-carriers. Those had sailed down the River Yarrow to its confluence with the great River Meadham, accompanied by Mundoan warships. From what Meir had told Voada in the dark quiet of their bed, Savas would sail onto the Western Sea and northward along the coast to Onglse. The land forces of the army would continue overland to the same island to surround and besiege the draoi's island fastness from across the narrow strait that separated it from the Albann Bràghad.

Voada wondered how the draoi and the warriors of the northern clans could possibly resist a force as large as that commanded by Savas. It seemed impossible.

She had little time to worry over such distant events. Meir's efforts to help Commander Savas over the days after the banquet had exhausted him. Archiater Boann, whom Voada had brought to the house, had ordered him to his bed, then sent Voada out of the room while she examined him. Now Voada and Boann sat in the courtyard under a sky that threatened rain at any moment. The sky matched Voada's mood.

Boann sipped at the wine the servants had brought them, then put the goblet down on the table alongside her chair. She pulled her cloak tighter around herself and regarded Voada with solemn eyes without saying anything, though her gaze held a statement that Voada couldn't escape.

"No . . ." The denial sounded more like a moan as it emerged from Voada's mouth.

Boann's regard softened but remained unblinking on Voada. "We all have our time," the old woman answered. "This is his."

"No," Voada said again, more firmly this time. She shook her head. "I won't allow that."

"Even the draoi of old, for all that they could reputedly do, never had that kind of power. *She*"—her voice gave the word a resonant emphasis—"doesn't permit that. Power over death is reserved for the gods."

"How long . . . ?" Voada couldn't finish the sentence, but Boann shrugged under her cloak.

"A hand of days. Or less. A day. Tonight. Any moment. Only Goddess Elia knows." The mention of that name made Voada look guiltily around to see if anyone had overheard her, but none of the servants could be seen.

"What will I do? Afterward?"

Boann sighed. "Only you can answer that. But his time isn't yours; I see that much."

"There's nothing else you can do?" Voada pleaded. Boann remained silent, and Voada took in a breath that broke into a sob. She made herself to take in another, calmer breath, forcing down the grief that threatened her. "I thank you, Archiater, for all you've done. Your potion . . . He was breathing much better, and I thought . . . I hoped . . ."

Boann bent toward Voada, her hand closing on top of Voada's. "Hand-wife, you know better than most that your husband's is a journey all Cateni eventually take. One day, at the end of the sun-path, it may be that Elia will bring the two of you together again, at least until it's your time to return. I know that what I'm saying means little at the moment, but take what comfort you can in that thought."

"Thank you," Voada managed to say through the emotion clogging her throat. Boann tightened her skeletal fingers against Voada's once, then stood with a grunt.

"Go to him," the archiater said. "He was asking for you."

Voada nodded. With a hush of leather sandals against marble, the archiater left the courtyard, one of the servants rushing from the shadows to open the road gate for her. Voada rose with a last glance at the lowering sky and went into the house. She could feel the gazes of the house staff on her, silent and sympathetic, as she passed them. At the door of their bedroom, she paused, looking in.

"Has that old hag gone away . . . with her nasty potions?" Meir asked. He broke the sentence in half, taking a breath in the middle. Despite the open shutters, the coming storm made the room dim. Boann, or perhaps one of the servants, had lit candles about the room; they seemed to amplify the darkness rather than alleviate it. Voada could see Meir's form under the quilt, with Fermac at his side and Meir's hand scratching his ruff.

"She has," Voada told him. She forced cheerfulness into her voice. "And you'd better have taken that nasty potion, too."

Meir gave a laugh that morphed into a barking cough. He spat into a linen cloth and took a long, wheezing inhalation. "I took it. It's helped. Some."

"Good," she told him. "I'll make sure the kitchen brews another potion for you soon. Archiater Boann said that you need to take it more often."

"Is that all she said?" Meir asked.

Voada tried not to show anything on her face. "She said you need to rest and get your strength back."

"Voada . . ." Another breath. Meir favored her with a lopsided smile. "Pouring honey over thorns still doesn't make them edible."

Voada sighed. "I've never been able to lie to you."

"You show everything on your face," he told her. "It's why I love you." His eyes closed. When they opened again, he was staring directly at her. "What did she tell you?"

She went to the bed and sat next to him, taking his hands in her own. Fermac rose, lumbered to the foot of the bed, and lay down there. "She's worried. She said there's really nothing she can do. The potion . . ." Voada sighed. "All it will do is make it easier for you to breathe."

"How long before . . . ?" He didn't finish the sentence. He didn't have to.

Voada looked at him, and she had to brush away the tears that threatened. "Soon." Then she pressed her lips together and sniffed. "She could be wrong, Meir. The archiater doesn't know. She *can't* know. Only Goddess Elia . . . The fates . . ." She stopped. She realized she was pressing his fingers too hard and forced her hands to relax.

"The archiater knows," Meir said into the quiet. Farther back in the house, they heard Hakan calling for Orla. "*I* know. I've known for a while. We always knew it was likely to end this way, Voada, even if neither of us ever said it. I'm so many years older than you. You should have married a younger man."

"I married the person my heart told me to marry," she answered. "And I've never regretted that."

"Even now?"

She leaned over and kissed his forehead. "Even now," she told him.

His hand lifted, and his fingers brushed away the moisture on her cheek. "You'll show me the sun-path if I can't find it? Promise me?"

Voada nodded silently, not trusting her voice to speak.

"Good. Don't worry—you and the children will be fine." He sucked in a rattling breath, and his hand dropped away. "The Hand's contract gives the emperor half the value of the estate . . ." Another breath. Another. She watched his eyes close with the effort. ". . . when I die," he finished. "The rest goes to you; it will be enough. You can even stay here . . ." Two more breaths. " . . . if you wish. That will be at the Voice's discretion, of course. I'm sure the new Hand . . ."

She put a finger to his lips. "Hush," she told him. "I don't want to talk of this now. Rest."

Meir shook his head. "I'll have rest soon enough . . ." He coughed and wiped at his mouth with the linen cloth again. "Now . . . send our children in. I want to see them. I want to memorize their faces and their voices . . ."

Voada had no idea what time it was or how soon morning might come. She'd spent the night alternately lying alongside Meir as he slept and sitting in the chair next to his bed. Fermac seemed to sense his master's illness as well; except for when Voada had Hakan take the dog for a walk, he stayed next to Meir.

Meir hadn't spoken since late morning. His eyes had closed not long after that and remained closed, though the eyelids fluttered from time to time as if his eyes were moving underneath them. His breathing had gone from simply labored to a slow cycle of a stuttering inhalation, a wheezing exhalation, and a terrifying pause before the next breath, the pauses growing steadily longer throughout the evening and into the night.

Inhale.

Voada had been at his side since dinner. The candle she'd lit on the table next to their bed at nightfall had gone down five stripes since then; dawn was probably only two or three more stripes away.

Exhale.

The servants shuffled in and out of the room quietly, leaving her cups of watered wine and small plates of fruit. Fermac lay on the bed. Hakan and Orla had sat with Voada for most of the night. They were still there, both of them sleeping in chairs just behind her.

Pause.

Voada had nearly dozed off herself a few times. She fought off sleep by talking to Meir, relating tales of her favorite times with him, telling him what they might do when he recovered even though she knew that for the lie it was. She wondered whether he heard her at all, wondered whether her voice was any comfort to him in whatever twilight between life and death he now inhabited.

She wasn't sure whether she'd drifted off for a time. She realized, with a sudden inrush of terror, that the room was too quiet, that she hadn't hear Meir take in that next breath. She stared at him in the shifting, uncertain light of the candles, looking at his open mouth and his chest under the linen sheet, trimmed with tiny embroidered roses. She held her own breath, willing him to suck in air once more, for his chest to rise. She waited until she had to let out her own breath, and with it, a word.

"Meir?" she asked, leaning forward, taking his hand in hers. It seemed colder than it had been last time, as if she were grasping an empty sack. "Meir?" Fermac lifted his head, staring at her with great mournful brown eyes. Across the bed, she saw Orla's eyes flutter open, saw Una slide into the room in the dimness, her hand to her mouth as if to stifle a cry. Voada looked back to the bed; there was a shadow moving in the room, sliding away toward the window. The curtains lifted in a sudden breeze, and the shadow was gone, and with it, the sense of Meir's presence. There was only an empty shell left on the bed. Fermac's head dropped down.

"Oh, Meir . . ."

Voada heard Orla sob, and Hakan woke at the sound, sitting up wide-eyed in his chair. "What—" he began, then stopped. From the doorway, Una began a keening wail. Voada released Meir's hand and stood. She leaned over the bed, and—as was custom—kissed his mouth to seal it after the passing of his spirit and slid her fingers over his eyelids to shut them completely. Then she gathered her children to her, clutching them as if they were something solid in a world rushing around her like foaming rapids.

Holding them, she closed her eyes and allowed her grief to well out of her in a sharp, throat-tearing cry.

7

The Fruits of a Life

"**D**ID YOU SEE IT, Mother?"

Voada knew what Orla meant. She nodded as she
brushed her daughter's hair. "Yes, I saw it too."

"And was that . . . ?"

"Yes, it was your father's taibhse."

Orla nodded, which caused Voada to pull the brush away for
fear of pulling her hair. Una had dressed Orla for the funeral at the
temple and was making sure that Hakan looked presentable while
Voada finished with Orla, sending away the servants who had offered to help. Doing this took her mind away from the grief that
had overwhelmed her several times during the last day.

She'd washed and anointed Meir's body, dressed him in his best
robes and placed the silver wreath of the Hand about his head,
then wrapped the body in a funerary sheet so the servants could
carry it to the temple.

But the ceremony and routine had done little to ease the loss.
She'd see something of Meir's, or smell his clothing as she pulled
it from the chest at the foot of their bed, or imagine she heard his
voice, and her eyes would brim and overflow, and she could do
nothing but sob for several breaths. She felt as if a limb had been
cut from her body. She'd married him the solstice after her first

moon-time; ever since then she'd been with him, and they'd grown together like two trees twined around each other. Now that support was gone. The emptiness was a dark, starless void that surrounded her and through which she struggled to move.

Even now. Even as she pulled Orla back to her chest and hugged her.

Una came back in with Hakan in tow. "Here's the boy," she said to Voada. "I'm not quite sure he understands."

"I *do* understand," Hakan insisted. "Father died. Maybe the Voice will make me the new Hand."

Orla sighed at that, causing Hakan's face to fall into a scowl, and Voada hurried to counter the argument she saw coming. "I'm afraid you're too young to be Hand right now," she told Hakan. "Voice Kadir will have to name someone else as Hand, at least for the time being."

"Then I'll be Hand when I'm old enough," Hakan stated with a glare toward his sister. "Like Father."

"Perhaps," Voada told him. "We'll worry about that later. For now we have to go to the temple, and you'll need to show the Voice that you are the Hand's son. Can you be brave and do that?"

Hakan nodded. Voada smiled at him and resumed brushing Orla's hair. "Then go with Una now, and tell the servants that we're nearly ready to go to the temple. Una, send someone to tell the Voice that it's time. I'll meet you in the courtyard."

Una nodded and left. Hakan bowed, a mimicking of Meir that made her press her lips together, and ran out of the bedroom. Voada gave Orla's hair a final brushing, burnishing the already-glossy strands, and patted it into place. "There. That's done. Let's go and give your father back to Elia."

It should have been simple. The ceremony was to be small and private, per Meir's wishes: just the Voice and Hand's families as well as a smattering of the more distinguished families of Pencraig, those who *had* to be invited for the sake of politeness. In

Mundoan fashion, the servants had laid the body before the altar with Emperor Pashtuk looking down on him, but a traditional Cateni pyre had also been prepared outside the temple. Since Emperor Pashtuk now worshipped the One-God and had established that as the state religion, the Mundoa preserved and buried their bodies rather than burning them, a custom that Voada found incomprehensible and a waste of space. Still, the Mundoa allowed those Cateni who followed their old customs to continue to burn their dead so long as the ceremony for the deceased invoked the emperor rather than the goddess Elia.

For Meir, as Hand, the appearances were especially important. There had been a flurry of communications between Voada, Voice Kadir, and Voice-wife Dilara regarding the rites that would be observed. The Voice would give the formal panegyric in praise of the deceased, but would a sow or a goat be sacrificed to the One-God and Pashtuk? Had Voada already purchased a funerary urn from the local potter for the ashes? Would she want Orla and Hakan involved in the rite by anointing the body with aromatic oils, and did the children know the proper invocation to Pashtuk?

Voada had answered as well as she could, but her mind was elsewhere. She would get through this ceremony somehow, and then she could allow herself to collapse and grieve fully.

When she walked into the temple holding Orla's and Hakan's hands, she knew this would not be a simple, easy ceremony. She saw the expanse of faces gathered around the altar and Meir's wrapped body, saw their tight-lipped, solemn glances. A soldier in full armor stood near the altar, holding the lead of the sacrificial goat and a ceremonial knife with a bejeweled hilt to slit its throat. Voada had expected to see the strange ghost still pacing the temple, as it had been for days; it was indeed still there, mouthing wordless pleas and gesturing.

But she'd not expected to see another ghost there with it: this one a true taibhse, a spirit of the dead.

Orla saw it too. She dropped Voada's hand and gasped. "Father?"

The taibhse was standing alongside Meir's body, staring down at it as if transfixed, ignoring the others gathered in the space, none of whom noticed either ghost at all. The taibhse of Meir lifted its head as Voada, Orla, and Hakan entered the temple.

<Voada . . . My family . . . > She heard its faint, breathy voice in her head, as she had heard the other spirits she'd helped in the past. <I'm lost, Voada . . . >

"We're so sorry, Hand-wife," Voice Kadir said as he came up to her.

Voice-wife Dilara was alongside him, wearing the red that was the Mundoan funerary color. "I can't imagine how you must feel," the woman said, her voice as dry as her kohl-darkened eyes. "I know Voice Kadir has prepared a fine speech about all that the Hand has done over the years . . ."

Voada heard almost none of the platitudes. She was vaguely aware that Dilara's voice had trailed off and that her careful expression had drifted into a frown. Voada was staring instead at Meir's taibhse, which had come forward. It stood at Dilara's right side, and it was speaking to Voada, its pleading a sibilance in her ear. A quick glance at Orla told Voada that she heard Meir's voice as well.

<I'm lost, Voada. I tried to stay for you, and I shouldn't have. Now I can't find the way. I can't see it. Please, Voada, I know you can show me the sun-path . . . >

"I will," Voada told the taibhse. Her voice broke into a sob. "Follow me, my love." She stepped past Dilara, who gave a huff of exasperation at Voada's dismissal of her and the strange reply she seemed to have made to Dilara's comments. Voada could hear a ripple of surprise and shock moving through the rest of the on-lookers as well. "Mother?" Hakan called out, obviously not understanding what was happening, but Voada saw Orla shush him, holding him in her arms as Voada moved past the wrapped body of Meir, not looking at the shell he'd once inhabited but at the spirit at her side.

"Hand-wife, what in the emperor's name are you doing?" she heard Voice Kadir call out. She ignored him, walking to the altar and the paler floor tiles that formed a wide X from the two eastern

windows to the matching western ones, the altar set at their intersection: the sun-paths marking the solstice dawns and sunsets,
which the windows framed. The Mundoan One-God represented
by the Emperor Pashtuk didn't care about the solstices, though
the Cateni religion did. Mundoan souls didn't have to traverse the
sun-path to reach the land beyond—at least, Voada had never
seen their taibhsean here. The other Mundoa in attendance were
calling out to her along with the Voice now; she ignored them all.

"Follow me, darling," she told Meir's taibhse again. It nodded
gratefully. The other strange taibhse had stopped its restless pacing. From behind the altar, it seemed to watch Meir's ghost and
Voada, though its many-faced gaze often flicked over toward Orla,
which alarmed Voada.

<*Thank you . . .* > Meir's taibhse whispered. <*I looked behind in-
stead of ahead. I tried to stay with you, Voada, and I became lost . . .* >

"You aren't lost now, Meir," she reassured it. "I can show you
the path."

Sunlight glimmered through the northernmost eastern
window—not solstice light, but the beams still plucked out the
grains in the tiles, making them sparkle and flare as she stood at
the altar. She placed her feet on the sun-path and held her hand
out to Meir's taibhse. "Come here," she told him. "Come into me,
Meir, so I can show you."

"Disgraceful!" she heard Sub-Commander Bakir spit out. "This
is an insult to Emperor Pashtuk and Voice Kadir, and it's forbidden! Hand-wife, I order you to stop this nonsense! Stop this sihirki foolishness immediately!"

Voada ignored Bakir, ignored Voice Kadir and the Voice-wife,
still holding her hand out to Meir's spirit. She could feel the cold
touch of the taibhse, and she drew in her breath harshly through
her nose at the chill and the sense of intrusion as the taibhse entered her body. Her vision shifted, the temple around her now
overlaid with glaring light and glimpses of a twisted, otherworldly
landscape sculpted from fog, sea foam, and ice that threatened her
with jagged upthrust spears. A cold, biting wind tore at her,
plucking at her clothing, and her nose was filled with the odor of

rot and corruption, so strong that she nearly gagged. Holding the taibhse inside her was exhausting; she fought to hold on to herself and not to lose herself in Meir's pain and fear as it filled her mind. No matter how many times she'd seen this afterworld, no matter how many taibhsean she'd guided along to the path, it was always the same. It was no wonder to Voada that the taibhsean often seemed so frightened and confused; she would be terrified to be lost in this inhospitable place between the world of the living and the world of the dead.

And this experience was far worse. Not only was this Meir and not some stranger or acquaintance, but she could see the other taibhse far more clearly now, and its visage was terrifying. A dozen faces seemed to flicker and fade across its features, appearing and being replaced so quickly that Voada couldn't hold on to their appearance in her mind at all. The grave-clothes it wore were torn and ragged, fluttering in the storm of this world, and it screamed, a wail of despair that nearly made Voada lose her concentration on Meir and the sun-path. She could sense that if she allowed that to happen, she might fall away into madness herself. She tried to shut the sound from her ears, concentrating on the feel of Meir's taibhse inside her.

(In the world of the living, now muffled and indistinct, she could hear angry shouting and arguments, but that tumult was now distant and easy to ignore.)

Below her feet, in this doubled view, she could see the sun-path arrowing out toward the misty horizon beyond the windows of the temple and into a blaze of brilliant sun. *Tirnanog: the Other-world . . .* She concentrated on that, looking at nothing else. "There. Use my eyes, dear," she said aloud to Meir. "Do you see the path now?"

<*I do . . .* > Meir's voice was almost too loud, like hearing herself in her own head. <*I miss you, my love. I will always miss you. . . .*>

"And I will miss you as well," she told him. "Always."

<*Come with me now. We could take the path together.*>

"No." She shook her head into the firm denial. The taibhse's plea tugged at her with Meir's presence. All she needed to do was give herself fully to that interior existence and become one with it, but she couldn't do that, not when it meant abandoning Orla and Hakan. She clung to her memory of their children but didn't dare look for them in her doubled vision. She stared at the sun-path. Only the sun-path. That was the only solidity, the only solace. "I'll come to you in time, but that time's not now."

<Then I will wait for you in Tirnanog . . . > She felt Meir pull away then, and as he tore loose from her, the world of the taibhsean began to recede and fade, dropping her back into the familiar sight and sounds of the temple, which now felt drab and colorless in comparison. She saw Meir's taibhse walking away from her, fading as it went until, when it reached the eastern window, it vanished entirely. The other ghost remained. Indistinct and silent once more, it had moved close to Orla. The exhaustion of joining with Meir's spirit washed over Voada. The ghost shook its head as if scolding her and glided toward Orla as Voada collapsed to her knees on the hard tiles, unable to stand any longer. She heard Orla cry out and felt her daughter's arms come around her—she was safely away from the strange taibhse. "Mother!"

Voada grabbed Orla and held her tightly. She saw Hakan a few steps away, staring at the two of them as if they'd gone mad. She looked around the temple. Voice Kadir and Voice-wife Dilara had left, along with Sub-Commander Bakir, the rest of the Mundoan citizens, and even all of Voada's own servants except Una. There were a few other Cateni still remaining—merchants from the market, mostly—but they looked frightened. Orla lowered her voice to a near-whisper, her lips close to Voada's ears. "That was Father's ghost, his taibhse?"

Voada nodded, silently.

"And did you . . . ?"

"I showed him the path. He's gone on to Tirnanog. The Voice . . . ?" Voada asked Orla.

"He was terribly angry, Mother. He kept calling you a sihirki, saying that you were insulting the emperor. He said . . ." Her eyes widened. "He said that Father had insulted him and the emperor too, at the banquet for Commander Savas. The Voice-wife was shrieking the same things, and she said you'd deserve what you get. Sub-Commander Bakir looked furious, and he threatened to kill you if Voice Kadir gave him the order. Then they left, and most of the others followed them. Mother, I'm frightened, and poor Hakan . . ."

Voada hugged Orla tighter and stood slowly. She gestured to Hakan, but he remained stubbornly where he was. The taibhse had retreated to the back of the temple, staring from the shadows. Voada looked at the people who had remained in the temple: not the elite of Pencraig, but Cateni who still harbored some of the old beliefs. "The Hand's body must still be burned," she told them. "The pyre outside . . ."

"We'll help you, Hand-wife," Una said loudly. "You," she said, turning to a man Voada recognized as the local fishmonger. "You and your sons will help the Hand-wife, and you"—that to the coallier—"take a torch from the brazier and bring it. The rest of you, gather up the oils and unguents. Quickly, now; you've seen that the Hand-wife is menach here, and you don't want her angry with you . . ."

Under Una's scolding direction, Meir's wrapped body was carried outside to the oil-soaked pyre. They laid the body on the small platform over the logs, and Voada, her head still fogged with the effort of showing Meir the sun-path and the uproar she'd caused by doing so, took the unguents handed to her and lathed the wrappings of the body with the aromatic contents. She spoke in Cateni, not caring about the additional insult of using that language on the Temple summit, trying to remember the few fragments of the Cateni burial ritual that came to her.

The coallier handed her the torch. Invoking Elia, Voada plunged the torch into the midst of the pyre, then stepped back quickly as it ignited the oils. At first, only a meager few flames arose, but they were quickly joined by more and more until they engulfed the platform and Meir's body, hissing and fuming. The heat drove them all backward and away. Black smoke whirled upward, and the fire was bright even in the daylight with sparks like orange and yellow stars.

Voada wondered whether Voice Kadir looked up toward the temple and saw the flames and smoke, and what he thought.

It was past midday when Voada, along with her children and Una, finally left the summit. The other Cateni had departed as the pyre began to collapse into explosions of sparks and embers, but Voada had remained until it had gone to smoking ruins. Then she had carefully gathered up a few handfuls of ash and charred bone with the help of Orla and Hakan, placing the remains in the small funerary jar and stoppering it with wax.

As they walked toward the estates along the road, they could hear the hubbub coming from farther down the hill, could see the crowd that had gathered: a mob of people around the gates of the Hand's home. Their home.

Voada began to run, Orla and Hakan trailing her and Una puffing well behind. As she came closer, she could see the individual faces—a mixture of townspeople and soldiers from the Pencraig garrison—looting their house. There: someone was carrying out a handful of her best linens, and two men were lumbering away with the chest from the foot of her and Meir's bed. "Stop this!" Voada shouted, rushing into the courtyard, where it seemed that most of the household goods were now sitting, surrounded by a shouting, surging crowd. She recognized Sub-Commander Bakir, leaning against one of the portico supports and watching the sack of their house. "What are you doing, Bakir?" Voada shouted at him. "Tell them to stop! Where's Voice Kadir?"

The response was not what Voada expected. Bakir simply gave her a grin. "We're here at Voice Kadir's order, woman," he said, not using her title and addressing her as if she were nothing more than a peasant. "The Hand's estate is to be . . . distributed."

"No!" Voada shouted. "This is *my* house. Half the estate goes to me. That's what the Hand's contract says." She put herself in front of another soldier carrying chairs out of the main room, but she was not prepared for Bakir's reaction. The sub-commander brought his baton of office down hard on her arm, so violently that Voada screamed from the pain. Another blow caught her on the side of the head, and Voada crumpled to the flagstones of the courtyard, her knees cracking as they impacted the polished stone.

In the shadows of the portico, where Bakir had been standing, she saw a heap of yellow fur: Fermac, his eyes and mouth open in death. Voada's vision swam with tears of pain and loss. Bakir saw her looking at the dog's corpse, and he laughed. "Your beast came at me, so I gave it what it deserved. Hand-wife, the Hand's contract has been voided," she heard Bakir say through the red-hazed agony. "And you're the sihirki bitch who's responsible." She saw him lift the baton again, and she raised her hand against the coming blow, but he stopped, looking toward the gates.

"Ah, the spawn of the traitor," Bakir said. "Bring them here." Blood dripped into Voada's eyes from the cut on her forehead, and she blinked it away, mouthing a wordless, sobbing denial as soldiers grabbed Orla and Hakan and dragged them roughly toward where Bakir stood.

Orla was staring at her mother, crouching bloodied in the courtyard, but as she started to run toward her—"Mother!"— Bakir grabbed Orla's arm. He lifted her chin with the butt of his baton, smearing Voada's blood on her throat. "Well, this one's comely enough for a Cateni," he said. "And about the right age. She might make a good wife, don't you think? For me, or perhaps even for one of you fellows," he said to the soldiers gathered around. "Or I hear that the renderer's son needs a wife and doesn't care what she looks like as long as she'll work hard and can stand the stench. What do you think?"

The guards laughed, and Voada heard a chorus of obscene offerings. Orla struggled in Bakir's grip. "I suppose she could be my wife, perhaps, if she's untouched," Bakir continued, looking directly at Voada. "Otherwise, well, there are other uses for her. Let's see . . ." He started to lift the hem of Orla's dress.

"No . . ." Voada gasped. "Don't . . ." She tried to rise, and again Bakir raised his baton, bringing it down hard on her shoulder.

Voada screamed in pain, grabbing at her injured joint, and she saw Hakan break away from the guard holding him.

"Get away from her. I'll kill you! I'll kill you all!" One of the guards stuck out his foot as Hakan rushed toward Voada, and Hakan went sprawling on the flagstones. The same guard kicked the boy as both Voada and Orla shouted at them to stop.

"Now, the boy should make a decent slave," Bakir commented, looking down at Hakan as he lifted his face, his nose and mouth drooling blood. "Small enough for the emperor's copper mines, I should think. Get the child out of here. The Voice can decide where to send him." Bakir gestured to his men, and one of them reached down and lifted up Hakan, carrying him away as if he were just another piece of furniture, albeit one that kicked and screamed. Bakir looked at Voada, reaching out with her good arm toward Hakan. "And I'll take the girl," he said to her. To his men, he nodded his head in Voada's direction. "As for this one, make sure she understands how traitors to the emperor are treated."

Bakir's baton struck Voada hard between her shoulder blades and drove her face down onto the flagstones. A boot slammed hard into her ribs; screaming, she curled herself into a fetal ball, but another boot struck her from the other side, and someone was hitting her again and again, the blows raining down on her from everywhere until the torment overwhelmed her in a black wave and she felt nothing at all.

8

Merging with the Unknown

WHEN VOADA RETURNED TO consciousness, the first movement and her initial gasping breath sent pain flaring through her ribs like a lightning bolt ripping through her body. She managed to scream once through thick lips and a jaw that didn't want to move before the darkness rolled over her once more.

She drifted in the dark for a long time before she found the world again.

When she returned, she forced herself not to move and to only sip at the air. She tried to open her eyes, but only her left eye responded, and the light that poured in through her lashes was nearly as painful as moving. She closed her eye to just a slit; after a few breaths, she realized that she was looking at the flags of the courtyard awash in moonlight. She could see broken furniture scattered in front of her and the black edge of a stain on the flagstone. She lifted her head slowly, moaning, and her hair pulled reluctantly and stickily away from the congealed blood in which she'd been lying.

They left me here for dead . . .

"Help me . . ." she tried to call out, but her voice was cracked and her mouth dry, and the words sounded like the cawing of a raven. She licked her puffy and split lips, tasting blood, and tried again. "Please help me . . ."

She laid down her head again, closing her eyes, and drifted for a time in a darkness haunted by nightmares. She remembered Orla screaming as Bakir pawed at her and Hakan being dragged away. The horror of the memories pulled at her, and she opened her left eye and tried to push herself up. It was night, with a moon leering at her over the wall of the courtyard. Her left arm could not support any weight at all, and she screamed at the agony in her ribs caused by her movement, but she persisted, pushing with her right arm until she was sitting. Gasping with exertion and the pain, she looked around, her head throbbing. The courtyard had been trashed, littered with broken remnants of her and Meir's life.

"Orla? Hakan?" she called out. There was no answer other than a cat slinking away near the courtyard entrance as the moon slid behind a cloud. There was a mounded shape near where the cat had been, and the cloth covering the mound was familiar. "Una? Is that you?" The moon emerged again from the cloud, and in the wash of light, Voada recoiled from the sight of Una's face turned toward her, her eyes open and staring blindly, her mouth gaping in a soundless scream. "Una!"

Voada tried to lever herself to her feet. The broken ribs stabbed at her, but she managed to fold her legs underneath her. A length of broken pole that had once been used to hold up the laundry lines was lying within reach. She grabbed it with her right hand, then used it to help push herself up on legs that quivered and nearly buckled. She took one shambling step, cradling her left arm to her waist and leaning heavily on the pole as she stopped and took a careful breath. The world spun around her as she stood, and the memory of Orla's and Hakan's abductions threatened to overwhelm her with grief and panic. *I can't think of that. Not yet. Not now. Not if I want to live to do something about it.* She forced the thoughts away, concentrating on taking another step toward the entrance of the courtyard and Una's body. *They thought*

*so little of me that they didn't even bother to make certain I was dead.
Just a Cateni woman. Useless. Powerless. Just leave her to die on her
own.*

A step.

Another.

Each movement took an eternity, the moon sliding in and out
of fast-moving clouds above her and draping the world in alter-
nating light and shadow. She was next to Una now, and she could
see that there was no hope there—the body was eerily still, the
woman's face terrifying in its fixed agony. There was no soul there
either; even through the pain, Voada knew that. Una's essence had
vanished from the sprawled, empty corpse. She could only hope
that Una's taibhse had found the sun-path easily. Voada continued
past the body, slow step by slow step, grunting and moaning with
the effort.

She reached the courtyard entrance. The wooden doors there
were open and askew on their hinges; the street beyond was
empty and silent. She looked down the hill toward the town;
there were few shimmerings of light there. Upward was the same.
Pencraig was asleep. Uncaring. Oblivious.

Voada wanted to shout, to call out for Orla and Hakan, but she
knew that the only answer she might hear would be the garrison's
guards, coming to finish what they'd begun with her. She looked
upward to Voice Kadir's estate, its roof visible in the moonlight
above the walls sheltering the Voice and his family from the night.

Beyond, at the summit of Pencraig Bluff, was Pashtuk's temple,
white marble gleaming against the star-and-cloud-wrapped sky.

Elia's Temple. The polished stone almost seemed to glow, and
looking at it, Voada could feel the presence of the taibhse there, as
if it were calling to her. *Come to me. Finally. Come . . .* She took a
stumbling step toward the temple, catching herself with the makeshift walking staff. The jolt made her cry out in pain once more,
the sound sharp and loud in the quiet, and she paused, hoping no
one had heard her.

She couldn't trust anyone in Pencraig. The Mundoa had all
turned on her family because of what they thought she was, and

any Cateni who might be tempted to help would be too frightened after seeing what had happened to her. No one would help her recover Orla or Hakan, and she couldn't try to do so alone.

Come to me . . .

She had to be imagining the voice that pulsed along with the throbbing pain in her head. But she put her face toward the temple again and took another step up the slope, then another. She thought she would fall from the pain of movement, from exhaustion, from her injuries. But she didn't. She passed the Voice's estate, not daring to look at the closed courtyard doors there, afraid that the Voice or Voice-wife might look out and see her limping toward the temple. But the street remained silent and empty but for her and the shifting moonlight, and once past the Voice's home, there was only the path and the trees and the temple beckoning her ahead.

Come to me . . .

There: Meir's pyre, still smoldering in the dark with faint red streaks running along the edges of coal-black wood. "Meir . . ." Voada sighed. "I'm so sorry. This was my fault. I've lost them. I've lost our children . . ." Tears made the night swirl in her vision, and she sobbed aloud. She almost fell down there. The staff trembled in her hands, and she nearly gave in to the exhaustion and pain. *I could die here. I could be with him again. I could end the pain. It would be easy just to die here.*

But that would be abandoning Orla and Hakan entirely, and she couldn't do that yet. Not if there remained any hope at all.

Hope. She wasn't certain such a thing existed. Not anymore.

She turned away from the pyre. Slow step by slow step, she entered the temple.

The taibhse was no longer pacing. It stood motionless before the altar, silvered by the moonlight, staring at her as if it had been expecting her arrival. Voada thought she saw a sadness in the visages that flowed across the taibhse's face: ghosts within ghosts within ghosts. "Were you trying to warn me?" Voada asked it, her voice breaking with a sob. "Why couldn't you just *tell* me? I've lost everyone I cared about. Everyone . . ."

She sagged against her walking stick, which bowed under her full weight. She could feel the darkness coming toward her again, and she wanted to embrace it, to sink into its nothingness and let the world fall away. *Maybe this time forever. Maybe this time to join Meir . . .*

Something touched her with the ice of winter. Her eye opened to see the ghost directly in front of her . . . no, it was passing *into* her with a breath of ice and snow, and she could *hear* it now, speaking to her, cajoling her.

<*This isn't your time or your place. Stay awake. We will help you. North. We must go north . . .* > The taibhse's voice was not a single one; it was a dozen voices or more, all speaking in unison, female and male, old and young.

"Why?" Voada asked it. With the taibhse inhabiting her body, her blood-smeared vision was tangled with its own; the temple was impossibly bright in front of her as if the moon were a midday sun, and images of the interior shifted and moved in the same way she'd seen different features racing across the ghost's face. On the altar was Emperor Pashtuk; no, it was Elia's statue as she remembered it; no, it was a different Elia, painted in blue and trimmed in gold leaf . . . Voada blinked, trying to clear away the overlapping images, but she could not.

Thankfully, the pain of her injuries receded as well, as if the torment were muffled and dampened as it moved through the ghost. Voada's breathing was easier, and she managed to stand erect, though she still needed the staff to help her.

"Who are you? Whose taibhse?" she asked it. "Why are you here if you don't want me to show you the sun-path?"

<*We are . . . many. Draoi all, in our lives. Many, not one. Not a taibhse at all. And we need to go north. With you.*>

"I can't," Voada protested. "Orla, Hakan . . . I can't . . ." As she said the names, Orla appeared in the too-bright shared vision of the ghost, weeping inconsolably on a bed in a candlelit room that

Voada didn't recognize, and there was someone moving in the shadows beyond the bed. On Orla's breast, Voada saw the gleam of a silver oak leaf: the pendant she'd given her. Then the vision of Orla wavered and vanished, and she saw Hakan: asleep in a pile of straw, his skin dappled with dark bruises, his hair hacked short in a slave's fashion, and an iron collar set around his neck. "You see," Voada cried, her voice cracking and echoing in the chamber. "I can't leave. I can't. I have to . . . have to . . ."

<There is nothing you can do for them, not as things are. You would only waste your own life uselessly.>

Voada felt the truth of that, but she shook her head stubbornly, which only increased the throbbing. "No," she said again. "I can't. I'll go into the forest. I'll hide there and rest until I'm stronger, then I'll—" She stopped. There was no plan beyond that.

<We can lend you the strength you need. More strength than you can imagine. We can help you find those who will heal you. In the north.>

"Why? Why must I go north?"

The not-taibhse seemed to sigh in her head, sending a winter breeze through her that raised gooseflesh on her arms. <We don't know. It has been too long since we were last bound to a body. We've lost that understanding, but it will return. We only know that you should go. You can't stay here, or you will die. They will finish what they started when they find you again.> The not-taibhse gave a howl of distress, and Voada's own mouth opened to release the sound, like the shivering wail of a Gray Wraith. She could hear the sound echoing out from the temple. She wondered if those hearing it down in the village might not quake with fear that it was their own deaths the Wraith was foretelling.

Voada drew herself up, her throat ragged from Wraith-wail. "I can save Orla and Hakan if I go with you?" she asked.

<We promise nothing. We can only tell you that if you stay, you will die, and your children will have no hope at all. We can glimpse that future. Go north, and you may live; while you live, there remains a chance to help them.>

"How can I know that what you're telling me is the truth?"

She heard a trill of shared laughter in her head. <You can't. You

*must trust us, and you must trust your own judgment. Come with us.
We should go now, before the village wakes.>*

The ghost stepped away from her. As the world snapped back
to normalcy, no longer imbued with the apparition's vision, the
pain and the weariness also came back to her. Voada nearly fell,
leaning heavily on the stick. Her head pulsed in time with the
beating of her heart; she could barely see with one eye puffed and
closed, and when she tried to move her left arm, she cried out at
the sensation of searing, interior tearing, and rending that followed. The ghost watched her from a step away, its multiple faces
in turn impassive, sympathetic, accusing.

If you stay, you will die . . . She could sense the truth of that. She
was broken inside; it was only sheer will that had allowed her to
come this far from the wreckage of her house and her life, and
that will was fading, buried under the onslaught of her injuries.
Go north, and you may live . . .

"I'll go with you," she said to the ghost. "But I will need your
help."

The not-taibhse nodded and came forward again, sliding into
her, occupying her body and her mind once more. She let herself
sink into it this time, gratefully accepting its presence and the
soothing touch of it. The pain receded.

<We should go,> its multiple voices whispered in her mind.
<Walk, and we will stay with you. Go down to the river.>

"They'll see us."

*<Not while we are with you. We will shield you. Go. We must leave
now.>*

With a groan, Voada turned. She began to shuffle toward the
door of the temple, the staff tapping on the tiles. Outside, the brilliance of the moonlight threatened to overwhelm her. The landscape laid out below seemed to be alight, the trees glowing, the
roofs and windows of the houses of Pencraig incandescent, the
River Yarrow far below a shining ribbon set in land gleaming like
cold, green fire. The air above the remnant of Meir's pyre was
alive, shimmering in glowing curtains.

She walked on through this strange world overlaying her own, down the lane to where the estates of the Mundoa stood. A servant was awake and standing at the gate to Voice Kadir's estate, a freshly emptied chamber pot in her hand; Voada halted, her breath catching. The woman squinted in the moonlight as if she had caught a glimpse of something where Voada was standing, but she looked away quickly, closing the gate again behind her as she went back into the Voice's courtyard.

<You see? We protect you. Hurry, for in the light of Elia's lamp, there can be no deception.>

They continued down the street, and Voada halted again at the yawning, broken gates of her house. She glanced inside at the wreckage and destruction, at the body of Una still lying there, at poor Fermac's corpse. "Una," she said to the taibhse. "I should burn her body, and Fermac's too."

<The woman's body is empty. Her soul has already taken the sun-path to Tirnanog.>

"You know this?"

<Yes. We saw her go. And now you must also go. Please. Walk on . . . >

With a final glance at the home that had sheltered her since her marriage to Meir, Voada obeyed: down the hill and into the cluster of buildings huddled near the river, then past them to the docks, where the taibhse instructed her to step into one of the small cur-raches tied up there. It swayed as she entered, rocking under her feet and the Yarrow's current.

<Untie the line. Lie down. Let the water take you to the River Mead-ham. We will stay with you, and we will watch for you. Sleep now. Sleep . . .>

Lying in the round bottom of the small boat, Voada let the gentle rocking and the stars drifting overhead lull her to sleep. If she dreamed, she had no memory of it.

9

Over the River

THE GENTLE BUMP OF the currach grounding on a bank was a physical blow to her abused, violated body. Voada nearly screamed with the shock and pain of the movement that awakened her from sleep. It was daylight, the sun filtered by high gray clouds, and she could also see the green canopy of trees along the riverbank: drooping willows brushing the currach's gunwale while farther back from the river loomed the more emphatic and stern emerald of hardwoods, laced with thick black branches. She could smell mud and water and hear the river's current thrashing against the skin of the currach and the scrape of the hull against the rocky bottom. A chill wind caressed the arm she raised to pull herself up into a sitting position.

"Where . . . ?" Voada began, speaking to the ghost, but she realized that the not-taibhse was no longer with her and there would be no answer. She had no idea where she was, but the river behind her looked nothing like the winding and lethargic Yarrow—it was much wider and flowing too fast. Was this the River Meadham, then? If so, which bank was she on, the north or the south? Was she in Albann Bràghad or not?

She looked for the sun to orient herself; for the first time since the beating, she was able to open her right eye, if only a slit. The sun was low in the sky in the direction the river was flowing, so it was either morning or evening, but the Meadham flowed primarily east to west. If this was River Meadham, then the sun was setting, and she was on the right-hand bank as she faced the sun, which meant she was on the northern bank. She had no idea how long she'd been sleeping or how the currach could possibly have traversed the confluence of the Yarrow and the Meadham and crossed the river besides. Perhaps the ghost had somehow done that?

Where *was* the specter? She couldn't see it in the sunlight, couldn't feel its cold presence. Had it left her?

Too many questions, and the answers didn't matter right now.

The bank here was grassy and high, roughly the same height as the currach's sides. Voada reached over with her good arm, grasping at the foliage and pulling the boat tight against the shelter of the bank, the bottom of the currach grating against the riverbed. Holding onto the grass, grimacing and trying not to cry out at the pain in her ribs and in her other arm, she half pulled, half levered herself until she was laying on the bank, her legs still in the currach. She panted from the exertion for several breaths before reaching back into the boat for her makeshift staff. As she lifted it out, the currach—sitting higher in the water after the loss of her weight—caught the flow of the river as if it realized it was no longer needed, drifting out into the faster water and gliding toward the setting sun.

It was her last link with Pencraig. With Orla and Hakan. With Meir and her former life. All lost now.

As she was herself. Lost.

She saw a crow regarding her from a branch of the closest tree, as if trying to decide whether she was something on which it could dine. "If I were going to die, I'd have died at home," she told the bird. "I don't intend to do that here."

Using the staff for support, she pulled herself up slowly: first into a sitting position, then—painfully—to standing. The crow watched her with black and impassive eyes. "There," she told it when she was finally steady on her feet. "You see? I'm not for you. Not yet." She took a step away from the river and toward the crow.

With a caw and a rustle of large wings, it dropped from the branch and flew away northward. Far more slowly, Voada followed it.

She stumbled along until the sun was throwing long shadows from the trees and the light had turned golden, moving upstream along the boggy, willow-lined path of a small creek that was flowing toward the Meadham, stopping now and then to quench her thirst and to rest. Hunger was beginning to gnaw at her, and at first she thought it was that feeling that caused her to imagine she smelled a cook fire, the delicious scent of meat grilling mingling with the odor of burning peat. But as she walked slowly on, step by slow, deliberate step, the smell became stronger, and she thought she could see a smear of dark smoke rising from a copse of trees on a small hill ahead.

It took nearly the rest of the light to walk the distance and climb the rise. There in a small glade overlooking a lake was a collection of round-roofed, thatched huts: a Cateni village, little more than an encampment. Her presence was noticed before she could enter the glade; two men stepped out from behind trees, both with arrows already nocked on drawn bowstrings. In the fading light, she could see the muscles in their arms standing out from the tension. "Who are you, woman?" one of the men grunted in the Cateni tongue, a slight young man with light gray eyes and a shock of ruddy hair who appeared to be little more than Orla's age. His words were nearly indecipherable; his accent far stronger than any Voada had heard before.

"My name is Voada Paorach," she told him in her own halting Cateni. "I mean no one any harm."

"She's a southerner," the young man said to the other. "Listen to that awful accent . . ."

"She's also been beaten," the other answered—a taller, heavier, older man with graying, receding hair at his temples. Voada wondered if he was the younger one's father. "Look at the blood on her

face and clothes, the bruises. We both saw how she can barely walk."
Then, to Voada: "Why are you here? Are you spying for the Mundoa?"

Voada shook her head. "The Mundoa did this to me," she told
them. "I came from Pencraig."

"Pencraig? Down the Yarrow? You're a long way from home,
lass," the man commented, but his arm relaxed on the bowstring,
and the arrowhead dipped, though he kept the arrow on the
string. The two looked at each other again, and then the older
man inclined his head toward the huts. "We'll have Ceiteag talk to
her and decide what to do. You—Voada—walk on."

Voada did as she was ordered, the two men walking a few steps
behind her. As she passed the first of the huts, she saw faces staring at her with open curiosity and a few with suspicion. There *was*
a cook fire in the center of the circle of huts, a deer roasting on a
spit over it and a steaming stock kettle smelling of fish and vegetables also suspended over the fire. A rock-lined well was at the
far end of the circle, nearest the lake. There appeared to be perhaps several hands of Cateni adults living in the village, most of
them out of their homes or leaning against their doorways watching her pass. Children ran toward her, only to stop short as their
parents called out to them.

One of the buildings in the village was larger than the others
and set back from the main circle, surrounded by old oaks. Voada
saw tall windows cut into the wood-and-daub walls, the arrange-
ment familiar to her; echoing the temple on Pencraig Bluff. As
Voada approached the cook fire, a woman came out the door of
the temple. Her hair was pure white and long, cascading over her
shoulders and down the back of the brown bog dress she wore.
There were bracelets of horn around her thin arms, and her face
was well worn with wrinkles. A bronze torc hung around her
neck, the metal polished near the knobs as if she often touched it
there.

"Menach Ceiteag," the older man escorting Voada called out to
the woman, "we found this one coming from the river."

"And it's mighty dangerous she looks, Seor," Ceiteag answered
as she came toward Voada, her walk steady and firm. "It's good

that you have your arrows ready in case she tries to run away."
The open sarcasm in her voice was biting, and Voada heard chuckles from the onlookers.

"We thought she could be a Mundoan spy," the younger one said sullenly behind Voada's back. "We all saw the Mundoan soldiers in their ships on the Meadham a hand of days ago, ready to go to war."

"We did. And undoubtedly she's one of their mightiest champions, who fell off the commander's own ship." Ceiteag stopped in front of Voada, looking her up and down, then—strangely—glancing sharply off to Voada's right, her eyes narrowing as if she were appraising something in the empty air. Then her gaze returned to Voada, who noticed that the not-taibhse was with her once more. "Elia's spit, Seor, the woman can barely stand, and she looks famished. Put your bows away and help her into the temple. Now! Before she falls down."

With that, Ceiteag turned on her heel, obviously expecting compliance, and walked back toward the temple. Voada felt Seor's hand on her good arm, and she followed the old woman into the cool darkness.

The sun had already touched the horizon, and it took several breaths for Voada's eyes to adjust to the lack of light inside, but when it did, she saw that the building *was* a temple of Elia. The four solstice windows showed the dusky landscape outside, and the sun-path was marked with polished granite stones on the wooden floor. A small wooden altar was placed at the intersection of the paths with a crude carved image of Elia set atop it.

And there were two not-taibhse inside as well, visible in the dark. One stood alongside Ceiteag, regarding her as closely as the old woman. And the other was the ghost from Pencraig, standing near the wall to Voada's right.

"Put her on my bed," Ceiteag said to Seor, pointing to a rush-filled mattress near the door. "Gently. We don't know how badly she's hurt. Good. Now take my bowl and bring me back some of the stew for her. Go on, now."

With that, Seor bowed his head to Ceiteag and left the temple. "What's your name?" Ceiteag asked.

"Voada Paorach. You're the menach here?"

"I am. Menach for the temple, and also draoi." She touched the bronze torc as she gave her titles. "I am Ceiteag of the Dark Water." She paused, rubbing at her chin; loose skin wiggled underneath her jaw. She gestured toward the two ghosts in the room. "You see them, don't you?"

"The taibhsean? Yes. I've sometimes helped them find the sun-path." That made her think of Meir, and she had to bite back a sob.

Ceiteag cocked her head, as if she had noticed the grief that colored Voada's voice. "You *are* from the south if you think that," she said, but her tone was gentle. "You see them, but you obviously don't understand what you see. These two aren't taibhsean— not lost ghosts of the once-living. The two in this room are *anamacha*. An anamacha is a collection of the souls of a line of draoi who have come before—what we once were, and what we'll become ourselves. Did the draoi who taught you not tell you this?"

Voada shook her head. "My seanmhair should have been draoi, or so I was told, but she died when I was very young, and my mother never taught me anything she knew of the draoi." She nodded toward the ghost who had helped her. "I thought that this one that you call an anamacha was another taibhse."

"You see taibhsean, and you see anamacha—and you've brought one along with you as well." Ceiteag gave a long sigh as Seor reentered the temple, holding the bowl of fish stew. "Well, you and I have a lot to discuss, then. But the first thing we have to do is get you healed. The bruises will go away on their own, but those cuts on your face need to be cleaned and sewn. I can tell that you've broken ribs; you won't take a deep breath. Your left arm—can you move it at all?"

"Only a little."

"Then it will need to be set." Another sigh. Ceiteag scowled toward Seor. "Get the fire stoked and burning in my hearth, and bring water from the well to boil. Then go find Anabia and Isbeil and tell them I need their help. Go on, now. Hurry, man."

As Seor left the temple again, Ceiteag looked down at Voada with her hands on her hips. "We'll take care of you. And while we do, you can tell me how you came to be here."

PART TWO

ALBANN BRÀGHAD

10

Onglse

ALTAN SAVAS WISHED HE could simply return to his bed and Lucian, but Lucian had slipped out earlier to begin preparations for this morning. Two days ago, a message had been delivered to Altan from Great-Voice Vadim III in Trusa, the mouth of the Emperor Pashtuk, the words direct and not open to interpretation. The Great-Voice expected Altan to "root out the Cateni sihirki on Onglse before the change of season" and, following the accomplishment of that task, to "take the emperor's army and stamp out any remaining tribal resistance north of the River Meadham, preparatory to establishing Mundoan settlements there."

Altan thought it an easy message to send when the Great-Voice slept undisturbed in his comfortable palace in Trusa and didn't have to confront any of the Cateni warriors or their damned shrieking draoi himself. The Mundoan version of the draoi, the sihirki, for all their boasts of possessing magic greater than any of the "barbarian pretenders," couldn't accomplish anything at all beyond minor pyrotechnics, while the draoi were decidedly effective and deadly. Two of Altan's troop ships had foundered in a storm that impossibly erupted from a clear sky as they emerged from the mouth of the River Meadham. A quarter of the men aboard were lost, along with supplies and weaponry, and the remaining ships of his borrowed fleet had only barely managed to limp to the shore of Albann Bràghad, south of Onglse. Altan's overland troops had faced pouring rain that turned bogland and glades into swamps, as well as attacks from packs of wild dogs that ripped the throats from those they bore down to the ground. According to the men Altan's officers had interviewed, the mad dogs had glowed in the dark and vanished as quickly as they came. Showers of arrows and spears pestered them as they passed between the steep mountains and slopes of the Cateni northland, and though there had been no major battles during their march across the narrow strait from Onglse to the shore, they had glimpsed war chariots and blue-painted troops shadowing them.

Altan's ships had been patrolling the straits between Onglse and the mainland for nearly a moon now, to little effect. Altan knew that his naval line was too porous, but he didn't have the ships or the soldiers to complete a proper encirclement that would stop supplies, warriors, and equipment from getting through to the island. He had told the Great-Voice before he'd started this campaign that he felt a siege of the island might fail; now that possibility was all too real. A thick and unnatural fog that no wind could move clung to the shore of Onglse, and frequent storms swept the straits and pummeled the boats Altan sent to intercept Cateni vessels. They'd managed to capture a few supply boats, but Altan suspected that far more had slipped through the wide-laced net he'd attempted to erect around the island. The Mundoan sihirki cast their own spells toward the island to dispel the fog and thwart the storms, calling upon the power of the One-God, but Altan never saw any effects from their efforts at all.

And the longer Altan's troops remained here in hostile territory, the more the length of their supply lines became an issue. They could not remain here indefinitely.

Root out the Cateni? Stamp out their resistance? That would not be an easy or swift task. The history of the Albannian Wars should have taught Emperor Pashtuk and his Great-Voice that much. A century ago, then-Emperor Beris had sent an army easily

five times the size of Altan's to conquer the gentler and less popu-
lous south of Albann—Albann Deas—and despite his sobriquet
of "The Victor," even that great force hadn't been able to hold any
territory north of River Meadham. Altan had been able to take
only half of the troops he commanded northward; the rest were
needed to keep peace in the towns and cities of the south.

"We're expected to extinguish a forest fire by spitting on it."

"Sir?"

Altan shook his head, brought back to the moment. He glanced
at Lucian, standing at the flap of the tent. He smiled at the man:
his companion, his driver, his shield, his friend, his lover. Through
the opening, he could smell the salt wind and see torches guttering throughout the encampment, blurred by fog in the early predawn light.

"Is everything ready?" he asked Lucian, who nodded silently.
"Help me with my *krug*, then." He gestured to his chest armor: a
cuirass with iron-plate segments bound together with links of iron
mail and a large central polished rondel of bronze in the center.
The mirror was supposed to reflect the evil eye and ward off
spells; it had been blessed by the Mundoan sihirki and adorned
with symbols of the One-God and the emperor. The triple-star
symbol of his rank as commander sat on either shoulder. Altan
had seen enough dead soldiers in bloodied and broken mirror
armor to be skeptical of its efficacy, but the higher officers were
expected to wear the protection, though the foot soldiers generally depended on iron mail alone. For that matter, so did Lucian,
who lifted the cuirass and slipped it over Altan's head, then tightened the laces and buckles around him.

Lastly, Lucian handed him the plumed and polished helmet,
and Altan slid it on over the leather skullcap that cushioned his
head, tightening the lacing under his chin. Lucian attached a short
cape of ultramarine trimmed with gold thread to his shoulders,
then stood back. He nodded approvingly. "The men are pleased
that we're finally moving."

"I hope they'll still be pleased after this day's over," Altan answered.

"Those that are still alive will be," Lucian answered. The grin he gave Altan was devoid of humor. "Especially when we're standing on Onglse proper."

"I hope you're right," Altan said. "We'll know soon enough. Let's go. We need to move before full light."

The fog was heavy, but above it Altan could still see stars in the brightening sky. The camp was alive with fog-dampened sounds: the clashing of metal, the snorting neighs of horses being readied, the murmur of the soldiers as they gathered in their companies. The strait that separated Onglse from the bulk of Albann Bràghad was littered with sparsely settled islands that were poorly defended. The Cateni fished the seas around Albann, but they had no established navy to speak of and no standing army, unlike the Mundoa. The clans allied when they felt it was necessary, but more often they fought amongst themselves.

Altan had slowly moved the bulk of his troops to the largest of the islands just to the south of Onglse, nearest to where Onglse's intimidating seaside cliffs gave way to a sequence of harbors and rocky beaches. The Mundoan ships were anchored about the island. From the forest nearest Onglse, they'd cut down trees to construct additional boats—little more than oar-driven rafts, but sturdy and high-walled enough to counter the swells of Onglse Strait. The single cohort of five hundred soldiers still on the Albann Bràghad mainland had lit fires all along the coast with the intention of making the Cateni on the island think that the main forces remained encamped there.

Altan had little expectation that their deceptions would be entirely successful. The Cateni on Onglse were led by Greum Red-Hand, the ceanndraoi—High Draoi—of Onglse. Altan knew enough of the man from previous encounters to know that he was competent and aware of the usual Mundoan military tactics. If the Cateni were waiting for them with their painted warriors and spells, this might well be the last morning Altan himself would see.

They would know soon enough.

Lucian drove Altan in his war chariot to the shore, which was alive with activity: troops being loaded onto the ships along with horses and equipment; swarms of small boats carrying people and supplies out to the larger vessels anchored in deeper water; officers in their krug barking orders. The strait was calm enough in the early morning, though the shore of Onglse, a quick sail of a single sandglass away, was still shrouded in gray clouds. As the soldiers saw Altan driving up, a cheer arose from those nearest him; Altan raised his arm in salute. The salute was returned, and then everyone returned to their tasks. Lucian reined in Bella and Ardin, the warhorses hitched to his chariot. They both tossed their armored heads as Lucian reached out and patted Ardin's rump. "I'll get the horses onboard and settled, sir," he said to Altan. "Do you want to stay here?"

Altan shook his head and dismounted the chariot. "They know what they're doing and what's ahead. I'll come with you for the moment."

Lucian slapped the reins once on the horses' backs, nudging them forward onto a gangplank for one of the makeshift flat-bottomed troop ships grounded in the shallows. Altan walked alongside, helping to make sure that the beasts stayed on the narrow walkway. When the chariot was set in place and the wheels chocked, Lucian came down to take the reins, standing alongside Altan, who was staring outward over the gray swells toward Onglse, as if the intensity of his gaze alone could pierce the fog. "We've been through this many times before," he heard Lucian say sotto voce. "We've always survived. We will this time, too."

Altan smiled at that. Hidden by Bella's flank from the hubbub and swarms of troops and sailors around them, he let a hand trail down Lucian's side, a gentle caress. "I know. It's just . . . Onglse. This isn't the battle I would choose or the way I would wish to attempt it. That's all."

"We'll survive," Lucian said again. "I promise."

Their fingers intertwined, and Altan squeezed once before he released Lucian's hand. "I'll hold you to that," he said. "I should get to the command ship. I'll see you again on the island."

"We'll be waiting for you there," Lucian told him.

Onglse emerged from the fog slowly, gray and cold. From his vantage point on the upper deck of his command ship, Altan watched his troop ships approach the shore in the first dim light of veiled dawn, like black insects crawling over a fluttering carpet of gray-green sea and white foam. It appeared that the report Altan had received from his spies among the Cateni tribes had been correct: Onglse was poorly defended from a standard battle perspective. Greum Red-Hand might have sent messengers to the clan leaders, but so far there'd been little response except from the Cateni clans who lived nearest Onglse. *No more than a thousand warriors have responded to the summons*, one report had claimed. *The Red-Hand relies on his draoi to hold the island.*

Not only the draoi—the land itself was Greum's ally. Set back from the shore on a tall, steep hill was one of the hill-forts that girdled the island, a single point in a double circle that protected Bàn Cill, the sacred temple amongst the sacred oak groves at the very center of Onglse. Traditionally, it was there that the Cateni draoi were trained and there that the draoi would gather for their seasonal rituals. Bàn Cill was the heart of the Cateni religion and culture, which the Great-Voice knew well. If Bàn Cill could be taken, if the heart could be pierced and those sacred groves cut down and burned like the abomination they were, then all resistance to the Mundoa throughout Albann might collapse as well.

That was the hope. Altan had no illusion that doing so would be an easy or simple task.

However, it seemed that those on Onglse certainly hadn't expected this invasion. The troops' passage across the waters of the strait had been quiet and rapid, with a good wind from the south. They had been seen now, though—that much was obvious. Torches and lights gleamed along the towers of the fort, and a great flare of white fire erupted from the summit on the tallest tower, sending stark shadows racing along the ground. In the flash, Altan could see the first boats grounding and disgorging their foot troops and mounted cavalry, which the officers quickly ranked up into battle formation.

Among them would be Lucian, awaiting Altan's own arrival on the shore.

Over the sounds of the waves and the wind, Altan could hear the shouted orders of his sub-commanders and officers. He could also hear the shrieking of the draoi in the fort, now chanting spells. The wind picked up suddenly and unnaturally, a bank of fast-moving dark clouds scudding toward the beach from the ramparts of the fort. The roiling clouds walked on legs of jagged lightnings, the sound of low thunder coming belatedly to Altan's ears. Where the lightning touched the ground, boulders and dirt flew into the air. The cloud-creature stalked down the hill toward the beach, toward the Mundoan troops there, then swept over the first of their ranks. Amidst the thundering roar of the spell-beast, Altan could hear all-too-human screams. The Mundoan sihirki, in their boat, were shouting their own counterspells, but the Cateni-made storm continued on until it enveloped the troops entirely. Altan watched, helpless, his hands tightening on the deck rail as if he could grind the polished wood to dust under his whitening fingers.

Then the cloud-creature vanished as quickly as it had come, and Altan could see that the troops were in chaos, dark craters filled with dead men dappling the formations. The officers called out orders in the confusion, trying to regroup their troops. Up the long slope, the gates of the hill-fort opened, and blue-painted warriors, several of them mounted, surged out over the earthen mounds erected before it. They screamed the Cateni war cry, waving spears and swords as they charged madly down the slope toward the Mundoan invaders. Arrows from the fort arced high and fell like deadly rain onto the closest Mundoan soldiers, who raised linked shields against the assault.

Altan could stand back and watch no longer. The need to be there among his men, leading them directly, was a fire inside him. *It's your worst defect as a field officer*, his previous commander had once told him when he was still leading his first cohort. *You want to be at the front of the battle, not at the back where you properly belong.*

"My boat. Get my boat in the water," Altan barked to the ship's captain, standing aghast near the commander.

"Commander Savas, sir . . ."

"Did you not hear me?" Altan grunted. "My boat. Now!"

The captain called down to his sailors, who quickly lowered a small craft into the swells, a half-dozen sailors taking up oars as Altan put on his helmet again and strode down onto the main deck. A rope ladder had been thrown over the rail; Altan took hold of it, half sliding down into the launch. A squadron of soldiers—his personal guard—followed him wordlessly. "Row!" he shouted to the sailors when they were all aboard. "Put your backs into it!"

Impatient, Altan jumped from the boat as soon as he heard the hull grate against rocky sand, plunging into waist-high surf and immediately feeling the coldness of the northern sea. His guards followed; together, they splashed stiff-legged out of the waves and onto Onglse. They could hear the shouts of battle and the clash of metal on metal. Farther up the slope, Mundoan troops were push-ing slowly forward. From the right, Altan saw Lucian with Bella and Ardin in the harness of the war chariot, a spear in one hand and reins in the other as Lucian raced across the wet shingle toward him. Altan raised his hand; Lucian lifted the spear in ac-knowledgment. *He knows what I want of him without my saying a word . . .*

"Follow as you can," he told his guard squadron as Lucian slowed the horses to a high-necked canter. Altan vaulted aboard the open-backed chariot, and Lucian urged the horses back into a gallop.

"Forward," he said to Lucian as he gripped the side and took up a spear and shield himself. "Get me to my officers and my men." Lucian quickly grinned back over his shoulder. He noticed that Lucian had a long streak of blood down his left arm and splashes on his armor, but none of it appeared to be his.

"Can't bear to simply watch, Commander?" Lucian said, but he didn't wait for an answer. "Go!" he called to the warhorses, turning them toward the roar of battle. Lucian shouted to the troops ahead, who gave them room as the chariot lurched up the beach and onto trampled grasses strewn with white-flowered sea campion and dotted with lichen-covered boulders. For a moment, Altan had a vision of this place as it might have been in peace: quiet, remote, and beautiful.

Then they passed through into battle and the smell of blood.

The scribes always wrote of battles as if they were delicate, deadly, and ornate dances, with lines advancing or retreating and troops gliding over the land in orderly formations. They might appear that way to someone watching from a safe distance. But Altan knew that for those at the front of the battle and in the killing zone itself, there was only the eternal moment and the single threatening foe they confronted. Battles were a series of small and very personal encounters, hundreds of them happening at once all over the field of combat, and one either survived them or not. There was no time to think or react or reflect. There was only the *now* of iron and bronze weapons, of arrows that could impale you in a moment from nowhere at all. There was the stench of mud and blood and sweat. The battle was a constant din surrounding you, deafening and shrill, and the drumbeat of your own blood pounding in your temples.

A mounted Cateni, a female with blue paint smeared across her forehead, her hair flying under the conical helmet she wore, came at them from the right. Unlike the Mundoa, whose soldiers were entirely male, Cateni women sometimes fought alongside their men, a trait that Altan found personally abhorrent—too many Mundoan soldiers had died from hesitating to engage a female warrior. The rider hurled a spear toward Altan's chariot, and Altan brought up his shield. The leaf-bladed spear hit the metal rondel of the shield and glanced away as Altan brought up his own spear, and Lucian, knowing from experience what Altan needed him to do, yanked the horses hard to the right. Altan's long spear, braced under his arm and against the rim of the chariot, slid over the shoulder of the Cateni's mount and slipped through her ringmail into the woman's guts, driven by the twin force of her own charge and Lucian's turn. Her mouth opened, thick red strands flying from her lips, her eyes white and wide with shock and pain. Her fingers released the sword she'd drawn, and the blade went spinning wildly past Altan's head. The spear's shaft bent, then snapped as the warrior fell, dragging her horse down with her. Altan heard the dying screams of warrior and horse alike. He tossed away the broken shaft and plucked another spear from the chariot's holder.

Another moment. Another small, personal battle.

They found themselves momentarily in a lull. The Cateni had begun a slow retreat, giving ground and disengaging as if they were about to surrender the field to the Mundoa. It was a tactic that Altan had seen before; there were likely but two or three draoi in the fort, and it took time for them to recover from casting their spells. The attack from the fort was intended to give the draoi time to gain back the energy they needed and for reinforcements—both troops and additional draoi, who would have seen the white fire erupt from the tower as a signal—to come from the nearest strongholds.

Altan glimpsed two of his sub-commanders, their cuirasses spattered with gore, one of them missing his helmet. "There!" he said to Lucian, pointing, and Lucian called to Bella and Ardis. They galloped up to the officers, mud and sand spattering from their hoofs and the metal-shod wheels. Altan pointed at the hill and the retreating Cateni. "Ilkur," he shouted to the helmetless one, whose disheveled brown hair glistened with oil and blood. "Take these men here, and give chase to the Cateni. This battle's not over. You, Musa," he said to the other. "Gather your cohort. Take the left flank, and get behind the Cateni. Don't let them get to their embankments. Put them between the horns of the bull, and keep them engaged. The draoi will be reluctant to send their spells if it means killing their own. Move! Both of you!" The officers saluted and began shouting orders, and Altan gripped Lucian's shoulder. "Lucian, take us back down to the beach to our engineers. I want the siege engines assembled and ready and the barrage started *now*. We need to give the damned draoi something to worry about."

"Sir!" Lucian nodded. He yanked hard on the warhorses' reins, and they moved down the slope through a landscape of dead and wounded soldiers, discarded and broken weapons, and torn earth.

Altan pushed his engineers even as the battle raged a few hundred strides upslope. Within a half turn of the glass, two of the half dozen ballistae had been assembled and moved midway up the hill, close enough that their skein-driven springs could hurl boulders into the stone walls of the Cateni fort. Altan had the artillery experts concentrate their barrage on one point in the wall, each subsequent boulder opening the hole wider.

At the same time, protected by a full cohort of soldiers, a siege tower was trundling toward the earthen ramparts around the fort, drawn by eight armored packhorses and bristling with archers, with drawbridges to cross over the embankments. Altan had Lucian drive his chariot forward again, exhorting the men and occasionally charging into the fray to relieve wounded and pressed foot soldiers. Other officers in their own chariots swept up the slope with them, driving back the Cateni's own charioteers, few as they were.

For what seemed forever but was likely only a turn of the glass, the battle raged, with the Mundoa moving slowly forward until the siege tower was nearly touching the wall the ballistae had breached.

It seemed they would take the field this day, and that made Altan scowl suspiciously. The draoi should have recovered by now. At any moment, he expected to hear the mages begin shrieking their mad spells, for fire and lightning to descend on them, followed by another wave of Cateni warriors. But instead, from the hill-forts to the right and left, white fire hissed and fumed, visible even in the daylight. In response to the signal, the remaining Cateni turned their chariots and horses as one and fled the field, their warriors on foot hurrying after them. Though Altan expected arrows and spells to come from the fort, nothing at all harried them as they continued to advance, faster now, in pursuit of the Cateni, who were vanishing into the folded hills to either side of the fort.

"Take the fort," Altan shouted to his officers, to his men. From the chariot, now parked alongside the siege tower while Bella and Ardis stamped impatiently, Altan watched as a cohort led by Ilkur flooded through the breached wall and into the fortifications. Several minutes later, Ilkur appeared at the summit of the wall nearest to Altan.

"Commander Savas, they've abandoned the fort," he shouted down. "There's none left but the dead."

A cheer went up from the soldiers gathered around, and they clashed weapons on shields in triumph and celebration, the shouting slowly moving down the slope to the beach. Altan, looking downslope, could see men waving banners on the boats still anchored in the small bay.

"Why aren't you smiling?" Lucian asked Altan in the midst of the clamor. "We've won this battle. We're standing on Onglse and have taken the first fort."

Altan shook his head. "This doesn't feel right. This isn't how the Cateni have fought before. Greum Red-Hand knows we intended to take Onglse. I'd hoped to catch him sleeping, but . . ."

"You *have* caught him napping. This proves it."

"Perhaps," Altan sighed. "Let's go in and see what it is we've won."

Altan continued to shake his head as he looked around the courtyard of the hill-fort. Had he been the commander here, he wouldn't have abandoned this place so quickly. Yes, the outer wall had been breached, but he could have held the stronghold long enough with the resources inside for help to arrive from the nearest forts: archers on the walls, men working to repair the breach, draoi (not the useless sihirki he had) to cast spells, enough charioteers and warriors to harry and perhaps destroy the siege towers the enemy might bring forward. The inner walls were still intact, and the inland gates were untouched and available to allow reinforcements to enter . . .

No, he would not have retreated, which meant *they* shouldn't have retreated.

Something was wrong . . .

The day had gone gloomy. Altan looked up at the clouds. They were dark, swirling, and unnatural, gathering directly above the newly taken fort. He felt the chariot move under his feet, and Bella stamped hard on the grass of the courtyard, both of the warhorses' eyes wide and nostrils flared. A strange smell pervaded the area, causing Altan's nose to wrinkle. He felt his stomach lurch with sudden fear. All around them, his soldiers were crowded into the area.

"Sorry, sir," he heard Lucian say. "I don't know what's wrong with them."

Altan paid no attention. He could feel the hair on his arms standing on end and a prickling on the back of his neck. There was a tension in the very air, and a terrible premonition came to him. He imagined he could hear a chorus of draoi chanting distantly.

"We have to get everyone out of—" That was all Altan managed to say before a cold wind rushed over the hilltop and the sky became as dark as any night he had ever seen.

He was never certain afterward exactly what had happened next. There was a flash, a simultaneous roar of thunder, and a sensation like falling from the edge of a tall cliff, an impact that tore a scream of pain from him, then . . .

Nothing.

As Altan slowly regained consciousness, he first heard the screams of his men. Through the fluttering screen of his eyelashes, he saw smoke rising from a black hole torn in the earth at the center of the courtyard, and around it, broken wood and stone. And broken men as well, some of them struggling to rise but too many of them still and silent on the ground. "Lucian!" he called as he tried to stand and found that he could not; his left leg dangled strangely, broken, and with the realization, nausea and pain washed over him, leaving him sweating. "Lucian!"

He saw Bella and Ardis then—or what had once been the war-horses, lashed into the harness of the chariot. The broken remains of his chariot were to one side, and in the midst of the shattered wooden planks, unmoving . . .

"Lucian!" he called again, but not far from Ardis' savaged corpse, he could see Lucian's open eyes, the terrible wound that had ripped through mail, bone, and flesh. His lover's arms and legs dangled at impossible angles from his torso, and he knew that Lucian would never again answer.

The scream Altan gave then was not one of pain, but one of loss.

11

Recovery and Lessons

THE MOON HAD GONE from crescent to full and back to crescent again.

For Voada, the moon-cycle had been full of pain as her body slowly healed under Ceiteag's ministrations; of horrible, wracking grief at her loss of Meir, the abduction of her children, and the sacking of her home; of searing guilt at her own survival and the fact that she didn't know what had happened to Orla and Hakan; and most strangely, of calm wonder as Ceiteag began to teach her what her own mother had refused to (or perhaps simply couldn't) teach her. She was slowly learning what it meant to be draoi and beginning to understand what the call of Elia might mean to her.

All that left her simultaneously exhilarated, repelled, and even more guilt-ridden.

If I'd known these things, could I have saved my family? Could I have prevented it all from happening?

She would never know.

"Again," Ceiteag said, forcing Voada to concentrate once more on the spell she was learning. Her left arm, still healing from the break, was tired and sore and was refusing to cooperate with the movements it was supposed to make.

"I can't, Menach Ceiteag. My arm, and I'm still tired from the last . . ."

The old woman looked as if she'd tasted a worm in an apple. "It's not your arm, Voada; it's your mind. It's not your energy you need, but that of your anamacha. Draw from them. Again . . ."

Voada sighed. She knew from her short time with Ceiteag that the woman would not relent. She would push her and push her until she'd done what Ceiteag wanted. Voada opened her arms and closed her eyes, and her anamacha—invisible in the sunlight but standing close to her, as it always did—responded to her gesture, sliding into her as it had on that awful final day in the temple at Pencraig. As Ceiteag had taught her to do here.

As the anamacha entered her body, Voada found herself immersed in the Otherworld of the dead draoi—not Tirnanog, where the souls of dead Cateni waited to be returned to new bodies, but Magh da Chèo, as Ceiteag called it. That place swept around Voada and overlaid her own vision. Magh da Chèo was a dark, grim landscape, a storm-swept bitter plain that had terrified her the first time she'd seen it. It still frightened her, knowing that this was where the souls of the draoi lived, where she would one day dwell herself as part of the anamacha that had chosen her. Inside the anamacha, she would become one of the many voices going back long generations: a collective of those who had been draoi.

Voada opened herself to the voices. <*Here . . .* > she heard them whisper. <*We give you the words . . .* > The skein of ancient words, the pattern of the spell, came to her from the anamacha, their multiple voices slow but distinct, and Voada echoed them, chanting the high song that shaped them, trying to ignore the twinges as she made the hand motions that would contain the spell.

You must be very careful. You're not ready yet to meld completely with your anamacha, Ceiteag had told her when they'd first started this study. *The draoi inside can consume you if you're not strong enough, and you must push them away. Above all, don't call them forward individually; some of those inside the anamacha are too powerful and dangerous, and you won't be able to control them. Stay*

away from them, or they'll send you into madness or death. Don't
listen to them if they call you; don't let them approach you in Magh
da Chèo. Listen to the anamacha only when it speaks with multiple
voices . . .

As Ceiteag had taught her, she flung the spell away from her as
the chant ended, stifling the whimper that the motion threatened
to cause.

Across the glade in which they stood, not far from the Cateni
village and close enough to the river to hear the water, a stroke of
lightning arced from the clouds above them to the fallen maple
tree that Voada had been told was her target. Thunder cracked,
and Voada's vision blurred with the purple afterimages of the
flash. She saw shredded bark fly away and the trunk start to smolder, a puff of smoke rising from it.

The exhaustion that followed the casting of spells hit her then,
threatening to buckle her knees. Her anamacha left her, and Voada
forced herself to stand erect, trying to show nothing. Smoke
curled away from the maple's trunk and vanished, leaving behind
a small, insignificant blackened circle touched at the edges with
white ash.

She heard Ceiteag sigh and thought she also heard an echo of
internal laughter from both her own anamacha and Ceiteag's.
"Well," Ceiteag said, "this time you hit your target, at least. That's
progress."

"I'm sorry, Menach Ceiteag."

The woman's face softened then, and a faint smile wiped over
her dry, thin lips. "If you'd come to me two or three hands of years
ago, when you should have had a mentor guiding you, when you
would have been sent to Bàn Cill for the ceanndraoi to evaluate
you, because . . ." Ceiteag seemed to bite off what she might have
said. She shrugged instead. "But you didn't, and yet this anamacha still managed to choose you. That's something. We should get
back. You're strong enough to walk?"

Ceiteag didn't give Voada a chance to answer. The old woman
turned and strode toward the village with her walking staff, Voada
trailing after her. As soon as they entered the clearing, several of

the villagers came running up to Ceiteag. "The Mundoa, Menach!" A dozen voices seemed to speak at once, so that Voada had to untangle the threads of their words to understand them.

"Have you heard . . . ?"

"They've attacked Onglse . . ."

"A battle's been fought . . ."

"Hands upon hands dead . . ."

"Greum Red-Hand wants all draoi who can come . . ."

". . . calling for the clans to send those warriors to fight . . ."

"Enough!" Ceiteag pointed to Seor, the older man who had first found Voada. "You. What is all this uproar?"

Seor ran a hand through his thin graying hair, as if that might stimulate his memory. "A rider came while you and Voada were away, bearing Greum Red-Hand's seal. He said he was going to each of the villages, to all the clans. The Mundoan boats we saw on the river hands of days ago, the army marching on the far side—they were on their way to Onglse. The rider said that there's been one battle already and that the Mundoa are on the island. Greum Red-Hand calls for all draoi to come to him with as many warriors as the clans will send so that he can push the Mundoa back into the sea." Seor could not quite keep the stern grin from his face. "It's war in Albann Bràghad again, Menach, and it's Onglse itself that we're called on to save this time. I'll go, and my son, and many others . . ."

"You should do as you feel you must," Ceiteag told him. Then her gaze swept over the others. "All of you should."

"And you, Menach? Will you go?"

Voada saw Ceiteag nod slowly, and she felt her own stomach knot in response, uncertain of what this might mean for her. "I will. At dawn tomorrow. For now, go and make whatever preparations you need, and let me do the same."

With that, she started to walk slowly toward the temple, and the others in the village began to disperse, talking loudly among themselves as they went to their own houses.

"What are you waiting for?" Ceiteag had stopped, looking back over her shoulder at Voada.

"I . . . I don't know . . ." The confusion roiled in Voada's head. She could hear her anamacha's voices as well, but they were all a muddle.

"No, you *don't* know nearly enough yet," Ceiteag answered. "And that's the problem. Come with me. You can help me get ready." With a final sniff, Ceiteag continued on.

After a moment, Voada followed.

"What is it that you want?" Ceiteag asked Voada.

Darkness had fallen outside, and a brief supper had been eaten. Ceiteag had said nothing about Greum Red-Hand's summons; Voada wondered if the woman had forgotten it or if she'd decided to ignore it. Now, across the small table near the bed, Ceiteag gnawed on the end of a loaf of brown bread and regarded Voada. The menach's eyes glittered in the light of the fire in the hearth, which also shivered the walls of the temple around them. Ceiteag's anamacha stood near her, as Voada's did with her; she'd almost become used to the ghost's constant presence at her side and its shifting, uncertain visage.

"Menach, what do you mean?"

The lines of the woman's face fell into a familiar scowl. "What is it that you want more than anything else? What kept you alive when you might have died? What drove you to come here?"

That was easy enough to answer. Voada thought of the response to that question every day, and often. "Thinking of my children kept me alive," she said firmly. "I want them back, and I want to pay the Mundoa back twentyfold for every pain they've inflicted on them." She couldn't look at Ceiteag as she said the words. The rage filled her. She could feel fury burning on her face as the bitter taste filled her mouth and her hands curled into fists. The memory of that awful day in what had been her house danced before her eyes: Meir's taibhse leaving her, Orla's terror, Hakan's pain, Una's and Fermac's bodies. A helpless tear tracked down her cheek, and she rubbed it away angrily.

"So you want revenge."

That brought her attention back to the moment. In the dim firelight, Voada couldn't read the woman's face. "If that's how you wish to phrase it."

"And how are you going to gain revenge? You, one small person, against all of those who did this?"

Voada wanted to shout at Ceiteag for her mockery, but she forced herself to remain calm and shrugged. "I don't know yet. But my own injuries are mostly healed—I will always be grateful to you for that, Menach—and if you're going to leave for Onglse, then I suppose I'll go back across the river to Pencraig."

"You're not much of a draoi, and you're a worse warrior. You'll die if you do that."

"You asked what I wanted, Menach, and nothing you can say will make me change my mind. Anyway, I don't care what might happen. You don't understand . . . What they did to them, to me . . . I have to try to get my children back. I *have* to."

A slow nod. "A draoi with her full power might not die. Might even succeed. Your anamacha—it's a strong one."

"Then teach me how to fully use my anamacha, and I'll try to be a good student."

Voada heard Ceiteag sigh before she had even finished speaking. "I wish I could. But I'm only a very minor draoi with a weak anamacha, which means that I'm a poor teacher for you. My calling is more to be a menach, and you're not interested in serving Elia that way. As much as I wish I could, I can't teach you what you need to know." She pushed herself away from the table and rose to her feet with a groan. "And I'm to bed. You should do the same." Ceiteag lifted her hand before Voada could protest. "No. You've nothing to say that can't wait until morning. May Elia bless you with dreams of your children tonight."

I dream of my children every night, Voada wanted to tell her. *I've awakened you several times this moon screaming their names. What I see is a horror and not a blessing.* But Ceiteag was already shuffling to her pallet; it seemed a very few breaths later that she heard Ceiteag start to snore.

"I want Orla. I want Hakan. I want to hold them again." Voada spoke softly into the night air, looking at the statue of Elia on the altar stone at the center of the sun-paths. She could feel the cold brush of her anamacha as it moved closer to her. "Can you give me that, Mother Goddess? Is that within your power to grant me?"

<*We aren't yet at the place we need to be . . .* > She heard the whisper of her anamacha's voices as the ghost touched her. <*Not the place. Not the time. Not yet . . .* >

"Then when?" she asked the anamacha.

<*Not this place. Not this time . . .* >

Voada sighed. Standing, she went to her own pallet on the far side of the temple. Sleep, when it came, was troubled and confused, and she heard both Orla and Hakan wailing and crying for her. In her dream, she cried along with them.

The morning light slashed in through the east windows of the temple and across Voada's face. She shielded her eyes from the light. She could hear Ceiteag, already up, singing softly to herself in a quavering voice. Voada lifted her head from the pallet to see the old woman packing clothing and supplies into a sack. In the shadows of the temple, she could see both Ceiteag's anamacha and her own, watching.

"You're leaving?" Voada asked sleepily.

"Soon. You should also."

"You'll die if you do that." Voada remembered the menach's comment from the night before, and it rekindled her anger at what was done to her family and her fear of what Orla and Hakan had experienced since. *I've waited too long here. Orla and Hakan need me . . .*

Voada tossed aside the blanket from her pallet. After her morning ablutions, she began rolling up her own few belongings: clothing gifted to her from the villagers, a spare pair of leather shoes, a wooden mug, a water skin, a fire stone. The silver oak leaf pendant Meir had given her was already around her neck, where it always stayed. She rolled the rest in a blanket and tied it with leather thongs, ready to carry. Ceiteag had finished packing and was watching her.

"Thank you again for all you've done, Menach," Voada told her. "I will always be grateful, and may Elia reward you for your kindness."

"You're leaving to seek your revenge?"

"I seek my children first." Involuntarily, Voada's hand went to the oak leaf pendant. She clutched it, remembering how excited Orla had been when she'd been given her own silver oak leaf, remembering how she'd glimpsed that pendant around Orla's neck as she'd been taken away . . .

Ceiteag nodded. "What does your anamacha tell you?"

"I do what my heart tells me, Menach, not the will of ghosts." The silver warmed in her hand. Her fingers caressed the serrations of the leaf.

"Hearts are fickle muscles. They can lead you to be rash and too quick." Ceiteag paused. She watched as Voada slung her pack over her shoulders. "I told you that I can't teach you what you need to know. That's true. But there are those who can. Come to Onglse. The draoi at Bàn Cill can show you how to fully use your anamacha, how to open it completely so you can wield its power. They can make you the draoi you'll need to be to have any chance to rescuing your children."

Voada shook her head, but without conviction. She looked at her anamacha: <*Yes. Listen to her. We aren't yet at the place we need to be* . . . > "That would take yet more time, and my children are south and east, not north and west. I would lose them."

"You've already lost them, my dear. Do you know where they are at this moment?" Voada had to shake her head, and Ceiteag continued. "As a draoi, you might find them again with your anamacha. And you might survive long enough to get the rest of what you want. The Mundoa—they hurt you because of what you are, Voada: because you're Cateni, and the life of a Cateni is worth nothing to them. We're chattel. To them, we're no more than possessions and slaves. As Hand-wife, you were blind to that. But we're also what they most fear. They're afraid that if they don't beat us down and keep us there, we'll rise up against them and push them back into the sea from which they came. What happened to you and your children happened because you're Cateni, because you forced them to face that fear and acknowledge it. Here in the north, we've never forgotten that. I'm telling you to embrace what you are. I'm telling you to be a bright sword, to be one of those Cateni who make them shiver in their fine boots and cower in their marble halls. But if you go back now, as weak as you are now, you'll never be that. You've not been tempered in the fire. That fire waits for you on Onglse. You have to find the courage and the faith in Elia and your own people to go there. You have to *become* Cateni, not something that is neither Mundoan nor Cateni and therefore less than either. Then—possibly—you might be able to recover your children and have your revenge."

It was the longest speech Voada had ever heard the woman make, and her fervor pulled at Voada, making her recall every time Voice Kadir and Voice-wife Dilara had made some disparaging comment about the Cateni or treated Voada and Meir like they were errant children or pets to be scolded and chastised. She remembered her early youth, before she met Meir, and how her parents had bowed whenever a Mundoan had approached them, how their voices changed whenever a Mundoan talked to them, going lower and softer and never daring to contradict what they were being told, how the elders had mused at night about the great exploits of old Cateni warriors and draoi and spoke of legends that had been told to them in their youth but were now only ghosts and whispers. She remember the statue of Elia that her family had buried in order to save it from being destroyed, of the statue of Emperor Pashtuk that stood in Her place in Her temple.

They stole our past from us—at least in the south.

Voada's anamacha had glided close to her as Ceiteag was speaking. Now it slid partially into her, the cold presences inside seeping into Voada's blood. *<Onglse,>* their chorused voices echoed in her head. *<We remember. We must go there. Home.>*

"Can you promise me that I'll be able to find my children, at least?"

Now it was Ceiteag who shook her head. "I promise you only that possibility. Nothing more, because nothing in the future is certain. The future is in Elia's hands and your own."

Voada was still cradling the silver oak leaf. She saw Ceiteag looking at her hand. She released the pendant and tugged her pack higher on her back. Voada glanced at the altar, at the statue of Elia caught in sunlight.

"I'll come with you," she said.

"Good," Ceiteag said. "I have something for you." She reached into her own roll and pulled something out: a bronze torc, the metal gleaming. On the face of one of the knobs, Voada could see the incised mark for "oak"—a vertical line with two short horizontal lines meeting it on the left side. "This is for you. You're draoi, and you should be marked as such."

"I can't . . ." Voada protested.

"You will. I won't have someone I taught going to Onglse without it. Lower your head, woman."

Voada did. Ceiteag pulled the torc open enough to slip the knobbed end around her neck, then pushed it closed so that the metal was cool against her skin. "There," she said, sounding satisfied. "Now everyone will know you're a draoi."

Everyone but me, Voada thought, but she said nothing. Instead, she managed to smile at Ceiteag as her fingers caressed the polished torc.

12

On the Path

ONGLSE, SHE'D BEEN TOLD, was the long gray smudge on the horizon past a few darker lumps of closer islands, all set on a gray sea that flailed at the rocks of the shore on which Voada stood and crashed with cold, white fury against the low cliffs. Behind her, in a makeshift village of tents and crude shelters, were those they'd gathered up in their walk to the shore of the aptly named Storm Sea, a journey of two hands and four days. They'd gone well north of the closest approach to Onglse, warned that there were several Mundoan cohorts there guarding the shore as well as Mundoan ships patrolling the channel between. Worse, the news had come to them that the main force of the Mundoan army was already on Onglse, though there was no immediate danger to Bàn Cill.

Voada wondered how they would reach Onglse if it was so well guarded, but Ceiteag seemed unconcerned.

The wind off the Storm Sea was cold and wet with salt spray, and Voada pulled her woolen cloak, beaded now with water, tighter around her shoulders. She couldn't see her anamacha in the broken light of the day, but she could sense its presence near her, colder than the wind. She turned away from the vista before her and began walking back to the village through a stand of wind-twisted aspens, birches, and wych elms. The wind swirling through the branches carried a wisp of speech to her.

". . . you've all felt the anamacha who has claimed her." Voada recognized the voice: Ceiteag. A male voice, one she couldn't readily identify, answered. A chill touched Voada. <*They speak of us,*> her anamacha said, <*and of you.*>

"Aye, we've felt it. We thought that one lost and dead forever." Another male voice, with a tone of disbelief woven through it. That voice Voada remembered: Conn, a draoi from another tribe they'd met on the journey.

"Aye," yet another voice agreed, this one female. "That's what I was told as well by the ceanndraoi himself. Greum Red-Hand always claimed that the anamacha of Leagsaidh Moonshadow died when the last image of Elia was taken from the temples of the south."

Voada moved slowly and quietly through the trees and black-thorn brush toward the voices. She stopped when she could see the speakers just inside the tree line with the encampment a hundred strides beyond them: Ceiteag and four others—two men, two women—huddled together. She'd been introduced to them by Ceiteag over the last several days; all of them were draoi who had responded to Greum Red-Hand's summons to come to Onglse.

"Then it seems the ceanndraoi was mistaken." That was Ceiteag again, but the others seemed unconvinced.

"Greum Red-Hand, mistaken? That's not something I'd care to tell him to his face," Conn answered with a laugh. "We can't be certain she has the Moonshadow's anamacha. Maybe we're the ones who are mistaken."

Ceiteag's laugh was dry and unamused. "You know that's not the case, all of you, or you wouldn't be troubled by the possibility."

Leagsaidh Moonshadow. Voada knew the name; all Cateni did. She was a draoi of legend, one of the Eldest, her accomplishments more myth than reality. In the tales Voada had been told as a child, when the sun failed to rise for a full summer, it was Leagsaidh Moonshadow who called down the moon from its place in the sky to replace the sun so that the crops could grow in its light and heat, causing the sun to grow jealous and return. It was Leagsaidh Moonshadow who had pulled Onglse up from the Storm Sea to become the haven for all draoi. It was Leagsaidh Moonshadow . . .

"Does *she* know?" asked one of the women: Marta, if Voada recalled their brief introduction correctly.

"Why not ask her?" she heard Ceiteag respond.

The woman's gray head turned, and her gaze found Voada's. "Well, Voada?" she asked.

The others had followed her glance. They were all staring at Voada through the intervening branches. She walked toward them, her fingers scissoring the oak leaf on its chain. "I didn't intend to overhear you, Menach Ceiteag. I was only out walking, and—"

"I know," Ceiteag said, waving her hand impatiently. "I wasn't accusing you of spying. Answer the question we've asked. Is the Moonshadow part of your anamacha?"

"I don't . . ." Voada started to answer, but her anamacha slid partially into her, unasked, at the same moment. <*That name. . . . we thought it forgotten. Yes, one of us was called by that name. She is among us, as one day you will be.*> The voices of the anamacha sounded almost gleeful, as if the name had opened up memories that they had misplaced or lost. Voada wondered at that, but the other draoi were still watching her, waiting. "Yes," Voada finished. "It seems she is. What does that mean?"

"Much. Or nothing at all."

"Still talking to your students in riddles, Ceiteag?" Conn laughed. "You did that with me as well. Let's be more plain with our words. Voada, many of the anamacha have vanished since the Mundoa came, and without the anamacha, there are no draoi. Yet one of the oldest known anamacha thought lost with all the others evidently remains, and somehow it has found you. Greum Red-Hand has to know about this. If the anamacha that holds the Moonshadow still exists, then so may all the others, which means there may be more draoi in the south who—like you—aren't aware of their full capabilities."

"Worse would be if the Mundoan sihirki subvert them," Marta added. "What if those draoi of the lost anamacha are turned against us?"

"That's why we must go to Greum Red-Hand as soon as possible," Ceiteag said. "The answers to all questions will be at Bàn Cill. Tomorrow. We've been promised that tomorrow the ships will be here and we can sail."

The others nodded in agreement, but their smiles were too broad and too forced. Voada had the sense that they hadn't told her everything they knew, nor had they explained why her anamacha had alarmed them so. There were gaps and omissions in the information she'd been given.

But that could wait. As Ceiteag had said, the answers were at Bàn Cill. At least Voada hoped so.

<Bàn Cill . . . Yes, that is where we must go . . . >

So Voada attempted a smile and walked back to the village with the other draoi.

The ships did come the next morning: several four-oared, single-masted vessels of sturdy oak with leather sails, emerging from the morning fog and anchoring just off the rocky shingle below the cliffs. The ships were from Cateni coastal villages to the north, and they smelled heavily of fish and brine, with nets of twisted linen draped over the rails.

At Ceiteag's order, the draoi were placed on separate vessels— "If the Mundoan warships are out there waiting, we don't want one lucky ram to sink us all"—though Voada remained with Ceiteag. They approached Onglse from the north and east, coming in from the Storm Sea side. They remained unchallenged, the ocean empty of any other vessels, and pulled into a small harbor to be met by grim-faced warriors and a single draoi, who had come from the hill-fort above the harbor. "Menach Ceiteag," the draoi said. "Well met. It's good to see you once again and to see so many with you. Who have you brought with you?"

"Well met yourself, Daibhidh. It's been too long. We have five full draoi, one acolyte, and two hundred and more clan warriors."

Daibhidh nodded. "They're all needed. The warriors I'll leave to the fort commanders to distribute. The draoi should follow me. We go to Bàn Cill."

It took most of three days walking the steep hills of Onglse, but eventually Voada looked down into the central valley of the island and Bàn Cill. The sacred home of the draoi was surrounded by steep-walled green slopes with a ring of hill-forts along the ridge-line. In the valley stood another circle: a narrow band that was a forest of tall, imposing oaks. The sight of them made Voada touch the pendant at her neck. Surrounded by the oaks loomed a ring of dark standing stones capped with granite slabs, with taller open-ings at the solstice points and flagged paths marking them as well. Where the paths intersected at the center of the stones, a large temple stood, its walls the height of three tall people, crafted from polished stone that caught the sun's light and threw it back, daz-zling Voada's eyes. The door stood open, and the windows of the sun-path weren't simply openings cut into the stone like in the temples on Pencraig Bluff and in Ceiteag's village. Instead, they were filled with panes of translucent white crystal.

Rings within rings within rings.

In all of Cateni history, Bàn Cill had never known the touch of an invader's boot. "As long as there remains a draoi in Bàn Cill, it will never fall," Voada heard Ceiteag say, as if she were having the same thoughts as Voada. Led by Daibhidh, they followed a road through the gates of a stone wall that connected the towers of the forts, then wound down through the brush and bracken to the oaks. As they approached the oaks, Voada saw a cloaked form move from the shade of the trees onto the path they followed. The man was tall with a warrior's build, long black hair braided down his back, and a thick oiled beard also heavily speckled with gray. His face showed years of exposure to sun and weather, the skin tanned and chiseled. Under thick eyebrows, eyes as dark as his hair regarded them. The bronze torc of a draoi, this one wrapped with silver wire, collared his neck.

Daibhidh stopped a few paces from the man and bowed low. "Ceanndraoi Greum," he said, "more draoi have answered your summons."

Greum inclined his head to the group, holding out his hand in greeting. The Red-Hand: Greum's right hand was mottled past the wrist with a rash or perhaps the scars of an old burn, the blotches a bright red-orange. "I thank you all for arriving so quickly," he said. His voice was a rich, deep baritone—much like Altan Savas' voice, Voada thought. "I know most of you, and it's good to see you all again. We've need of your skills." Voada felt his gaze move to her; she held it with her chin lifted. His eyes slid just to her right, as if he saw her anamacha standing alongside her. His eyes narrowed slightly, his lips pressing together under his beard as his regard came back to Voada, slipping down to the torc around her neck so obviously that Voada had to resist the impulse to put her hand there. "I don't know you," he said. Voada wasn't sure whether he was referring to her or her anamacha. She noticed that he pointedly didn't use the word "draoi" to refer to her.

"I'm Voada Paorach," she told him. "Menach Ceiteag told me that I should come here to learn from you."

"You're southern. Your accent is Albann Deas. Almost Mundoan."

"And your accent is northern. We can't help where we're from, Ceanndraoi. I'm not a spy, if that's your worry. I've as much a reason to hate the Mundoa as you. Perhaps more."

He gave a laugh that was mostly a cough, but there was no amusement in his face. "That may be, but you've chosen a bad time." He spread his hands as if to encompass the entire island. She saw the red stain on both. "Onglse is besieged by Commander Savas and his army."

"And my coming here was as little a choice of mine as where I was born," Voada told the man. There was an arrogance to Greum Red-Hand that reminded her too much of Voice Kadir. She could feel everyone staring at her. "As it happens, I've met Commander Savas," she said. "In Pencraig, where I was once Hand-wife. I even liked the man—he did my husband and me a kindness. But if you believe that makes me a friend of the Mundoa after what was done to me, you're mistaken. I didn't choose the time to come here."

"A Hand-wife," Greum said slowly, as if trying to taste the words. "A friend of Savas. And yet also claiming to be a draoi, the very thing the Mundoa hate and fear most. You have to admit those are strange and conflicting attributes."

"She only recently found her anamacha, Ceanndraoi," Ceiteag broke in quickly. "She was touched by Elia even in Albann Deas, and she might have been a menach alone, as she can see taibhsean and guide them to the sun-path and peace. But this anamacha also sought her out—the anamacha of the Moonshadow, Ceanndraoi, that was believed to be lost. The others here have felt that also, and Voada has confirmed it. She *is* draoi, and she needs your mentorship."

Voada saw Greum's gaze flick over to where her anamacha stood, and this time he regarded the emptiness there for a long time, his head cocked as if he were listening. She wondered whether his own anamacha was talking to him.

"We'll discuss this," Greum said finally. "I'll let Daibhidh show you where you'll be staying, and we'll meet in the temple in two stripes. I have other things I must attend to now. Daibhidh, after you've shown them where they can rest, have the clan heads come to me."

With that, he inclined his head once more, turned, and walked quickly toward the temple. Voada watched him go, his stride that of a person certain of himself.

"This way," she heard Daibhidh say. "I'll have food and drink sent to you as well, though there's little enough of that here of late."

"Do you trust him?" Voada asked Ceiteag.

"Ceanndraoi Greum? Of course I do. Why would you ask that?"

"I don't know. There's just something . . ." Voada shook her head. "He reminds me of someone I wish I'd never come to know."

The room to which they'd been shown was in the gate tower of the high fortifications: a stone-walled chamber that was barely large enough for the two beds it held, with a single small window looking out over the valley of Bàn Cill and admitting a dim shaft of light. The food and drink that Daibhidh had sent them was a hunk of dry bread, a slab of hard cheese, and a jar of tepid, watered small beer. Voada plucked off a bit of the bread and chewed the stale crust.

"Greum Red-Hand has forgotten more about being a draoi than I ever knew," Ceiteag said, sipping at a mug of the beer. "He's a hard and ungentle teacher, but a far better mentor than I. He always said that I was more menach than draoi, and he was right. Greum is who you need to show you how to be a draoi, Voada. But you need to understand that with the Mundoan forces here . . ."

"I do understand that. He has far more important and pressing matters to worry about than me. Maybe I've made a mistake, coming here."

"Does your anamacha believe that?"

In the darkness of the room, they could see their anamacha easily, Ceiteag's near her and Voada's a stride away to her left. The multiple faces were watching her; Voada wondered if any of them heard or understood their conversation. Voada lifted a shoulder. "No," she admitted. The anamacha had said little to her since their arrival, but it had made its feelings clear before they'd taken ship. "They wanted to come here. All along."

"Then this is where you should be," Ceiteag responded, as if that answered all the questions and uncertainty Voada might be feeling.

It didn't. Voada went to the window, gazing out at Bàn Cill. She could feel the chill of the anamacha's presence at her shoulder. She wondered what it saw and what it felt at seeing this place where the souls that composed it had once lived and walked.

13

The Shadow of the Moon

THE TEMPLE AT BÀN Cill was far larger and more elaborate than any that Voada had seen before. The central eye open above the altar was bordered with blue and white tiles in an elaborate knotted pattern. The crystalline windows of the sun-path allowed in a milky, thick light. The altar was a jet black, glossy stone, unlike any in Voada's experience, and the statue of Elia was as tall as Voada and painted in eerily lifelike colors. The sun-paths were gilded and broad, and there were small private rooms along the walls, something Voada had seen in no other temple at all. Their footsteps echoed loudly off the distant roof as they took the long walk from the door to the altar.

Greum Red-Hand emerged from one of the side rooms as they approached, along with two men bearing weapons and shields, their cloaks mud-spattered and torn. One of them had a jagged, old scar running white through his dark beard along his left cheek and jaw and long black hair in a braid down his back. He wore an outer cloak of deep red, sewn at the hems with silver threads in a knot pattern, and his forehead was stained with streaks of blue. "This news is troubling. Keep me informed, Ceannàrd Iosa," they heard Greum say to the scarred man. "Let me know how Commander Savas responds or if he tries to move from the fort he holds."

Both of the warriors clashed spears on shields and strode quickly away, giving the draoi only fleeting glances.

"I apologize," Greum said to the group. His gaze seemed to linger on Voada and her anamacha—barely visible in the temple's brightness—for a breath longer than any of the others.

"We understand, Ceanndraoi," Ceiteag answered. "The Mundoan army is on Onglse. How can we help? That's why we've come."

"Once I've reacquainted myself with your individual abilities, you'll be sent to the south and east of the island. The Mundoa have only a tenuous hold here. They have a beach on which to land men and supplies, and they hold one hill-fort. That's more than they've ever taken before; their Commander Savas isn't the total fool that his predecessor was. If it came to warrior against warrior alone, there are so many of them that I would despair of holding Onglse, even though we Cateni are more fierce than these southern people." His lips tightened under his beard. "Despite that, we've managed to stop them. They've more fighting men than we have, aye, but they've no answer to our draoi, especially not their useless sihirki."

Laughter rippled through the draoi at that, echoing in the temple, but Greum's stern look quickly silenced the laughter. "Our draoi are increasingly drained," Greum continued, his ruddy hands slicing through the window light. "I myself spent the last hand of days casting spells at the Mundoa and at the fort where they huddle. My anamacha can no longer help me. I came back to pray to Elia for her aid and to allow my anamacha to recover before I go back. There are two more hands of draoi here now who are doing the same." Greum drew himself up with a sigh. "But enough. I would know each of you again so I know where you'll be best used. Ceiteag, come with me . . ."

Greum took each of the draoi, one by one, into his room in the temple. Ceiteag emerged after half a stripe. She merely told Conn to go in, then left the temple without another word, with only a glance and a shrug to Voada. Voada waited, pacing the temple as the others went in and departed, and finally knelt down before the altar and looked up to the statue of Elia. She brought the silver oak leaf pendant out from under her *léine*, closing her hand around it for the comfort it gave her. She tried to pray but found it difficult to keep her concentration. Being in the temple brought back memories of Pencraig, of Meir, Orla, and Hakan, of the day when her old life had been wrenched away from her.

Why am I here? Why did I come when Orla and Hakan are so far away and lost? Did I do the right thing? Elia gave Voada no answers to those questions. There was only silence and the wintery presence of her anamacha at her side.

It was perhaps two stripes of the candle later when Marta, the last of the draoi, came out of the room. Greum emerged with her. As Marta left, Voada could hear Greum's footsteps approaching her where she knelt. She heard him stop a few strides away, could feel his gaze on her, or perhaps he was looking at her anamacha.

"So that *does* contain the Moonshadow," he growled. "Her anamacha is still with us."

Voada brought her head down and looked over her shoulder. "That's what I'm told."

"Why did it choose you?"

"I don't know." Voada let the pendant drop to her léine. She groaned as she leaned back, flexing her knees—which protested with twin cracks—and sitting cross-legged on the floor of the temple. Slowly and more gingerly, Greum imitated her, sitting so they were facing each other with Elia's statue gazing out over their heads.

"Ceiteag told me what happened to you in Pencraig," the Ceann-draoi said. "I have four children myself—three sons and a daughter—and I sent them to fosterage with their uncles on Beinn Head only half a moon ago. It wasn't safe for them here. And if the Mundoa can reach them on Beinn Head . . . well, then we are lost indeed, and it won't matter."

"Do you miss them?" Greum nodded. "And their mother?" Voada asked.

"She's in Tirnanog. She died a moon after birthing our last child, two summers ago." What might have been a bitter smile touched his lips. "And aye, I miss her also."

The unshielded pain in his eyes made Voada regret what she'd said to Ceiteag about Greum earlier. At that moment, he seemed all too vulnerable, all too normal—no different from herself. "I'm sorry."

He shifted his gaze to Elia's statue, then back to her. "I know you understand that loss. Tell me, Voada, what is it that you hope to gain here? If you could have your full ability as a draoi, what would you do with it?"

Her answer surprised even her with its ferocity. "I would have my stolen children returned to me. Then I would drive the Mundoa from their homes the way I was driven from mine. I would make every last one of them feel the pain I've felt, doubled and redoubled. I would send them all back across the Barrier Sea to Rumeli, wailing bitter tears. I would give them fire and blood and death."

She wondered whether she'd spoken too harshly, but Greum's fingers only spidered through his beard. "Ceiteag said there was rage inside you. I don't think she understood how much." With a groan, Greum pushed himself up from the floor. "Stand," he told Voada, holding out his hand to her. She ignored his proffered hand, standing on her own, and she saw Greum grin momentarily at that. "What do you know about the anamacha?" he asked.

"Only what Ceiteag has told me—that an anamacha is the collected souls of all the draoi it has chosen before, and that it's through the anamacha that a draoi gains power."

"True enough, but far too simple. You need to understand this, Voada—a living draoi is simply a vessel to hold what the anamacha can give. A draoi can only be as powerful as his or her anamacha, and then only if that draoi can bear to merge completely with them—an anamacha is properly a 'them,' not an 'it.' Plural, not singular, though we all sometimes think of them as one entity or refer to them that way. A draoi has to be a perfect vessel and strong enough to contain the anamacha. And if you aren't able to contain your anamacha, they will consume you."

"Why does everyone whisper about my anamacha containing Leagsaidh Moonshadow? Why should that matter?"

"It doesn't, perhaps. The Moonshadow is a great figure among the draoi, but as I said, an anamacha isn't one but many, and some who held the anamacha of the Moonshadow were mediocre draoi at best. But not all. The anamacha of the Moonshadow was last held by Iomhar of the Marsh, who was killed in the first battle with the Mundoa at Íseal Head; he was ceanndraoi at that time. We thought this anamacha gone—lost, as many of anamacha from Albann Deas remain lost."

"So this Iomhar is in my anamacha too."

Greum was nodding. "And hand upon hand upon hand of others, all the way to the Moonshadow, who is the Eldest of those we know. That's why the anamacha are dangerous. To be *with* them, to use what they can give you . . . that can be like trying to swallow glowing coals from a hearth."

"You want to frighten me."

"I want you to understand the risk you are undertaking. As I said, the draoi is a vessel, and sometimes a vessel can't hold what's poured into it and bursts."

"I don't care about that," Voada told him. She glared at Greum defiantly. "Let them break me, if that's what they demand. I want my children; if this is the only way I can have them, then this is what I'll do. Show me how. Teach me."

"If I do and you can't hold this anamacha, they will shred your mind. You'll become mad, lost in the Otherworld Magh da Chèo, and you will die. They will consume you completely. Forever."

"Teach me," Voada repeated.

Greum's gaze held her own for several breaths, neither of them speaking. She could see his anamacha alongside him; like her own, the faces caught within flickered across its face like shadows from a fire.

"Then we'll begin, since that's your wish. Give me your hands." He held out his own hands toward her; reluctantly, she obeyed. His grip was stronger than she liked, on the verge of hurting her, but she forced herself not to react. "Call your anamacha at the same time that I call mine," Greum said. "Bring them into you so you can hear their voices."

Voada looked at her anamacha. "Come to me," she mouthed, and the ghost slid toward her silently. She felt their cold touch entering her, felt Greum's hands tighten even more on hers as his anamacha did the same to him.

Then her anamacha was entirely inside her. <We're here,> they said in their multiple voices.

"Open yourself, Voada," she heard Greum say, his voice doubled with those of his anamacha. <Open yourself.>

"How?" she asked. "I don't know what you mean. That's nothing Ceiteag showed me."

<Like this . . . > Both her anamacha and Greum's spoke at the same time, a chorus of voices and tones. Voada felt something change inside, as it had when Ceiteag had first shown her how to bring the anamacha into her, but this . . . this was far stronger, and painful besides, as if she were allowing herself to be ripped open. She cried out as she *felt* the anamacha filling her, becoming her, seeping into her, and her vision was no longer her own.

She gasped.

She'd glimpsed Magh da Chèo before with Ceiteag, but she realized now that what she had seen had been like looking at a landscape through a fog.

Now, the temple where they'd been standing was gone. Greum was gone, though she could feel his touch on her hands. She inhaled, smelling a storm-odor, as if the very air had been altered by lightning and rain. In front of her, in a terrible world lanced with brilliant colors—shifting, swirling, sparking—stood a crowd that moved endlessly around and through her. Ghosts, all. As they passed, they stared at her: faces she didn't recognize, male and female, some wrinkled with time and some smooth-skinned and young. Yet when she tried to focus on any one of them, the image slipped away, as if she could only glimpse it in her peripheral vision no matter how she turned her head.

There was sound, too: their voices calling to her, shouting, cajoling, comforting, a cacophony which no one voice dominated, from which she could catch only fleeting phrases. And the cold—she was wrapped in ice, shivering as if she would never be warm again.

<The power is here, all around you. Can you feel it? We are part of it. You will be part of it with us.>

This wasn't like the other times she had merged with her anamacha. There'd been the feel of cold, yes, and their voices, but she had always retained her vision. She had always been able to see her own world in front of her. Now she was fully in their world, and there was no solid ground underneath her, only more light and more confusion. The dance of bodies, the flickering of light and color, the noise, the movement—all of it made her stomach churn, and she fought not to be sick, choking back the bile that rose, burning, in her throat.

<Just let go of the Red-Hand. We will take you. We will show you. Let go of him, and you will be with us.>

"Be calm, Voada," she heard Greum say, though she couldn't see the man, only feel the pressure of his hands. "This is normal."

"Where are we?" she asked.

"You know where you are: Magh da Chèo, the world the anamacha inhabit," he answered. "This is the world from which the draoi take their power. I brought you here so you could see it as it really is."

<Let him go . . . >

"It's frightening, this place."

She thought she heard Greum laugh through the chaotic noise. "I'd think you a fool if you *weren't* frightened. If I let go of you right now, you'd be lost—especially with this anamacha. But if you wish to be draoi, you need to learn how to come here, how to find the souls within the anamacha that are safe for you to use, how to make them do your bidding. Menach Ceiteag has been very careful with you so far. Too careful, in my opinion—she's too cautious a teacher. If you want what I can teach you, you'll also have to accept the danger. Will you do that?"

"Yes, Ceanndraoi," she told him. "Yes."

"Then we'll start. Cast out your anamacha."

<No! Don't listen to him. Stay with us! Be with us!>

"How? I don't know how."

"You do. Simply close your mind to them. Don't allow them to touch your thoughts. *Order* them to leave you. Tell them that *you* are in control, not them."

<Stay with us. He lies. We can show you everything. Just stay with us . . . >

Voada shut her eyes to the glowing world, to the crowd of ghosts around her, to the smells and the tastes and the odors. She pushed the anamacha's voices away, wanting to clap her hands to her ears to block them out but not daring to break contact with Greum.

A breath. Two. Three.

Slowly, she felt this interior world fading, and when she opened her eyes again, she was in the temple once more. Greum was still holding her hands, but their anamacha had moved away, now appearing like the taibhsean Voada had shepherded to the sun-path and their rest in Tirnanog. Greum's fingers relaxed, and she pulled her hands away from him quickly. He smiled under his beard at that. "For a first time, you did well," he said. "I've had many that I had to pull back myself. Do you need to sit?"

Voada realized that she was exhausted, as if she'd been involved in some tremendous physical activity for several stripes of the candle. Her legs felt weak. She did sit, letting herself slide to the floor of the temple. Greum's own face showed traces of the same weariness, and he sat with her again, saying nothing until she spoke. "I never had to do that before to cast a spell."

"And how impressive were those spells you cast?" Greum asked. When Voada didn't answer, his smile widened. "I thought so. Ceiteag . . . well, she's a good and kind menach, but as a draoi, she wasn't one of my better students. Perhaps that was my fault—I pushed her hard, and she resented that. She treated you too gently, the way she wanted to have been taught herself."

"Perhaps if you had been a better teacher, Ceanndraoi Greum, Ceiteag would have become a better draoi."

If he took offense, Voada saw no indication on his face. "Perhaps. It's common enough for a student to blame the teacher for their failure to learn. But you should know this. Draoi have little to do with the power of the spells they cast; that comes mostly from the anamacha, who draws the power from Magh da Chèo. Some are more powerful than others; some are weak."

"And mine?"

"Yours?" He laughed, a bitter sound. "Yours is hardly what I'd call weak."

"Because of the Moonshadow?"

Greum shook his head. "Not entirely. But . . . Do you know the story of Leagsaidh Moonshadow?"

Voada could only shake her head. "I've heard the name, but that's all."

Greum sighed. "Listen, then . . ."

"Leagsaidh Moonshadow was the Eldest," Greum said, "the First Draoi. She was Leagsaidh of Clan Mac Cába then, the wife of the clan àrd, and she was said to be comely enough, with auburn hair that the summer sun would touch with gold and eyes the color of a deep sky late in the day. Clan Mac Cába was from the southwestern shores of Albann Deas, near where the town of Darande is now.

"That was long ago, in the time when the White Ships arrived from the farthest south and their bloodthirsty people spilled out to ravage Cateni towns and villages, killing everyone who stood in their path. That included Leagsaidh's husband and family and most of their clan. In the diaspora that followed, when many of the clans went north across the River Meadham and into the mountains where no people lived, Leagsaidh led the remnants of her clan north to Onglse. It was she who found the circle of blackstones, already in place and waiting—erected there, she always claimed, by Elia and the demigods.

"It's said that when Leagsaidh touched the central stone—which is now the altar that you see in front of you, Voada—a presence trapped in the stone leapt out: the Moonshadow. The Moonshadow was the source-anamacha, the first being to bring a Cateni into Magh da Chèo, the guide who would show Leagsaidh how to use the power there, and the Mother of all the anamacha to come.

"Being first, being the only, Leagsaidh became the most powerful of the draoi as well.

"And eventually, wielding that power would drive her mad.

"As Ceiteag undoubtedly warned you, Voada, using any anamacha can be dangerous to a draoi. You've just barely begun to understand that. Just think of how it must have been for Leagsaidh, with no one to guide her and whose anamacha contained a demigod, its fierce power burning in her mind, a presence wild and difficult rising constantly within her. I find it amazing that she was able to remain sane for as long as she did.

"But she did. For the next several years, others came to Onglse who had the ability to draw their own anamacha from the blackstone—drawn, perhaps, by Leagsaidh unlocking it—though none of these new anamacha were comparable in power to Leagsaidh's own. Yet she helped guide the new draoi so they could use these other, weaker demigods.

"When it seemed all the anamacha that the blackstone contained had been freed, Leagsaidh Moonshadow led her draoi followers southward once more as their ceanndraoi—to war. To wipe those of the White Ships from Albann. All the tales of that time say that the war was both terrible and long, though it's impossible to know whether those stories are true or simply fanciful, grand legends. What we *do* know is that the spells of the new draoi slowly pushed the enemy back and back, and where Leagsaidh Moonshadow walked, none could stand against her. But the power she held was already tearing at her, consuming her more with each passing moon, and she was becoming more irrational and difficult to deal with even as her ability to wield spells grew.

"In the final battle with those of the White Ships on Ìseal Head—the same place where, long years later, the Mundoa would first come to Albann—the people of the White Ships surrendered the field, but the Moonshadow fought on, wanting to kill them to the last and refusing to listen to those who counseled her to stop.

"In the end, she turned against her own draoi and warriors when they tried to interfere.

"They killed her, because she left them no choice. Because she was insane with power. Because she could no longer be reasoned with, and she considered anyone who stood against her to be an enemy.

"That was Leagsaidh Moonshadow. That is who is hidden deep within your anamacha. And that is who you must be careful to never bring forth.

"But," Greum finished, "the story of the Moonshadow's life ended ages ago, and the older the soul, the more difficult it is to find and to use. You haven't met the Moonshadow yet. No, those presences you've felt were the most recent of the draoi inside—Iomhar, perhaps, and those before him who had the anamacha you now hold—but not the Moonshadow. Had it been her . . ." His shoulders lifted and fell again under his tunic. "I would have pulled you back here immediately. You would not have survived her touch, Voada. Not yet. Maybe never."

She took that in, nodding gravely. "What I just did . . . will I have to do this every time?"

"If you want to be more than some sad bog draoi that people come to for herbs and spells to make their livestock breed, yes. You need to know how to open yourself fully and how to best use the souls within your anamacha for what they can give you."

"Then show me." Voada felt the anger and grief surging up in her. She *wanted* this, wanted to have the power Greum hinted at.

Wanted to *use* it. *Orla, Hakan, I've not forgotten you or abandoned you. I will come back. Soon. I promise. Soon.*

"Not today," Greum said, as if answering her internal thoughts. "We both need to rest and recover first. Come to me here tomorrow at midday, and we'll begin." His dark gaze bored into her. "And I'll push you far harder than I ever did with Ceiteag, Voada. I'll push you because there's so little time. I'll push you because that's the only way to see if you'll shatter under the pressure."

"I don't care."

Greum chuckled at that. "Oh, you will, despite everything you think right now. You'll hate me for what I'll do, but you'll be a draoi who can make the Mundoa tremble." He paused a moment and laboriously rose to his feet. "Or you will if you don't break in the process, friend of Savas," he added.

14

A Challenge Offered

ALTAN'S SLOWLY HEALING BROKEN leg throbbed under the wrappings and splint. It was also raining, which didn't help his mood, but then it seemed as if it had been raining and storming every day since they'd established their tenuous hold on Onglse. The rain was decidedly unnatural, in his opinion, a product of draoi spells. Certainly no one, not even the Cateni, would voluntarily live in a place that was constantly being drenched.

Water dripped from every surface in the ruined fort they held, flowed in rivulets that carved increasingly deep ruts in the sandy earth, cascaded in rippling sheets over moss-covered stone walls, flowed down the slope through the encampment to the sea, where it seemed the clouds picked up the moisture once more, only to toss it down at them again.

The sky wept for the Mundoa. The sky wept for all the dead. The sky wept for Lucian.

It had been nearly a moon now that they'd been on this accursed island. They'd buried their fallen here, including poor Lucian. They'd survived attacks by draoi (with little help from their own impotent sihirki) and repulsed waves of assaults by Cateni troops from the surrounding forts. Altan had been unable to gain more ground than what he'd taken in those first days, but the

137

Cateni had also been unable to force him to retreat from the island. The two sides had settled into an uneasy stalemate, a situation that Altan found supremely frustrating, an attitude undoubtedly shared by Greum Red-Hand on the other side.

"I *will* take this island," Altan said, realizing belatedly that he'd spoken aloud. But the fervor burned in him. He'd sent runners back to the Great-Voice in Trusa with the request that more troops and resources be sent to him now that they had established a supply route and a hold on Onglse itself, even though Altan's more rational side argued that they'd already left the south dangerously undefended. The Great-Voice evidently didn't share Altan's unspoken misgivings, for in the last hand of days, more ships had arrived with fresh troops, supplies, and military equipment.

He *would* take this island. He'd take it because it was here that Lucian would rest forever, and he would not allow that to be Cateni soil. It was a promise that he'd made to Lucian's memory.

"Commander Savas?" Sub-Commander Ilkur's voice intruded on Altan's reverie. "There's movement from the fort to the east."

"I'll come look," Altan answered. Grimacing, he swung his bad leg off the improvised stool that propped it up and reached for his crutch. Ilkur slid Altan's oiled cloak over his shoulders. Placing the crutch under his arm, he followed stiff-legged after Ilkur, awkwardly and slowly climbing the crumbling stone steps that led to the fort's battlements. Several of the Mundoan archers were gathered there, looking out through the rain over the ridgeline of the low hills and eastward to where the next hill-fort stood, grayed with distance and indistinct through the weather. There were men moving along the ridgeline, but Altan couldn't easily see how many there were or what threat they represented.

"Your eyes are better than mine, especially in this accursed weather," he said to one of the archers. "What do you see?"

"A group of about three double hands of warriors, Commander, with two war chariots in front."

"Draoi?"

"None that I can see, sir, though they could easily be hidden in the rear."

"There's been nothing seen to the west or approaching from the interior?" Altan asked Ilkur.

"No, sir."

"Then we wait. I want men at the interior gate, ready to defend the fort at need, and archers on all the walls, just in case this is a feint or diversion. I think I know what they want; I saw it with Tamar One-Eye a long time ago. If I'm right, they won't be getting what they're after."

As Ilkur relayed orders from the wall, men scurried to their places. Altan continued to watch the slow advance from the east. The group was making no attempt at stealth; they were shouting and calling, their voices faint through the mist and fog at first, then growing louder as they came nearer. Their jeers and insults were in Cateni; Altan understood some of what was being said, though he doubted most of the men around him could, but their tone was clear enough. The group of men halted just out of easy bowshot of the walls, where the wooded ridgeline flattened to a cleared glade. One of the war chariots rumbled forward, the driver racing up and down in front of the Cateni troops, the blue-adorned warrior rider behind him brandishing his spear toward the wall. Altan heard the nearest archers' bowstrings being pulled back, ready to release on command. "Archers! Hold!" he said to them, lifting his hand, and the bowstrings relaxed.

The rider in the chariot was shouting in heavily accented Mundoan now, his words clear and ringing in the morning. The man had a long scar down one side of his face, his bare chest was slathered in the thick sky-colored clay that the clans used to paint themselves, and he was wearing no armor beyond leather pants. "I give challenge!" he cried. "I am the Ceannàrd Maol Iosa, and I command the warriors of the clans here on Onglse. I have already sent hands of Mundoa as blood-slaves to serve our dead fighters in Tirnanog. I am the champion of the Cateni. Send out your own champion, if you dare, Savas! Let me send him into the afterlife as the chief blood-slave. Or are Mundoa just cowards like those weaklings who command them, who would rather hide behind walls than fight, who cower like children under the storms our draoi send them?"

At the final insult, the man spat on the ground between himself and the walls of the fort. In response, the Cateni ranked behind him clashed spears on the stony ground or against their long, iron-wrapped hexagonal shields. They began a slow chant: "Come out! Come out! Come out!"

"Sir?" asked Ilkur.

"Do nothing," Altan said. Then he raised his voice so that the men gathered in the courtyard below could also hear him. "Do nothing," he repeated. "I will cut down any man who makes to step from his post to respond to this man before he has the chance to draw sword. I don't care what this fool Maol Iosa says or does; we will *not* give him what he wants. Am I understood?"

"Yes, sir," came the responses, but Altan could sense an uneasiness in their answers. Ceannàrd Iosa continued to shout and bray, his war chariot digging ruts in the muddy ground as he hurled a barrage of insults toward the fort.

But Altan knew that the Cateni had to have seen the arrival of the new ships and men; they had watched the encampment growing on the slope below the fort Altan held. They knew that soon enough, the Mundoa would leave this fort and advance. Altan crutched to the wall. He called down, his voice matching the roar of the Cateni. "Maol Iosa," he shouted, "I am Altan Savas, and I command the Mundoa."

The driver brought Iosa's war chariot to a halt in front of Altan, the twin gray horses yoked to the chariot rearing up. "Then come down, Altan Savas, and we'll fight," the man responded, his bearded and scarred face uplifted. "You in your chariot and me in mine. Let us settle this conflict between us honorably and waste no more lives."

That brought back the memory that had haunted Altan every night since the fort had been taken: Lucian dead in front of him with Bella and Ardis torn open nearby. Altan closed his eyes briefly, then opened them, banishing the interior sight. He wondered, if Lucian had still been alive and their warhorses in his chariot harness, if he would have been able to resist the temptation that Iosa represented. He shifted his weight on the crutch, his leg protesting the movement. "I'll show you that our gods are greater than yours," the Cateni continued ranting below him, "and after your blood has been spilled on this ground, your soldiers can slink back across the River Meadham and know that you'll never threaten Onglse and Bàn Cill again."

Altan laughed, theatrically and derisively; that silenced the man. "The ceannàrd is a stupid fool if he thinks a war is won by a single man's efforts. Wars are won by *many* soldiers, whose fate it is to risk their lives. Wars are won by superior strategies, by superior resources, by superior numbers. I have all of those."

Iosa roared in defiance. "So Commander Savas is nothing more than a frightened child, hiding behind his soldiers and his walls."

"Commander Savas is someone who wins battles for his emperor. Nothing more. And nothing less. As I will win this one. I give you fair warning, Ceannàrd Iosa. You should retreat now."

Iosa spat again. "Cateni do not retreat."

"Then you tell me that Cateni are fools," Altan answered. He turned to Ilkur, standing at his left. "What do you think? Can our archers hit that man?"

Ilkur glanced over the battlements at Iosa and his chariot, gauging the distance. He grinned. "I think so, sir," the man said.

"Then let's see if he can outrun arrows."

"Archers!" Ilkur called immediately. "Nock, draw, and loose!"

Iosa evidently heard the command also—he touched the arm of his driver, who pulled hard on the reins of the warhorses, slapping them down hard. The chariot canted over on one wheel as the horses broke into a gallop, and a storm of arrows rose into the gloomy rain and fell again toward the fleeing chariot. Iosa lifted a shield from the rail, holding it over himself and the driver. Most of the arrows fell into the mud behind the racing war chariot as it hurried back to the group of Cateni warriors, but Altan saw several plunge into the wooden shield like the bristles of a hedgehog.

"Hold!" Ilkur called before a second volley could be released. "He's out of range again, sir."

The ceannàrd's driver drew up the horse at the edge of the clearing, and Iosa threw down the shield. One arrow had found his calf, piercing his leggings; Iosa plucked it out and brandished the bloody arrow toward the fort and Altan.

"Coward!" The single word was faint through the drumming of the rain.

"I'll meet you on the field soon enough," Altan shouted back at the man, "and we'll see who's the coward then."

Jeers in Cateni answered him.

With that, Altan stepped back from the battlement. "Have watchers placed here in case," he told Ilkur. "But I don't think we have to worry about them for the moment. I'd like you and all the sub-commanders to come see me in my rooms tomorrow morning. I'm as tired of sitting here as Iosa and Greum Red-Hand are."

The hand of sub-commanders gathered around the table in what had become Altan's office in the fort: a former stable that had managed to escape significant damage in the hail of furious draoi attacks that had followed the first few days of the Mundoa's occupation of the fortress. The table itself had once been the door of the granary, now set on crude trestles. The walls had severe cracks, and moisture ran down the massive stones, as if the room wept at their presence. The five men—Ilkur, Musa, Haidar, Cumhur, and Volkan—straightened and rose as Altan entered the room. He'd abandoned the crutch against the advice of his archiater, though his leg was still heavily wrapped and splinted. He forced himself to walk as normally as possible despite the pain as he waved them back into their seats.

"Ilkur?" he asked. "What of our friend outside the walls?"

"He hasn't returned, Commander. Hopefully we left him a painful reminder of his visit."

Altan smiled briefly at that as he sat at the head of the table. Soldiers from the kitchen hurried in to place wine, flagons, bread, and cheese on the table, then left. "Good. I suspect you're all as tired of this miserable place as I am. Musa, did the messengers return from the Great-Voice?"

"Yes, Commander. We have all the soldiers here that the Great-Voice is willing to spare. A full hand of cohorts has arrived, and another hand is expected in the next few days, assuming good winds."

Altan nodded. "That should be sufficient. Cumhur, your engineers have been working?"

Cumhur was a burly knot of a man, his head nearly bald except for the length of a braid at the back. His arms and hands were massive and showed the wear from decades of work. "We have, sir, using trees from the bluffs and from across the strait. We've engines for a siege if need be or for our own bombardments. The men are eager, sir, and ready."

"As we all are. Here . . ." Altan unrolled a map on the table. "This is Onglse as we know it. We're here." He placed his finger on the southeastern edge of the island. "The island is ringed with hill-forts; I want us to take the forts directly to our east and west so that we widen the breach we've already made. Then we can hold the breach and move through with less worry about being attacked from the rear and surrounded. But . . ." He stabbed his forefinger at the center of the island. "Bàn Cill is there, a hard march of three days, and that's where we ultimately must go. Once Bàn Cill falls, the entire island falls, and with the draoi's stronghold gone, all of Albann Bràghad will be suddenly vulnerable."

"What about the draoi?" Ilkur asked.

The vision of Lucian arose before Altan again, and he closed his eyes to banish it, taking a breath. "They've done nothing but bother us with this accursed rain since we won the fort. That will end once we advance; they'll come at us again with their damned shrieking spells, and we'll lose soldiers to them. But we know they'll tire; we'll wear them down. And we know from our experience here that when they *do* retreat, they'll leave behind trap-spells for us to set off, so we won't be so easily fooled this time. But—and this is the important fact—the draoi are a finite resource. We'll make the Cateni use them until they're exhausted, and that's when we'll begin our push on Bàn Cill."

"They'll make us pay for every stride," Volkan said, and Altan looked up. Everything about Volkan was dark—his hair, his skin, his glowering eyes, his expression—but there was an eagerness to the set of his mouth, as if the man relished the thought of the coming battles. "There's another ring of hill-forts to penetrate past this one. The land is wrinkled and treacherous, and we don't know the best paths."

"None of us ever expected this to be easy," Altan answered. "But the Great-Voice has given us most of what I've asked for, and now he expects payment in the form of Onglse's fall. So let's put our heads together now and determine the best way to accomplish that."

It was late that night, candles guttering to waxen mounds on the table, before they finished.

15

Thrust into Battle

THERE WERE DAYS WHEN Voada thought she might not survive Greum's attention.

For the first few hands of days, she at least had Ceiteag's sympathetic ear to complain to when Greum's insistent and blunt attentions frustrated and angered her. But Ceiteag and the other draoi Voada had come with, as well as most of the remaining draoi in Bàn Cill, were sent out by Greum when the Mundoan forces suddenly left the fort in which they'd been huddling and renewed their attack.

She'd thought—no, she'd hoped—that Greum would go with Ceiteag and the others, but that wasn't to be. She was left largely alone with the man and his harsh lessons.

She couldn't decide whether she admired him or hated him. Perhaps both at once. After all, that was one of his constant reminders. "You have to be able to hold two contradictory emotions in your head at once: your own feelings and those of the personality in your anamacha that you're using."

Voada wondered whether he entirely trusted her, since the mocking term "friend of Savas" had continued to come up in their discussions. She wondered why he was paying so much attention to her, barely a draoi at all, given the invasion of the island. At the same time, she could see how the situation on Onglse wore at the man. He seemed to be in daily consultation with runners from the forts and with other draoi, and Voada had seen Ceannàrd Maol Iosa in Bàn Cill at least three times. Still, Greum found time to spend a few stripes of the candle with her every day, sometimes more. He gave her exercises and spell incantations to memorize, and he accompanied her into Magh da Chèo when she called her anamacha to her. She had to admit that she'd learned more from him in a hand of days than she had during her entire time with Ceiteag.

Under Greum's tutelage, Voada now understood how to separate the massed voices of the anamacha, how to keep her equilibrium when she entered into the anamacha, and to harness the power of a few of the draoi who composed her anamacha, though he would not let her reach out to find Leagsaidh Moonshadow, hidden deep in the shadowed interior. "The Moonshadow would rip apart your own mind and leave you mad or worse," Greum insisted. "You wouldn't be able to hold her. You'd die and become just another minor voice inside, forgotten forever like too many other new draoi who tried to bond with this anamacha."

She found it easy to follow that advice, since it was difficult enough to handle the lesser personalities in her anamacha. Voada felt herself not at all tempted to try to pluck the Moonshadow from her refuge. Today, Greum had told her that she would be entering Magh da Chèo entirely on her own. "Ceiteag told me you could barely set dry wood on fire. Prove her wrong."

He gestured around them. They were in the ring of oak woods outside the circle of standing stones. Above them, a breeze played with the canopy of green and brown like a parent tousling the hair of her child. The air was filled with the smell of rich loam and vegetation. The forest made Voada touch the oak leaf pendant under her torc. Greum noticed her gesture; he shook his head. "There's nothing magical or sacred about these trees. What's sacred is what we teach the draoi here. Show me what you've learned, Voada. Show me that I haven't been wasting my time with you, friend of Savas."

The comment scraped at her irritation, making her release the pendant on its leather string. She could see her anamacha standing a few steps away, its form half lost in the play of sun and shadow. "Come to me," she called, opening her arms as if inviting them to embrace her. The anamacha responded, gliding toward her and slipping into her without hesitation. There was cold, and then there was the sense of being ripped from this reality into another. Ceiteag had never let her enter fully into the anamacha; Greum insisted on it, but before he had always been with her as a guide, using his own anamacha. Now she did so on her own.

As Greum had taught her, she fought to retain her own vision so that the nightmare world of Magh da Chèo was overlaid on the landscape around her. Without Greum's help, the feat was far more difficult to manage; what she saw through her own eyes kept slipping away, tossing her into the anamacha's dark and chaotic land even as she fought to push it aside like a curtain. She could feel her fingernails pressing into the palms of her hands as she battled to retain control.

It was Iomhar who came to her first, as it usually was—whether it was because he had been the last draoi to become part of the anamacha or because there was some affinity between them, Voada wasn't certain. But he was the easiest of the personalities inside the anamacha to separate out and was one of the more powerful, at least according to Greum.

<You're alone . . . Your guardian isn't here,> the multiple voices chorused. There was curiosity, there was encouragement, and there was also a sense of menace. Some of those within the anamacha would happily destroy her, because it would give them pleasure to see someone else succumb as easily as they had, or perhaps they felt it a mistake that the anamacha had come to her. <Ah, we can feel the fear. She stinks of it.>

"I'm not afraid of you," she answered them. "Of any of you. I call Iomhar to come to me now."

< . . . Not afraid . . . not afraid . . . not afraid . . . > the voices echoed—some mocking, some not—but their voices and the feel of multiple presences were already fading as Voada concentrated

on bringing Iomhar forward. The world lightened around her, her own sight becoming dominant. A single shade now stood with her, and Voada could feel it pulsing with the energy that the ana-macha had gathered from the world it inhabited, so near that of the gods.

The ghost that was Iomhar glowed as if a sun burned inside him. *<This is what you want? Can you shape it? Can you take what I hold?>*

"I know the shape. I know the words," she told him. With that, Voada began to move her hands in the spell pattern, weaving an imagined knot before her, the shape more complex than the simple patterns Ceiteag had taught her. Invisible in the living world, she could see it through the anamacha's vision. As her hands passed through the crossing of the knot, she shouted the words that would bind the net, spoken in a language that resembled Cat-eni, but was—Greum had told her—much older. Already Iomhar was releasing the energy he had gathered for her, placing it in the knot work that pulsed between Voada's hands. *Make fire*, Greum had told her, and she spoke the word: *Teine!*

<Our power is yours . . . My part here is done . . . > Flames burst into existence inside the knot work, the heat and light lashing the front of Voada's body. She could feel its desire to be released; it was difficult to contain even in the net she'd woven. When she could bear the pain no longer, when she could make the knots no stronger, she gestured and spoke the words of release.

She'd chosen a medium-sized oak set a bit apart from the others. The spell she released flew true, striking the target at head height with a furious clap of thunder. The tree shuddered at the impact, the trunk shattering into splinters as flame rolled like liquid further up the tree, crackling and fuming. The upper boughs fell, engulfed in flame as they struck the ground. Sparks spiraled away into the sky.

In the sudden silence, Voada and Gruem could both hear the fire consuming the tree and spreading to the nearby brush. Tendrils of white smoke coiled away on the breeze, the smell of ash and fire overpowering. The anamacha slid away as Voada stag-

gered, exhausted from the effort of creating the spell and casting
it. She could feel her body trembling. "Adequate," she heard
Greum say. "Now get rid of what you've made. We can't have a fire
here in our wood."

"Ceanndraoi, I can't," she said. "I'm so tired . . ."

"Quit complaining," he barked. "Just do it. Do you think your
friend Savas would stop attacking you because you're tired? Do it."

"He's not my friend."

"You're angry with me. Good. Use that. Put out your fire."

Voada scowled at Greum. She forced herself to stand taller and
opened her arms again to her anamacha. "Come to me," she commanded it.

This time, the anamacha was much more difficult to control and
to keep apart from herself. The massed voices called to her, a din
that made it difficult to find the voice she wanted: Iomhar's. When
at last she did manage to isolate him, he seemed recalcitrant and
slow to gather the energy required, and she could feel her control
slipping away even as she created a new knot work web and allowed him to release the energy into it. She hurried, speaking the
necessary words and shaping the container as quickly as she could,
using her irritation at Greum to push away the fatigue. "*Uisge*," she
commanded this time: *water*. She could barely hold it, barely manage to pull herself from the anamacha's world.

When she released the spell, a small storm cloud coalesced
above them, dark and foreboding. A stroke of lightning pierced
the air, followed by thunder, and then the rain poured down, cold
and fierce, soaking not only the tree but herself and Greum. The
fire before them hissed and complained, then went out completely, leaving only a blackened and fallen tree trunk as the storm
she'd created became caught in the winds above the canopy and
went scudding off to the east, still pouring rain.

Voada fought to stay upright under Greum's regard, refusing to
collapse as she wanted. She looked at him. Water dripped from
the ends of his beard, hair, and torc, plastering his robe to his
body. "Adequate?" she asked, mocking his tone.

She thought he nearly smiled. "It will do," he answered.

"Neither spell was as precise as it could have been." As if to demonstrate, he shook drops of water from his fingers.

"Are you never satisfied, Ceanndraoi?"

"Never," he answered. "Not even with myself. In fact, generally less so with myself."

His somber tone and his gloomy demeanor made her laugh despite her irritation and weariness. "Why does that amuse you?" Greum asked.

"I don't know," she told him. "Perhaps because you're so much the opposite of Meir, my husband. He always told me that the best way to have someone work hard for you was to praise their good efforts and remain silent otherwise. He said people required the same care that a good potter gives her clay, so that it works for her and remains solid and whole. That approach seemed to do well for Meir—and for me. Your way . . ." Voada shrugged. "It seems that you risk shattering and cracking your pots by handling them roughly."

"If my pot shatters, then perhaps it was flawed from the very beginning. Better that it breaks *here* than when it's desperately needed elsewhere. We don't have the luxury of time." He sniffed and looked past her to the blackened ruins of the tree. "We should go back to the temple and rest. It's time we were both placed in the potter's kiln."

"It's time for me to return to the battle," Greum said as they walked back toward the temple. "And time for you to relieve those who have been there too long. Be ready to leave at sunrise."

Voada didn't protest; Greum had made his attitude toward shattered and broken apprentices clear enough. She was prepared for this task, or she was not—she knew it wouldn't matter to Greum either way. Horses and packs were made ready for them by Daibhidh and the temple staff, and when the sun rose the next morning and the menach of the temple had performed the morning prayers, Greum, along with Voada and a half dozen other draoi, set out.

It would be a three-day journey over rugged terrain. Voada found herself physically sore and tired from the constant jostling and balancing and mentally exhausted from the lessons that Greum insisted on inflicting on her when they stopped for the evening. She would drop into sleep as soon as she could afterward, and her dreams were haunted by images of Orla and Hakan. Her children called to her for help, and in the dreams she could not reach them, though she struggled and fought through the hands that held her back: Voice Kadir's hands, Voice-wife Dilara's hands, Altan Savas' hands. Mundoan hands.

She woke without feeling rested.

On the evening of the third day, they finally came within sight of the island's outer defenses, a stone wall running along the ridge-line of tall, rounded hills studded at intervals with fortifications. To the south and east of where they were, storm clouds pouring gray sheets of rain blanketed the hills, masking them, and under them she could see columns of black smoke rising to blend into the gloom.

Battle. Silent and still hidden, but near.

The acolytes set up open-sided linen canopies in a circle as warriors scouted the nearby area. They found nothing, but guards still patrolled just outside the range of the light from the central fire. As Voada approached Greum's tent for her nightly instruction, she heard Greum's low voice talking to Daibhidh. She stopped in tree-shadow. She could see the two of them only a few strides away, silhouetted against the camp's fire and the fading afterglow of the sunset, their heads close together as they talked.

". . . you might tell her that she's impressed you." That was Daibhidh, his voice thinner and reedier than Greum's low rumble.

"There's no need for that. It's the anamacha who has claimed her that lends her power, not the woman herself." Greum's voice, quieter and lower, made her lean forward.

"Yet she can hold that power, and Ceiteag says that when the woman speaks, she has the gift of making others listen. She says Voada could be a menach as well, or a clan àrd."

"Might be. Could be," Greum answered. "I only care about

what she *is*. In this moment." His head lifted, looking in her direction. Voada shuffled back deeper into shadow. "And she is here now," Greum said.

Voada stepped forward into the light. "Ceanndraoi, Daibhidh," she said, inclining her head toward the men.

"You heard us?" Greum asked.

"I thought I heard my name. Nothing more."

Greum sniffed at that. He waved his red-splotched hand to Daibhidh, and the younger draoi stood, bowed to Greum, then Voada, and walked away. Greum gestured to the blanket where Daibhidh had been sitting, and Voada ducked under the canopy and sat facing Greum. "You lie easily," he said to her.

"Apparently as easily as you do, Ceanndraoi," she responded.

In the growing darkness, it was difficult to read the expression on his face. She could see his anamacha near him, and her own as well, both glowing softly in her vision. "I don't care whether you like me or not, Voada."

"You've made that very clear to me, Ceanndraoi. We evidently both feel the same way. But I do thank you for what you've given me."

"And what is that?"

"Far more than Ceiteag, you've given me the ability to use my anamacha. That gives me hope that I can one day accomplish what I most want."

Greum glanced in the direction of the storm clouds and smoke, now nearly invisible in the darkness. "And what is it that you most want? Simple revenge?"

Voada shook her head. "I want my children back. I want that more than anything else."

"And if you can't achieve that?" he asked her blandly as firelight moved over his face. "What then?"

"Then those who took them from me will pay," she answered, and she felt her lips draw back in an unbidden snarl. She could only imagine how that must look in the red firelight, but Greum simply raised his eyebrows. "And if you consider that simple revenge, then so be it."

"You'll begin making them pay here," he said. "We have to win here in Onglse first if you ever hope to return to Albann Deas and Pencraig." His head tilted as he regarded her. "That much, at least, you owe me for what I've taught you."

She didn't answer him. She heard him take a long breath. "We *will* defeat them, Voada," he told her. "That isn't a matter of hope, only of fact. And yes, since you heard me, I know your anamacha will be of great help to us here."

Her anamacha moved nearer to her, slipping into her enough that she heard its voice. *<Here isn't where you need to be. Now you need to go back. Go back.>* One voice seemed to dominate the chorus, a woman's voice that she'd never heard before, and Voada found herself echoing the statement. "Here isn't where I need to be," she said aloud, and she heard the anamacha's voice sigh in affirmation.

"Yet here is where you find yourself," he answered. "And here you'll be used. Now, sit down, and we'll begin your last lesson, because tomorrow you'll be needed."

Voada had never seen so many Mundoan soldiers gathered together in one place. She'd not imagined that there *could* be that many of them. In the midday gloom of the storm clouds, their troops spilled over and around the stone walls girdling Onglse's shore; their siege engines trundled noisily and ominously toward the fort on the battlements of which Voada stood; their war chariots raced before and around the main mass of the advance; flags and banners fluttered above them in the rain and wind as their drums beat a slow cadence; their ships were massed in the half circle of the harbor far below. Boots clashed in time on the stones of the island, the rhythm pounding like some mad god's pulse.

The sight made her despair at the fate of the island and the ability of the Cateni to defeat the Mundoa. If this was war, then war was more chaotic, confusing, and loud than she'd ever thought it could be.

Greum had brought a hand of draoi to the summit of the fort's tower, where they could look down and see where to cast their spells. Already, Voada could hear some of them chanting, their hands weaving the patterns of their spell-knots in the air. As they cast their spells, lightning flicked down from the clouds and exploded in the midst of the Mundoan ranks, fires burst up among them, winds tore at their ranks, and stones erupted from the earth underneath them, but there were always more men to take the place of those who fell.

The drum beaters' cadence quickened, and now the Mundoan army moved faster. Below, in the courtyard of the hill-fort, Ceannàrd Iosa bellowed orders as the gates opened and the Cateni warriors—pitifully few, Voada thought—rushed outward toward the Mundoan front, led by Maol Iosa's war chariot.

Most of the draoi on the tower staggered back from the battlements, their faces weary and drained. Voada felt Greum's touch on her shoulder. "It's our task now, Voada," he said. "Our task . . ." Greum wasted no more time; Voada saw him open his arms, and his anamacha slipped into his embrace. His eyes went distant; he began to chant, and his hands wove patterns in the air. His spell finished faster than Voada thought possible, certainly far quicker than any of hers. He gestured, shouting the release word, and from the storm clouds a quartet of lightning strokes descended, leaving brilliant streaks in Voada's eyes, and the thunder that followed immediately was so loud that Voada nearly clapped hands to ears. She ducked involuntarily, as did nearly everyone around her.

As she rose, blinking away the afterimages, a shout of triumph erupted from the Cateni troops. Voada looked down to see the front ranks of the Mundoan army torn open, four gaping holes gouged out of the wall and great boulders torn from the earth and hurled to either side as if they were no more than pebbles. Amidst the rubble were the twisted, broken remains of soldiers and the closest siege engines. Voada could hear the screams of the wounded and maimed. She could smell charred wood and flesh, and underneath, the tang of blood.

Voada gaped. She'd not realized just how powerful Ceanndraoi Greum was. He was looking at her now, and if what he'd just done had taken any toll on him, she could not see it. "Well, woman?" he asked, pointing down. "There's your enemy. There are the people who stole your family and your home from you. Show them what I've taught you."

The screaming of the Mundoan wounded continued. Ceannàrd Iosa had halted his own assault for the moment, waving his spear in salute toward the tower where the draoi stood. "Look out there—there's Savas himself," Greum said. He pointed farther down the line of Mundoa to where the rest of the siege engines had halted. A war chariot moved there, and behind the driver was a man in shining krug, the mirrored armor of the officers, and a plumed headpiece. She couldn't see his face, but the banner of three yellow stars on a blue field fluttering from the chariot said that yes, it was Savas. "The coward stays far enough back that our spells can't reach him." Greum spat over the side of the tower. "What are you waiting for?" he asked Voada. "There are still Mundoa within reach, even for you."

Well out along the ridge, soldiers were milling around the ballistae, and Savas' chariot was nearby. She saw the ballistae being loaded and men turning the cranks. With a wave of Savas' hand, they released as one, loosing a hand of boulders toward the tower. She felt the wooden floor shudder underneath her as the massive stones struck the tower's base, gouging out huge chunks of masonry and stone as the draoi staggered back from the battlement. Now it was the Mundoa who shouted and cheered as the tower swayed. Voada steadied herself, opening her arms and calling the anamacha to her. She plunged into their dark world, quickly finding Iomhar's presence and taking his energy into herself. She let it burn and sear inside her as she formed a spell-net larger than any she'd made before, taking in more and more of the power that Iomhar continued to feed her. She faintly heard Greum shouting at her—"What are you doing, Voada? Release the spell!"—and ignored him, letting the power pound at her, throbbing in her skull until she thought it might burst.

Her vision was blurred. She could see Savas, could see the wooden structures of the ballistae and other siege engines.

<They're your enemies. Kill them. Destroy them. This is what you wanted.> The voice was loud, and it wasn't Iomhar's alone, but also that of a woman. *The Moonshadow's voice.* Voada realized that with a start.

She could reach Commander Savas. She felt that. In her doubled vision, he looked closer, close enough that she could see his face and know it was him, close enough that she saw him peering upward toward the tower and herself. She recognized that face, and she remembered how he'd scolded Voice Kadir for his treatment of the Cateni and the kindness he'd shown Meir after the dinner.

She held the power to kill him.

"Not all Cateni are our enemies, Voice Kadir, and we shouldn't speak so strongly against them all . . ." She remembered Savas' words at the Voice's banquet in Pencraig, remembered how he'd not allowed Meir to walk back to the house but had instead driven them in his chariot.

Voada spoke the release word and flung her arms outward, a ball of glowing lava rushing away from her. The brilliance dripped liquid fire as it rushed over the Cateni, past the front ranks of the Mundoan troops, and flashed over the head of Commander Savas to plow into the earth and explode in the midst of the ballistae as their slings were being reloaded. Molten lava cascaded over the wooden beams and over the men but spared Commander Savas.

Voada could hear their screams and their terror even as she reeled backward from having cast the spell and releasing her anamacha. Greum was peering over the stones; below, Voada could hear Maol Iosa's bellow of triumph. "I could not have thrown a spell that large that far," Greum said. "But you missed your friend Savas."

"The engines were more important than the commander," Voada told him. The words were hard to speak; most of her concentration was going toward keeping her on her feet. She badly wanted to sleep.

Greum was staring at her, his gaze dark and appraising. "Perhaps," he said. "Or perhaps your aim isn't all I would have hoped for."

16

Victory and Defeat

SAVAS GAPED AT THE ruins of the ballistae smoking behind him. The rain hissed against the high flames. The fireball had soared a bare arm's length over him, the heat palpable through his armor, and his new warhorses had reared up in fear as it passed. His banner was scorched with its drippings, and what it had done to the ballistae and the men assigned to them . . .

Four of the six ballistae were shattered, and most of the men with them were dead. The ones who weren't dead were worse, writhing and screaming on the ground with blackened, charred skin. The flames continued to lick at their flesh even as the rain poured over them. One was crumpled near the chariot, a black-ened claw of a hand reaching toward him; Altan ripped a spear from its holder and plunged it into the man's chest to end the poor soldier's agony.

The hand dropped to the ground.

"Get those fires out!" Savas shouted. "Move the other ballistae away quickly! Find the survivors, and get them to the archiaters! Go! Move!" The men around him were shaken out of their shock by his voice and scurried to their tasks as Altan looked back at the tower of the fort ahead. He'd glimpsed the draoi who had cast the spell: a woman, not young but not yet old, with long auburn hair.

Many Cateni women would look much the same from that distance, but this one . . .

There was something about her that nagged at him, though he couldn't place the memory. Had he seen her before? Where?

There was no time to think about that. He'd also seen Ceannàrd Iosa lead the Cateni warriors from the hill-fort gates. The sooner he engaged them, the sooner the cursed draoi would be unable to cast their spells for fear of killing their own. "You men!" he shouted, pointing to the two untouched ballistae. "I want that tower down before we reach it!"

He didn't wait for their answer. "And you!" he said to the nearest soldier. "Run and tell the drum captains to call the advance." Finally, he leaned forward toward his new driver, Tolga, a young soldier whom Musa had recommended as being an excellent charioteer. "Take me to Ilkur," he told the man, and Tolga shouted to the warhorses as he slapped the reins down on their muscled backs and climbed forward on the yoke.

"Go, Bora! Go, Jika!" They moved forward alongside the ranked men as the drums began to pound out the call to advance and the entire army surged forward with a massed, wordless cry. Altan gripped the rail of the chariot, cursing his stiff and splinted leg. Once he'd ridden the chariot easily, balanced and shifting his weight without thought as it jounced over uneven ground. Now he rode like an old man, holding on desperately in order to remain upright. Still, the men cheered as he passed, and he lifted a spear to them in response, pointing the tip toward the fort before them. The air smelled of smoke and fire as they approached the front, and they passed craters with dead men in Mundoan armor scattered around them: the work of the draoi. Tolga took him up the slope of the ridgeline, then—more slowly—up the tumbled stone of the wall until they stood atop it. He stopped there, where they could look down and see the battle in front of the hill-fort just ahead of them.

The first ranks of the Mundoa had already struck the Cateni with a clash and roar and a swirl of chariots, along with the discordant blatting of the tall bronze trumpets the Cateni called *carnyx*, which they used to signal during battle the same way the Mundoan armies used their drums. The Cateni's chariots were also thrashing into the melee, scythe-bladed wheels cutting their way through the ordered ranks of the Mundoa.

Altan saw Ilkur's banner in the midst, swaying above the fray. He saw Maol Iosa's banner close by as well; the Cateni champion wielded his sword in the midst of a clot of Mundoan soldiers, then jumped back onto his chariot as his driver whipped the horses into a gallop. That was the Cateni tactic with chariots: drive them madly into the front ranks of the enemy, knocking men aside, tearing at them with the blades attached to their wheels, or running them over as the rider threw javelins and spears or loosed arrows. Then, when the spears and javelins were exhausted, the rider would jump from the carriage and into the midst of the battle with his sword, only to be picked up again and moved quickly elsewhere.

It was a tactic that the Mundoa had adopted after their first contact with the Cateni, with some modifications. Most Mundoa used their chariots more like swiftly moving platforms for archers, though Altan had fully emulated the Cateni tactics with Lucian— a dangerous tendency for a commander, but one that had won him grudging respect from the Cateni. He knew it was the reason that Maol Iosa had thought to challenge him directly.

Altan could see Ilkur's banner as his sub-commander led a wave of chariots forward to release arrows at the Cateni warriors, cutting them down like wheat being scythed in a field. They were answered by arrows from the hill-fort, but even as the first volley fell, the remaining Mundoan ballistae returned to action, one boulder striking the tower halfway up, another chunking into the base. Splintered rock and shattered mortar flew as the tower visibly shuddered; Altan saw the draoi gathered on the roof vanish as Greum Red-Hand ordered them down and out of the tower. Altan allowed himself a smile: good, not being able to easily see the battle to place their spells would cripple the draoi. That was especially important, given how that accursed woman draoi had taken out so many of the siege engines as well as the engineers working them. Keeping her and Greum Red-Hand out of the battle as much as possible was paramount.

Voada saw Greum preparing a new spell when another round of ballista-flung boulders slammed into the tower. The building lurched under her feet with a groan, sending Voada and some of the others on the roof off their feet and ruining Greum's spell preparations as his incantation faltered and his hand movements went awry. She could feel the structure sway, the wooden floor of the roof no longer level. "Down!" she heard Greum shout. "Down to the courtyard!"

She pushed herself up and joined the others hurrying toward the stairs. The stairs were also damaged, creaking under their weight, and the interior of the hill-fort's tower was filled with choking dust. Voada could hear the sounds of the battle, too close now. She felt vulnerable and frightened, but she couldn't stop her flight downward; Greum was directly behind her, the last of the draoi to leave. The descent of four floors seemed interminable. It seemed that the archers and other tower-defenders were also abandoning the unsafe structure. More people crowded the stairwell, and the stones underneath them when they reached the second floor were cracked and broken, making their footing treacherous. More than once, Voada nearly fell.

Then, somehow, they were outside in the open courtyard of the fort, rain pouring down on them from the spell-induced storm above and the clamor of the battle outside the walls echoing around them. The courtyard was largely empty except for the injured, and a few of the fort's servant staff, though a few archers remained on the surrounding walls. "Voada!" Greum called. "Another spell—what you did last time."

"I can't see to aim the spell," Voada protested, pointing to the wall and the tower in front of them.

"Just send it."

"But . . ."

"Do it!"

Before Voada could even start the spell, they heard the impact of more boulders against the tower, which groaned like a dying animal, leaned over and collapsed. The wreckage spilled mostly outside the walls, though stones also bounded into the courtyard as everyone scrambled away.

"Voada! Now!" Greum shouted.

The Cateni, Altan had to admit, were incredible hand-to-hand fighters, fierce and dangerous, but he could see that the Mundoan numbers would eventually overwhelm the Cateni. They had taken this hill-fort, and Volkan was leading the attack on the other to the west, which meant the Mundoa had cracked the first perimeter wide open and established a hold and supply line that would allow them to move into the interior of the island.

Altan began to hope that they might be able to accomplish what Emperor Beris' army had never been able to manage: defeating the draoi's stronghold and beginning to secure the land north of the River Meadham.

Already the landscape of the battle was shifting. The Cateni were being pressed backward by the disciplined ranks of the Mundoan infantry. The ballistae opened up again, both striking near the base of the tower, which groaned, leaned to the right, and collapsed entirely, smashing into the rearmost Cateni troops and taking a portion of the fort's wall with it. A shout went up from the Mundoa forces, and Altan plucked his banner from its holder, waving it side to side: the signal for a full-out assault on the fort. The Mundoan army surged forward as Maol Iosa leapt into his chariot and retreated back to the fort, those around him following. Tolga grinned at Altan over his muscular shoulder. "We've beaten them, Commander," he said.

"Not yet," Altan reminded him. "Take us forward, Tolga."

"Sir!" Tolga answered. He crouched on the yoke and slapped the reins down on the horses. "Go!" They snorted, reared up, and leapt forward.

The chariot lurched down the slope as Tolga picked his way through and over the rubble at a breakneck pace, Altan holding on to keep himself upright. They reached the smoother cleared area in front of the fort, now littered with bodies, Mundoan and Cateni alike. From the storm above, lightning flared again from cloud to earth, and thunder barked: draoi spells. Altan heard men crying out from near the tower's rubble but couldn't see what had happened. More light: another fireball went careening over the remnants of the fort wall and exploded a few dozen strides in front of Altan's chariot, scattering bodies and gouts of thick lava. He could feel the heat, and the impact of the concussion tilted the chariot. Tolga pulled back on the reins momentarily as the horses reacted, nostrils flaring and eyes wide. Then he yanked the reins hard to the left, taking them around the flames. Soldiers scattered in front of them, scurrying out of the way. "To the fort!" Altan shouted to his troops. "Now!"

Voada opened her arms to her anamacha, letting herself fall into the other world and find Iomhar once again. *<You don't want to kill your own,>* she heard the voices of the anamacha proclaim, again dominated by a woman's tones.

Is that the Moonshadow herself? Voada wondered. *Is she moving out of the shadows?* The warnings Ceiteag and Greum had given her regarding the Moonshadow made her hesitate, but voices continued to croon and cajole.

<We understand your feelings. Send the spell far enough, and you hurt only the Mundoa. Remember your children. Remember what they did to them.> The words called back the memories. She was again in her old house as it was looted and destroyed, and she screamed at the soldiers and the staff as she created the spell-netting as quickly as she could. She shouted her love and her promise to

Orla and Hakan once more as she released the spell blindly into the air, letting it arc up and away. She fell backward into supporting arms.

<We can help you. We can give you the revenge you desire, that you need. It's time to return . . . To return . . . > And amidst the chorus, there was Iomhar's voice, alone, and she clung to it as a refuge. <The clans could have won at Íseal Head, as they could have here. They only need the right àrd and the right draoi to lead them . . . A ceannàrd and ceanndraoi they can believe in . . . . > The voices faded as the anamacha receded from her.

On the far side of the wall, light bloomed in the dimness of the storm, and screams followed. Those around her cheered.

But a few breaths later, Maol Iosa's war chariot came racing through and over the rubble near the gate, followed by retreating Cateni warriors on foot and more war chariots. Voada saw Iosa shake his head mutely at Greum Red-Hand. Greum seemed to draw himself up, sighing. The ceanndraoi opened his arms, calling up another spell. This time he was slower, more deliberate. He waited as more Cateni came through the gate, and when the first soldiers in Mundoan armor and livery appeared, he released the spell. Lightning flared around the gate, and thunder boomed. The walls and roof of the gateway collapsed, crushing those underneath.

Ceannàrd Iosa had already taken his chariot through the gates of the fort in retreat, and the rest of the Cateni chariots and warriors were following quickly. The Cateni were pulling back; Altan knew they'd continue to retreat from the gates on the far side of the fort toward the refuge of the next hill-fort and the folded hills nearby. "Ilkur!" he shouted, but the officer couldn't hear him over the roar of battle. The archers' war chariots might have a chance to move quickly enough around the walls of the fort to pursue the retreat, but Ilkur was already moving toward the tumbled gate in pursuit of Ceannàrd Iosa.

The chance to capture ceannàrd and ceanndraoi was slipping away from them, and Altan cursed.

A draoi's spell flared, and the remaining stones of the gate fell, nearly burying Ilkur. When the dust cleared, there was no easy way through. Ilkur left his chariot to scramble over the stones toward the fort with a cohort of soldiers.

Altan could only shake his head in frustration.

It would take turns of the glass and the loss of more men than Altan wished, but they'd taken the fort. They would not find Greum Red-Hand and his draoi, nor Maol Iosa.

There were no Cateni left inside but the dead.

"Through the west gate!" Maol Iosa shouted. "Quickly! Chario-teers, take the draoi!"

Voada felt herself being picked up and placed on the bed of the ceannàrd's own chariot. Under the pounding and concealing rain, the retreat began.

"That was impressive," Iosa shouted back to her as his driver took the chariot through the gate at a breakneck pace.

"Ceannàrd?" Voada shouted back to him as they lurched out onto open ground amidst the confusion of mounted warriors and those on foot, all heading toward the fort looming on the next hilltop.

"The spell you cast," Iosa told her. "Impressive." The rain was washing the blue paint from his face, streaks of it running into his beard and uncovering the scars on his cheek. His hair hung in wet strings around his face, and a Mundoan sword had laid open a wound across his chest, liberally spattering his skin with blood. The ceannàrd bore the signs of the battle, but he was grinning as if the fighting had only revitalized him. "The Red-Hand could have done no better. In fact, I suspect he might not have been able to match it."

Voada didn't answer, didn't know *how* to answer. Instead she clung to the rails of the chariot and wondered how the ceannàrd managed to stay so easily balanced on the swaying platform. "You should be careful," Iosa said.

"Why?" she managed to ask.

"Greum Red-Hand doesn't like competition, and he can only see one path: his own," the ceannàrd answered. "You may find that what the ceanndraoi wants ultimately isn't what you want, and you'll be forced to make a decision."

"That sounds disloyal, Ceannàrd," she told him. The man only laughed at her comment.

"Does it?" he said. "I've talked to Menach Ceiteag about you. You and I . . . it may be that we want the same thing."

"I have no idea what you mean." Voada found herself unable to hold the man's gaze. She looked away, toward the fort they were approaching.

She said nothing more to the ceannàrd, nor did he speak to her again. She slid from his chariot as soon as it entered the courtyard of the fort.

17

An Alternative Offered

CEITEAG LOOKED AS EXHAUSTED as Voada felt. The bread and cheese they'd been given on their arrival at the hill-fort had been eaten quickly, even the crumbs picked up with their fingers and licked away. The wooden flagons in front of them had been drained of ale, refilled, and refilled again by servants who kept their eyes averted.

The two women were draoi, after all, and thus dangerous to offend.

When the servants came in to clear away the dishes, Voada and Ceiteag visited the middens in the tower, trying to ignore the stench. One of Voada's unpredictable moon-times had begun without warning; she blamed the wild bouncing of the chariot during the ride from the fallen fort. Voada placed a soft linen pad filled with blood-moss between her legs, and Ceiteag watched her tie the strings of the pad tightly around her hips beneath her undertrousers.

When they returned to their room, Ceiteag went immediately to her bedding while Voada stared listlessly toward the inner courtyard of the hill-fort from her vantage point on the second floor of the tower. Torches flared throughout the fort, and the moon shone through torn clouds—some of the draoi had cleared the weather. The Cateni injured in the battle were lying on the ground while archiaters moved among them, tending to their wounds. She could see Maol Iosa as well, kneeling down occasionally next to one of the warriors to give comfort and encouragement. There were too many wounded and too few healthy men below. She wondered if Commander Savas was feeling the same to the east as he looked out over the ruined fort he'd won.

Voada looked back at Ceiteag, who was slumped against the wall, sitting on her blankets. With her gray hair still damp from the rain and hanging in ragged strands, illuminated only by the single candle in the room and a small mound of glowing peat in the hearth, she looked impossibly old. "It's more exhausting than you believe possible," Ceiteag said, "this kind of usage of your anamacha." Ceiteag cocked her heard slightly. "Even one like yours. Surely you feel it."

"I do." Voada shook her head. "So many died."

"Not enough of our enemy did," Ceiteag answered with a wry twist of her lips, "or we wouldn't be here. Does the death bother you, Voada? Did you think that being a draoi in war would be bloodless? Weren't you telling me how you wanted revenge for what the Mundoa did to you and your family? I would think you'd be pleased at the chance to strike against them."

"I'm not bothered," Voada told her. "I would do it again, and more." She could hear the false bravado in her own voice and softened her tone. "It's just . . ." She stopped, taking a long breath as she looked out to the courtyard again and thought of her decision to spare Commander Savas. She wondered whether Greum was right and that had been a critical mistake. "I saw the Mundoa crawling over the land like maggots over a rotting corpse, so many soldiers that they couldn't be counted. Why *were* we so few in comparison?" Voada asked. "Why did so few of the clans come when Greum Red-Hand called for help? We brought him only a paltry number of hands of warriors and only a hand-and-one of draoi. Out there with the northern clans there must be many times more, but they didn't come. Not even for the sake of Onglse."

A shrug answered Voada. "You've never known anything except the way things are in Albann Deas. Up here in Albann Bràghad, the clans keep to themselves and protect their own first. But they'll do what they must when the time comes. Greum sending a messenger to ask for help is one thing. Had he gone to them himself and spoken to the clan leaders . . ." Ceiteag repeated the shrug. "It might well have been different. But he chose not to do that."

They only need someone to lead them. Iomhar's words. "I can't see Greum holding out that red hand for help. I can see him expecting and demanding the help as his right."

Ceiteag laughed quietly at that. "So you've discovered that he doesn't make it easy to like him."

"From what I've seen, he doesn't care whether anyone does or not."

"He's taught you well, then."

Now it was Voada's turn to laugh. "He says it's not me, it's only Leagsaidh Moonshadow's anamacha that matters. Nothing else." Voada glanced to her right, where her anamacha stood impassively. The flickering, moving faces seemed to watch her.

Ceiteag only nodded. "You should sleep. We'll all need the rest, because soon enough there won't be time for it. How do you feel? I remember when my moon-times came that the pain was sometimes bad. I have willow bark; I could make tea."

"That's kind of you, Menach, but I'm fine. My moon-times have been rare since I gave birth to Hakan, and they don't bother me much."

Ceiteag blew out the flame on the candle next to her bed, leaving only the low, blue flames of the peat fire. Voada could see Ceiteag's anamacha, silent and still as it stood next to the older woman's bed. Ceiteag's eyes closed.

Voada glanced out the window to the courtyard once more. *So many of the Mundoa. Savas and the Great-Voice must have emptied Albann Deas of every last solider . . .*

The thought seemed to echo around her; she could feel the cold touch of her anamacha, and she wondered if it was its voices she heard. Movement below caught her eye: a ghost—a taibhse gliding around the cot of one of the dead. The body had been covered with a cloth by an archiater, but the taibhse circled around it, unseen by the archiaters, servants, or other wounded men. Voada could also see Ceannàrd Iosa not far from the taibhse, moving from man to man, crouching down alongside each and speaking to him.

Voada took a blanket from her bedding and wrapped it around herself, then left the room, padding down the stairs in bare feet until she reached the door of the courtyard, her anamacha gliding behind her. She nodded to the guards there and went out among the men. She could hear some of them moaning, could hear the archiaters as they tried to comfort those who were hurt. The taibhse stood over its corpse, but it looked up as she approached, appearing to see not only her but her anamacha as well. She could hear its whisper as well.

<*I'm lost . . . I tried to follow, but I hesitated and couldn't see the path anymore . . . I'm lost . . .* >

"I can help you," she said to the ghost. Iosa, tending a man nearby, looked up from where he knelt and saw Voada. His scarred, battle-worn face nodded to her, understanding what must have happened. "Give me just a little time . . ." she said to the ghost. In a temple, she could have looked down to the sun-paths engraved on the floor, and she could have ushered the taibhse along them. She tried to imagine the temple at Bàn Cill and how it would be oriented if it were here, tried to remember where the dawn would come and where Elia's lamp might sit. Her anamacha evidently understood her intention as well; it moved to her, not entering her as fully as when she cast a spell, but enough that she could hear its voices.

<*Look with our eyes. We can show you the sun-paths. Look with our eyes . . .* >

Two crossed lines of shimmering yellow light glistened on the flags at her feet, the ends sliding outward over the bodies of the men there. Where the lines struck the walls of the forts, doorways of blinding white brilliance opened. "There," Voada said aloud to the taibhse. "Can you see? All you need do is follow one of the sun-paths to Tirnanog."

<I see them . . . > The ghost nearly sobbed the words. It turned and began to move along the path. With each step, the taibhse grew fainter and more difficult to see, until it vanished into the glare near the wall of the courtyard. The sun-paths vanished as one at the same time.

Voada was standing in the gloom among the torches and the men. <This is not where you should be.> The statement came from her anamacha, and again a woman's voice dominated the others.

<Are you the Moonshadow?> Voada asked internally.

<You already know, as you know what you should do. You've already taken from Onglse what it had to give you. Now you must go back.>

<Why? Why must I go back?> The torc of the draoi felt heavy on her neck. Voada found herself with the silver oak leaf pendant between her fingers, staring at it as if to give her stability in the twin worlds in her vision.

<You know why. You know why. You must tell them. This is why we came to you.>

The voice was receding. Her anamacha was alongside her but no longer touching her, and with her return to the reality of the fort, her exhaustion was complete. A sudden cramp rolled through her stomach. The woman's voice still echoed in her mind. She clutched the oak leaf, pressing it into her palm against the cramping. She lifted her head and saw Iosa still watching her, standing now, his lips pressed tightly together under his dark beard, his scar standing out white. His eyes were black pits, and she saw him take a step toward her.

She didn't want to talk to anyone else, especially a man. She didn't wish to know what the warrior might say, think, or want. The ghost was gone, and there were no more waiting to be guided to their rest; that was enough. She turned, walking along the rows of prone men and back to the tower. She thought Iosa might call to her, but he did not. Without looking back, she climbed the steps again.

She was asleep as soon as she lay down on her bed in the tower room.

The draoi had been invited to Greum Red-Hand's conference with the Cateni war leaders, but Voada knew she was expected simply to listen and remain silent. She huddled in a corner of the stone-walled room, a blanket wrapped around her, as Greum paced the room's perimeter, accompanied by his anamacha. Her moon-time was on her heavily, and she wanted little more than to be alone and to drink some of Ceiteag's willow bark tea. *Tomorrow it will be better; the day after, it will be nearly gone . . .*

"The Mundoa left hands upon hands of their dead sprawled before the two forts they took," Greum said. "We slew four of them for every one of our warriors now receiving his or her reward in Tirnanog. They'll spend time tending their wounds and burning their dead before they move again. We'll keep chipping away at them; we'll make them miserable and wet, and every time they try to move toward Bàn Cill, we'll take more of their men until only a few hands of them survive to run back to Albann Deas. Bàn Cill and Onglse have never been taken, and I promise you they never will be, not while any of us still live."

There was a cheer at that statement, led by Maol Iosa, though Voada thought some of the affirmations felt halfhearted. *So stupid. They don't see what's in front of them . . .*

"The Mundoa's next move must be to drive their forces inland," Ceannàrd Iosa declared, stepping forward into the center of the room. The scar on his face was now joined by the deep, puckered, angry red cut on his chest, which an archiater had sewn together, as well as wounds along each arm. If they bothered the warrior, it didn't show in his easy movements. He cocked his head, long, braided black hair swinging with the motion. "Greum Red-Hand and I are in agreement about that. Strategically, it makes no sense for Savas to continue to spread out his forces along the outer perimeter. His goal is Bàn Cill, both for its symbolic value and because he knows that we will defend it to the death. From here, he will try to punch through into the second wall of forts, but the land between here and the second wall is our ally. We know it. We know its twists and turns and folds. They don't. If we killed four to one here, we can kill two hands for every man of ours out there. They won't meet us champion to champion, so we'll use the land as our shield and shower them with arrows, descend on them like an avalanche from the heights, and have our draoi send death down upon them in the valleys." The warrior looked at each of the men in the room, then lowered his voice, which pulled everyone forward to listen. "I tell you this: they will leave their bones here. All of them."

With that, he stamped his foot on the stone flags as cheers erupted around him. Voada could only shake her head.

"We're making a mistake." The words emerged from her seemingly without volition, sounding loudly in the room as the cheers began to die. Heads turned toward her immediately as she stood, letting the blanket fall from her shoulders. On her léine, the oak leaf glittered in the sunlight entering from the window, and Voada brushed her fingers over the smooth metal of the torc around her neck. Next to her, she heard Ceiteag whisper a warning, but she remained standing. Iosa and Greum Red-Hand were both glaring at her. Iosa started to reply, but Greum lifted his hand. Iosa scowled but swallowed whatever he'd intended to say.

"So, our new draoi wishes to tutor *me* now? Tell us, friend of Savas, newest of the draoi: what mistake are we making?"

His tone was mocking and dismissive. Voada knew he wanted to intimidate her, wanted the others to laugh at her and render her silent. Once, perhaps, she would have wilted under his glare, made an apology and sat again, but the echoes of the voices in her anamacha as well as the memories of what had been done to her family and home remained with her and stiffened her spine. She drew herself up, inhaling hard through her nose. "You're thinking only of Onglse, Ceanndraoi Greum," she said. "That's the mistake. Yes, Onglse is in genuine danger, and that must be considered, but look at what the Mundoa have done to create that danger.

They've brought nearly all of their army here. How many of their cohorts are left in Albann Deas? How many of those are disciplined and strong troops? How many protect the cities and towns they've taken from us over the last several generations? Leaving those sites unguarded is *their* mistake; ours would be not taking advantage of it."

Greum snorted as if amused, and a few chuckles sounded from the others in the room. He waved his hand at her. "And how should we do that?" he asked.

You must go back . . . Voada had spent the night thinking of what the voices were saying and feeling the truth of it. "We should keep enough of our draoi and warriors here to slow down the Mundoa and to keep them engaged here in Onglse," she said to Greum, Iosa, and the others. "But we don't need to stop them, only keep them engaged here for as long as possible. We take the strongest draoi and our best warriors, and we gather more warriors and more draoi from the clans of Albann Bràghad. Then we march our own army south across the River Meadham. We burn the Mundoa's houses and destroy their cities. The Cateni they've subjugated and enslaved for three generations now will rise up with us, and our army will only grow stronger. By the time Savas realizes what's happened, it will be too late. We'll take back the land they stole from us. We'll drive the Mundoa back over the Barrier Sea. We will make *all* of Albann, both north and south, Cateni land once more."

Greum was shaking his head long before Voada had finished. "You'd let Bàn Cill and Onglse fall?"

"Onglse would be the bait in our trap. It may not fall in any case, but if that happened, that one small defeat would lead to a far greater victory."

"Onglse is the home of the draoi, and it has always been so," Greum responded, his voice rising now. His face was nearly as red as his hands. "Bàn Cill is sacred ground, and I *will not* allow it to be stolen from us the way Albann Deas was stolen. I won't let Onglse be dangled in front of the Mundoa like a lure. I will defend it to my last breath, and so will all of us here. Anyone who dares to say otherwise is a traitor and should not be wearing the torc of the draoi." He looked directly at Voada. "The strength of your anamacha doesn't make you ceanndraoi, Voada Paorach, nor does it give you the right to question my orders. The Mundoa have foolishly come here, and as Ceannàrd Iosa has said, they will leave their bones here. A mistake?" His laugh was loud and cutting. "Savas has made the mistake, not us. The clans of Albann Deas were weak when they allowed themselves to be conquered in the first place. We of Albann Bràghad are neither. But then, *you* wouldn't realize that, being of Albann Deas yourself. Sit down, Voada Hand-wife. Sit down, and stop making yourself look foolish."

The faces surrounding her were either accusing and angry or carefully averted from her, as if everyone were embarrassed to meet her eyes. Even Ceiteag was staring carefully toward the window as if the clouds drifting past and the splash of rain on the sill were somehow intensely interesting. Voada clenched her jaw so tightly that she heard her teeth grinding.

Greum's regard was harsh and unrelenting. Iosa was also staring at her, though it was hard to guess his thoughts behind the scarred and bearded face. The silence fell heavy around Voada, pressing down on her, and she did sit once more, wrapping her blanket tightly around herself.

At last, Greum looked away. "Unless someone else here feels we're making a *mistake*," he said with a significant pause after the phrase, "then here's how I believe we should best place our resources . . ."

18

An Alliance Offered

"**Y**OU'RE UPSET WITH ME," Voada said. Ceiteag shook her head.

"Not upset, child. Worried for you."

The two were taking their midday meal in their room. After Greum Red-Hand's meeting that morning, the decision had been made that the outer perimeter of forts would be abandoned except for a skeleton crew of warriors and messengers who could relay any unusual movements to Ceannàrd Iosa or Greum. The draoi and the bulk of the warriors would move inland to the smaller second ring of hill-forts and walls, which they would defend while launching assaults against the Mundoa. Greum Red-Hand strode away from the meeting with Iosa at his side without speaking to Voada again. The other warriors and draoi had given her glances that seemed equally amused and angry and went away whispering to each other.

Voada could only imagine what was being said.

"You don't think I should have said anything."

Ceiteag lifted a shoulder as she broke off a piece of hard bread. She turned it in her hand as if appraising a yeasty gem. "You contradicted Greum in front of those he commands," she answered, speaking more to the bread than Voada. "What in Elia's realm did you *think* would happen?" Now she brought her gaze to Voada's face. "You're no longer the Hand-wife who can expect to say something and have everyone at least pretend to listen. You're a draoi, and a new one, no matter whose anamacha has bonded with you. Greum is a proud man; even if he might have agreed with you, you made it so he could not."

Voada bit her bottom lip, taking in Ceiteag's mild scolding. "I should have gone to him in private."

"Ah. Finally some wisdom." Ceiteag popped the bread into her mouth and chewed before saying more. "He may have still disagreed, he may have still said no, but he would have heard you out, and there would have been some small chance of him taking your advice. As soon as you claimed in front of the others that he was making a mistake, he stopped listening to anything you said."

"It *is* a mistake if he wants to defeat the Mundoa once and for all. That's not going to happen by protecting Onglse."

"If it *is* a mistake, you've just assured that he's going to continue to make it." Ceiteag leaned forward. She stroked the torc around Voada's neck, then let her fingers trail down to the oak leaf pendant before taking Voada's hands in her own wrinkled, thin ones. "The truth is, Voada, that you frighten the ceanndraoi," she said. "He looks at you, and he worries that you not only want to take his place but that you have the power to do so."

Voada gave a dry laugh. "I don't. I barely know what I'm doing with my anamacha. He's told me so many times."

"Yes. And what does that say about your potential?" Ceiteag patted Voada's hands and leaned back. "He knows your story, and he knows the others have heard it as well. He sees that people have sympathy for what happened to you. He—and every other draoi here—also knows the history of your anamacha. He's seen the others watching you and wondering. He's heard the passion in your voice when you talk about bringing the clans together, and he wonders whether you might be able to do just that."

"Then why doesn't he help me? If he wants to lead the way, I'd be happy to follow him."

"You'd be happy as long as he went the way you wish him to go." Ceiteag's rebuke was gentle but firm. "Isn't that what you're saying?"

"Menach, we have the chance to do something that the Cateni haven't been able to accomplish before." There was exasperation in her voice, and Ceiteag responded to it with a wry smile. "I know how prideful that sounds," she told the woman. "But it's true nonetheless. The voices of the Moonshadow's anamacha, they all tell me that."

"The voices of the anamacha sometimes try to deceive the draoi they serve. They aren't always truthful, and sometimes they're as jealous of the draoi who uses them as any living person. Listening to them can be dangerous."

"Maybe, but . . ." Voada looked away, not wanting to see the kindness and sympathy in Ceiteag's eyes. "Ceanndraoi Greum is squandering our chance."

"I know that's what you believe," Ceiteag answered. "But only Elia knows the truth, and Her voice is the most difficult of all to hear." She went to the pot steaming over the hearth and spooned stew into a wooden bowl. She brought it back to the table, placing it in front of Voada. "Dip your bread in this," she said. "It'll soften it and make it easier on your teeth—something that might not bother you yet, but it does me. And I've added rue and shepherd's purse to help ease your bleeding."

Voada glanced from the bowl to the bread to Ceiteag. The old woman lifted her hands, palms up.

"At least that's good advice you might take," she said.

The sun was setting the clouds in the west afire as it set, but Voada was looking east and down the line of the wall, where under banks of low, scudding black clouds, the fort that Savas had taken stood like a broken tooth in an old man's gums.

"What Greum said is correct," she heard a low voice say behind her. "The Mundoas' next attack will be toward the inner wall and

Bàn Cill. More of their ships stuffed with soldiers will arrive in a few days, and that's when Savas will make his next move."

Voada glanced over her shoulder to see Ceannàrd Iosa standing a few strides from her. Lost in her own thoughts, she hadn't heard his boot steps approaching. The sentries posted along the wall were standing well away from them, not looking their way and out of easy earshot. She wondered if that was deliberate.

"I never suggested otherwise," she told him.

"But you would have us abandon Onglse."

Voada shook her head as she turned to face the man. He was standing close to her, a looming silhouette against the setting sun. He smelled of smoke and oil. "No," she said. "Not abandon it. We need to keep Savas engaged here for as long as possible."

"While you set fire to the south."

Voada took a long breath of the cool evening air. "As long as Savas and his army are here, Albann Deas is open to us as it hasn't been before. The commander knows that the Cateni—and especially the draoi—think of Onglse as sacred; he's convinced that we'll do everything possible to defend it, and he's certain that's the weakness that will allow him to defeat us. But his certainty about what we'll do is *his* weakness, yet you and the ceanndraoi don't see that."

Iosa didn't answer immediately. He took a step toward her. She remained where she was. She could see his shadowed eyes, and she held their gaze, her chin lifting. "You would need the cooperation of many of the Albann Bràghad clans for your plan to have any chance of working, Draoi Voada. And you'd still need a large force of both draoi and fighters left here on Onglse to convince Savas that he needs to remain here for as long as possible."

"Greum Red-Hand could go to the clans. They'd listen to him if he went to them personally."

"But he won't," Maol Iosa answered even before she finished. "And you won't be able to convince the clans yourself."

"I can try."

"Your accent's southern, and the northern clans think of their southern cousins as weaklings—you heard that yesterday from the ceanndraoi himself. You've no reputation yet as a draoi. None of the clan àrds will listen to you."

"Just like Greum," Voada said bitterly.

Another step. He was very close to her now, and she resisted the impulse to take a step back. "*I* listened to you," he said, his voice low and soft. "I heard you. I told you already, you and I—we want the same thing. We want an Albann that is ours once again."

The sun slipped below the horizon, and around the fort, watch fires and torches were being lit. The sentry behind Voada put a torch to his watch fire, and Voada could see the flames reflected in Iosa's pupils as the ruddy light painted his cheekbones and the scars there. He leaned forward slightly, though he didn't touch her. "And the clans . . . well, their àrds might listen to me as one of their own."

"What are you saying?"

He tilted his head, speaking nearly into her ear as she stood still, wondering whether she should back away, wondering what he'd do if she tried. His breath was warm against her ear and the side of her neck. "I'm a warrior," he said. "I lead men into battle, but I prefer those to be battles that can be won. I listened to what you said, and I think your strategy is worth considering. You've proved yourself as a draoi, but you don't know war. You don't understand it. I do, and the clans will listen to me because they know me—because I am Ceannàrd of Clan Iosa, and because Greum Red-Hand chose me to lead our warriors." Now he leaned back away from her. "I wonder what could we accomplish together?"

Voada could feel her stomach tightening. She wanted to take a step away from the man but forced herself to remain where she was. "Together?"

"You lead the draoi. I lead the warriors. We take them south. Would that be something that interests you?"

"What would Greum Red-Hand say if he heard you asking me this?"

"He would say we were both traitors and cowards. He would take your torc from you and mine from me. He'd have the draoi kill you and the warriors kill me—if they could." A trace of a smile touched his lips. "Which is why I've said nothing before and why I'm speaking to you here, where anyone who sees us together might assume that I'm simply trying to persuade the new draoi to share my bed tonight."

She reacted as if the man had just slapped her face. Her fingers went to her cheeks, to the scars that remained from her beating in Pencraig. Then she stepped back and opened her arms as she turned to where her anamacha waited a few steps away. Maol Iosa's smile widened. "There's no need to call your anamacha to you, Draoi Voada," he continued. "I'm no threat to you, and I'm asking nothing more of you than what you wish to give freely. I know what you've lost and how recent that was. I know you must still grieve for your husband and family."

"I do," she told him firmly.

"Then I'll leave you to consider what I've said. We'll talk again. But if we follow your path, we need to do that soon."

With that, he gave her a brief salutation, turned, and walked toward the tower staircase. She heard the guard stationed there chuckle as he passed. "It's a cold bed tonight, eh, Ceannàrd?" His voice carried too loudly in the still air.

Maol Iosa lifted a finger to his lips, shaking his head, and the guard grinned. The ceannàrd slapped the man—not unkindly—on the shoulder as he passed into the shadowed interior of the tower.

Voada's moon-flow had lightened considerably by the next morning. She prepared another linen pad, then washed out the stained one and placed it in a pot to boil. She'd removed it to dry when Ceiteag entered the room. "Ceanndraoi Greum wants the draoi in the main hall," she told Voada. "He's also called for Ceannàrd Iosa and the other chief warriors. I suspect we're leaving today."

The prediction proved correct. Greum Red-Hand wasted no time with niceties, standing to speak as soon as everyone had gathered. "We'll be leaving two hands of warriors and one draoi here," he said without preamble. "No more. Draoi Conn has volunteered to remain and continue to cast his weather spells over the Mundoa. He'll also be in charge of the warriors. Everyone else will leave through the western gates in three stripes of the candle. We'll follow the wall over the next ridge, then follow the valley north. The Mundoa won't be able to see us; we'll use our land itself as a shield until we reach the inner fortifications. I sent a messenger to the eastern hill-forts to tell them to do the same. The Mundoa will assume that all the remaining forts are still fully manned. Get yourselves ready."

The draoi and officers gathered in the room muttered their agreement, but Iosa stood to address Greum. "Ceanndraoi, let me take my chariot and a hand of mounted warriors as you leave. I would like to give a last challenge to Commander Savas or his champion before I rejoin you."

Greum shook his head. "You already know that the cowards won't accept challenges."

Iosa persisted. "I don't expect them to, Ceanndraoi. But issuing the challenge will make them believe that we intend to make our stand here. That may delay them a few days more, or at the least make them plan for that. We'd slow them and give ourselves more time to prepare."

Greum shook his head. "It's too dangerous. We can't afford to lose you, Ceannàrd."

"You won't," Iosa answered. "Draoi Voada has agreed to ride with me to ensure that."

Voada, sitting on the stone floor with her back to the wall, lifted her head belatedly upon hearing her name. Greum was already glaring toward her, but Iosa's back was to her, and she couldn't see his expression. "Her?" Greum questioned, a ruddy hand gesturing to Voada. "Why?"

"Draoi Voada's spells will keep the Mundoa's heads down and their archers nervous," Maol Iosa answered. "And if they see a draoi with me, they'll be doubly certain that we intend to stay here. You can't deny, Ceanndraoi, that Draoi Voada's anamacha has power."

"It does," Greum responded, though it looked to Voada as if the words were bitter on his tongue. "And we wouldn't care to lose that power, either."

"You won't lose either of us, Ceanndraoi. I give you my word. I'm your ceannàrd; you've given me that title because I can best defend Onglse. That's why I ask this."

Greum looked unconvinced. "Draoi Voada has agreed?"

Now Iosa turned to Voada, his long braided hair moving. The wounds on his arms were dark with clotted blood, just beginning to heal. "She has," he said easily. He tilted his head in her direction. "And I believe Draoi Voada trusts me. Draoi Voada?"

"I trust that the ceannàrd understands war," she said, "even if he doesn't understand *me* in the slightest."

There was laughter around the room that told Voada that gossip about last night had spread widely through the fort. Iosa laughed with them, then half turned back to Greum, spreading his hands wide. "You see, Ceanndraoi?"

Greum didn't look pleased. He glared at Voada again, and she gazed back at him placidly. "As you both wish, then. Ceannàrd, I expect you to rejoin us quickly."

Iosa bowed. "As quickly as we might," he told Greum. "Draoi Voada, come with me so I can introduce you again to my driver and my horses."

He held out his hand toward her. She ignored it, standing up on her own. "That would be good," she told him, "since it might be difficult to distinguish the ceannàrd from the rears of the others."

There was louder and longer laughter at that. Iosa smiled thinly and bowed his head to her. They left the room to whispered comments.

"If you were a man, Draoi Voada, I would have challenged you then and there for insulting me in front of the others," Iosa said as they rode out of the fort, the bed of the chariot bouncing over the stones. Four more chariots carrying other warriors followed them.

The leather suspension creaked underneath them, and the warhorses snorted as their hooves pounded the grass and earth. Iosa's driver, Tadgh—young, agile, and muscular, wearing only leather pants—crouched in the webbing of the harness between horses and chariot, the thick leather reins in his hands as he shouted at the two steeds, seeming to ignore the conversation behind him.

"If I were a man," Voada retorted, tightly clutching the rails next to Iosa to stay on her feet, "I doubt there'd have been a need for the comment. If you want to challenge me, tell your driver to stop the chariot, and you can have your challenge: your spear against my spell."

She saw Iosa's jaw clench and his knuckles go white where his own hand held the rail. They were following the line of the island's outer wall, descending into a small valley. Dark gray clouds hung low in the sky here—the creation of the draoi, she knew—and rain began to pelt them as they rode, the drops striking hard on the skin. Voada shielded her eyes with a hand. The hill-fort that the Mundoa had taken loomed at the summit of the next hill.

"I would never be draoi even if I could be," Iosa said. His dark hair and beard were dripping and plastered to his face now, and the paint he'd applied was streaked and fading. "There's true honor in fighting with a spear or sword, one against another, staring into each other's faces, knowing one of you must kill the other. An archer's bow, a siege engine's stones, a spell, all the killing done from a safe distance . . . there's no honor in those ways."

"Yet an army uses them all. The Mundoa have their engines, the Cateni have the draoi."

"We have them only because we must," the ceannàrd answered. After a breath, he spoke again. "Ceanndraoi Greum believes that you had the opportunity to kill Commander Savas but chose not to. Is that true?"

They'd reached the bottom of the slope. Tadgh slapped the reins hard down on the warhorses' backs as they began to climb toward the hill-fort, and the chariot lurched hard over the rocks of a small stream at the bottom. Both Voada and Iosa had to cling to the rail of the car to avoid being tossed from the chariot and into the water and mud. Through the rain, Voada could see movement along the tumbled wall of the hill-fort—they'd been seen. "I knew Commander Savas before I came here," she told him. "I liked the man. He treated me and my husband well—far better than the Voice of Pencraig did. He would never have done to my family what they did."

"I admire the man as well," Iosa said, "as I would any competent enemy. I honor his bravery, his skills as a warrior, and his intelligence."

"'The officer who doesn't appreciate the skill of his enemy is nothing more than a fool.' Commander Savas told me that once."

"As I said, he's an intelligent man. But he's also my enemy, and I would kill him without hesitation. Will you?"

"I thought you didn't believe there was any honor in killing your enemy from a distance."

Iosa grinned over his shoulder at her and laughed. "And that's why I admire you, Draoi Voada. You always have an answer."

There was no more time for talk. The small group of war chariots moved out onto the open ground before the fort's northern gates, staying out of the archers' range. Voada lifted an arm, calling her anamacha to her; she fought to remain focused between the swaying movement of the chariot and the chaos of the anamacha's interior world. Her vision swung wildly between the two and finally settled. "Iomhar!" she called.

<We are here,> the answer came.

While the other chariots stopped, Iosa had Tadgh race back and forth in front of the fort's wall, the wheels of his chariot and the warhorses' hooves churning the turf into black mud. He roared his challenge toward the rain-soaked walls. "Commander Savas, come and meet me or send your champion! You know me. I am Ceannàrd Maol Iosa, and I would enjoy seeing how well the Mundoa can fight, warrior against warrior! Come out! Show me!"

Heads appeared along the wall: archers with arrows nocked and ready. Finally, a figure dressed in a brilliant blue cloak emerged. Even from this distance, even through the haze of rain and the overlay of the anamacha's world, Voada knew it was Savas. "Ceannàrd

Iosa!" he shouted, his voice thin and faint. "I gave you my answer once before, and it will be the same every time you ask. Let our armies meet on the field, and perhaps you'll have your wish."

The man in the blue cloak turned, and the archers loosed a barrage of arrows. At the same time, Voada gathered the energy Iomhar held and threw it outward with a gesture. The arrows immediately turned to flame and smoke, and arrowheads plummeted far short of them like an iron rain. The Cateni cheered, and there were shouts of consternation from the walls. Iosa laughed. "Back to the fort, Tadgh," he called. "The ceanndraoi will have left by now. That should keep the Mundoa back for today and make Savas think again if he wants to pursue us."

Tadgh turned the warhorses, and they rode back the way they'd come. Voada craned her neck back toward the fort as they left. Savas still stood there, impassive, in his blue cloak.

<It's time,> Voada heard the woman's voice say in her head, echoed by the others. <We must return . . . >

But Voada remembered Savas and the way he'd treated her and Meir, the way Meir had spoken admiringly of the man and his honor, and the manner in which Savas had spoken of the Cateni. Voada reluctantly released the anamacha without answering. *Could there be another way?* she wondered. *If I could speak to Savas somehow, perhaps we could stop the fighting . . .*

"Draoi Voada," she heard Iosa say to her, bringing her attention back to him, "we've not much time before we're back with the others. Have you thought more of what we talked about?"

"Yes," she told him. "But I still don't know that I can trust you." *Or if there's another way I must try first . . .*

"That's wise of you," he answered. He smiled as the chariot lurched and started back down the slope, the others following behind them. She felt his arm touch her waist as if to steady her, and she looked at him warningly.

He continued to smile, but he removed his hand.

That night, they camped well inland, nearer to the second ring of forts, hidden from the Mundoa by the high ridges between them. Voada shared a small tent with Ceiteag, who was already snoring in her blankets, but Voada found sleep elusive. The terror of the battle and the tense excitement of her ride with Ceannàrd Iosa still pounded inside her, while the voices of her anamacha whispered to her, insistent:

<*Remaining here is a mistake. You must leave. You weren't meant to be here this long . . .* >

<*Be silent!*> she shouted back at them in her mind. <*I might go. I might not. First I want to try to parley with Savas, but I don't know how to do that yet.*>

<*That's foolishness . . . You think you can broker a peace? That's not possible . . . You can't wait . . . Stupid woman! You waste your time here . . . You squander the power we give you . . .* > Dozens of the voices inside the anamacha raged at her, though none of them seemed to be the one she thought of as the Moonshadow. That one had gone silent again, withdrawing deep into the shadows.

<*I don't care what you believe,*> she railed at the voices. <*I must see Savas.*>

<*We can help you with that.*> A lone voice: Iomhar's, the one among them she most felt she could trust. <*We can show you . . .* >

She had listened to the anamacha once before, and to Iomhar, and that had brought her to a greater understanding of what being a draoi meant. How could she ignore the voices now, especially when the guilt of having left her children behind still haunted her?

She wanted to hold them again more than anything else.

<*We can bring you to Savas,*> Iomhar said again.

<*Then show me,*> she said.

A sense of satisfaction washed through her from the anamacha. <*Open yourself to us . . .* >

Voada closed her eyes, opening her arms in invitation as the cold touch of the anamacha pressed against and into her. The world of Magh da Chèo opened around her, storm-filled as always, and she saw Iomhar there, standing near her. <*You want to talk to this Savas? There's a way. You won't be able to touch him or do anything to him, but he will see you and hear you. Is that enough?>*

Voada nodded.

<Then make your spell cage and take what we give you . . . >

She felt Iomhar begin to draw power from Magh da Chèo, and Voada moved her hands in the pattern she'd been taught, chanting the words to bind the net and pull the energy from Iomhar to herself. This spell felt draining and slippery to hold, but it was quieter than the spells of war. Softer. When the net she'd woven was full, Iomhar gave her the release words: *bruidhinn nam fhochair.* "Speak in my presence."

As she intoned the words, she imagined herself standing before Savas.

And she was. She was no longer in Magh da Chèo but somewhere within the half ruined fort Savas had taken, standing inside a small chamber with a single window. A candle burned on a table, giving the room a wavering, dim glow. Savas was sleeping there. She reached out to touch him, to awaken him, but the hand and arm she extended were nearly transparent, shimmering insubstantially in the candlelight, and her hand simply passed through him. "Commander," she said then, and the word sounded as if she were speaking from some great distance, echoing. "Commander, I would speak with you."

His eyes flew open, and he reached instinctively for his sword, drawing it suddenly. He slashed at her even as he rose, though he moved more slowly and awkwardly than she had expected; his left leg was still bandaged and stiff. The weapon slid through her body as though she were made of smoke. Savas stared at the useless sword, then at her. She saw recognition touch his scarred features, narrowing his eyes.

"You can't touch me, Commander," she told him. "And it seems I can't touch you. I supposed we should both be grateful for that."

"Why do you look familiar?" he asked. "Who are you? *What* are you?"

"You knew me as the Hand-wife Voada of Pencraig," she told him. "You did a kindness to my husband and me."

Savas blinked at that. His free hand rubbed at his eyes as if he were trying to wake himself. "Hand-wife Voada? Yes, I remember . . . But you're *dead*. Why are you here haunting me?"

"I'm not dead, though my husband, Meir, is. I am Draoi Voada now. I am on Onglse, but elsewhere."

Savas shook his head in denial and confusion. "You're draoi? Here? I don't understand . . ."

"It was my spell that destroyed your ballistae, Commander. Certainly you remember that? I could have killed you just as easily, but I didn't, because I remembered the kindness you showed my husband and me in Pencraig, because you defended the Cateni when Voice Kadir insulted us. For that I spared you. Now I want to talk with you, Commander. Nothing more."

Savas gave a bark of a laugh. He sat on his bedding again, his injured leg unbending, though he still held his sword. "What use is talking to a dream?"

"I'm not a dream, Commander. We are able to speak through a draoi spell, but I don't know how long it will last. I'd rather we didn't waste that time." Savas said nothing, only stared at her. Voada sighed and continued. "I came to tell you that you won't win here, Commander. Your sihirki are laughable against Cateni draoi, as you've seen, and our warriors easily match your soldiers. What you don't realize is that there are more draoi and warriors coming to Onglse every day." Voada knew that last statement for a lie, but she hoped that Savas wouldn't perceive it. "All that you can accomplish by remaining here is more death, and your own will inevitably be among them. It doesn't have to be that way. I want a truce. I'd rather have peace between our people. We could accomplish that, Commander, the two of us. We could make a start."

Savas was shaking his head before she finished. "Hand-wife . . . or ghost or dream or whatever you are . . . you think me more than I am. I'm just a soldier. No more. I have my orders and my duty. You want peace? Then tell Ceanndraoi Greum to surrender Onglse. Tell Ceannàrd Iosa to have his warriors lay down their arms. Have the two of them put in chains, and I'll deliver them to the Great-Voice in Trusa to be tried, but I'll let the rest of you go to your homes in peace."

"That won't happen," Voada told him. "That's not peace. That's defeat."

Savas nodded. "I know. But that's what Emperor Pashtuk demands, and thus what Great-Voice Vadim demands of me in turn. I'm sorry, Hand-wife. I heard what Voice Kadir did to your family after I left—though I was told you died as well—and I'm sorry. But none of us can change the past, even though we might want that. I certainly do." Voada could see a sadness pass over Savas' face, a grief that seemed nearly as deep as her own. "The past is done and finished, and the future can't be known. We can only do what duty and honor binds us to do and hope we're taking the right path."

"This isn't the right path. We both know that."

"So my dream continues to argue?" Savas put the sword down on the bed. He exhaled loudly. "If our path's the wrong one, it's nothing either of us can change. If I refuse to act according to my duty, someone else will take my place to do so. And you . . . if you go to the Red-Hand and tell him that you'll no longer do his bidding, what will he do to you?" When Voada didn't answer, Savas gave her a sad, weary smile. "Ah," he said. "You see, dream? So we can only hope and keep walking our paths. I'm sorry, Hand-wife. For both of us."

"So am I," Voada told him. "More than you realize."

With that, she willed the spell to dissolve, and she found herself collapsing onto her blankets back in her tent in the darkness.

19

Separations

THE CATENI REACHED THE nearest of the hill-forts in Onglse's inner defensive ring wall by midday. Iosa and Greum spent the rest of the day in conference with some of the other warriors and draoi, but after her previous outburst, Voada was pointedly not invited to join them.

Instead, she sought out a small garden facing Bàn Cill near the fort's gates. The inner defensive ring wall had less the look of a fortification, possibly because unlike the outer ring, it had never actually seen war. The Mundoa had attacked Onglse more than once since they'd come to Albann, but they had never before breached even the outer wall. On the inside of the ring, the land was heavily wooded and sloped down gently until the tree-covered slopes that enclosed Bàn Cill itself rose a short day's ride away. Someone had created the garden alongside a pond, fed by a stream cascading through the gorse. At the end of the pond, the stream fell away again into a chattering waterfall and disappeared once more under the brush alongside the rutted roadway leading toward Bàn Cill.

She was sitting on a moss-covered boulder near the waterfall, the crystalline sound filling her ears and the smell of clean water and the flowering gorse in her nostrils. She held a clump of the flowers in her hand when she saw the ceannàrd enter the garden and stop a careful stride away from her.

"Just how did you plan to leave Onglse, Draoi Voada?" he asked her. "Were you going to swim across the channel?"

Iosa's tone was gently mocking. Voada scowled at the man. "I hadn't made any plans to leave at all until you came to me," she told him. "And I still don't know that I will." *Or rather, for me to do so alone would be foolish.* To Voada, that seemed likely, despite the yammering of her anamacha, intensified now since her failed conversation with Savas. "Have you betrayed me to Ceanndraoi Greum?" she asked. "Is that why you're here?"

"Is that what you think I'd do?"

"That makes more sense to me than you abandoning Onglse to go on a fool's errand with me."

Iosa crouched down near her. He plucked at the moss on the bank of the pond. "Why?"

"I've little to offer you. You are the ceannàrd. I've seen you in battle. I've seen the pleasure you take in fighting—and there *will* be fighting enough for you here if you stay. Glory and honor and perhaps even a hero's death to take you into Tirnanog, where the gods will be pleased to have you sit with them. Go with me . . ." She shrugged. "Perhaps we'll be discovered leaving, and Greum Red-Hand will have us put to death as traitors. Or let's say we actually manage to steal away from Onglse, but none of the clans can be persuaded to join us. Perhaps—"

Iosa's laugh cut her off. "Perhaps we'll gather an army of the clans and sweep into Albann Deas before Commander Savas and the Great-Voice realize what's happened. Perhaps the southern Cateni will rise up with us. Perhaps we'll give the Mundoa a mortal wound and send them running and weeping back to Rumeli and their emperor." He tossed the moss into the pond; they both watched it swirl away in the current. "I like my 'perhaps' better than yours," he said. "Glory and honor and a true hero's death— those are all more likely if I leave. So you see, I believe in you perhaps more than you do yourself." He paused, his gaze finding hers. "I'm intrigued by everything you have to offer, Draoi Voada."

Voada held his gaze. "As long as you don't think I'm offering more than what I've already suggested, Ceannàrd. I'm not. I won't ever be your lover. I won't be your consort or your wife."

His smile was slow, the muscles moving under his beard and scars. He plucked more moss from the bank, dropping his gaze to look as he rolled it in his fingers. "Your anamacha—it still wants you to leave Onglse?"

She nodded.

"Then if we're truly to do this, we need to move quickly, before Commander Savas decides to attack us here. We need to be gone before that happens, and we need to give ourselves several stripes of the candle before Greum notices our absence. We can't move toward Bàn Cill and the northern coast—we'd be found and captured before we could reach it. Ideally, we need to leave Onglse altogether before we're missed. *If* this is something you still want."

"How do I know I can trust you? How do I know that you aren't just looking to betray me to Greum Red-Hand?"

"You don't know," he answered. "You *can't* know, because I've no way to put you inside my head and show you whether I'm lying. You have to trust yourself and me." He dipped his fingers in the pond, cleaning them of the moss. As he stood, he wiped them on his cloak. "As for betrayal, you did that yourself when you spoke up in the meeting. Greum Red-Hand doesn't need my testimony; he already thinks of you as arrayed against him. You need to decide now, Draoi Voada. We haven't time to waste."

You either trust him, or you must go yourself. There's no other way. It was difficult to tell if the thought came from her or her anamacha. "So do you have a way for us to leave Onglse other than swimming?"

Iosa cocked his head. "Then you're saying yes?"

Voada nodded silently in reply.

"Ceanndraoi Greum has requested that Draoi Voada and I go to the mainland to bring more warriors and draoi from the clans to the defense of Onglse. I'm sure you understand how vital our mission is."

The àrd of the fort nodded, but he looked unconvinced and worried. "Ceannàrd, we've had no such orders from the Ceanndraoi, and taking a boat across the channel in the middle of the night . . ."

Voada tried to calm the fear burning in her stomach. Iosa managed to look bored and irritated all at once. "Àrd—what's your name again? I want to make certain to remember when the ceanndraoi asks—I truly don't have time to waste arguing. The tide is already beginning to go out, and we need to go with it. You know who I am. Do you think that Greum Red-Hand sent me here to have his plans delayed by you? Do you wish to challenge me, Àrd? Because that's what will happen if you don't arrange for our passage *now!*"

The last word was a shout that echoed through the courtyard of the hill-fort. Voada wondered whether even Commander Savas, a day's ride away, didn't also hear it.

Voada and Maol Iosa had slipped away from the fort while the last light of evening still lingered, taking two riding horses from the stable. Voada didn't hear what Maol Iosa told the stable hands, but she heard the chuckles and laughter and saw them looking back toward her with knowing glances, so she could guess the excuse Iosa had given them. They'd ridden out quietly; the guards at the gate had already opened the smaller door, and the guards on the walls remained silent—Voada assumed that Iosa had given them similar stories. As they rode, Voada had opened herself to her anamacha and Iomhar, creating a fog that boiled and rose like a wall between them and the fort. They had slipped quickly into a valley, turning the horses to ride hard eastward, toward the outer wall but away from the hill-forts nearest those held by the Mundoan army. By the time they had approached the outer wall and hailed the guards to awaken their àrd, the moon had risen and slid halfway up the sky while the constellation of the Warrior dipped low in the west. The àrd—gap-toothed, gray-haired, and slack-muscled, long past his prime as a warrior—had obviously been sleepy and annoyed at being rousted from his bed, though his demeanor had changed somewhat when he'd recognized Ceannàrd Iosa in the torchlight.

Now, at Maol Iosa's mention of a challenge, he took a step back and wiped at his cloak as if brushing away stray crumbs. "There's no need for that, Ceannàrd. Certainly I'll help you and the lady draoi. You!" He snapped his fingers at a guard trying hard not to appear like he was listening from the shadows of the doorway. "Rouse the boatmaster and tell him to get his crew up. He's to take two passengers across to Albann Bràghad immediately."

"And tell him to be quick about it," Iosa added, "or Draoi Voada might be tempted to use her powers to curse him with something that'll make him and his wife regret his slowness. And while he prepares the boat, we require food and wine. It's been a long and hard ride."

"Go on," the àrd told the guard. "You've heard the ceannàrd." The guard hurried away, calling for the boatmaster and the kitchen staff as the àrd rubbed at his balding head. "If you and Draoi Voada will follow me, Ceannàrd. I'm sure Cook will find something for you."

It seemed but a stripe later that they found themselves on the rolling deck of a Cateni vessel, its single sail full-bellied with a wind conjured up by Voada to speed the ship across the water. In the moonlight, they could see the anchored ships of the Mundoa near the mouth of their harbor well to the south. If anyone saw their vessel, they made no move to pursue them, though Voada was confident that had one of them done so, she could have easily dealt with it. Her anamacha was nearly singing as they moved away from Onglse, as if they were all pleased by her decision. That pleased her as well.

Ceannàrd Iosa stood alongside her near the prow of the ship, watching the water churn white with their passage. He seemed dour and pensive. "You're troubled, Ceannàrd?" Voada asked him. "Are you thinking it would have been better to tell me to swim?"

He gave a brief chuckle at that. "No." He continued to look out over the water. A wave lifted the boat's carved prow, spraying droplets of cold salt water over them. "Just wondering what awaits us there."

He pointed eastward. On the horizon, there was a line of greater darkness: the mountainous terrain of Alban Bràghad and the northern clans.

"The honor and glory you want," Voada told him. "And for me, the children who were stolen from me."

"And revenge," Iosa added.

She nodded. "And that. For all of us."

"I wonder if it will be enough," Iosa said.

"Are you worried that you've made the wrong choice, that you should have stayed back there?" Voada inclined her head toward the bluffs of Onglse.

"You're not?" Iosa asked her, and Voada shook her head quickly.

"No. Now I'm certain this is the right choice for me. The only choice, if I want to see my children again. I've already been away so long . . ." The thought brought tears to her eyes, and she brushed at them almost angrily. "Do you have a wife?" she asked Iosa. "Children?".

"A wife, once. She died giving birth to our child. A boy it was, who also died that evening."

"I'm sorry."

Iosa shrugged. "Elia's will, aye? I was destined to be a warrior and nothing more. Not a father. Not a husband."

"Is that enough for you, Ceannàrd Iosa?"

Now he laughed, a full and loud sound that rang out over the water and caused the boatmaster and crew to look at them. "That, I think, is what I'll discover in the next few moons. And you might as well call me Maol, if we're going to be traveling together."

They both watched the land slowly approaching them until they could see the waves breaking white at the bottoms of the sea cliffs.

20

The Moonshadow's Storm

IN THE DIM DAWN light, they glimpsed a village to the south with small fishing vessels just setting out for the day's work. "That's Clan Mac Tsagairt's land," the captain of the ship had told them. "They've sent a few hands of warriors to Onglse, but that's all. Not the friendliest of folk. Keep to themselves, they do."

They landed on an empty beach on the headland of Albann Bràghad not long after. Tired to the point of exhaustion, they took their supplies and horses from the ship, then watched it depart again for Onglse. They remained on the beach, lighting a fire from driftwood to keep themselves warm and dry and sleeping for a few stripes of the candle. Voada woke to find Maol—she wasn't sure she'd ever get used to calling him by his familiar name rather than title or his clan name—with the horses already in their livery and their supplies packed onto them.

"Shall we go meet Clan Mac Tsagairt?" he asked, inclining his head in the direction of the village.

She shrugged. "We have to start somewhere," she answered.

A few stripes later, they found themselves in a village smelling of peat and fish. Out in the channel, they could glimpse the islands between the mainland and Onglse as well as the faint gray hump of Onglse on the horizon, looking more like a cloud than land. Eyes stared at Voada and Maol as they rode into the village, little more than a collection of round huts. The people they passed put down their work or stepped out from their huts to watch them. "Who is your clan àrd?" Voada asked the nearest of them, a stooped, gray-haired woman who'd stopped sweeping the dirt from her home and leaned against her doorway.

The old woman spat on the ground, showing pink gums adorned by only a few teeth. "Who is it wants to know?" She was staring at the glint of silver from the oak leaf on Voada's chest as well as the bronze torc around her neck.

"I'm Draoi Voada; this is Ceannàrd Maol Iosa from Onglse," Voada told her.

The woman's eyes widened a bit at the second name, and she stood slightly straighter, her gaze traveling to Maol with his own torc, the glint of ringed mail under his cloak, the pommel of a sword at his side, and a spear lashed to the pack of his horse. She pointed toward a fold in the hills beyond the village. "Àrd Comhnall Mac Tsagairt lives there, in the stone house. You'll find him there." With that, she vanished back into her dwelling. They could see her watching them from the shadows as they rode on in the direction she'd pointed, following a well-worn path.

The stone house wasn't much larger than the wattle-and-daub huts of the village, but it looked as if it had been standing for generations. The sides were covered with vines, the thatched roof was green with moss and lichens, and the rocks holding down the thatching swayed in new ropes. There were workers in the fields around the house, who leaned on scythes and plows to watch their approach. Several small children were playing in front of the house; they ran inside when Voada and Maol appeared, and soon after, two young men armed with long pikes emerged from the doorway, moving to stand on either side of it. A fair-haired woman with piercing, pale eyes followed them, holding a bow with arrow nocked and ready to draw. "You'll stop where you are," the woman called out before they could approach. "What is it the two of you want?" To Voada, her accent was thick to the point of near-incomprehensibility.

Voada introduced herself and Maol—who appeared more amused than worried by their reception. "We've come to talk to Àrd Mac Tsagairt," she added. "We've come to ask for his help."

"For *my* help? What would a draoi and Ceannàrd Iosa be needing from the likes of us, I wonder?" A man had stepped out from the house: brown hair beginning to be woven with gray, a well-worn, bearded face, and hands that had seen much work. He stood next to the female archer, his hand on her shoulder. "Ceannàrd Maol Iosa, is it? Truly? The Ceannàrd of Onglse himself has come here? Why, this must be terribly important." He pressed his lips together.

Voada's horse stirred restlessly under her. She watched the woman with the bow, ready to call her anamacha to her should she raise the weapon.

"Well, Ceannàrd Iosa, if that's who you really are, I've already sent along those who were willing to fight on Onglse," the àrd continued. He gestured toward the village and the channel beyond. "And given the number of Mundoan ships out there in the strait, we're not likely to see any of 'em again."

"If you don't believe that I am who I say I am, then look at my torc and the insignia on my cloak," Maol Iosa said. "And if you still don't believe it, then I'll happily accept your challenge, Àrd."

Àrd Mac Tsagairt stared at Maol at that, then grunted. "We've a proposal for you, Àrd Mac Tsagairt," Maol continued. "One for all the àrds of the clans. Can we come inside and discuss it, or is this the best hospitality Clan Mac Tsagairt can offer the ceannàrd?"

The àrd shook his head. "Talk is cheap enough, I suppose." He gestured to the two young pikemen—to Voada's eyes, they resembled the àrd far more than the woman. "Boys, take care of their horses," he said. Then, to the woman: "Magaidh, our guests will be wanting some food after their journey." Magaidh glared at the two of them a moment longer, then released the tension on her bowstring, turned, and went back into the dwelling. Àrd Comhnall waved a hand at the darkness beyond the door; Voada could see children's faces staring out at them. "Come on in, then, and you can tell me about this proposal of yours," the àrd said.

The stone house's common room was filled with movement as children and servants bustled about and set the table. Voada and Maol were gestured toward the seats nearest the hearth, in which a peat fire hissed and fumed. As was proper, Maol leaned his sword against the hearth, though within easy reach. Mugs of ale were set in front of them along with plates of bread, cold meats, and cheese. Àrd Comhnall settled into a high-backed chair at the table's head; Magaidh, who Voada realized must be his wife, sat to his right. Voada wondered if the two young men were the àrd's sons. If so, Magaidh must be his second or even third wife; she couldn't have been more than a hand of years older than the two brothers. They came back into the house and stood, arms akimbo and with sour faces, near the door. The servants finished setting the table and went into the kitchen on the other side of the hearth, taking the children with them.

"So," the àrd began without preamble, "what's this proposition of yours, Ceannàrd?"

Maol leaned forward, elbows on the table. "Àrd Mac Tsagairt, the Mundoa have put nearly all their resources into their attack on Onglse," he told the man. "As a result, they've left the south poorly defended. While they're occupied with Onglse, we have an opportunity to strike at their head and heart: Albann Deas. We intend to call the northern clans together to march with us."

Comhnall looked unimpressed. "The Red-Hand named you as ceannàrd to defend Onglse. So why are you here telling us we should take our warriors from our own lands to those below the River Meadham? Is that what Ceanndraoi Greum wishes?"

"No," Maol admitted. "Greum Red-Hand worries only about Onglse and the fate of Bàn Cill. Draoi Voada and I see that the ceanndraoi's concerns have blinded him to the gift Elia has given us, and it's our duty and honor to answer Her call."

"Ah. You and Draoi Voada, eh?" He looked from Maol to Voada and back again. Magaidh looked at Voada as well, and Voada noticed that her gaze snagged on Voada's anamacha, standing just behind her and—to Voada's eyes, at least—easily visible in the dimness of the house. Magaidh stared at the anamacha, then brought her pale gaze back to Voada.

She can see it, but she doesn't have an anamacha herself . . .

Voada realized that she'd missed some of Maol's answer. ". . . join us, because now is the time for the clans to rise and stamp out the Mundoa, to reclaim the lands that were once ours, to have the southern clans rule once more instead of being made servants, slaves, and chattel."

"And you're going to accomplish that, are you? Just the two of you?" Voada saw Comhnall glance at Magaidh, who was still watching Voada. That brought the àrd's attention to her. "And is that what you're after too, Draoi? The way you talk—you've come from below the river."

Voada nodded. "I'm from Albann Deas, aye. What the ceannàrd wants and what I want are aligned, but they're not the same. My children were taken from me by the Mundoa, and I want to get them back. I want to punish the ones who took my family and my home from me."

Over the next turn of the glass, she told Comhnall and Magaidh her story: how she'd been the Hand-wife of Pencraig; how Leagsaidh Moonshadow's anamacha had found her in the temple; how Meir had died, and what Voice Kadir and Voice-wife Dilara had done in the wake of his death and funeral; how they'd wrecked her home and broken or stolen everything she owned; how Orla and Hakan had been torn screaming from her side; how she'd been beaten when she'd resisted. "Elia's done so much for me. She's made me a draoi, and She's given me a way to go back. I *know* She wants me to return. I *know* that it's Elia who has set me on this path, and I will take it with Ceannàrd Maol Iosa or without him, with or without the help of the clans."

"Your companion has fire in her, I'll admit," Comhnall said to Maol Iosa. "So we have the pleasure of hosting both the Ceannàrd Iosa himself and the draoi who holds the Moonshadow's anamacha. It's all a fine, fine tale—if any of it's true. Perhaps I should

send one of my boys across the channel and have him ask the
Red-Hand himself."

Maol stood at that, his chair tumbling over behind him. "You
doubt my word, Àrd? You doubt who I am?" He touched the scars
on his face and displayed the healing wounds on his arms. "You
think these came from a plow or a fishing line? Then call your
champion, and let me prove myself." He snatched his scabbarded
sword from the hearth, drawing the blade as the àrd shoved his
own chair back and away, as the young men at the door started
toward the table. They shouted in rage and challenge, and Voada
saw everything they'd intended to accomplish falling to ashes as a
result.

Voada rose, opening her arms to call the anamacha to her. She
let herself drop quickly into their world—the nausea and confusion was far less now that she knew what to expect.

<Iomhar!> she called into the storm, but only multiple laughter
answered.

<That one can't help you . . . You can't stop them without harming
them . . . What you intend requires great skill . . . You will kill them if
you interfere . . . Foolish woman . . . >

<Listen, Voada. Listen to me . . . > A voice rang out in Voada's
mind, drowning out the others. A woman's voice. The Moonshadow's voice. She could feel the presence emerge, a darkness contained in darkness: a tall, slim woman in a draoi's robes with
auburn hair touched with gold. Deep blue eyes regarded Voada.
<I can show you . . . Let me be with you . . . > Unlike the others, the
Moonshadow spoke not of "we" but of "I"; Voada could feel her
singular presence, looming but unseen. She remembered Greum's
warnings not to use or engage that spirit, to go no deeper into the
anamacha than Iomhar's presence, that the Moonshadow would
swallow and consume her.

But Greum wasn't here, and this was not his anamacha, and
blood was about to be spilled, and her children might be truly lost
as a result. "Come to me . . ." she said aloud, and a storm erupted
in her head and in Magh da Chèo. The other voices went wailing
away as if driven by a wind.

Voada could see the anger around her in the real world as well: blood-colored flashes across her vision.

<This will be easy for you, for us. Scatter them . . . > The Moonshadow's voice called from within the twilight, echoed by the others. *<Scatter them like seeds in a gale . . . Take what I give you. Take it . . . >*

The living world slowed, as if those in it moved through air thick as honey, as Voada's hands wove a net in the air, as she chanted the words that the Moonshadow fed her, as she gathered up the energy, her head throbbing as she tried to contain it all.

Voada could see what the Moonshadow wanted to do, but it was more difficult and more painful than any spell she'd cast before. This required precision and using the anamacha's power slowly rather than releasing it all at once. It burned her to hold it all. Voada's hands almost ceased to move, and the power she was holding threatened to spill out without any control at all; she knew if that happened, no one around her would survive. Lightning crackled and snapped, and the wind howled. The Moonshadow's voice was the thunder.

<Move as I move . . . > it commanded. *<Say what I say . . . Be me . . . >*

Voada *was* the Moonshadow. The ancient draoi's presence filled her, crowding out everything else, and she knew that Greum had been right: it would be easy to become overcome by this personality, to lose her own sense of self and go tumbling away into that storm to be lost forever. But she thought of Orla and Hakan's faces and forced herself to remain where she was. The Moonshadow's hands moved in a pattern Voada had never seen before, and she copied it. The dead draoi chanted words, and Voada opened her mouth to echo them.

<Now . . . > the Moonshadow whispered. *<Let it go . . . Direct it . . . >*

Voada obeyed, gathering the power in her hands. The new web that she'd fashioned in the world of the anamacha allowed her to hold the power of the spell, to control the amount of energy she permitted to flow from her. *Scatter them,* the Moonshadow had said.

"*Anail!*" she shouted, pointing at the combatants frozen before her, and it was as if she'd released a howling hurricane gale into the room, but one she could direct, which touched nothing but what she wished it to touch. She sent Maol sprawling, the sword falling from his hand, and did the same to the àrd and his sons. Wielding the powerful storm wind, she sent them stumbling and falling as they tried to rise, pushing the four of them until they tumbled through the door, as she walked calmly outside after them. In the muddy yard, she separated them, sending the àrd and his sons toward the pigs' pen and Maol to the stone wall of the nearest field. The power was still trembling and roiling inside her, demanding release. She sent the remainder of the energy the Moonshadow had given her into the sky, where it blew apart the rain clouds, allowing the sun to break through. Magaidh and the rest of the household had followed them outside, and the field workers stopped their labor once more, gaping at the sight of a warrior and the àrd's family rolling in the mud like mad creatures, pursued by a draoi.

"Fools!" Voada shouted at Maol Iosa and Àrd Mac Tsagairt, who were groggily trying to stand. She could still feel the Moonshadow's presence within her, and the dark world of the anamacha was doubled in her vision. Her shout was the Moonshadow's as well as her own: a god's bellow that boomed and roared and echoed, a din so loud that the pigs bleated and squealed and the sheep in the meadow reared and fled. Voada heard horses neighing in alarm from the stable alongside the house. The children clapped hands to their ears. "Idiots! No wonder the Mundoa could push the clans back into their hideaways in the mountains! We fight amongst ourselves more than we fight them. You're all mad, stupid, and stubborn! Go ahead and brawl if you want, but you're only hurting the Cateni!"

Then the Moonshadow left her, and Voada was only in her own world again, feeling empty, feeling as if she'd lost part of herself.

She was nearly drained; she had to force herself to remain standing. But the anger helped. Voada turned and stalked back into the house, knowing that she had to sit down or she would fall.

She managed to make it back to her chair before her legs gave way. She closed her eyes, trying to slow her shaking breath and pounding heart, all her limbs still trembling. She concentrated on simply breathing. It was enough.

"You are the true ceanndraoi," she heard Magaidh say somewhere close to her. "I heard the Moonshadow. I felt the power you held."

Her eyelids felt as if they were made of lead, but Voada managed to open them. Magaidh was standing on the other side of the table. Her eyes were wide and troubled. "I'm not . . ." Voada began to say, but the doorway darkened, and they both turned their heads to see the àrd and Maol entering. Their clothes were torn and soiled, and they were scratched and bruised and bleeding.

It was the àrd who spoke first, his head bowed toward Voada. "I'm sorry I doubted you, Draoi Voada," he said, the simple words a growling whisper. "Perhaps there is a way Clan Mac Tsagairt can help you."

"You've convinced Comhnall to come with you, to help raise the other clans?" Magaidh asked.

"Yes. Ceannàrd Iosa has promised him that he will be First Àrd under him, and in turn your husband will bring as many warriors as he can muster," Voada answered. She'd left Maol and Àrd Mac Tsagairt still talking around the table with several flagons of ale consumed between them. She'd gone into the kitchen to find Magaidh there with only a kitchen hearth and a few candles providing light, as if she'd been waiting for her. The rest of the household was in their beds.

"You can see my anamacha, can't you?" Voada asked Magaidh.

The woman nodded in reply.

"There have been draoi in your family?"

Another nod. Voada saw Magaidh's gaze flick over to the ghostly presence near her. "A few. My seanmhair was . . . That's the reason that Comhnall pursued me after his first wife died. An àrd whose wife was draoi—he thought that would give him prestige." She ducked her head, blond hair falling past her shoulders. "But no anamacha ever came to me, so I couldn't go to Onglse and learn the craft."

"Mine didn't come to me," Voada told her, "until I was much older than you. Do you see taibhse, too?"

This time Magaidh shook her head. "Our menach, down in the village, can see the ghosts of the dead, but I can't. Is that why I've no anamacha?"

"No," Voada told her. "Not all draoi are menach, nor all menach draoi. Greum Red-Hand can't see the taibhse either. Ceannàrd Iosa can't see my anamacha, but I think he can see the taibhse. Perhaps he could have been a menach if he hadn't become a warrior." Voada watched the flickering of the blue flames above the peat for a moment. "Greum Red-Hand told me when he was teaching me that there are only so many anamacha, that there are more people who could be draoi than who are, and that sometimes a draoi has to go where an anamacha might find her."

"Then I'll come with you and my husband," Magaidh told Voada, "and if I find my anamacha, you can teach me."

"Your children—you'd leave them?" *Could I have left Orla and Hakan in order to become draoi?* Voada had no answer to that question. Perhaps she could have for a short time, at least, if Meir had been there for them and Una had been watching over them. But this . . . going into war . . .

Magaidh's questions and her insistence brought back echoes of Orla to Voada. She could imagine her daughter asking the same things. She could imagine Orla desperately wanting to know what Voada knew, wanting to become a draoi like her mother.

She wondered if Orla would ever have that experience, and that thought made the world shimmer through the water that filled her eyes.

Magaidh brought her knees up to her chest, hugging them to

herself and propping up her chin. Voada knew that she saw the tears gathering. "Don't worry. The clanfolk will care for my children as if they were their own. They'll be safe here no matter what happens. Ceanndraoi Voada—"

"Please don't call me that," Voada interrupted. She wiped at her eyes as if they'd betrayed her.

"Others will name you that soon enough," Magaidh told her. She took in a long breath. "I've felt something missing inside me for a long time now. I thought the children Comhnall gave me would fill that space, and they're wonderful, and I do love them, but that emptiness is still there. I think . . . I *know* that it's the part of me that is supposed to be draoi. Please, help me to find that."

Her sincerity and her need tugged at Voada. Even Voada's anamacha stirred, touching her enough that she could hear their voices. <*Yes . . . Let her follow you . . . We will help you teach her . . .* >

The Moonshadow's voice was gone from the chorus. For that, Voada was grateful. *I felt her once, and that was enough. I'll be careful and never call her again.*

Voada sighed and gave Magaidh a tight-lipped smile. "I'll help you," she said.

PART THREE

ALBANN DEAS

21

The Battle of Muras

VOADA AND MAOL SPENT the next moon moving from one clan to another, crisscrossing Albann Bràghad and asking the clan àrds to lend them any fighters or local draoi who wished to join them or for the àrds themselves to join and command their own warriors. Voada told her tale hands upon hands of times as she had to the Mac Tsagairt clan: outlining their plan to attack the south, telling them whose anamacha she held, and demonstrating the power her anamacha could command. She heeded Greum's warnings and avoided calling forth Leagsaidh Moonshadow again, instead continuing to use Iomhar as her conduit to the anamacha's power.

It seemed Magaidh had been right; Voada found herself being called "Ceanndraoi" very quickly as news spread that a new draoi held Leagsaidh Moonshadow's anamacha.

And soon it was Voada rather than Maol Iosa to whom the clan-folk most listened. Her story—the loss of her children, her desire to recover them, her anger and resentment of the Mundoa who had done this to her—sparked the northern clans' ire and passion. She became the figurehead around which this new rebellion began to coalesce. She was its leader, a strange sensation to her. But as the days went on and more clans came to them, she slowly became more comfortable with the role.

After all, it was Elia who had guided her fate. Moonshadow's anamacha had come to her unbidden. As Greum Red-Hand had told her, it wasn't the draoi who was powerful but the anamacha that draoi held. Voada gave herself up to the path that had been laid before her.

"Join us!" was the song she and Ceannàrd Iosa crooned over and over around communal village fires and around tables. "Join us!" The clan àrds listened, if grudgingly at times. They listened, and they responded; a few at first, then more, and finally a flood. The news of their call to arms traveled faster than Voada and Maol and their ever-larger entourage, passed on and enhanced by word of mouth. They soon found the àrds and the clanfolk waiting for them when their burgeoning army arrived in a new place.

They also heard the news from Onglse: how the battle for the island continued, with Commander Savas' army pressing slowly but steadily inland. Of Voada and Maol's betrayal, nothing was said at all; the gossip remained silent on that. The rumors were that the Mundoan army had breached the second wall but had been thrown back again; that the battles were fierce and wild; that Ceanndraoi Greum Red-Hand himself had been injured, though the details on his injuries and their seriousness varied wildly depending on who was telling the tale; that Great-Voice Vadim III in Trusa had sent even more troops to Savas; that the Red-Hand was renewing his call for help from the clans.

But the clans were now listening to another more seductive voice, and the àrds were witnessing the gathering of an army of the northern clans unlike any they'd seen before. By the time the moon had returned again to full, Voada and Maol found themselves at the head of a formidable force: men and women both, warriors and a few draoi, though fewer than they'd hoped—most of the draoi, trained in Bàn Cill, had already left to bolster the defense of Onglse. A train of family and camp followers accompanied them as they moved south in earnest.

Toward River Meadham. Toward their first true battle.

The bridge at the town of Muras was one of the few crossings of the River Meadham and was the westernmost point at which the river could be crossed on foot, horse, or cart. Beyond Muras Bridge, the Meadham became too deep for fording, too wide to be bridged, and the current too strong to fight. Even at Muras, the bridge was only possible because it was actually two bridges, one coming from the Albann Bràghad bank and one from the Albann Deas side where the town proper sat. Both bridges linked to a large island in the center of the Meadham, clustered with shops and inns.

There was one additional ford not far west from the confluence of the River Yarrow that was seasonal and erratic; the clans largely avoided that ford after years of losing carts, horses, and those who were unable to swim when the water was too high. The other more reliable fords were all east of the Yarrow.

Too far for the Cateni army. No—lacking ships, they would have to cross over the bridge at Muras.

The army—hands of clanspeople beyond counting—had encamped a half day's march north of the river. Voada had sent a few of the family groups ahead to Muras to report on the military presence in the town; they'd returned that evening, coming to the command tent where Voada and Maol, along with First Àrd Comhnall, the other clan àrds, and the hand and three of draoi, were waiting.

"If they're aware that we're here, they don't show it," one of the women, wearing a plain bog dress, declared as she took a bowl of stew offered to her by Magaidh—still without anamacha, but often at Voada's side. "There were only a hand—two at the most—of their soldiers checking those crossing the bridge from this side, and they looked mostly bored. They just watched us, then waved us past. It was the same on the Muras side of the island; not much of a watch on the second bridge."

The woman's husband nodded in agreement. "There are more soldiers in Muras itself, of course, but from the numbers of them we counted when we passed the garrison in the town, I'd suspect it's half a cohort in total. Certainly not many more, and possibly fewer. And the ones we saw there were poor soldiers: too old or too young, most of them, and none of them look used to war or fighting."

"The Mundoa," another woman said, and spat on the ground at the word, "won't cross north past the island unless they must, and the Cateni who go into Muras from the north to sell their sheep and grain would say nothing about us even if they knew."

Maol looked at Voada, who nodded. "You all have our thanks," Maol said to them. "Go, take more food and rest. Tomorrow . . . well, we'll see what that brings." They bowed and left the tent, and Maol turned to Voada and the àrds. "Ceanndraoi?" he asked Voada. "I rode close enough to see the bridges and the approaches myself. My worry as ceannàrd is that bridges themselves are our main tactical problem, not the garrison there. Once our forces cross the final ridgeline, there'll be nothing but the floodplain of the Meadham in front of us—we'll be seen well before we reach the bridges. The Mundoa don't even need soldiers; if those defending Muras can take down the bridge, we'll be trapped on this side of the Meadham for leagues. If I were defending Muras, I would have made certain that the bridges could be destroyed quickly either by my soldiers or by the sihirki."

"The sihirki," one of the draoi—Tormod, a tall young man with hair the color of ripe hay—"are nothing to the draoi." He spat on the ground in front of him.

"And how many sihirki have you actually pitted yourself against, Draoi Tormod?" Voada asked, her voice as cutting as the edge of a honed axe. Tormod scowled and dropped his gaze to examine the matted grass and mud beneath his feet; to Voada's eyes, his anamacha seemed to shudder. "I know the sihirki well. I've been in battle against them. Yes, they're weaker than we draoi, but to think them powerless is simple foolishness."

Even as she spoke the words, she felt a coldness fill her: the anamacha's presence. <*He will understand soon . . . Soon . . .* > The chorus of voices was dominated by the Moonshadow, but Voada ignored the anamacha, and she felt it move away from her again. She stared at the young man, who refused to meet her gaze.

"But," she said after a pause, "it is the draoi who can overcome our ceannàrd's worry. Ceannàrd Iosa, here are my thoughts . . ."

Just before dawn, a fog crawled through and over the tall birches and oaks of the ridgeline opposite Muras, cascading down the verdant slope and onto the meadows and grazing fields of River Meadham's floodplain. Like a gray, cloud-wrapped wave under the moonlight and stars, it swept toward Muras Bridge, moving far more quickly than any natural fog.

The best and most competent soldiers of the local garrison had been sent to Commander Savas at Onglse half a moon ago by the local Voice; those who remained in Muras were grizzled veterans near the age of retirement or raw and largely untrained recruits. The night watch at the Muras Bridge's entrance on the Albann Bràghad side of the Meadham consisted of a hand of soldiers: two hardly more than boys, the other three men in their fourth decade, scarred and wearied by their time in the army. All of them were bored. Muras hadn't seen a battle with the Cateni since the Mundoa had taken the town generations ago; the watches on the bridge had long ago become used to uneventful nights. They were all inside the guard house—three of them engaged in a game of *zar atmak*, casting bone dice on the table and wagering the few coins in their purses, while the remaining two huddled against the stone walls, snoring. All of them had loosened or even removed their armor; what need was there for its heaviness during the long, monotonous nights when travelers only rarely came to the bridge?

They first noticed the fog when cold fingers wafted in through the open windows of the guard house, accompanied by the sudden, alarming sounds of galloping hooves and rattling chariots on the wooden planks of the bridge and the wild chanting of Cateni draoi, the clamor all strangely muffled. The guardhouse shook and trembled as the soldiers at the gaming table rushed outside—the older one first taking the time to sweep the coins on the table into his purse—and the remaining two guards struggled sleepily to their feet, following belatedly.

The fog and the early dawn dimness made it difficult to ascertain exactly what was happening, but they could see war chariots as well as Cateni warriors on horseback, hand after hand of them, rushing past them and over the bridge. One of the guards started to shout an alarm, but a spear came from the fog bank, and his shout was lost as he toppled, clutching desperately at the shaft that impaled him as blood poured through his fingers. As the others stared at their fallen comrade, at the invaders rushing past them, more spears came flying out of the fog as the ghost-like horde continued flowing by them.

One by one, the other four guards fell to join their companions, slowly painting red the gray wooden planks of the bridge.

Voada rode in Maol Iosa's chariot, bound upright to the railing so that she could create the patterns of the fog spell and send it sweeping out before them. They'd passed over the first bridge and onto the island, rushing past the knot of stores and inns that lined the dirt road and onto the second bridge, as poorly guarded as the first. In her doubled vision, the lightnings and storms of her anamacha's world were bright against a real world filled with dull gray.

Her heart was pounding with the thrill of the moment. She felt somehow more alive than ever before. Maol shouted, and his new chariot driver—Comhnall Mac Tsagairt's eldest son Hùisdean—slapped the reins hard on the horses' backs, urging them onward. The wind was tangling their hair, the fog rolled before them, and they clattered over the bridge and into Muras itself, the mounted Cateni swarming after them.

Voada had returned to Albann Deas, and the realization made her shout in exultation along with the ceannàrd even as she sagged against the ropes that held her upright from the exhaustion of using the spell, which had come from Iomhar's spirit in the anamacha.

Maol and the other charioteers wheeled about the head of the bridge, making room for the mounted fighters who followed them. They'd left more fighters of the clans at the other bridge-heads, ready to hold those positions against any counterattack until the Cateni on foot could cross. They could hear shouts and calls of alarm from all around them now as the townspeople woke and realized they were under attack. Voada opened her hands, stopping the chant and releasing the fog to clear on its own. Already a breeze from the west was shredding it, and the eastern horizon smoldered with the first rays of sun, turning the waters of River Meadham a fiery orange.

"Hold the bridge!" Maol shouted to the others. "We must continue to hold the bridge!"

They were in the market square of Muras, deserted in the dawn, and across the square, they could see the gates of the Muras garrison. As Voada watched, they swung open and disgorged a clot of Mundoan soldiers. To her right, Voada saw Tormod's hands moving, and his voice rose in a chant. He gestured, and a wave of water from the river behind them lifted into the air, flew above them, and crashed down on the soldiers, sending the first ranks of them sprawling and flailing. Tormod grinned at Voada. But more soldiers were now pouring out of the garrison, and Voada could hear the Mundoan sihirki chanting from the upper floor. Ceannàrd Iosa was shouting at Hùisdean, directing him to turn and attack the onrushing soldiers. Already the other Cateni charioteers were doing the same. Their chariot lurched and turned sharply as Voada began a new spell; from the side of her vision, she saw a ghostly spear—a sihirki spell—arc out from the second floor of the garrison.

The conjured weapon wobbled, poorly formed, but Voada saw Tormod's chariot, turning to meet the soldiers, move into the path of the sihirki's spell even as the young man began creating a new one of his own. Voada called out a warning to Tormod, abandoning her own spell, but he either didn't hear her or chose to pay no attention. She saw the sihirki-created spear—already beginning to fade and fail—strike Tormod full in the chest, tearing into the young man's body. Blood erupted from him, spraying out behind the moving chariot as it plunged into the line of soldiers and showering Maol's chariot with red droplets. Voada shouted in wordless anger and grief and ripped open the anamacha's world once more. She called Iomhar to her, stealing the energy that he quickly fed her to create a spell. In the real world, she could hear the sihirki continuing to chant even if she couldn't see them. She wove the net to hold the spell, and even before it was full, she gathered it and gestured.

A ball of light arrowed away from her, so bright that it cast shadows across the square and the tumult of fighting bodies, chariots, and horses, and plunged into the open upper windows of the garrison. For a moment, it seemed that the sun itself had materialized inside the building, rays of brilliance stabbing outward into the morning sky and the remnants of the fog. Voada could see the black shadows of the sihirki nearest the windows. Then the sun pulsed and went from light to heat. The upper floor burst into sudden and complete flame, screams echoing across the market as Voada sagged against the ropes holding her upright. One of the sihirki flung himself from the window, his clothing afire, his skin blistered and charred. The sihirki's body lay twitching on the cobbles of the square.

The entire garrison was aflame now, the noise of the blaze loud and the heat palpable even near the bridge. The flames were beginning to leap across to the nearest buildings, and townsfolk were running out, fleeing and carrying their children and possessions.

Voada's chariot lurched as Hùisdean turned the horses once more, and Maol flung spear after spear into the soldiers confronting him. Hùisdean had the horses rear and strike out with their hooves, then let the scythe blades mounted to the chariot's wheels tear at the Mundoan soldiers milling around them as the they galloped across the square.

More Cateni warriors were beginning to stream over the bridge on foot now, and their arrival ended the confrontation. Soon the Mundoan soldiers were all dead or fleeing for their lives. Maol shouted in triumph from his chariot as Hùisdean drove the horses in a mad, wild circle around the square. He howled as he looked back at Voada.

"We've taken Muras!" he screamed. "The entire south will soon be ours! We'll take them all!"

22

A New Draoi

THE AREA SOUTH OF the market square of Muras was burning. The fire Voada had started at the garrison spread rapidly in the wind, devouring the wood-and-thatch structures. Voada could have stopped that destruction. Certainly she could have called down a rain that would have at least slowed it and saved some of the houses.

She did not. She had other concerns.

The market square was filled with bodies, most of them Mundoan. Near her, the war chariot in which Tormod had been riding was stopped, and the warrior and his driver were trying to untie the sagging, broken body of the draoi from the rail. Here and there, Mundoan soldiers and a few Cateni fighters were moaning, holding up their hands in supplication. Cateni archiaters were moving among them, crouching down and making their assessments, then calling over men to take the wounded where they could be treated. Cateni fighters simply killed any of the wounded Mundoan soldiers who were stubbornly alive.

The pillaging of Muras had begun. The army of the Cateni was flowing across the bridges of the River Meadham, unstoppable, and they were looting what they found as they spread out through the town. Looting, and worse. At the eastern end of the square,

Voada saw a girl who looked to be little older than Orla—a local Cateni, from the blond hair and shape of her face—pulled from one of the houses by three Cateni fighters, who were tearing at her clothing and laughing. "Stop that!" Voada shouted, still bound to Maol's war chariot, but her voice went unheard in the general chaos around them. "Ceannàrd Iosa, look!" She pointed to the assault, but Maol only shrugged.

"It's war, Ceanndraoi," he said. "This is what the end of any battle looks like."

"Not this one. Not *my* war . . ." Voada opened her arms again in invitation, ignoring the weariness as she let her anamacha enter her. Iomhar was there, waiting for her as if he'd expected her return, but she ignored him.

<*It's me you want . . . I'm here . . .* > The Moonshadow came as if the thought of her had been a summons. Without another word, she began to funnel the power of her world toward Voada, who started to shape it, letting it fill her as she chanted and shaped the spell with her hands.

Greum's warning about the Moonshadow was but a whisper in her mind, one easily ignored in the heat of the battle's aftermath.

Voada gestured widely, leaving the power inside her, and the Moonshadow's presence filled her voice so that it boomed and roared, echoing throughout the town and rebounding off the buildings around them and the ones across the bridge: a voice like that of a god. "Listen to me and hear me. I am Ceanndraoi Voada, and this is *my* victory. I will not have it tainted. Do what you will to the Mundoa, but do not harm or take anything from any Cateni. Do no harm to Cateni children or women. Those Cateni are our brothers and sisters, and I call on them to join with us. Those who harm the Cateni of Albann Deas I declare to be my enemies, and you have seen what I do to my enemies. Hear me, and understand what I say. Stop this!"

Maol and Hùisdean had clapped their hands over their ears against her voice; everyone in the square had stopped to look at her, including the men around the young Cateni girl. They saw her staring directly at them, her arm pointing in their direction.

They stepped away from their victim and dropped to their knees, bowing their heads low. Voada saw the girl clutch the remnants of her clothing around herself and run. No one pursued her.

"Cateni of Muras," she continued, the god-voice bellowing. "We've come not to hurt you but to free you. Join us, and together we will set free the whole of Albann Deas. Go to any of our warriors or any of our draoi; they will help you. I am Ceanndraoi Voada, and I promise you this: no more do you have to serve the Mundoa. No more!"

She shouted the last two words with all the power left in her. The words were incandescent, shimmering in the very air with their energy. The world spun in Voada's vision. She sagged against the ropes holding her, and the worlds—both of them around her—vanished.

She was lost, but someone had her hand, and even though she couldn't see in the darkness, she allowed it to pull her forward until light fluttered around her . . .

"Ceanndraoi! I was so worried about you."

Magaidh's face came into focus in front of her. Voada could feel a cool cloth against her forehead and a blanket over her. She was laying on a makeshift bed, and the surroundings seemed oddly familiar: a temple. Moving her head slightly, she could see the tiles marking the sun-paths and the traditional four large windows. On the central altar plinth of the round structure, a crude statue of Elia had been placed, while on the floor around the altar were the shattered remnants of a bust of Emperor Pashtuk.

The air of the temple was filled with the scent of wood fires, and Voada could hear voices outside, punctuated by the occasional shout.

"Who brought me here?"

Magaidh looked away as if embarrassed. "After your spell in the square, no one could rouse you, not even the other draoi or the archiaters. The ceannàrd sent a runner for me, and I came and told them to move you here. It seemed the best place. You were murmuring in your dreams, and I held your hands . . ."

"I felt your touch," Voada told her. *The Moonshadow was so strong a presence, like trying to hold the sun. She nearly consumed me. I can't call her again. I can't.* "That allowed me to follow you back. Thank you, Magaidh. You brought me back to the living world."

Magaidh blushed at that, but a grateful smile touched her lips. "I didn't know what else to do. I was just as useless as the others, but I knew you weren't gone—your anamacha was still standing alongside you."

Voada smiled. "You did exactly right. How long has it been?"

"Three, maybe four stripes of a candle." Magaidh's gaze left Voada and traveled to a different area of the temple. There was another anamacha there with them, one whose shifting form Voada remembered: Tormod's anamacha. It stood there as if waiting. Magaidh's attention returned to Voada. "It follows me," she said in a whisper, as if afraid to let the anamacha overhear her. "It appeared not long after dawn, before the ceannàrd called me to you. I . . . I think I can hear its voice."

"Tormod died today," Voada told her. "His anamacha went looking for another draoi. They want you."

Magaidh drew back slightly. The straw in the mattress under Voada crackled with her motion. "I don't know . . . I don't know how to . . ."

"I can show you." Voada grunted as she pushed herself up into a sitting position. Every muscle in her body groaned and protested at the movement. She fought the urge to lie back again and give herself up to the darkness once more. *You can't go back there. She'll take you if you do. You need to be stronger to hold her.*

"Ceanndraoi. . . ." She felt Magaidh's hand on her again, pressing the cool, damp cloth against her forehead once more.

"No," she told the young woman. "I need to be up. I need to see what's happening here. And I need to help you most of all, and this is the proper place to do that." Voada saw that Tormod's ana-

macha had slid closer to them. In the shifting faces of the apparition, she thought she saw Tormod's features appear briefly in the
barrage of faces. She remembered how Ceiteag and Greum had
taught her, in their very different ways, to use her own anamacha.
She called her anamacha to her reluctantly as she swung her legs
over the side of the bed and stood. "Watch me," she said to
Magaidh. "Then copy what I do with Tormod's anamacha. You
must make them yours and bond with them. I'll be with you in
their world; I won't let them harm you."

"Them?"

"The anamacha holds every draoi who has ever been part of it.
Now it holds Tormod as well, and one day it will hold you. Greum
Red-Hand told me that the draoi are forbidden to ever enter Tirnanog; instead, we remain forever in Magh da Chèo, the otherworld of the anamacha." She found Magaidh's gaze and held it.
"This is a decision you need to make now. Do you still want to be
draoi, knowing this? If you take this anamacha, you'll never be
with your husband or your children in Tirnanog. That's the draoi's
curse."

Magaidh nodded, though her eyes were wide. Voada imagined
that she must have looked the same to Greum—frightened, uncertain, yet strangely eager. "Do as I do," she repeated, and she
opened her arms. Her anamacha slid toward her quickly at the
motion, entering her and plunging her into the dark world. "Iomhar!" she called, making certain that it was he who connected
with her and not Leagsaidh Moonshadow—she didn't even dare
think that name. She felt Iomhar's comfortable, familiar presence,
and that calmed her. But she also sensed the Moonshadow moving closer to her.

<No!> she thought to that presence. <Stay away from me! I don't
want you!> Voada thought she heard laughter in reply, but the
Moonshadow's presence slid away from her, back into the shadows.

A few breaths later, Voada saw Magaidh appear near her, surrounded by the flowing presences within her anamacha as she

was surrounded by her own. "Magaidh," she said, and the young woman spun about wildly, seeking her voice. "Don't worry. I'm here with you."

"The voices. I hear them. I see them. So many . . ."

<We hear them also . . . We hear all of them . . . >

"Can you find Tormod's voice? Concentrate on that. Call him to you. He's the most recent soul here; he'll be the easiest link and the safest for you. Call him."

"Tormod!" Voada heard Magaidh's voice, faint against the storming of the anamacha's world and the insistent voices of Voada's own anamacha.

<She's not as strong as you . . . You're no Greum Red-Hand, who has taught hand upon hand of draoi . . . They'll take her . . . She won't survive . . . > the chorus told her, with Iomhar's voice dominating, and she sent a wave of irritation toward them.

"Be quiet! Let Magaidh do her work."

"I see him, Ceanndraoi. I . . . feel him," Magaidh said. "He's laughing at me, mocking me. All of them are. Why? Why do they hate me?"

"They don't hate you," Voada told her. "They're testing you. They want to be certain you're strong enough to handle them. Call him again. Make him come to you."

Voada could feel her hesitation. Lightning flared in the anamacha world; thunder cracked. A wind that couldn't be felt shrieked around them, and it tore the name from Magaidh's mouth and hurled it into the void: "Tormod! Come!"

A figure detached itself from the crowd around Magaidh and approached her. Voada watched carefully. "Good," she told Magaidh. "I don't know the other draoi within your anamacha, but Tormod will. For now, use him alone—he can gather the power here and pass it to you, but that's another lesson. Later, he can tell you which of the souls within your anamacha is most powerful, which ones he used, and which ones he trusted. For now, calling him to you is enough. Tell them all to leave you now, Magaidh. Cast their voices out of your mind, and let yourself come back to our world."

Voada watched, ready to snatch Magaidh away herself if she needed to do so—and wondering what would happen if she did—but she saw Magaidh's anamacha suddenly vanish, and she released her own at the same time. The storm-riddled world of the dead draoi fell away from her, and she was back in the temple in Muras, seeing Magaidh sway and nearly fall. Voada caught the young woman and lowered her to sit on the bed alongside her.

"Ceanndraoi, I never thought . . . How do you manage . . . ?"

Voada smiled and patted Magaidh's hand. "I was exhausted and overwhelmed too the first time I did that. I promise that you'll get used to it, and you'll learn how to use what's there. I'll teach you."

Voada closed her eyes for a moment, taking in a long breath, then rose to her feet again. "And now," she said, "I have to find the ceannàrd. We're done with Muras. We need to move on while we still have surprise on our side."

"The capital of Trusa is open to us. The entire south is open." Maol grinned at Voada, clapping his hands together in satisfaction. The ceannàrd had taken the Voice of Muras' villa on the bluff above the Meadham as his temporary residence. Beyond the balcony on which Voada and Maol stood, she could see the Voice and the Voice-wife's bodies, hung splayed, bloody, and naked on either side of the villa's gates: a warning to the Mundoa.

Inside, in the grand dining room of the villa, dishes clattered and voices were raised as Hùisdean—Maol's driver—and several of the clan àrds, among them Comhnall Mac Tsagairt, availed themselves of the best dishes of the Voice's estate, as well as the rich plunder of his larder and wine cellar. Magaidh had accompanied Voada here and was also inside, having joined her husband. Through the open doors, Voada could see the two of them embracing and kissing, Magaidh's anamacha standing alongside her. Magaidh seemed to feel Voada's gaze on her; she looked over and smiled. Voada remembered similar times she'd had with Meir and how she'd hoped to see Orla just as happily married, and though she smiled back at the young woman, the grief of her loss surged through her again, as sharp as ever. Meir was already gone, but would she ever see Orla and Hakan again?

She turned away before Magaidh could notice the tears that threatened.

"We'll sweep into the capital like a gale from the Storm Sea. We'll roust the Great-Voice himself from his throne and send his head back to Rumeli as a gift for Emperor Pashtuk," Maol continued, a little too loudly. Voada could smell the wine on his breath. He gestured southward with a golden cup, and scarlet liquid sloshed over the rim. His steps toward her were stumbling.

"No," Voada told him flatly. She sniffed away the remnants of the moment with Magaidh. "First we're going to Pencraig."

"Pencraig?" Maol laughed, the dry sound echoing in the courtyard below. "Voada, I understand why you want to go there, but Trusa is the prize we need to capture. We can't let it slip out of our hands because we delayed. Pencraig can wait until after Trusa. Strategically, Pencraig has no value at all."

Voada was already shaking her head long before he'd finished. "Trusa is *your* prize, not mine," she told him. As she spoke, her hand went involuntarily to the silver oak leaf pendant on its chain, the twin of the one she and Meir had given to Orla. Maol's gaze followed the movement of her hand. "I told you from the very beginning what I want. I want my children back, and they were in Pencraig when I last saw them, and it is Voice Kadir who let them be taken and who nearly cost me my own life. *I* am going to Pencraig, Ceannàrd. If you like, I will tell our army that they need to choose who they follow: you or me. You can take those who will go with you to Trusa, and I'll take those who wish to follow me to Pencraig."

Even Voada could tell that her own voice had changed. Her declaration sounded like a faint echo of the god-voice the Moonshadow had lent her. The thought troubled her, though she allowed none of it to show on the stern face she turned toward Maol. *Is it truly her I hear? Have I somehow brought her out of the anamacha? Has she already taken a part of me?* But no, the anamacha was standing well to her right, and she couldn't hear their voices at all.

Maol's mood darkened, and his intoxication seemed to vanish in an instant. He threw his goblet angrily to the side; wine splashed over the white marble rail of the balcony, and metal rang. "You asked *me* to lead this army, Voada. What you're proposing is a mistake. News of the fall of Muras will reach Great-Voice Vadim in Trusa in less than a hand of days. No more. As soon as he hears it, he's going to send his fastest riders to Commander Savas and order him to bring the army home. If we march directly on Trusa *now*, immediately, then we'll arrive before the Great-Voice learns about Muras or at nearly the same time—certainly before he has any chance to respond or pull more troops to the city. We'll be in Trusa before they have a chance to prepare. If we take the days to go to Pencraig instead, we'll lose that chance. They'll know we're coming. Voada, you need to listen to me as the ceannàrd."

Perhaps it was the exhaustion of the day and the use of her anamacha, but a matching anger flared in her at the man's insistence. Voada put her hands on her hips, glaring at him. "You aren't listening to me, Maol. I asked you to lead our warriors into battle, but no more than that. This is *my* war, and it was my story that brought the clans together. I don't *care* whether Savas learns about us a few days before he might otherwise. Trusa can wait until I have my children with me again. And as for Savas . . . no matter how quickly he abandons the attack on Onglse—if he does that at all—he still won't reach Trusa before we do."

"You can't be certain of that."

"Perhaps not. But I know that I and those who wish to follow me will be going to Pencraig first. So I ask you, Ceannàrd, will you go there with me or not?"

"Voada . . ."

She waited, holding his gaze. Finally, Maol sighed. He blinked. "As you wish, Ceanndraoi." He put heavy emphasis on the title. "I know who the army would follow if you made them choose. I'll go with you to Pencraig. But it's still a mistake."

"I hear you, but I disagree," Voada told him. "In any case, the decision's made. Let's join Magaidh, Àrd Mac Tsagairt, Hùisdean, and the others. We'll give them the news: we'll leave tomorrow at dawn. In the meantime, I'm famished, and we have a long march ahead of us."

As they moved toward their companions, Voada stepped close to her anamacha, feeling the cold brush against her skin, and in that moment she heard its multiple voices, the Moonshadow's tones dominant among them. <*We will be one soon . . . We will show them how strong we are . . . You and I . . . Together . . .* >

Voada didn't answer her.

23

Returning Home

"**T**HAT'S ENOUGH FOR NOW," Voada said to Magaidh. "You're doing well. Better than I did, truthfully, and learning faster."

Magaidh smiled and sat down next to Voada at a small campfire on the edge of the army's encampment. They'd gone there in order to continue Magaidh's lessons; Voada had watched Magaidh pull the flowing water from a creek bordering the field where they'd halted for the night, reversing the flow and sending it upstream as a tumbling, roaring wave before letting it crash down on its rocky bed once more. Her anamacha seemed particularly adept at manipulating water.

"You're being very kind, Ceanndraoi," Magaidh said, "but I find that hard to believe. After all, my anamacha isn't yours. I can't imagine being able to handle the Moonshadow. Even those inside my anamacha whisper about it."

"Do they?" Voada asked, and Magaidh nodded, her hair glistening in the firelight. Voada could see the weariness in the young woman's face from opening herself to her anamacha without Voada's aid and using it, but she'd done well. She'd bonded easily with the shade of Tormod, and if there were deeper, more powerful, and dangerous shades within that anamacha, Tormod was shielding Magaidh from them.

Not like her own anamacha. Neither the shadow of Iomhar nor any of the other dead draoi inside could hold back Leagsaidh Moonshadow if she wanted to step forward. Nor could Voada, it seemed.

"They say that the Moonshadow is too powerful, that she's fey and wild," Magaidh was saying, as if echoing Voada's own thoughts. "They say that it's her will that drives you, that you won't be able to control her power or go against her." Magaidh's shoulders lifted and fell. "I'm sorry, Ceanndraoi, if that offends you. I . . . it's only that I worry about you. I owe you so much."

"You've been a good friend to me, Magaidh," Voada told her. *And you remind me of what Orla could have been—no, no, I can't think that way. Of what Orla will be once I find her.* "And you shouldn't worry. I can contain the Moonshadow. I promise you." *Or maybe I should have stayed longer with Ceanndraoi Greum. Perhaps he knew how to hold back the Moonshadow. But it's too late for that . . .*

Her anamacha was standing just behind her. Voada glanced over her shoulder at it, at the fleeting faces of the draoi it contained. One face—a woman's, with hair fiery in the storm-light and eyes of piercing blue—stared at her, staying fixed on the anamacha's face for a breath longer than the others and regarding her almost with sadness. *The Moonshadow . . .* But then it was gone again, lost in the next face and the next, all the draoi who were part of this specter.

"If you say that I shouldn't worry, Ceanndraoi," she heard Magaidh say, "then I won't, and I'm pleased that you would call me a friend. I hope to always be that for you."

Voada could only smile again. She wanted to pull the woman close to her, to hug her as she would Orla. Instead, she placed her hand over Magaidh's. "Thank you. I need your friendship more than you could possibly know. It's not something I've experienced much of late."

"Ceannàrd Iosa . . . he's also your friend, isn't he?" Magaidh's voice was almost shy as she said it, and Voada could hear the un-subtle implication under the question.

"Ceannàrd Iosa and I share a common goal," Voada answered. "But beyond that . . ." She shook her head. *The last friend I had was Ceiteag, and I left her behind in Onglse. Only Elia knows if she is even still alive. And Maol is only interested in how he can use me as a weapon or how he can entice me into his bed.*

"Ah," Magaidh breathed. "I wondered. The two of you—well, Comhnall and I sometimes argue as I've heard the two of you do, and so I thought perhaps . . ." Magaidh caught her lip between her teeth, stopping the words. "You loved the Hand of Pencraig? Your husband?"

That brought images of Meir to her mind. *His face, his touch, his laugh . . . I still remember. I'll always remember.* "Meir? Yes, I loved him. He was . . . well, he was everything I wanted in a husband and in the father of our children. I can't imagine feeling that way about someone ever again."

Voada blinked, feeling sudden and unbidden moisture run from her eyes and down her cheeks. Now it was Magaidh's hand that covered Voada's for a moment, warm against the evening chill before it left again.

Voada sighed and sniffed away Meir's memory. She rose, Magaidh rising with her. "We should sleep," she said. "I'll ride with you while we're traveling tomorrow so we can continue to practice, and when we reach Pencraig, you'll be ready."

Pencraig.

Voada's breath caught as soon as she saw the mist-blue lump on the horizon that was Pencraig Bluff, rising high above the flood-plain of the Yarrow. She wanted to be there already, but they were still a half day's march away and had yet to ford the Yarrow. She wondered if someone on the bluff had already run to inform Voice Kadir, if he were already staring down from near the temple as

Voada's army moved inexorably toward the town. She wondered if he trembled at the sight.

She hoped so.

"I hope you've heard of Ceanndraoi Voada, and I hope hearing that name makes you piss yourself."

"Voada?" Maol asked, looking over his shoulder at her.

"It's nothing," she told him. "I was just speaking my thoughts aloud."

She was riding in Maol's war chariot at the head of the army with Magaidh and Comhnall Mac Tsagairt's chariot alongside them. Behind them, other chariots and riders were clustered, followed by legions of those on foot, and trailing the foot soldiers came the vanguard of supply wagons as well as the camp followers: wives, children, those too injured to walk, as well as untrained Cateni who had simply joined them along the way.

In the past hand of days, they'd swept largely unopposed through several small villages in the farmlands that comprised the lower floodplain of the Meadham as they moved east to the confluence of the Yarrow, where they finally turned south. Those Mundoa who chose to resist had been killed; most had simply fled southward, toward Trusa and the Mundoan cities of the lower half of Albann Deas. The Cateni army had swelled in size, and from necessity, they plundered the ripe fields and farms through which they moved in order to feed themselves.

Toward Pencraig. Toward the answers that Voada was seeking. Toward, hopefully, her reunion with Orla and Hakan.

"We'll be at the ford before midday," Maol told her. "You still believe we'll encounter no resistance before then?"

Voada nodded. "I doubt we will. Pencraig sits on the other side of the Yarrow—there's nothing but a few fisherfolks' huts on this side. The Pencraig garrison has always been smaller than that of Muras; I don't think they'll be at all eager to meet us." She scowled, remembering Sub-Commander Bakir and his treatment of Orla. *I will pay you back for that tenfold.* "I suspect their ranks have been thinned to join Savas at Onglse, just like all the rest, and they were never that impressive even before that. They may simply flee rather than fight. We'll have the town before the sun sets. I'll promise that."

She clenched her jaw as she finished. Already she could see the white speck that was the temple at the top of Pencraig Bluff. *I'll take Pashtuk's bust and throw it from the bluff. Then I'll dig up Elia's statue and put Her back on that altar myself. It's time She sat where she belongs once more . . . Long past time . . .*

She could feel Maol's regard on her as she started toward the place that had once been her home. If he thought otherwise than she, he said nothing.

They marched on, a storm ready to break upon the town.

As promised, they reached the banks of Yarrow Ford, just upstream from Pencraig, as the sun stood high in the sky. Across the river, several hands of Mundoan archers and soldiers were arrayed, most of them beardless youngsters with frightened faces. They were directed by an officer Voada didn't recognize: an old graybeard who seemed to sit uneasily on his horse and whose krug—the Mundoan armor—seemed to have been fashioned for a man half his girth, the straps gaping and straining at the sides. She wondered where Sub-Commander Bakir might be, and sudden worry gnawed at her stomach.

Yarrow Ford was wide but shallow, with grass growing here and there where there were tiny islets when the river ran low, as it did now. Maol halted their advance force several strides from the water. The Mundoan archers, at the barked orders of their officer, brought their bows up, aimed them toward the sky, and unleashed a barrage of arrows, nearly all of which were misaimed and fell into the river or onto the muddy bank, where they stuck upright in a mockery of the water grass of the ford.

Maol laughed. He gestured to Voada. "Old men and half-children . . . If this is the best they can do, you're right: we'll make short work of Pencraig. Talk to the fool, Ceanndraoi."

Stepping down from the chariot, Voada approached the river,

wearing the dark red robe she'd adopted as ceanndraoi, the torc—now wrapped in silver wire—polished and bright around her neck and the silver oak leaf glittering beneath it. She wondered if the Mundoa would even recognize her or the symbols she bore. Stopping where the furthest arrow had pierced the mud, she called across the river. "I am Ceanndraoi Voada. I was once Voada Paorach, Hand-wife of Pencraig, and I have returned."

The aged officer didn't seem to react, but some of the men with him did. She saw them turn to each other, speaking and pointing at her. The officer shouted at them—"Quiet! Get back into your ranks!"—then turned toward her. "I am Sub-Commander Adem Nabi of the Pencraig garrison." So Bakir was no longer sub-commander? Worry grew inside Voada at that news; could it mean that Orla was also gone? Where was she? "Your name means nothing to me, Ceanndraoi Voada. You and your filthy Cateni are not permitted to pass here."

Now it was Voada who laughed, and Maol and the Cateni warriors within earshot gave voice to their amusement as well. "I and this group of 'filthy Cateni' have taken Muras and burned her to the ground. We intend to do the same to every Mundoan city in Albann Deas. You don't have enough arrows for all of us or enough soldiers. You're as bothersome to us as a slow, fat summer fly, and we'll smash you as easily. Listen to me, Sub-Commander. I'm giving you a chance to save your life and those of your men. Leave the ford, and leave Pencraig. I have business with Voice Kadir, and I won't be stopped here. Or, if you prefer, we'll simply walk over your dead bodies as we pass."

Again she could see the soldiers breaking rank and whispering, and again Nabi snapped at them. His horse was restless under him. "I have my orders from Voice Kadir," he called across the river to Voada. "I am here to protect Pencraig, and I will do so."

"There is no protecting Pencraig from us, Sub-Commander. Use your old eyes. This is an army at my back, and with me are the greatest warriors of the northern clans. With me are draoi who can call the elements to do their bidding. I'm giving you a chance to live long enough to return to Rumeli and the near-children

you're commanding the opportunity to live long enough to have
families of their own."

Nabi didn't respond immediately. Once more, the soldiers with
him broke rank. Some of the ones in the rear turned and began to
run back toward Pencraig, tossing their weapons aside. This time
Nabi said nothing to them. "I have my orders," he said again, his
voice barely audible over the rustling of the willows on the riverbank and the rippling waters of the Yarrow.

"As you wish," Voada told him. She gestured to the war chariot
alongside Maol's; Magaidh stepped down from her position next
to Àrd Mac Tsagairt and strode toward Voada. In the midday glare,
her anamacha was invisible, but Voada could feel its presence.
"Do you remember what I've taught you, Magaidh?" she asked the
young woman, who nodded. "Good. Then it's time you demonstrate what you've learned for these Mundoa."

"Yes, Ceanndraoi," Magaidh answered. Voada saw uncertainty
in her eyes, and she leaned in close, gently touching the young
woman's cheek.

"You can do this. I know you can. Elia is with you," she whispered, and Magaidh nodded. She opened her arms, calling in her
anamacha as Voada stepped back from her. She saw Magaidh's
gaze go distant as it entered her, no more than a shimmering in
the air. Her hands began to weave a knotted pattern, and her
voice—clear and loud—spoke words in an older form of the Cateni tongue. Magaidh's eyes opened wide; she stared across the
river at Nabi and his remaining troops, and as she did so, Nabi
ordered the archers to ready another volley.

Water lifted from the shallow bed of the Yarrow, the wall of it
green in the sunlight and growing taller with every passing breath,
fed by the water pouring downstream. Voada could see fish trapped
within the wall, and more flapped helplessly on the wet grass and
mud where the water had once been. "Loose!" she heard Nabi command the archers, and as the arrows flew into air, Magaidh gestured sharply. The green wall foamed, rose, and fell, engulfing the
arrows, crashing down on the soldiers and sending them sprawling. Nabi was unhorsed and thrown down into the mud.

Voada caught Magaidh as she staggered back from the effort. "You did very well," she whispered in Magaidh's ear. "You make me proud."

From his chariot, Maol gave a shout, and Hùisdean slapped the reins down on the horses. The chariots surged forward into the returning water of the Yarrow, splashing and churning white under the hooves and wheels. The mounted warriors followed, as did the warriors on foot.

The Mundoan soldiers scrambled to their feet, nearly all of them breaking and running now, leaving their swords, spears, and bows scattered on the Yarrow's bank. Voada saw Nabi trying to rise, only to be trampled and broken under the hooves and wheels of Maol's chariot. The few soldiers who resisted were quickly dispatched. Maol called back the Cateni warriors who were pursuing the retreating backs of the rest of Nabi's men. He pointed downstream: to the rising bluffs, to the temple atop them, to the cluster of dwellings they could see where the river curved away toward its source.

"Pencraig is waiting for you, Ceanndraoi. Let's go find its Voice, and then we can move on to Trusa and the Great-Voice there."

The battle for Pencraig wasn't entirely bloodless. The remainder of the garrison had been alerted; they put up a running, grudging resistance as they retreated slowly up the hill toward the Voice's estate, but it was mostly bodies in Mundoan armor that sent bloody rivulets running back down toward the river. Voada, back in Maol's chariot, could only shake her head at the youth of some of them. *So young, and too many of them just Cateni conscripts . . .*

That was yet another debt to be laid at the Voice's door for payment.

It was strange to ride up Pencraig Bluff once more, to see the buildings and houses that had been so familiar to her. It seemed ages ago that she had last seen them, but it had been less than a year. Halfway up the road to the temple, she looked down at the older section of the town. There were fires there, sending columns of smoke into the sky; there was also, she knew, looting and death there, but she had warned her people once again that she would not tolerate mistreatment of Cateni unless they actively opposed them. *"Kill the Mundoa, but leave any Cateni who isn't resisting untouched."*

That resistance seemed to have melted away as they rose higher on Pencraig Bluff. Voada wondered if the respite would last, expecting the last remnants of the garrison to attack a final time at any moment.

They passed her old house, the sign of the Hand freshly painted on the pillars of the gates, which were yawning open. There was no sign of anyone in the courtyard beyond, but the furniture there was new and set differently than it had been when Voada had lived there: no longer her home, but a stranger's house. She wondered who this Hand might be, if he had a family as she and Meir had, and where he and that family were now. Maol noticed her attention as they moved slowly up the road toward the Voice's estate, the road now empty of anyone, Mundoan or Cateni.

"This was once your home as Hand-wife?" he asked, though he kept his eyes on the road ahead and to either side.

"Yes."

One side of his mouth lifted as he sniffed. "A Hand is evidently treated well."

"The Mundoa treat the Hand the way you'd treat a favorite dog; you're rewarded as long as you do what they expect you to do and you don't bite. Fail that . . ." She didn't complete the sentence. She tore her gaze away from the house, staring ahead of them to where the Voice's estate awaited. *What happened to Orla? Where is Hakan? That's all that matters. They could be here still, very near, and I might be with them today . . . and I will make Voice Kadir and Voice-wife Dilara suffer for every torment they've inflicted on them and for every day since they were taken from me.*

Voada set her mouth in a firm line, pressing her lips tightly together. Maol glanced once at her. He gestured to Hùisdean to move forward. The other war chariots clattered alongside and behind them. Warriors on foot moved quickly onto the grounds of the houses on either side, but Voada heard none of the clamor of fighting. The inhabitants had all fled elsewhere.

A stone wall as tall as two men appeared to their left: the wall that surrounded the Voice's estate. As they approached the marble pillars that marked the estate gates, Voada called her anamacha to her and found Iomhar among the souls in the otherworld. She began to prepare a spell.

In her doubled sight, she saw that the gates of the Voice Kadir's estate were closed . . . and heads suddenly appeared along the wall. Even through the roar of Magh da Chèo, she heard the groaning of bowstrings under tension.

"*Doineann!*" she shouted, casting the power away from her. As the archers released their arrows, as Hùisdean and Maol belatedly raised their shields, a storm-wind went howling outward, and the arrows flew backward and scattered as the archers vanished. The stone wall bowed inward against the spell-gale and cracked, massive stones falling. As the wind screamed, Voada shifted her focus. The wooden, steel-reinforced gates rattled and chattered, then were finally torn from their hinges and flung madly into the courtyard beyond. Maol barked an order—"Forward!"—and his chariot was first through the gap and into the courtyard, Àrd Mac Tsagairt and Magaidh following close behind. The spell done, Voada hung in her harness, watching as fighting raged around her and Mundoan soldiers poured in from the sides of the courtyard. She saw Maol flinging spears and the maddened hooves of their horses striking wildly as more Cateni followed them, loud with battle-rage.

And as suddenly as it had started, the battle was over. The Mundoan soldiers were down, as well as a few of the Cateni. Voada saw their faces staring blindly as they had at the ford, as they had in Muras, most of them too young or too old to be soldiers. Cateni warriors had already entered the house; Voada heard shouts and screams, male as well as female, and several of Maol's warriors emerged again into the courtyard, dragging with them two couples dressed in Mundoan finery.

One of the couples was obviously Cateni, and the silver wreath the man wore—the same wreath Meir had once worn—told her that they were the new Hand and Hand-wife. The other couple she recognized immediately: Voice Kadir and Voice-wife Dilara. Voada unstrapped herself from the rail of the chariot. She leapt down, striding toward the two captives with the bright robe of the ceanndraoi swaying around her, with the torc of the draoi around her neck and the silver oak leaf on its chain at her throat.

She stood in front of the two and saw both recognition and terror wash across their faces.

"Where are my children?" Voada demanded.

24

An Empty Revenge

"**H**AND-WIFE VOADA," Voice Kadir stuttered. "We thought you . . ."

"Dead?" Voada finished for him. "I'm certain that was your hope, but I'm far from dead. And I'm not Hand-wife. I am Ceanndraoi Voada of the Clans. I am the Bane of the Mundoa and the Vengeance of Elia. And I demand to see the children you stole from me. Where are they?"

Voice Kadir looked at Dilara, and Voada saw a glance of despair pass between them. "Where are they?" Voada repeated. "If you value your lives at all, you'll answer me."

"Hand-wife . . . I mean, Ceanndraoi Voada," Voice Kadir said. He wouldn't look at her, instead staring down at the bloodied tiles of their courtyard and the corpses of his guards. She could see his hands trembling. Dilara was weeping, her distress so loud that Voada thought they must be able to hear it at the river. The Hand and his wife were huddled together behind Dilara, clutching each other but otherwise silent. "I'm afraid . . . I don't know . . ."

"Answer me!" she snapped at him, the command echoing off the facade of their house and causing Dilara's weeping to stop momentarily. "*Where are my children?*"

"Ceanndraoi," Voice Kadir began. He lifted his gaze to hers and

dropped it again. He licked dry lips. "Hakan . . . Well, Hakan . . .
It was Officer Bakir's suggestion, after all . . . He was sent as a
slave to work the copper mines, and he . . . You see, I was informed there was a tunnel collapse, and he . . ." Kadir lifted his
face to Voada once more. His eyes pleaded silently. "I'm sorry," he
said.

Voada's breath caught in her throat. *Dead. My son is dead.* And
worse: a soul that died trapped underground could never find the
sun-path. A soul there was doomed and lost, never to reach Tirnanog and never to be reborn unless the body could somehow be
found. A wail of grief was torn involuntarily from Voada, and she
couldn't see through the tears that filled her eyes. She felt
Magaidh's arm go around her waist and Maol's hand on her shoulder. She let them support her while the anguish and loss and rage
buffeted her, an emotional storm that threatened to overwhelm
her and take her spinning away with it. She felt the cold touch of
her anamacha as well, drawn to her by the turmoil inside.

<*Many of us have suffered such losses . . .* > The voice that domi-
nated the chorus was the Moonshadow's. <*The death of a child is
something that never leaves us. It is a burden we bear eternally, but we
bear it. You must also. This will hurt you, and terribly, but you must
put it aside for this moment.*>

"I don't know if I can," Voada answered.

"Ceanndraoi?" she heard Magaidh say, and Voada took in a long,
gasping breath. She pulled her shoulders up. She stared at Kadir.

"And Orla?" she managed to ask, trying to control the quavering that threatened her voice. "Where is my daughter?" *I don't
know if I can bear it if they're both dead. I don't know . . .*

<*You must. You must . . . We will help you . . . It's not yet time for
you to join us . . . Listen to me . . . Let me be with you, and we can
punish them all for this . . .* > The Moonshadow. Insistent. Voada
heard the voice and her promise and made no effort to push her
away. Her voice was a comfort.

"Orla?" Kadir said. "We don't know . . ." Voada heard Dilara
sigh, and she looked at the woman, who held up her hands as if
in supplication.

"Sub-Commander Bakir took her as his second wife, to attend to his first wife and their children," Dilara said. "But he left Pencraig moons ago, under orders from the Great-Voice to join Commander Savas. His family traveled with him at least part of the way. Orla went with them. She was . . ." Dilara stopped. Her hands dropped.

"She was *what*?"

"She was with child. At least that's what Bakir's first wife told me." Dilara started to lift her hands again, then brought them protectively around her waist. "That's all I—we—know."

Voada could feel the slow rage building inside herself. It seethed in her voice, and her anamacha moved nearer to her. <*Join with me . . . With us . . .* > "So my son was enslaved and killed while my daughter was violated by that savage Bakir, the man you sent to plunder my house and steal everything I once had, who killed Una and slew our dog, and who took great pleasure in beating me nearly to death. Did the two of you hate me and Meir that much?"

"No . . ." Kadir began, but his voice trailed off. "No," he repeated in a near-whisper. Dilara went back to sobbing.

"Ceanndraoi, what do you wish me do with these people?" Maol asked, his voice stern and almost eager.

Voada looked first at the Hand and Hand-wife. "You're both Cateni?" she asked them. They nodded mutely. "The silver wreath of the Hand was my husband's, and I claim that. Then you're free to leave here. If you wish to join us, you may do so; if not . . ." She shrugged. "Then go where you will, but know that the Mundoan world will be shattered. I intend to destroy it entirely."

<*Yes! You and all of us, together . . .* >

The Hand lifted the wreath from his head; he passed it to Voada, the weight of it heavy in her hand. The two slipped by the Voice and Voice-wife, past Voada, and through the ranks of the Cateni, who moved aside to let them pass.

"You'll let us go also?" Dilara asked hopefully. Voice Kadir slipped the golden wreath from his forehead and held it out to Voada. She only stared at it.

<*No!*> the voices of her anamacha shouted as one, with the

Moonshadow's predominant among them, and Voada spoke as
one with them: "No." The golden wreath dropped from Kadir's
hand, clattering on the tiles. No one moved to pick it up. "We still
have business to attend to." Voada turned her back on them, gesturing to Maol and the others. "We're going to the Temple of Elia
to reclaim it," she said. "Bring these two prisoners with us."

☼

Before she'd allowed anyone to enter the temple, she'd had Maol
drag Voice Kadir into the woods just behind the temple. There
under the oak tree with everyone watching, she'd directed him to
dig with his hands. He'd protested, but Maol had shoved him
down, and the frightened Kadir had scrabbled and clawed at the
dirt with soft hands until—his robes soiled, his hands filthy and
bleeding—he had uncovered the wrapped statue of Elia. Voada
had taken it from him before he could unwind the cloth around
it. She began walking toward the temple, the rest following.

<Yes . . . We remember this place . . . > Voada heard the sigh from
her anamacha as they entered the temple. Seeing the temple again
brought back all that had happened to her, all the losses that had
so drastically changed the path of her life. She stepped into the
cool half darkness, the four windows illuminating the sun-paths,
the open roof allowing the sun to play over the central altar but
leaving shadows elsewhere.

There were no taibhse waiting for her this time. No anamacha.
The temple seemed so small and insignificant after Bàn Cill.

"Bring the Voice and his wife here," she said, going to the altar.
The two were alternately pushed and pulled forward by Maol and
Hùisdean and thrown down on the temple floor near Voada as
Àrd Mac Tsagairt and Magaidh watched in silence. Putting down
the still-wrapped statue, Voada picked up the ceramic bust of
Pashtuk from the altar.

"*This* is an abomination," she told Kadir and Dilara. "This filth
doesn't belong here in this sacred place, and I intend to destroy
every image of this man in Albann Deas." Deliberately, she spat on

Pashtuk's face, raised the bust above her head, and threw it down onto the marble tiles. Pashtuk's visage shattered as Kadir and Dilara raised their hands in defense, and jagged shards of fired, painted clay struck the Voice and Voice-wife like a hard, sharp rain. Voada ignored their cries. She crouched down and reverently unwrapped the statue of Elia, nearly smiling when she saw the chipped, faded face and body. "I will have Your statue restored, Elia," she said aloud to the image of the goddess. "You'll be magnificent again, and You'll once more have Your crown of gold." She placed Elia on the altar. "There. You are where You belong once more, and that's where You will stay. We'll find You a proper menach to care for You and this temple, to set the dead on the path to Tirnanog and to chant the rites of the seasons. You will have draoi to protect You. I promise You that."

She stepped back, looking at the altar and the temple. But then the brief satisfaction she had felt fled, replaced by the anger and grief that still filled her, that had never left her. "This place is soiled," she said. "It needs cleansing."

"I will wash the temple myself, Voada," Dilara husked out. "Maki and I . . . We'll sweep it and clean it . . ."

"That's not the cleansing it needs," Voada told her, her voice flat. She pointed to the Voice and Voice-wife. "Get them up," she said to Maol and Hùisdean. "Hold them."

Her anamacha slid alongside her, sliding partially into her. <We agree . . . This is what you want, what we want . . . This is what they deserve . . . We will help you give it to all of them . . . All you must do is join with us . . . > And another, stronger voice added, <With me . . . >

Urgently, Maol and Hùisdean grabbed the Voice and Voice-wife and dragged them to their feet. Voada stood in front of Voice Kadir, who was held by Maol. He had voided his bladder; she could smell the urine and see the spreading stain on his clothes. She lifted his chin with a hand, staring into his eyes. "You are no longer the Voice of Pencraig," she told him. "You are no longer anything at all. You are filth, like Pashtuk. You are vermin that must be removed from existence."

Still watching him, she slid her knife from the sheath on her belt. Without warning, she slashed it across his throat in a single, savage motion. Kadir made a strangled, wet cry as blood poured over Voada's hand and the knife, as bright red sprayed her clothing and face and spewed onto the floor. Maol released the body as Dilara screamed. Kadir's blood pooled on the tiles and slid thickly around the shards of Pashtuk's bust.

Voada stepped over his corpse to stand in front of Dilara, who was sobbing in great, gulping heaves while Hùisdean held her tightly. Voada grabbed the woman's braid and pulled it back hard until her eyes bulged and the tendons stood out in her throat. "Your husband was simply a fool," she said softly into the woman's terrified face. "But you . . . you are worse than a fool, because you're intentionally cruel. You don't deserve the quick death I gave him. Your death should be as slow and miserable as my son's was, as awful as the abuse that my Orla has suffered." Dilara tried to speak, but Voada pulled harder on her braid, choking off the woman's voice. "You don't deserve a quick death, creature, but I'll give it to you anyway. Let your blood and that of your husband wipe away the Mundoan taint in this place. In *Elia's* temple."

Voada's hand moved again, and a second grotesque mouth appeared on Dilara's neck. Her lifeblood gushed in a diagonal across Voada's robes, threw heavy droplets on the marble of the altar that dripped sluggishly down. Hùisdean released the Voice-wife as Dilara's breath gurgled and bubbled in the wreckage of her throat, and the woman fell to sprawl beside her husband.

Voada bent down and wiped the blade of her knife on Dilara's robes. She slid the blade back into its sheath. Maol, Hùisdean, Comhnall, and Magaidh were all watching her, their expressions carefully neutral. Only the anamacha spoke. <Yes . . . > they said, and their voices were full of eager satisfaction. The temple was silent except for the sounds of the birds in the wood beyond. Voada could smell the tang of blood in the air. She looked down at the gore coating her hands.

"Have someone remove these bodies," she said. "Impale them on spears in the market square so that everyone can view them, and leave them there to rot. Then have the temple properly washed so that Elia's faithful can worship here again."

She didn't wait for an answer. She walked to the door of the temple and out.

She should have felt some satisfaction. She should have experienced triumph with their deaths. A release.

She felt . . . nothing. She felt hollow.

Empty.

Voada walked alone down the hill to the Hand's house—her old house that was now strange and wrong—to find some of the Cateni women of Pencraig rummaging through the rooms. They started to scatter at the sight of her, but she sent two of them farther down the hill to the vanguard wagons to fetch her a new set of clothing and a few others to bring her water and a sponge to wash herself. She went into her old bedroom, the room she and Meir had shared, stripping off her bloodied clothing as she did so. The women obeyed her without protest. "The Ceanndraoi Voada . . ." she heard them whispering. "They say that she is Leagsaidh Moonshadow returned . . ."

The blood took time and effort to wash away, and she stared at her arms and hands, expecting to still see the stain there in the folds of her skin or under her nails. She stared at her reflection in the copper mirror she found in the bedroom, trying to see if traces were still on her cheeks or in her hair. Finally, dressed in the clothes that had been brought to her, she sat on the bed—placed now on the wrong side of the room—and stared at the walls she remembered so well. Here she'd lost Meir; here they'd made love and had their few inevitable arguments; here their children had been born; here they'd grown up.

Here had been love.

She could almost hear the ghosts of them. She found herself weeping without realizing she was doing it; all the emotions she'd been holding inside for moons now tumbled out, and she put her head in her hands and sobbed. Her anamacha watched silently from the corner of the room, making no move to come toward her.

"Ceanndraoi?" Voada heard the soft query from the door of the bedroom. She sniffed and wiped at her eyes, looking up to see Magaidh standing there. "I'm sorry . . . When you left the temple, I thought . . . I wasn't certain if you needed to be alone, or if . . . if . . ."

Voada managed to smile at the young woman—so much like Orla might come to look. "Come in," she told her. She patted the bed next to her. "And thank you, my friend."

Magaidh sat alongside her. Her hands found Voada's. "I can only imagine how you must feel. If someone did to my children what has been done to yours . . ." She stopped. "I think I would have done the same."

"Would you have?" Voada asked. Her voice cracked, comfortless.

Magaidh drew in a long, shuddering breath. "Perhaps," she said. "I don't know."

"That's honest, at least. Magaidh, killing them didn't help, even though I thought it would," Voada told her. "And what I did . . . I don't know how many people I've killed with the Moonshadow's anamacha, but that was always at a distance, always somehow impersonal. Killing someone like this, executing them with my own hand . . . it's different. Harder. Uglier. I thought . . ." She took a long breath that threatened to turn into a sob. "I thought killing those two would make me feel satisfaction, but it's changed nothing for me. Nothing. Meir and Hakan are still dead, and Orla is lost. Everything I had and loved is gone. My entire family. Gone . . ."

Magaidh's arm slipped around Voada's shoulders, and for several breaths, Voada relaxed into that embrace, neither of them saying anything. "What are you going to do now?" Voada heard Magaidh half whisper at last. "Will you leave us to look for your daughter?"

Voada straightened on the bed, and Magaidh's arm fell away as the young woman took Voada's hand again. "I don't know where she might have gone or how I can find her." A deep rage surged within Voada, its heat burning away the tears. *<There's a way . . . Listen . . . >* Voada found herself speaking the Moonshadow's words. "The ceannàrd was right all along," she said. "There was nothing in Pencraig for me, no resolution. We'll take Trusa as he wanted. We'll burn it to smoke and ash and ruin, then I'll do the same to the rest of their cities until the Mundoa scatter like frightened rats, fleeing for home." Voada nodded as if to herself. She turned to Magaidh, her face stern. "They'll pay for all the Cateni blood they have spilled with their own. Everyone will know who Ceanndraoi Voada is. And so will Orla. She'll hear of me. She'll hear my name from the terror of the Mundoa and know where I am, and she'll find me."

"And this is what you want?" Magaidh's hand slipped away from hers as Voada nodded, tentatively at first, then more forcefully.

"It's not only what I want. It's what I have to do." She looked at her anamacha across the room, and it seemed to nod to her. It was the Moonshadow's face that it wore. Magaidh's hand returned to hers, as if she'd seen the same. "I have no choice."

"Then, as your friend, I'll help you," Magaidh told her, but Voada could hear sorrow and worry in her voice. "We'll all help you."

25

Returning to the South

IT WAS TOLGA, ALTAN Savas' driver, who brought the scroll to Altan's tent just inside the second ring of hill-forts on Onglse. It was raining, pelting the canvas above them. It was always raining on them since they'd arrived on the draoi island; the Red-Hand's sorcerers saw to that. The promise of the sun and dry clothes that would result when they finally took this accursed place was a large part of what drove the Mundoan army as the fighting dragged on.

Altan glimpsed Great-Voice Vadim's seal impressed into the leaden tag enclosing the copper wire that wrapped the heavy parchment in Tolga's hand and raised an eyebrow. Tolga shrugged. "Sub-Commander Musa said I was to give this to you immediately. A messenger ship brought it to our Onglse harbor this morning with orders to place it in your hands as soon as possible. I told him I'd bring it to you." He held out the scroll to Altan, his hand covering most of the thick paper so that Altan's hand would have touched his as he took the scroll. Instead, Altan nodded to his field desk, and Tolga placed the scroll there, disappointment on his face. It was a game Tolga had been playing with Altan recently; it was obvious the man thought that he could replace Lucian as more than just Altan's driver.

That wasn't going to happen. Altan couldn't imagine ever feeling for someone else what he'd felt for Lucian.

"My bet is that the Great-Voice is getting impatient for his victory and wants to know if he can assure Emperor Pashtuk that we'll have Onglse by summer's end," Altan said to Tolga, picking up the scroll and hefting it. "But we should have it before then," he said. *Despite the fact that this offensive was never a good strategy in the first place.* That thought—a constant companion of his since their arrival on Onglse—he kept to himself. *You do what you're ordered to do, and you don't question those orders in front of your soldiers.* "The Red-Hand is nearly out of options. Maol Iosa seems to have abandoned Greum Red-Hand, and that cursed woman draoi is missing, too—hopefully she's dead."

He wondered at that last statement, remembering the strange half dream he'd had of Hand-wife Voada of Pencraig claiming to be draoi and here on Onglse. *Could she really have been the draoi she claimed to be? Certainly we haven't felt that power since she disappeared. What had she said? That if I stayed I would die here, that she wanted peace between our people? I haven't died yet, but maybe she has . . .*

Altan used his knife to sever the wire around the scroll. He unrolled it on his field desk. He read the words there with growing trepidation and anger. He smashed his fist down on the scroll as he finished, breathing heavily.

"Sir?"

And there are times when you should ignore orders entirely, no matter what it costs you . . .

"Sir? Altan?"

Had Tolga been Lucian, Altan would have stood and taken the man in his arms for the momentary comfort it might have given him regarding the statements on the scroll. But he'd never hold Lucian again, and Tolga's use of Altan's given name only fueled the anger that was already surging through Altan because of the words unrolled before him. "You *dare* to address me in such a familiar way?"

Tolga's eyes widened. "Sir," he said. "I'm sorry. It's just . . . I know that Lucian . . ."

"Lucian is dead." Altan stared at the man. "You are not Lucian."

"No, Commander. I . . ." Tolga swallowed hard. "I'm sorry, Commander."

If Lucian were alive . . . Altan would have confided in Lucian and told him all that he'd just read: that his worst fears had been realized; that the clans had attacked the poorly defended south while he was occupied in pursing the Great-Voice's ornamental victory; that the army of the clans had sacked and plundered Muras, Pencraig, and other towns in the north; that someone calling herself Ceanndraoi Voada, along with Ceannàrd Maol Iosa, were directing their army; that they were now moving toward Trusa; that the Great-Voice wanted back half the troops he'd sent to stop this invasion, to be commanded not by Altan but by one of his sub-commanders; that Commander Savas was to remain on Onglse with the main army and complete his mission of taking the island and Bàn Cill and bringing back the body of Greum Red-Hand.

So that's where Iosa and that draoi woman have gone . . . Sourness sat heavy and bitter in his gut. Altan found himself wondering, if only for a moment, what might have happened if he'd accepted the offer of the dream who claimed to be Voada. Perhaps she *hadn't* been a dream after all. Perhaps . . . But he shook the thought away and looked again at the orders in front of him. *The Great-Voice is ignorant. He knows nothing about war. This order is another terrible mistake, one that's potentially fatal for all of us* . . .

Altan straightened. Tolga was standing stiffly at attention, his face pale as Altan rerolled the parchment. Walking over to the brazier that warmed his tent, Altan placed the parchment on the glowing coals, watching the edges first curl and darken, then smolder, then finally brighten to flame. He waited for the scroll to turn to ash before he turned again to Tolga. "Go find Musa and Ilkur. Tell them to come here. The Great-Voice has given us a new task. I'll need a good driver like you in my chariot, so make sure our horses are readied."

As Tolga bowed in relief and left the tent, Altan watched the last of the scroll shrivel in the brazier. "Lucian, my old love, I think I might be with you soon after all," he said to the air.

Ilkur scuffed his feet as if movement alone could calm him, his gaze as restless as the rest of him. Musa stood solid and unmoving, his olive face impassive under his short-cut black hair. Altan regarded them, wondering how they would receive their new orders. "I've just received an urgent message from the Great-Voice," Altan told his two sub-commanders. "We know now where that troublesome woman draoi and Ceannàrd Iosa have gone; the two of them have left Onglse, presumably at the Red-Hand's orders. They managed to do the impossible and unite the northern clans àrds, and a Cateni army crossed River Meadham at Muras. They're ravaging the countryside and appear to be heading for Trusa."

Musa's eyes widened slightly. Ilkur took a step back, then forward again, his hands cutting the air. "Trusa, Commander?" he said. His face had gone pale. "My family's there . . ."

"I know," Altan told the man. "I have family there as well. My parents and many cousins live in Trusa or nearby."

Musa's jaw was clenched; Altan could see the muscles standing out against the scars on his face. He knew what the man, who had been his sub-commander in previous battles in Rumeli as well, was thinking. *There aren't troops enough in Albann Deas to keep Trusa safe against an invading army of Cateni warriors and draoi; the Great-Voice gutted the garrisons everywhere and sent them here because he was impatient and an idiot and has never been a soldier. We're days away, too far away . . .*

Altan sighed. *And now I have to tell my officers a lie with the hope that it's not too late already, knowing that if I'm convicted later for this mutiny, they might be taken down with me, their deaths laid at my feet. I have my orders, but I can't obey them. Not if we're to survive this.*

Altan took a long breath. "The Great-Voice has wisely ordered us to abandon our attack on Onglse entirely and return across the

Meadham to deal with this threat," he told them. "We'll move as quickly as we can. I want as many experienced cohorts as possible on the transports we have in the harbor by tomorrow evening—Musa, you know the ones I mean. They'll need to be ready for a fast march as soon as we're back on Albann." Musa nodded. "We'll sail down the coast for Gediz—going upriver to Muras against the Meadham's current would take longer than marching overland, and in any case, there are no longer any supplies or reinforcements for us there.

"Ilkur, I want you to take command of three cohorts. No more. Pull everyone back to the harbor hill-fort we first took; you may have to hold it against a renewed assault by the Red-Hand once he realizes that we've retreated. You shouldn't have to hold the fort more than a hand of days, certainly less than two hands. If you feel you can't safely hold here, then fall back across the strait and wait there. As soon as our transport ships have offloaded at Gediz, I'll send them back for you and the remaining cohorts. I'll leave orders for you in Gediz as soon as we know the situation better."

"We should never have come here in the first place," Ilkur said, and Musa growled at the younger officer.

"Soldiers do as they're ordered," he said, "and officers don't voice opinions about those orders, no matter what they think of them. Not even here. Not even with those officers you think agree with you." Musa looked at Altan and nodded slightly, as if acknowledging that he shared Altan's own thoughts. He held Altan's gaze as he added, "But it's good that the Great-Voice had the wisdom not to ask for only *some* of the troops to return, forcing us to fight on two fronts at once." Again that slight nod came, and Altan knew that Musa had guessed at the lie he'd just been told and what its cost might be and had accepted the risk.

Altan smiled grimly. "Indeed," he said. "It's far better to have one strong arm than two weak ones."

Musa tapped his cuirass in salute. "Is there anything else you need of me, Commander? If not, then I should start gathering my men. We might be able to get the troops ready and on the ships a few turns of the glass earlier if I'm there pushing my cohort officers."

"That would be excellent if you can accomplish it, Musa. Both of you, go and put everything in motion, and send Tolga back in to me. We'll meet you at the harbor fort later this afternoon. Everyone needs to understand that moving quickly is essential."

And we must hope it's not all in vain, he thought as he watched them go.

In his mind, he already had visions of Trusa burning.

26

The Swelling Tide

THE ARMY OF THE CLANS, with Voada and Maol at its head, crossed the Yarrow once more and moved slowly southward toward Trusa. Word of them, they knew, was racing ahead. There was little fighting to be done in the settlements and villages through which they passed. The Mundoa had already retreated in anticipation, or—as in a few settlements they passed through—the Cateni servants and slaves had already risen up and killed their Mundoan masters.

The ranks of Voada's army were growing every day. Hands upon hands of largely untrained fighters—both men and women—joined them in the rearguard, and their families followed in the wagons of the baggage and supply train.

As they moved through the low, rolling hills of middle Albann Deas, Voada sometimes paused at the summit of a hill and looked behind them. The Yarrow Road, built by the Mundoa, followed the old Cateni path. Voada marveled at the size of the force that spread out into the misty distance along the road, spilling out on either side in a great dark mass.

Voada's army was a wave of resentment and anger sweeping the Mundoa away from their land entirely. She nodded in satisfaction and heard the echo from her anamacha. <*Yes . . . We will do that . . . One day . . .* >

Each day brought them closer.

Each day the whispers and rumors and tales of Ceanndraoi Voada spread further throughout the land.

Each day she prayed to Elia that Orla would hear that name and would somehow find her way to her.

And each night, as the army slept around her, she tried to find Meir, Hakan, and Orla again in her dreams. But her dreams were too often images of war and death. The ghosts of Voice Kadir and Voice-wife Dilara haunted her still, pursuing her until she woke up screaming as their dead hands clutched at her.

<*You won't find peace until you've finished your task . . .* > she heard the voices of her anamacha whisper to her, the Moon-shadow loud among them. <*We will help you . . . We will guide you . . . Listen to us . . . Be with us . . .* > But the Moonshadow's voice dominated the chorus. <*Let us guide you . . . Let me guide you . . .* >

"Ceanndraoi?" Magaidh's query and the soft hush of the tent flaps being pulled back caused the anamacha's crooning to suddenly vanish. Voada felt warmth as its cold touch left her and lifted her head from the furs on which she lay. Magaidh stood, a shadow against the early morning light. "Ceanndraoi, I heard you call out . . ."

"I'm sorry," she told Magaidh. "It was just a bad dream. Go back to your own bed and your husband. I'm fine."

Magaidh nodded, but her gaze moved to the left, to where the Moonshadow's anamacha stood very near Voada. "I could stay," she said, "if you need company, if you need to talk. Perhaps I could help—"

"No!" The word came out too loud and harsh, and Voada saw Magaidh recoil. "No," she repeated, softening her voice. "I'm fine. Truly. It was just a dream. Go back and rest, and tomorrow we'll practice more. I'll need you to be strong at Trusa. Please, go on. I'm fine."

Magaidh bowed her head. She looked again at the anamacha. "Rest well, then," she said. A smile touched her lips and vanished like a morning frost as she left the tent. In the renewed darkness, Voada saw her anamacha glide close, seeming to kneel down alongside her. Its cold touch brushed her arm.

<We're here . . . > it crooned. <We will always be here for you . . . We're all you need . . . >

They passed through a village a day's ride from Trusa.

Like many of the others along the army's path, this village had already been abandoned by the Mundoa, though there were bodies dressed in Mundoan fashion lashed to poles just outside the settlement—evidently those who had been too slow to leave. The remaining residents, all Cateni, waved, shouted, and cheered as Maol's chariot, with Voada as passenger, passed along the road. Children tossed flowers as the chariot went by them, even as the outriders of the army were stalking through the fields within a few stripes' ride of either side of the road, taking any vegetables and fruit growing there, as well as the sheep and goats unlucky enough to be found out grazing.

All would be feeding the bellies of a ravenous army that night.

"They love us now," Maol said when the village lay behind them. "I wonder if they'll love us less when they see what we've taken."

"It doesn't matter," Voada told him. "We haven't left their houses burning. The Mundoa gave them the scraps from their tables. The Cateni had to work those fields for them, not for themselves—fields that a few generations ago had been their own. From now on, they'll be able to keep whatever they grow, whatever they raise. They own the land once more. Everything's changed for them. We've given them a gift."

Maol shrugged as the war chariot jounced over the ruts in the road. "I suppose. You've changed as well since I first met you, Voada, and especially since Pencraig."

"And you worry? You don't like the changes you've seen?"

"I always worry," he told her. "That's my job as ceannàrd of your army. As to liking the changes or not?" He repeated his shrug. "That's not my place. But I've been a soldier for many seasons now, and I know that there are times when even a long-awaited victory tastes sour in the mouth. You can't push away the pain of your loss, Voada, even with the deaths of the those who caused it. There's no remedy for it at all. You just have to bear it and know that those you trust are there to help if you need them. Magaidh, for instance—the woman loves you as a daughter loves her mother."

The comment made Voada draw back as a sudden suspicion came to her. "Has Magaidh been talking to you about me?"

Maol raised an eyebrow. "No. Should she? Is there something I should know?"

"No. Nothing. I just . . . wondered. Magaidh's going to be a fine draoi. She's progressing well." Maol looked unconvinced, and Voada reached out to put her hand on his shoulder. She gave him a momentary smile. "I should have listened to you after Muras, Maol. You told me that we should go immediately to Trusa, that I wouldn't find . . ."

"I'm not you, Voada," he said before she could finish. "I gave you the cold advice of a soldier, that's all. And look . . ." He waved his arm at the landscape around them. "Here we are despite going to Pencraig, with the Cateni rising up around us, ready to enter Trusa."

"A Trusa that knows we're coming."

He nodded at that. "Yes, and very soon it's not going to be easy for us. The scouts I've sent out are saying that the roads into Trusa are full of troops that the Great-Voice has ordered in from the nearest towns to protect his city. They've seen flags from as far away as Savur, Ladik, and Iseal. This isn't going to be like Muras or Pencraig, Voada. They know we're coming, and they're prepared for us. This will be dirty and foul and costly. They'll defend Trusa as fiercely as we defended Onglse."

"But we'll prevail." She fought not to add the rising inflection at the end that would make the statement a question.

Maol nodded. "We will. We have the larger force, and the

soldiers there don't have Savas guiding them. We'll take Trusa and silence their Great-Voice. I promise you that."

<*We will have victory . . .* > She hadn't noticed her anamacha pressing close to her side.

"And how will that victory taste?" she asked, not knowing whether she was talking to her anamacha or the ceannàrd.

Maol grinned back at her. "That's something we'll only know afterward," he said.

From the anamacha she heard nothing at all.

Trusa sprawled alongside the wide River Iska, a full two day's journey from its mouth but still close enough that the sea tides caused the river to swell and shrink dramatically twice each day. Trusa had never been a Cateni city, though there had been a modest village and farms near the current site. For the Mundoa, Trusa was well placed at the spot where the Iska was narrow enough for a bridge to be built over it, yet—with the tidal flow—still deep enough that the largest seagoing merchant ships from Rumeli could navigate upriver against the current and anchor safely in the deep middle channel.

Because of its bridge, Trusa became the nexus for roads in all directions: to the Mundoan settlements in the south of Albann Deas, to Muras and other northern locations, and to the west all the way to Gediz. While Savur, at the mouth of the Iska, had been the initial Mundoan capital, the massive tides in the Bay of Iska made it a less-than-ideal port that could leave an unwary ship on its side in the muddy flats. Trusa had quickly taken the title of First City from Savur. It had become an immediate trade and marketing center, and governmental functions had also rapidly migrated there from Savur. It was in Trusa that the second Great-Voice (and the first Vadim) had established his palace, now occupied by his grandson, Vadim III.

Trusa was surrounded by low, rolling hills. The army had seen men on horseback along the ridges of the hills as they traveled, men who vanished quickly if they sent their own outriders after them. Now Voada and Maol rode with their own scouts to the top of one such hill, well ahead of the main army. From the summit, Voada could see the city sprawled out along the banks of the Iska, a stretch of mud flats glistening in the sun just beyond the city's line of warehouses, and then the Iska's brown waters. Roads leading into the city came from the north, east, and west with carts and wagons, riders, and those on foot moving slowly along them. To the south, Trusa Bridge linked to the southern road. The river was dotted with the billowing sails of ships.

Outside the north entrance of the city, along the road the army of the Cateni was traveling, a sea of tents had been erected, and Voada and Maol could see armored men moving between them.

"The city's so large," Voada whispered. Maol grunted.

"They say Trusa's small compared to Kavak or Koruk in Rumeli and that those cities are tiny compared to Mundoci itself. But yes, that's hard to imagine, and it may not be true. You know how travelers' tales grow."

Voada glared at the town, snared in its tangle of roads and its watery link to the sea. The anger burned in her as she stared; this was the vile center of Albann from which the Mundoan empire spilled out its poison. This was where Great-Voice Vadim III lurked like a hungry spider, all of Albann Deas caught in his web, the ensnared Cateni providing food and nourishment to all the smaller spiders crawling the strands. "You were right, Ceannàrd," she said. "They know we're here, and they know how many we are."

Maol gave her a tight-lipped smile as Hùisdean, crouched over the harness, gentled the warhorses of their chariot, who were stamping restlessly, impatient to be moving. In that, they echoed Voada's own emotions. "If that's the entire force the Great-Voice has gathered to defend Trusa . . ." Maol spat on the ground. "Ours is larger still. Those aren't Savas' banners down there, so those aren't his cohorts. But there are still far more soldiers waiting for us than there were at the garrison of Muras, and, yes, they know we're coming. This won't be a simple fight, Voada. But honestly, it probably never would have been, even if we'd not gone to

Pencraig first. As I've already told you, this will be more like Onglse. Many will end up losing their lives here—and not just Mundoa this time." He peered down once again at the city. "But we'll take the city. The Great-Voice will quickly realize that's going to happen, and he'll try to flee rather than make his stand here. If I were him . . ." Maol rubbed at his scarred face. " . . . I would gather up a trusted escort for protection, and as soon as it's clear that we're close to entering the city, I'd take the bridge across the river to the south road for Savur or Ìseal or board a ship heading downriver. The Voices aren't soldiers, after all, not like our àrds. They're administrators. They've little interest in dying on the field along with their warriors."

"That won't happen," Voada said flatly, her regard still on the city. The coldness of her anamacha pressed against her. *<The Great-Voice . . . He can't be allowed to escape . . . >* "I'll make certain of it. I want the Great-Voice, and I'll have him."

She felt Maol's gaze on her, and she turned. "There's a problem with that?" she asked him.

He shook his head. "No. That's what *we* want," he said, with an emphasis on the plural. Voada decided to ignore it, though its implication annoyed her. *<We need him, for now . . . >*

"Good," she told him. She lifted her chin. "I'll talk to Magaidh and the other draoi when we return. Trusa will cower under the storm I'll have them send, and in the morning, they'll awaken to our spears."

"As you wish, Ceanndraoi."

She thought she heard a mild rebuke in his voice, but there was nothing in that battle-ravaged face, and his eyes regarded her calmly. Maol gestured to Hùisdean, and the chariot made its way back down the hill toward their waiting army.

27

The Harrying of Savas

THERE WAS SOMETHING WRONG.

Altan sensed it immediately upon their arrival in Gediz Bay in the dawn light: a tension in the air, a subtle difference in the way the dock workers—all Cateni—approached them, and their whispered gossip as Altan's ships tied up to the dock and started to unload men and supplies. A sullenness pervaded the atmosphere. There were more soldiers than usual stationed around the dock, and they displayed none of the boredom that such an assignment would normally engender. They were alert, looking around carefully, and their hands stayed near the hilts of their weapons.

"What's happened?" Altan asked the garrison officer, who had come aboard the ship to greet the commander. He was an old man with gray stubble below a balding head, and his cuirass was smeared and showed rust along the edges—the sign of a man who no longer cared about his position or appearance. Altan wondered how long the man had served the Voice of Gediz.

The officer scowled down at the dock. "You haven't heard? Those half-beast Cateni"—here the man paused and spat over the railing into the water—"are revolting in the east. Muras and Pencraig have been lost, and they're taking all the villages between

260

Pencraig and Trusa. Some cow of a draoi named Voada and one of
their northern warriors called Maol Iosa are leading a whole
damned army of 'em. The news is spreading, and now the Cateni
everywhere are becoming insolent and troublesome. I've had to
beat most of 'em to get 'em to do what they're told lately. Look at
'em—see how they're talking amongst themselves? I tell you,
they're plotting against us even now. There have been cowardly
attacks on the overseers, especially the ones they don't like. Three
of my lower officers have been killed in the last moon, last one
here at the dock. When they wouldn't tell me who did it, I had
twenty of the dock slaves put to death and their bodies hung on
the pilings for the others to see. Now no one goes out on patrol or
stands guard alone anymore. You don't want to turn your back on
'em anymore. Bastards!" He spat again. "Guess that's why the
Great-Voice has called you back, eh, Commander Savas? To take
care of this mess before it gets worse? Well, I hope you hurry on
to Trusa. From what I hear, you might be too late already."

"Then I'd advise you to keep treasonous gossip to yourself, if
you want to keep your tongue," Altan told him. The graybeard
snapped his mouth shut in response, ducking his head and giving
Altan a quick tap of fist on cuirass before he hurried away.

"If that man's an example of the officers and soldiers left to defend Trusa, then he's right. We really should hurry." Altan heard
Musa's low comment behind him. "Not that I enjoy agreeing with
the man," Musa added.

Altan managed a short, scoffing laugh. "Unfortunately, he's
right. We can't tarry here. Make sure that our officers get the supplies we need. Tell the cohort officers that I want to be ready to
leave Gediz in three turns of the glass, and the ships should be
sent back to Onglse immediately to pick up Ilkur and his men.
Make sure everyone stays alert—no one gets leave in the city. I
want us to be as far east as we can manage before nightfall. In the
meantime, I'll go to the Voice of Gediz and see if he actually knows
anything more than we do."

Musa clapped fisted hand to cuirass and nodded sharply. He
turned and strode away, already barking orders to the cohort

officers. Altan watched him depart. Then he sighed, shaking his head, and left to find the Voice.

The Voice of Gediz had been only slightly more than no help at all. The news he had from the east had been only a day or so newer than Altan's and was just as grim. "The very land is rising up against us," the Voice of Gediz had said. "You'll see . . ."

They saw. Altan's army, some seven thousand battle-tested soldiers, spread out over the land as they marched eastward. The line was nearly a morning's ride in length along the road and often spread out far to either side. They'd encountered no organized resistance over the last few days, but there were frequent quick sorties from Cateni rebels—arrows shot from wooded hillsides or armed men who rode into the ranks and ambushed them before melting away again. Once, as they crossed a creek, they encountered what must have been a draoi's spell, albeit a terribly weak one that dribbled in like a slowly thrown torch from a stand of willows and managed to hurt no one at all.

However, during the first day, Altan's force suffered a few hands of deaths and at least double that number of injuries, and there were even more the next day. The situation wasn't critical, but Altan felt like a dog being savaged by a cloud of mosquitoes: not in mortal danger, but irritated and unable to do anything to stop the annoyance.

The attacks slowed their progress, made the soldiers wary and restive—especially the outriders and scouts—and Altan knew the attrition could become more troubling if some of the cohort officers became targets. He ordered the officers to remove all insignia from their cloaks to make themselves less obvious and attractive to the Cateni prowling at the edges of the advance. He ordered Musa to stay well surrounded by the army, had Tolga do the same with his own war chariot, and made certain that Musa understood what to do should the worst happen and Altan be struck down.

He had the sickening feeling that what he'd been told in Gediz was correct: they were already too late to save Trusa.

They slogged on, and the sky conjured up a cold drizzle to accompany them—not anything of draoi origin but simply foul weather. The chill and dampness added to the misery of their march, the wheels of their chariots and wagons churning the roads and fields into muddy morasses that caked the hooves of their horses and the boots of the infantry and slowed them even further.

It was as if the physical land as well as its natives was against them.

A rider came hurrying back to Altan as the sun was starting the slow fall from its zenith. "Commander," he said, making a quick salute as his horse snorted twin white clouds. "There's opposition at the bridge ahead. Sub-Commander Musa said you should be alerted. He's halted the vanguard there."

"Tell the sub-commander that I'll be with him quickly and to stay where he is," Altan answered. "Go!" The rider saluted again, yanked hard on the reins, and was off. "Tolga," Altan said to his driver, "take us forward."

Tolga slapped the reins down on the horses, and the chariot lurched forward, the men in front of them moving aside to let them pass. Not long after, Altan saw Musa's banner fluttering ahead and to the right on a nearby rise; he tapped Tolga on the shoulder and pointed to the hill. Tolga followed his gesture, bringing them alongside Musa's chariot.

"Commander." Musa saluted from his chariot. "I thought you'd want to see this."

Musa gestured to the landscape that the hill overlooked. Below, the road was choked with his army. A fairly large stream ahead—a tributary of the River Slaodach that flowed from its source in the midlands of Albann Deas to Gediz Bay—was forded by a low bridge, a bottleneck over which their chariots and carts, at least, would have to pass. On the far side of the bridge, several hands of Cateni had gathered. Through the gloom of the drizzle, it was difficult to see details, but none of them appeared to be armed with more than farming implements, and Altan could see women and children among the crowd.

Musa knew what he was seeing as well. "Had it been warriors or draoi waiting for us, I wouldn't have hesitated, Commander," the man said as water dripped from the crown of his helmet and plastered his robe to his immaculately polished cuirass. "We'd already be across."

"I know," Altan said. "You did right, Musa. This . . ." Altan sighed. "Have you spoken to them?"

"Not yet."

"Then let's go down to them. We can't be delayed here, but maybe . . ." He didn't finish the thought. He nodded to Tolga, and they began moving down the hill toward the bridge.

As they approached, Altan could see that, yes, the mob looked to be largely Cateni farmers and their families, not an organized resistance. Unfortunately, the scythes, long knives, and improvised pikes they bore were no less dangerous than the weapons of trained soldiers. "Not too close, Commander," Musa cautioned him as they came near the bridge. "There may be hidden archers . . ."

"Archers, indeed," Altan answered. "Here's what I want you to do, Musa . . ." He quickly gave him orders, then instructed Tolga to take his chariot to the near side of the bridge. Glancing down, he saw that the water was running swift and deep under it—there would be no easy crossing if they couldn't use the bridge. *If I'd been one of those Cateni, I'd have burned the bridge or brought it down before we arrived and been done with it. They think like farmers, not soldiers. They need the bridge to move their crops and herds.*

"I am Commander Altan Savas of Emperor Pashtuk's army, Sword of Great-Voice Vadim III. Why are you rabble blocking our way?"

One of the men stepped forward: a young man in ragged clothing, muscular and with knotted hands that showed hard work in the dirt. His brown hair, slick with the rain, was cropped short and ragged as if someone had hacked at it with a knife. He leaned on his scythe in the middle of the road near the bridge's far end.

He spoke in Cateni-accented Mundoan. "I'm Labhrann of Clan MacÀidh, and we 'rabble' are blockin' your way because Ceanndraoi Voada has shown us that it's time for all Cateni to rise up an' join her. From what we've heard, half the east is already in flames an' she's at the gates of Trusa. Your Great-Voice is probably shittin' hisself in fear right now. The ceanndraoi will come for you next, and you'll do the same."

Altan ostentatiously looked around the area. "Strange. I don't see her here. I admire your bravery and that of your companions, Labhrann MacÀidh, and that's the truth. It's a rare soldier who's willing to fight against hopeless odds. You see, there's bravery, and there's foolishness. A brave man sometimes dies when it would be better if he lived to fight on another day when the odds were more in his favor."

Altan lifted his hand, Musa called out an order, and hand upon hand of archers near the front of the army lifted bows and drew back, leather strings under tension creaking as they readied to fire on the group across the bridge. MacÀidh lifted his pike in alarm, as if the weapon could stop the hail of arrows to come. Others in his group retreated a few steps, and some of those in the mob called out in alarm.

"Do you see the danger you and all your friends are in, Labhrann MacÀidh? Should my hand drop, you and everyone with you will be cut down before you ever have a chance to strike a blow. I've been a soldier all my life. I never regret killing someone who lifts a weapon against me, but I take no pleasure at all in killing innocents and children along with them. So I'm asking you right now to disperse. Go home. Go back to your farms. Leave the road to me and my soldiers, and perhaps when Ceanndraoi Voada comes here, you might join her, and we can meet again in battle. It's your choice. Do you stay, or do you go?"

A woman, heavy with a child and with a young one clinging to her skirts, came forward from the crowd and grabbed at MacÀidh's arm. "By Elia, listen to him, Labhrann," Altan heard the woman say urgently. "For our children's' sake . . ."

MacÀidh scowled and shrugged off her hand, but Altan could

see the uncertainty in his face and the way his body leaned back, as if he were trying to stop himself from running. "My archers can't hold their bows forever," Altan said. "Choose, and choose quickly."

They were already breaking, those at the rear of the crowd moving quickly toward the trees that lined either side of the road. MacÀidh glanced over his shoulder and saw the defections, and the man's resolve visibly collapsed. He bent down, pulling up a handful of wet grass and earth, holding it out toward Altan. "This land's not yours, Commander," MacÀidh said. "You don't belong here, and this land will spit your people out. Ceanndraoi Voada will make certain of it."

And with that, the man turned his hand over and let the muddy grass fall to the ground as the gathering scattered, vanishing into the gray drizzle. Altan nodded to Musa, who ordered the archers to lower their bows. "Well, that was enlightening," he said to Musa. "The bridge is ours. Let's take advantage of it. Tolga?"

Tolga slapped the reins down on the flanks of the warhorses. They rode across, the wheels chattering against the boards.

Greum Red-Hand and Menach Ceiteag stood at the summit of the long slope atop which stood the first fort the Mundoa had taken, its stones blackened and shattered from the fighting it had endured. They both stared down at the now-empty harbor that the Mundoan ships had left with the last of their soldiers. They could still see the sails well out on the strait between Onglse and Albann Bràghad, hurrying southward in the squall the draoi had sent to chase them.

Ceiteag pulled her cloak tighter around herself, shivering in the cold wind off the water. Her bones ached, and she was still exhausted from the efforts of the battles. If the war went elsewhere, she wouldn't complain. She shifted her feet, her boots heavy with caked mud. Gulls squawked their discontent as they circled overhead.

"Do we go too, Ceanndraoi?" she asked Greum. "The army that Ceannàrd Iosa has raised would certainly be grateful for the help of Onglse now that you've driven the Mundoa from the island."

Ceiteag very carefully avoided mentioning Voada or the fact that it appeared Savas' army had retreated on its own when it was on the cusp of taking Bàn Cill, but Greum Red-Hand glared at her nonetheless. He spat on the ground in front of him. "Iosa no longer has the title of ceannàrd," he said. "He abandoned us when we needed him most. He has no honor, and he will never be welcome on Onglse again. His name is forgotten. Don't speak of him again."

"But still," Ceiteag persisted, "most of the clans have sent people south over the Meadham. They've taken Muras and Pencraig and are marching on Trusa, if the rumors that we've heard are true. Surely they'll need help—"

Greum interrupted her before she could go further. "Onglse has done enough. The draoi will stay here and help us rebuild what the Mundoan army has destroyed. Let the clan àrds who have gone south deal with their own mess."

"Ceanndraoi, because we draoi cannot take the sun-path upon death, we can never be reunited with our loved ones who die. Tirnanog is forever closed to us; our essences are taken into our anamacha after we die. Therefore, as we both know, it's not uncommon for we draoi to become mad. Voada has lost so much— her husband, her children—and, well, if she is somewhat touched, perhaps that's why—"

Greum's arm slashed through the chilly air. "No. Enough. Don't make excuses for the woman. You brought her here with the Moonshadow, Ceiteag. You may still care about her, but I don't. She is *entirely* mad; the Moonshadow has taken her mind. The very fact that she fled Onglse to pursue this folly she's set upon shows me that. I know you have affection for her, but the Moonshadow . . ." Greum scowled. "That anamacha should have gone to someone who would have made better use of it."

You mean it should have gone to you . . . "We don't know that she's become lost in the anamacha. None of the news that's come here says—"

"She *dares* to call herself Ceanndraoi," Greum said, interrupting her again. "She *dares . . .*"

Ceiteag didn't say what was in her mind: *She didn't call herself that. The title was given to her by the clans, and for what she has accomplished, perhaps she deserves it more than you.* Ceiteag sighed. There would be no arguing with the Red-Hand over this; she knew him well enough to know that.

She looked at the ships stuffed with Mundoan soldiers fleeing south, on their way to confront Voada and the ceannàrd, then lifted her head to the clouds scudding across the gray sky. A lashing of rain splashed over her furrowed face. *Keep her safe, Elia*, she prayed to the clouds. *Watch over her as I would have . . .*

She didn't know if the goddess heard or not. When she brought her head down again, she found that Greum had left her. She could see him plodding back toward the broken fort.

After another glance at the ships, she turned and followed him.

28

Outside the Great City

BEFORE THE BATTLE BEGAN, Trusa's night was rent and torn by lightning, shrieking winds, and pelting rain. The tents of the reinforcements brought in to protect Great-Voice Vadim III and Trusa were shredded and blown away. Several soldiers were killed by lightning strikes, which also started fires within the city itself. The Great-Voice's sihirki, knowing that the storm was draoi-caused and not natural, shouted their own counterspells, none of which did more than slightly abate the whirling chaos that assaulted the city. The storm still boomed and crashed, and the inhabitants of Trusa cowered under the aerial assault.

The sihirki tried to convince the Great-Voice that this situation was acceptable. "Great-Voice," the chief sihirki said, "these spell-storms mean that the Cateni draoi will be drained and tired when the real attack comes, so they won't be as effective as they could be. They are wasting their efforts on flash and thunder. It's mere noise."

"That 'mere noise' has already killed hands of good soldiers we'll need," Vadim grumbled—a whip-thin man whose hair had receded to a mere gray fringe around his ears and the back of his head. He leaned back in his chair and plucked at the lining of his silken robe. *And that storm and the thought of the draoi spells to come has frightened every last one of the soldiers out there. I wonder how*

many have already deserted. "You'd best be right," he told the sihirki, "or I'll feed you to the Cateni myself."

The sihirki gulped and walked backward from the reception
room in the Great-Voice's palace, bowing the entire time.

The Great-Voice saw his wife at the inner door of the reception
room. She'd been listening and had a look of concern on her face.
He gestured her forward and rose from his throne on the raised
dais to meet her. "Don't worry," he told her softly so that the
guards stationed around the room could not hear. He pulled her
to him, his arms around her and his head nestled in her long dark
hair. She didn't pull away, as she so often did, but he felt her body
stiffen. "I've made arrangements," he whispered in her ear. "You
and the children will leave at dawn and go to Savur; if the battle
doesn't go well, I'll join you there."

"And do you think it will go well, husband?" he heard her say.
He wondered if her concern was for him or for the effect that the
loss of him might have on her. The Emperor didn't treat those
who failed him kindly.

"No," he answered bluntly. "That bastard Savas hasn't come
back with his army. I'll have his head as a wall decoration after
this is over; he's no doubt gloating over what's happened after all
his dire predictions. And even though the Cateni are just undisciplined rabble, there are too many of them, and they have those
damned draoi. I think they'll be plundering the city before nightfall . . . and I *will* leave Trusa as soon as I'm certain of that."

"I'm told the citizens began deserting the city as soon as this
draoi-storm broke, especially after the news about Muras and
Pencraig. They say the roads east, west, and south are choked
with them."

"You, the children, and I won't be using the roads; I've a ship
waiting for you and one for me. Don't worry." He kissed the top of
her head and stepped back from her. "Go on and prepare our family and servants. Sub-commander Cemal will come to you before
the sunrise and escort you, our children, and your attendants to
the ship. Get yourself ready now."

She bent her knee and head to him and left the room. Vadim

sighed and walked over to the windows, the shutters closed against
the storm. He opened one, looking out northward over the city.
Dark, foreboding clouds slid over the houses of Trusa, so low that it
seemed someone standing on a roof would nearly be able to touch
them. Curtains of gray rain hid the city gates just up the main Great
North Road. The storm slithered forward on legs of brilliant blue
lightning, and it roared and rumbled as it thrashed at the city, yet to
the east and west Vadim could see a hint of clear skies.

The damned draoi. The sihirki had better be right about them . . .

The wind shifted slightly, pelting Vadim's face with rain, and he
pulled the shutter tight again. The sound of the storm receded
slightly. Brushing rain from his ceremonial robes, Vadim returned
to the dais and his chair. "Go tell the city regent I wish to consult
with him," he said to the guard at the door. "And if you find that
he's already abandoned the city . . ." Vadim grinned humorlessly.
"Take anything you want from his house, then burn it down."

Voada had Magaidh and the other draoi end their spells a few
stripes before dawn, ordering them to rest and recover. She couldn't
sleep herself. From the rise to the north of Trusa, she watched the
spell-storm slowly cease its grumbling, and the westerly wind begin
to shred the false clouds and blow them away. The moon was a thin
sliver in the sky, the stars emerging through the clearing overcast.
Trusa lay before Voada, illuminated in pale blue light. It was easy
enough to pick out the Great-Voice's palace, rising above the roofs
on a low hill just east of the city center. She wondered if Vadim was
staring outward toward her and what he might be thinking.

All of the roads leading away from the city were crowded, except for the north road toward the River Meadham, where her
army waited. The citizens of Trusa were fleeing before the battle
with carts laden with whatever belongings they could carry, a long
procession of torches moving slowly away from the capital. They
were likely nearly all Mundoa; she suspected that many of the
Cateni would stay, knowing that they were safe from reprisals as

long as they didn't join in the defense of the city. Perhaps many of them were eager to join with the clans' forces. That was why she'd ordered that the lightning should largely avoid the poorer, Cateni sectors of the city.

Voada felt the presence of Magaidh's anamacha before the woman spoke, coming up to stand next to her. "I hope you don't mind," she told Voada. "I can't sleep. And Comhnall's been up with Ceannàrd Iosa for two or three stripes now, going over their strategy."

Voada nodded silently. The faint gleam of their anamacha glistened on the grass around their feet. "You're ready for this?" she asked.

"I don't know that anyone could ever be ready for what we're doing," Magaidh answered, her tone causing Voada to glance at the woman. Magaidh was still gazing out at Trusa. "But there are times when we do what we must," she finished.

"You don't think people like Maol enjoy war, that they don't take pleasure in what they accomplish on the field of battle? Do you think your Comhnall doesn't enjoy the victories he's helped to gain? Isn't this what warriors live—and die—for?"

Magaidh turned to Voada; there was a question and sadness in her expression. "As for Comhnall, yes, he's proud of what he's accomplished as àrd, but I also know he'll be happy when this is over and we can return to our own land with little to worry about but when the sheep need to be fed and sheared and the flock culled," she said. "As for me, I'd be wary of someone who took too much pleasure in killing. Even," she added, "when it's intended as blood payment for terrible deeds their enemies have done."

"Are you saying you're wary of *me*?" Voada asked, and the woman's eyes widened as she took a step back, and her anamacha moved closer to her. Magaidh stared at her as if she were seeing the face of a stranger before her, or worse, the face of someone she feared. *Who does she see?* "I'm no threat to you, Magaidh," Voada told her quietly. "It pains me to see you flinch away like that. You're my friend, and I want your honesty. I treasure it."

"Then I'll give it to you," Magaidh said, though Voada couldn't see relief in the lines of her face, only more of the fear. "Yes, Ceann-ndraoi, I am wary of you, because what's been done to you and your family by the Mundoa can't ever be undone, and so I'm afraid you'll never find peace, even after all this effort." Magaidh gestured with a hand toward Trusa. "I worry for you, Voada, because I'm grateful to you. You've treated me well, and I've come to think of you as a friend as well as my mentor. It's because of that friendship that I want you to find happiness again. I just . . ." She took a breath, looking away, then back again. "I just don't think you'll ever find it this way, with towns burning and Mundoan heads on spikes at their gates."

Despite Voada's words, Magaidh's rebuke stung her like a slap across the cheek. Her anamacha was near her, cold against her side. *<She doesn't understand us . . . She can't comprehend how we feel, how you feel . . . This isn't friendship; this is treachery . . . She weakens you . . . Show her your strength . . . >*

"You don't know how I feel," Voada told Magaidh, and she heard the chill of the voices in her head creep into her voice. "You can't, because you've never experienced what I've experienced. You belong to the northern clans. You've never been a Cateni under the yoke of the Mundoa; you've never been thought of as near-beast, fit for little more than servitude or slavery. Even as a Hand, my Meir was just a talking pet performing tricks at the Voice's command." Her voice rose in volume and sudden heat. "You've never been forbidden to worship as your ancestors did or seen your temples desecrated and all images of your gods smashed and destroyed. You've never had your children ripped away from you, your whole life uprooted and destroyed in front of your eyes. You don't *know* what will give me satisfaction. So please spare me your pity and your opinions."

It was as if she'd scolded Orla. Magaidh ducked her head, the curtains of sun-gold hair hiding her face. "As you wish, Ceann-draoi," she said. Her head came up again, her light eyes firm and steady as they searched Voada's face. "But I won't apologize. You told me when I first took my anamacha that they are dangerous, and I understand now how tempting it is to simply listen to the voices inside and do what they wish. I also know that the voices inside yours are far more powerful than those who inhabit mine. I worry, Voada, that I'm beginning to hear the Moonshadow in your voice and not you."

Her bluntness made Voada's head snap back. She could see Magaidh staring at her anamacha, at how it seemed to cling to her. *<The impertinence!>* the voices shouted, nearly drowning out her own thoughts. *<Strike her down!>* Voada knew that voice. Knew it well.

"No," Voada said, not knowing who she was answering. She took a step away from her anamacha so that the cold and the voices receded. "Magaidh, I am not the Moonshadow. I am simply myself."

Magaidh held her gaze for another breath, and then the young woman nodded. "Good," she said. "I don't want to lose my friend. Ever." She turned and began making her way down the hill toward their encampment. Voada reached toward Magaidh as if she could hold her back. She wanted to speak, to call to the woman, to apologize herself, but the words refused to come. Instead, she felt the cold touch of her anamacha and the chorused voice of the Moonshadow.

<They don't understand us . . . Stay strong . . . They will follow our strength . . . >

Voada let her hand drop. She returned her attention to Trusa and the growing predawn glow in the east, and she imagined herself standing in the city.

In that vision, there was blood pooling at her feet.

Maol, with Voada in his chariot, led the Cateni army as it progressed inexorably down the long Great North Road toward Trusa. They could see the Mundoan cohorts lined up in neat squares on the fields outside the city gates. As before, Voada had lashed herself to the frame of the chariot so that her arms were free and her body stable enough to cast spells. She could already hear the sihirki shouting their own spells from the rear of the Mundoan army. A fleet of arrows erupted from the archers behind the Mundoan infantry, arcing up as Voada opened her arms to her anamacha and let herself fall into their world. She had promised herself that she would not call the Moonshadow, but she quickly drew energy from Iomhar, her hands weaving the air in front of her as the chariot bounced over the ruts of the road.

A hard wind howled as she released the spell. It tore most of the arrows from the air.

Voada could feel anger rising within her, a complex rage born of her conversation with Magaidh, of the disappointment she'd endured at Pencraig, of the resentment she harbored toward the Mundoa. All of her frustrations now sat in front of her, crystallized in the city and the thought of the Great Voice squatting somewhere within like a gigantic, foul toad, ready to hop away before the boot of the Cateni came down upon him.

<Yes! Let the fire fill you! We can use it!> The Moonshadow's voice, bound up with all the other draoi captured in the anamacha. *<Here—take your anger back from us and use it . . . >*

<No!> Voada shouted back to the Moonshadow. *<I want Iomhar. Leave me alone. Iomhar, come to me!>*

But Iomhar didn't come. In her vision of Magh da Chèo, the shades of the draoi within her anamacha shuffled around her, and the only one who stepped forward was the Moonshadow, her suntouched hair the color of ripe wheat and a red setting sun, her eyes holding the deep sea. *<Iomhar can't help you here. Let me be the death that falls on them. Here . . . Feel the power we share . . . >*

With that, the Moonshadow's specter entered her, and Voada could not keep her out.

They merged.

They moved as one.

Voada began to weave a new spell the Moonshadow fed her, one more powerful and difficult to handle than any she'd felt before. The heat of it threatened to raise blisters on her skin as she wove the framework, and the words that came from her throat seemed formed of live coals. The world in front of her threatened to fall away entirely, to leave her soul trapped in the otherworld of the anamacha. Faintly, as if she were seeing a taibhse in the sunlight, she could see Maol turning to her, his eyes wide as if what he saw frightened him. His mouth was open; he was shouting at her, but she couldn't hear his voice over the roaring in her ears. Voada fought to retain herself, to keep some vision of what lay before her like a shield against the fiery chaos of the ghost world.

<*You hold it too long . . .* > She wasn't certain whose voice that was: her own, or the Moonshadow's.

"Ceanndraoi!" The shout came from alongside her: Magaidh, in her husband's chariot. She was staring at the inferno Voada held, her eyes wide with fear.

Voada shuddered at Magaidh's alarm. She screamed the final spell-words and spread her hands, breaking the webbing that held a glowing red sphere.

The spell went careening away from her, Maol throwing himself down in the chariot as it did so, the flames nearly touching Hùisdean as he ducked down over the harness. The warhorses reared up in alarm as the spell passed over them, the sphere growing and crackling as it rushed toward the waiting army. Voada could see the ranks already breaking, the soldiers in the vanguard shouting and pushing against those behind and around them as they tried to escape the roaring sun hurtling their way.

It struck them, the fireball exploding in their midst with a tremendous thunderclap that made Voada put her hands belatedly to her ears, that brought the charge of the Cateni to a momentary halt. Afterimages went from white to purple in her eyes, and when she could see again, the road all the way to the city gates was empty of anything but corpses and charred ground. The gates themselves hung askew and open, fire crackling along broken wooden planks.

Voada hung in her bonds, only half aware, empty of power now that Magh da Chèo was banished from her mind. The anamacha slid away from her, and she clutched at it as if to draw it back into her.

Maol and the other Cateni howled in triumph. Hùisdean slapped the reins on the warhorses' backs, and the chariot lurched forward, jarring Voada as Maol grasped a spear and brandished it skyward.

The Cateni charge resumed. With a massed roar, they hurtled toward the prize of Trusa.

29

A Voice Silenced

THE RESISTANCE BROKE QUICKLY and wildly after Voada's spell as the Cateni army pushed swiftly into the city and spread out. As with the villages they'd passed through, the Cateni of Trusa rose up at the same time, slaves and servants killing the Mundoa who had been foolish or brave enough to remain behind. Magaidh and the other draoi were casting their own spells, and columns of smoke began to rise from well within the city.

It was obvious that Trusa was to fall and that it would fall quickly and hard.

Voices called to Voada even as she watched her army swarm into the city streets, killing those soldiers who hadn't already fled, looting the houses of the Mundoa, setting more fires. Trusa would burn to the ground, and she would rejoice in the ashes.

Her anamacha touched her, cold at her side. *<You want more . . . We want more . . . The Great-Voice, he is already trying to slip away . . . You will lose your greatest vengeance for what they did to you. . . . >* It was the Moonshadow's voice leading the chorus, ringing in her head. *<Go . . . ! >*

"Maol!" Voada had to shout to the ceannàrd to be heard even though they were in the same chariot, the din of their victory was so loud around them. "The Great-Voice! We need to reach the river, quickly!"

Maol shrugged. "The city is ours. Let the fool run."

"No!" Voada screamed the word, using a touch of the power remaining within her to strengthen her voice so that it rang loudly enough that Magaidh, in her chariot several strides away, glanced toward them. Soldiers rushing past stopped momentarily to look. "I have given you an order. Do as I say! Hurry! The Great-Voice is our prize."

Maol scowled at that, but he nodded to Hùisdean, and the driver shouted to the warhorses. They surged forward, moving at a breakneck speed toward the Great-Voice's palace and the River Iska. Voada clung to the railing of the chariot as they moved, the voices of her anamacha howling within her in accompaniment to the screams of the citizens of Trusa they passed. She saw Hùisdean heading toward the city gate of the palace, still guarded by Mundoan soldiers, and she shouted at the driver. "No! To the river! That's where he is!"

Hùisdean yanked hard on the reins, causing Maol to lose his balance and, cursing, grab at the rails himself. They careened around the side walls of the palace and down a narrow alley. Voada could see the River Iska's brown waters ahead, mud flats glistening in its tidal flow while the palace's high stone walls still loomed on their left side. Then the wall abruptly ended, and Hùisdean had to yank back hard on the warhorses' reins in order to stop them from plowing ahead into the mud. Voada looked left; at a gate in the river wall of the palace, a tall, thin man in fine robes was being helped into a boat tied to a pier where a short channel had been dug from the low tide limits of the Iska to the palace wall, allowing boats to reach the steps of the gate even when the tide was out. The robed man was accompanied by several guards with gleaming mirrored cuirasses as well as a dozen or so other people in Mundoan finery.

"There!" Voada shouted. "That's Great-Voice Vadim."

Voada closed her eyes, letting the vision of Magh da Chèo fill her even though her exhaustion clawed at her. She felt the Moonshadow near her again, and this time she eagerly drew on that power, making the shape of a new spell, her lips speaking the words that came to her through the Moonshadow's presence. The shape of the spell was complicated, with a lacuna set in the midst of it, unlike any spell she'd ever seen before. Even as she marveled at the intricate shape, her hands finished weaving the net and the last words left her mouth. She cast the spell just as the guards saw their chariot; two of them drew back their bowstrings, and the others charged toward them through the mud with swords drawn.

None of them mattered. Voada released the spell, and the knot of flame and smoke sped away from her, the heat of it nearly singeing the manes of the warhorses, who whinnied in alarm. Voada loosed herself from the chariot, hopping down into the mud and starting to walk toward the Great-Voice as the spell touched the guards and the Great-Voice's companions. They screamed in agony, their clothing immediately going to flame, their flesh blackening before falling away to leave white bone glistening underneath. The bodies collapsed into the Iska's mud, the mouths of the skulls still open as the echoes of their screams reverberated from the palace walls. The wooden hull of the boat flared as well, the mast and sail going to quick flame. But the hole Voada had woven into the spell left the Great-Voice untouched. He was sobbing and wailing, even after all the other voices had gone silent, but his was a sound of terror and fear rather than pain. Frantically, the man tried to climb into the flame-blackened boat, grabbing at an oar and trying to row away. Voada continued to approach him as Hùisdean gingerly directed the war chariot along the mud flats closest to the palace wall.

Vadim was shouting for help in a reedy, high voice and frantically flailing at the shallow water with his oar. No one was responding. The smell of fire and burnt flesh was thick around them. The tide-exposed river bottom over which Voada walked was pebbled and strewn with the detritus of Trusa, broken pieces of pottery and other trash. The mud smelled of dead fish and brine. She came to the stone edge of the canal and stopped. She stared at Vadim until his wide-eyed gaze dared to find hers.

"Great-Voice Vadim III, you are the prisoner of Ceanndraoi Voada," she said. "And you will pay in kind for what you've done to my people."

The oar dropped from Vadim's hand at the words, and he began to scream.

"The Great-Voice is more valuable as a hostage than dead," Maol insisted.

They'd taken the man into his own palace, now controlled by the Cateni. Voada was standing at the balcony of the Great-Voice's private chambers. Everything about the room offended her: the extravagant opulence, the fine hangings around the walls, the expensive furniture, the obvious fact that it must have taken hands and hands of servants and slaves—all of them Cateni—to attend to it. Everything about the palace was an insult to her people, as Moonshadow's anamacha—pacing the perimeter of the room— reminded her every time they brushed up against her.

<*This place was built with Cateni blood . . . The very mortar between the stones is mixed with it . . . We remember that time, many of us in here . . . We still feel it . . .*>

Outside, much of Trusa was burning, the sky nearly hidden by the drifting smoke. The smell of it couldn't be escaped, and the fires were whipping up winds that coiled upward, the smoke wrapped around the flames like snakes. Even here, close to the river and behind stone walls, they wouldn't be able to stay much longer. Glowing embers were drifting in the wind like red snow; they would inevitably alight somewhere flammable, and the palace would suffer the same fate as the rest of the Mundoan capital. As Voada watched, an ember alighted on the marble railing in front of her and expired into dead ash.

"I don't agree," Voada answered Maol as she watched the ash fall away, leaving a smudge on the polished stone. She turned to him. "I didn't spare him in order to give him back."

"Voada, listen to me," Maol responded. "I *know* these people.

I've fought against them nearly all my life. I know how they think and how they respond. With their Great-Voice captured, they'll be willing to parley, perhaps even directly via Emperor Pashtuk. We can force change on them as payment for Vadim's safe return. We stand to gain much of what we want without bloodshed."

"You don't sound like a warrior," she told him.

"That's *exactly* what I sound like," he answered. "A good warrior knows the cost of war and when to end it. I'm not afraid of fighting—you of all people should understand that—but I'm also not afraid of peace. We've been given a gift here. Let's *use* it. And if they refuse to parley, well, then we fight."

<We can't trust the Mundoa . . . > The Moonshadow's chorus was louder in her head than Maol's real voice. She spoke the same words. "We can't trust the Mundoa. They lie. They'll make promises to us, but they won't keep them. We have to smash them entirely."

Maol shook his head. The scars on his face stood out starkly against flushed skin. His armor was soiled with blood and soot. "I would trust Commander Savas, Voada. Completely. He's a man of honor, and he'll keep any vow he makes. You've indicated to me that you feel much the same."

Voada swung her arms wide. "Savas says the right things, and yes, he was kind to Meir and me when I met him. But . . ." She spoke the word heavily, with a sigh. "I trusted a Mundoan's word once, a Voice's word, and it cost me my family and nearly my life. The Great-Voice must pay for that, because the Voice of Pencraig was just his echo."

"Revenge is a fine thing, Voada. I know that. I've acted because of that desire many times myself. But right now, we have a chance to do more, and we should set that revenge aside. You want to hurt the Great-Voice? What do you think will hurt him more than being the man who surrendered to the Clans and lost the Mundoa part of their empire? I'd be willing to wager that the Emperor will end up executing him."

<This isn't what we want . . . This isn't what you want . . . > The anamacha had come around again, sliding into Voada and out again with its whispers. "If he's going to end up dead anyway, then

let's not wait," she said. "This is my decision, Maol Iosa. You're ceannàrd on the battlefield, but the battle is over."

"Battles are not always won on the field. Sometimes they're won elsewhere, too." Maol spread his hands in supplication. "Voada, Ceanndraoi, I beg you to listen to me. The Great-Voice is more valuable to us as a hostage than as a casualty. Trust me on this."

< . . . *This isn't what you want, what we want . . .* > The voices warred inside her, tearing at her. She felt like she was being pulled apart. "I do trust you. I couldn't have asked for a better ceannàrd, and it's obvious to me why Greum Red-Hand chose you. But in this . . ." Voada pressed her lips together as the chorus of the Moonshadow's voices whispered in her head, and she found her own voice speaking the same words. "What you're suggesting isn't what we want."

"It isn't what *you* want," Maol responded. "That's the issue. Or is it that it isn't what your anamacha wants?"

<*Fool! Strike him down for that!*> Sympathetic rage surged through Voada at Maol's implication. She felt the temptation to move her hands, to say the spell words that the anamacha howled, to take the energy that they offered her. She clenched her fists, forcing her hands to remain still, but she could hear the echo of their harshness in her voice. "The Great-Voice dies, Maol. He *must* die."

Maol seemed to sigh. "Voada, I've spent the last stripe making certain that the Great-Voice told me everything. Commander Savas has left Onglse and is already here in the west of Albann Deas. We both know the commander isn't a trivial opponent. We couldn't keep him off Onglse, couldn't stop him from taking our fortifications. Now he's here. If you execute the Great-Voice, we'll end up having to face him again. With the Great-Voice as hostage, Savas will hesitate, and he'll be willing to parley. Without a hostage . . ." Maol shrugged. "We need to leave, Ceanndraoi, whatever you decide, because Trusa is burning. I need to see to my sub-commanders and our army. I only ask you to think about this decision. I'm going down to the river gate with the Great-Voice. Voada, make whatever decision about the Great-Voice that you must, but you need to come with me. It's not safe here any longer."

She knew he was correct about the danger. Ash and sparks were falling heavily over the palace now, and the buildings outside the walls were aflame. The city burned before her.

Voada nodded and followed Maol from the room.

With Great-Voice Vadim III lashed to the railings of Maol Iosa's war chariot naked and exposed, Voada rode with Maol Iosa out the river gate and along the muddy banks of the River Iska until they passed beyond Trusa's wall, blackened now with soot. Flames enveloped the bridge over the Iska, and the middle span had already partially collapsed into the river. The windows of the palace gleamed red with fire. The entire city burned behind them, the heat of the conflagration at their backs.

Once safely away from the city, Voada had Hùisdean turn toward Trusa's main gates and the Great North Road. There, per her instructions, a tall dais had been erected just to the side of the blackened and broken gates of the city. The banner of the Great-Voice had been taken from the palace and hung there upside down, mockingly. Voada's army and the swelling numbers of Cateni who had joined them were massed there before the dais, thousands upon thousands of them flowing out into the distance.

"Take him up," Voada said to the waiting quartet of Cateni who had once been slaves in the Great-Voice's palace. Almost gleefully, they came forward, cut their former master from his bonds, and half carried him to the rude stairs of the dais and what had been prepared there. Voada would look at neither Maol nor Magaidh, who watched from near the steps of the dais. Instead, she followed behind the protesting Vadim, feeling her anamacha close at her side. In her head, she heard the Moonshadow's satisfaction. They dragged the naked man up the steps, and Vadim moaned aloud when he saw the instruments placed on the table there—a table from his own bedroom in the palace.

When Voada reached the dais, she stepped forward and opened her arms to embrace her anamacha, borrowing from it the power to strengthen her voice. Though she called for Iomhar, it was the Moonshadow who answered. <*I don't need you,*> she told the shade. <*Let Iomhar do this.*>

<*We are one . . .* > the Moonshadow answered. <*There is no difference . . . Can't you feel that? Can't you feel what we have become, what we could become? Together . . .* >

The warnings of Greum, of Ceiteag, seemed distant against the warmth that she felt emanating from the anamacha in the storms of the Otherworld. Her protest withered in the emotions that she felt. She told herself that this wasn't the time to struggle against the anamacha, that she would reassert herself with the Moonshadow later. This moment, this demonstration, was what she wanted.

<*Come to me,*> she told the Moonshadow, and the presence swept into her.

As the energy of the Moonshadow filled her, she called out to the throngs before her, her voice as loud as the thunder of a summer storm, reaching all the way to the farthest of her followers. She wasn't certain where the words came from, but her throat moved with them.

"My friends, my people, we've taken the capital of the Mundoa, the symbol of their empire in Albann. We've begun the great task of freeing all the southern clans from the chains that the Mundoa have placed around us, with which they bound us when they first came to this land. *Our* land, which we are taking back from them.

"This won't be an easy task, even though we've made an important start under the direction of Ceannàrd Maol Iosa." She glanced down; Maol was staring impassively up at her. Voada pointed over his head to the road. "Out there, to the west and advancing toward us, is Commander Savas and his army. It's him we must go to meet next. It's his army that we *will* defeat, and once we have done that, both Albann Deas and Albann Bràghad will be ours once more. I need to know this from you: will you help me do that, all of you? Will you become the spear and sword of the Clans?"

The cheer that erupted then was louder than her voice, a roar that she could feel hammering against her, that caused the voices of her anamacha to respond with an interior exultation. Voada gestured back to the Great-Voice, held in the grasp of his former slaves. "Look at him. Stripped of his title, his clothes, his money, his palace, his soldiers, his slaves. Look at him. He is *nothing*. Just a puny, frightened, useless man. That's all he ever was."

Voada stepped toward him, plucking up a pair of steel tongs and a curved Mundoan knife from the table. She nodded to the Cateni, who held the man's limbs tightly, and one of them stepped behind the man, grasping his hair and pulling it back so that Vadim couldn't move his head. Voada could see Vadim's eyes widen further as the Cateni holding his hair also pressed the man's nostrils together. The Great-Voice held his breath, but he eventually had to open his mouth to gulp air, and Voada plunged the tongs into his mouth, grasping the end of the man's tongue and pulling it out. "He was once known as the Emperor's Great-Voice," she called to the crowd, who roared back at her. "Now we will take that voice from him. Forever."

With a single, harsh stroke, she severed the man's tongue with the knife. Blood drooled from his mouth, over his chin, and down Vadim's bare chest as he howled wordlessly. She held up the tongue to the crowd's approval, then threw it down on the ground in front of the platform.

She had intended for that to be all, to let the man go back to his own kind, humiliated and mutilated, as a message to his people. She would let Maol take him and use him as a hostage if he thought it would help. She thought she would feel satisfaction at this small vengeance, but there was only emptiness inside her.

<More . . . This is not enough . . . He deserves more punishment . . . >

She felt pressure building within her. The real world and the world of the anamacha were intermingled in her sight, and the touch of her anamacha was like being back in the embrace of Meir, familiar and comfortable. *<He is ultimately responsible for what happened to you and your family. Give him all he deserves . . . >* the Moonshadow's chorus crooned. *<How can you bear that he lives when Hakan has died and Orla's been lost to you . . . ?>*

It felt as if someone else controlled her hand. Voada turned quickly back to the man, and this time the knife slashed deep and hard across his abdomen as Vadim screamed once more. The blade tore at muscle and cartilage, resisting vainly as Voada's arm wrenched the weapon nearly from side to side. The gray coils of his intestines tumbled bloodily out from the wound, slithering to the floor of the platform. The Cateni holding Vadim released his arms, and the man fell to his knees, his hands clutching at the great rent in his body as if he were trying to stuff the ruins back inside himself.

He collapsed, and the crowd cheered, though Voada saw Maol grimacing in his chariot, and Magaidh's mouth opened in soundless horror as she turned away. Voada's anamacha glided away from her, and the real world snapped back into sharp focus. She could smell the blood and the smoke of the fire, could feel the shivers as she looked down at the Great-Voice's corpse, could see the gore that stained her arm to the elbow. The acclamation of the crowd filled her ears as she stared out at them.

She also felt the horror widening her eyes, roiling in her stomach and rising to burn in her throat. "I'm sorry," she said, looking at Magaidh, at Maol, but her voice was now only her own, unheard above the roaring of the crowd.

The oak leaf pendant around her neck, the brass torc of the draoi: both felt cold against her skin, as if the breath of some taibhse had touched them. She wanted to reach for the pendant, to stroke the silver and imagine Orla doing the same somewhere, but her fingers were too stained with blood.

Will you hear my name now, Orla? Do those around you talk of Ceanndraoi Voada, and do you know that it's me? Will you come to me? Will I hold you again?

She felt . . . empty. Alone.

She let the knife drop from her hand.

30

The Merging of Intent

THE ASHES AND RUINS of Trusa still smoldered, spewing a film of gray smoke that the wind smeared over the sky and blew eastward. Dogs scavenged the corpses of the city, eating the flesh and scattering the bones of the dead, including those of Vadim III—all except his head, which had been hewn from his body and placed on a tall post before the city gates with a sign underneath in Cateni script: *The Great-Voice is silent.*

Voada didn't know who had mutilated the body—the Great-Voice's former slaves, most likely.

Voada had sent word to Maol, Comhnall, and Magaidh to come to her tent in the encampment on the hillside outside Trusa where the Great North Road wound along the valley. The tent was dark enough that Voada could see Magaidh's anamacha standing at her right side, and she knew that Magaidh could see the Moonshadow's anamacha as well. Magaidh's husband stood to her left. The war, Voada could see, had aged Àrd Mac Tsagairt. He limped as he had entered the tent, and his hair had gone nearly entirely gray, even if under his armor his body still held corded muscle.

The two bowed to Voada as they entered. Magaidh's face was carefully arranged and neutral, and that saddened Voada. *We were friends. I wanted us to stay friends . . .* But that was her fault, not

Magaidh's. Or perhaps it was the Moonshadow's fault. Voada glanced at her anamacha in accusation. *I can't use the Moonshadow anymore. I can't . . .*

She wondered if she would still feel that way once she was in Magh da Chèo again, with the storm howling around her and the Moonshadow close to her.

Voada was seated in a velvet-cushioned chair, another item appropriated from the Great-Voice's palace before the fire had reduced it to a stone-walled and roofless shell. Her left hand was on the chair's gilded and intricately carved arm as her right touched the silver oak leaf she wore and stroked the polished brass of her torc. She gestured to the table to the side, set with flagons of wine and water as well as meat pastries. "Please," she said. "Magaidh, Comhnall, take some refreshment."

"Thank you, Ceanndraoi," Comhnall said, but neither he nor Magaidh moved. Maol arrived a breath later, announced by the guards at the tent's open entrance. *I must apologize to Maol for what I did with the Great-Voice,* Voada thought as the man made his own obeisance. Voada felt her anamacha press her left hand, their touch frigid as they merged with her. Voada could see that Magaidh noticed the interaction, while the two men did not.

<No . . . > the Moonshadow's chorus whispered back, hearing her thought. The single word echoed in Voada's head. <No apologies . . . We cannot appear weak . . . What we did was right and just . . . We did what had to be done . . . >

Voada would have argued with the anamacha, but the three were staring at her, waiting. She took her hand away and placed it in her lap.

"We've all heard the reports from our scouts and from those loyal Cateni coming to us," she said, nodding to Maol. "The Cateni of Velimese have risen up against their Mundoan rulers and have taken back the town. We've heard rumors of the same in Ladik and Var. We know that Commander Savas' army is very near Velimese and will undoubtedly move against them as they move eastward. The question we have to answer is this: from here, where should we take our army?"

"South," Magaidh said before either of the others could answer. "We should go south across the Iska. Savas' army is hands of days behind us. We have a multitude of willing bodies with us, and we have draoi; we could build a new bridge across the Iska in a few days using the ruins and pilings of the old bridge. We could then take the Great North Road south to Ìseal or go east to Savur." She spread her hands, and her anamacha mirrored her stance. Voada could hear the excitement in her voice. "If we have time before Savas' army nears, we could take them both. Think of it: we take their two great ports before the news of Trusa reaches the Emperor's ears and he decides to muster a new army from Rumeli. Maybe the Emperor would decide that Albann isn't worth the expense and the lives it would cost to take back all we've gained. Ceanndraoi, I *know* that once we take their two great southern cities, the Cateni will rise up in every town and village in Albann Deas. We'll have more Cateni to swell our ranks when we do face Savas, and we will crush him with simple numbers. All of Albann will be ours again, as you wanted it to be. As we want it to be."

Both Maol and Comhnall were nodding as Magaidh finished. The anamacha still pressed near to Voada, its hand now on her shoulder. In Voada's head, she heard Iomhar's voice: <Ìseal . . . We died there when the Mundoa first came . . . To be avenged for that would be pleasing . . . > but his voice was only echoed by a few of the other dead draoi in the anamacha, and Leagsaidh Moonshadow's voice was stronger and joined by more.

<No! This is your time, your moment . . . Strike the blow that must eventually be struck . . . Strike while you can . . . Do to the Mundoa what was done to those of the White Ships.> The plea warmed Voada despite the chill of the anamacha's presence. She could hear the ringing of heated metal being hammered into a sword, could see the glow hanging before her . . .

She shook away the image.

"I sympathize with what you've said, Magaidh, and your plan is well worth considering," Voada said. Magaidh smiled uncertainly at Voada, but her gaze was also on the anamacha of the Moonshadow. Voada wondered how she could tell them that while she understood, she didn't agree, without them thinking it was her anamacha speaking and not her.

For that matter, she wondered if she was entirely convinced of that herself.

"Unfortunately," Voada continued, "going south is exactly what Commander Savas expects us to do, because he would do the same if the situations were reversed . . . which is why I feel we can't follow that strategy."

"That makes no sense, Ceanndraoi," Maol said bluntly. "As Magaidh points out, we're days ahead of Savas. Even if he guessed exactly where we would go, he can't move quickly enough to reach us. The south *is* open to us. It's ours if we want it. We should take it while we can."

<*We agree . . .* > some of the voices in Voada's head clamored. But the Moonshadow's voice was prominent and compelling, and they went silent. <*No. We do* not *agree . . .* >

"As I told Magaidh, I hear you, and I sympathize, Ceannàrd." Maol's head cocked to one side, and his eyes narrowed, but Voada continued. "Yet . . . here's the problem with that plan, as I see it. You're all correct; Savas can't *stop* us should we go south, but he *will* send a ship flying to Emperor Pashtuk as soon as he learns that's the way we've turned. The message he'll send on that ship will tell the Emperor just how desperate the situation is for the Mundoa. Pashtuk will respond with more troops and more ships, and we'll be beset on *all* sides: from Savas' army to our north, the emperor's forces landing along the southern and eastern coasts, and the Storm Sea at our backs in the west. We'd be caught in a snare between them all, and even the power we draoi command and the troops we'll recruit from the Cateni wouldn't be able to withstand them. Eventually, we'd be caught and killed, and all resistance will collapse. Those of the northern clans who survive will flee across the Meadham and into the mountains again, and the Mundoa will rebuild their cities and their fortresses in Albann Deas. Only this time the walls will be taller and wider, more soldiers will be guarding them, and the Mundoan treatment of the Cateni will be harsher. Everything, *everything* that we've accomplished so far will be undone."

At the end of the statement, Voada paused, taking a deep breath. <*We must meet Savas now . . .* >

"We must meet Savas now," Voada said to them. "We must engage him now, while he's weak and while he's expecting us to run from him, not turn and meet him. We'll strike, and we'll crush him, and as Magaidh has suggested, all the Cateni will rise with us. The clans will once again hold Albann north and south, and if Pashtuk does bring another army here, we'll be waiting for him, strong and unified and ready."

She looked at each of them, holding their regard. She rose from her seat and moved away from her anamacha, not letting them touch her as she walked to where the trio was standing; Magaidh, at least, noticed that.

"You're my comrades and my friends: Maol, Magaidh, Comhnall. I want—no, I *need*—to make amends to each of you. I've seen that you worry about me. I've heard your concerns, and I understand them. And each of you has been right, at least partially. The Moonshadow's anamacha . . . it *has* been hard to stay in control of them, to keep the Moonshadow away from me. I was told by Greum Red-Hand and Menach Ceiteag how dangerous this anamacha can be, and I've learned that they were right. I've heard the Moonshadow's voice, and I've used her even though . . ."

Voada's voice broke. The anamacha moved toward her with those words, and Voada glared; the anamacha halted where it was. She gathered herself again. " . . . even though I shouldn't have. I don't intend to make that mistake again. But I'm still mostly the same person I was before I became a draoi. At least, I want to believe that. But I also know this: the responsibilities we've taken on, the battles that were thrust upon us and the battles we've begun, the deaths we've seen and the deaths we've caused, the terrible losses . . ."

She stopped, holding each of their gazes in turn and searching their faces for sympathy and understanding, uncertain of what it was she found there. "Those events have changed us all," she said finally, "and not always for the better. For the way I've treated you all because of that, I apologize. Especially to you, Magaidh," she said. "You have no idea how much I value your friendship and your advice."

"Then take the advice we gave," Magaidh answered. Voada could hear iron in the woman's voice.

Voada shook her head sadly. "I can't," she told Magaidh. "Not because you suggested it or Maol agreed, and not because the Moonshadow is making me say this, but because I simply don't believe it's best for us, and only one of us can lead the army we've gathered. So that's the question: am I the one who leads us, or aren't I? Magaidh? Comhnall?" Neither answered. Voada looked to Maol. "Ceannàrd?" she asked.

Maol remained silent, his lips pressed tightly together. He said nothing.

"Then we know what we'll do," Voada said to them. "Tell those you command to make ready. We go north and west to strike the head from the beast."

The town of Velimese sprawled along the lazy, swirling currents of the River Slaodach, the thatched roofs of its buildings like the warts on the back of a gigantic brown toad. Stormwind Road, the main west/east route in northern Albann Deas, originated in Gediz on the Storm Sea and passed through Velimese and Siran on the way to its intersection with the Great North Road near Trusa. Then it meandered northeast toward Pencraig, where it ended. Altan's forces approached Velimese cautiously.

The nagging harrying of Altan's army had continued as they'd proceeded eastward, but in the past few days, that annoyance had suddenly stopped. That alone was enough to make Altan uneasy. He'd sent a small advance party to Velimese the day before to consult with the town's Voice and arrange for reprovisioning and supplies. The party hadn't returned, which meant that the town must be approached with caution. Altan ordered Musa to spread out cohorts well to the north and south of the road, taking what they could from the farmlands they crossed, and to report if they met resistance.

The resistance became evident as they came within sight of the town. The road was blocked with fallen trees, and crude earthworks had been dug in a ragged arc to either side so that the war chariots could not easily pass. A small boulder was set at the end of the earthwork where it met the road. As Altan raised his hand to halt the advance short of easy arrow range, a man appeared on the earthworks alongside the boulder. His face was familiar, as was the armor he wore: the krug, the mirror armor of the Mundoa.

"Clansman MacÀidh," Altan called out as Tolga reined in the horses, who reared at their constraint. "I had hoped that you would have taken my warning to you more seriously. It appears you've ignored it."

"Aye, Commander Savas," the man shouted back. "I have, and we've done more besides. Were you hoping to meet with the Voice of Velimese? I'm afraid you won't find him particularly responsive." MacÀidh bent down and picked up the boulder next to him, and Altan realized that it wasn't a boulder but a head, which MacÀidh held by the hair. The man underhanded the gory thing toward Altan. It hit the bare earth of the road and rolled, stopping with its face and open mouth toward them. "There's your Voice of Velimese, Commander. Go ahead and talk to him if you'd like. But he's a rather quiet fellow now."

A sad anger built in Altan, and he closed his eyes before he spoke. "I gave you your life back once, Clansman MacÀidh. That isn't going to happen a second time. Not now."

"Is that supposed to frighten me, Commander? It doesn't."

"Then you're even more a fool than I believed you to be," Altan answered. He gestured, and the archers behind the war chariots loosed arrows as MacÀidh scrambled down from the embankment. "Go right," Altan shouted to Musa, then told his driver, Tolga, "Left!" Tolga lashed at the warhorses, and both he and Altan raised shields as arrows began to shower down from beyond the embankment. Half the war chariots and mounted soldiers followed Altan; the other half went with Musa. All of them raced around the arc of the earthen barricade as the officers of the infantry allowed the javelin-throwers to advance and hurl their weapons, then fall back through the formation as they urged their men forward along the road and over the embankment. Altan hung onto the chariot's rail as Tolga turned sharply around the end of the mounded dirt.

Beyond it, he could see a few hundred men and women: some arrayed in armor and weapons obviously taken from the town's garrison and the Voice's guards, others simply waving axes, scythes, and other farm implements or improvised weapons. Altan shook his head. *This is a rabble, not an army.* There were no lines, no formations. There was no discipline to the mob, no officers shouting orders and directing their defense. Already, the field just behind the embankment was chaotic and bloody, with Altan's soldiers hewing at the Cateni like they were a wheat field ready to be harvested. Altan could see the defenders already buckling, a few of those to the rear already dropping their weapons to flee.

This will be over quickly.

Altan's gaze found MacÀidh, mounted on a war steed, a horse that Altan recognized as that of one of the envoys he'd sent to the Voice. The realization made the anger flare even more in Altan's mind. He tapped Tolga on the shoulder and pointed at MacÀidh when the driver glanced back, thinking as he did so that this was something Lucian would have already done without words or contact. Lucian would simply have *known.* Tolga nodded and shouted to the horses. The chariot tore mud and grass from the ground as it surged forward, as Altan plucked a spear from the holder. MacÀidh's attention was on the melee in front of him; his head turned belatedly as Altan's chariot rushed toward him, as Altan hefted the spear and threw it. It struck the man with all the power of Altan's arm and the speed of the chariot. Altan couldn't see whether the blade had penetrated the man's krug, but the impact of the weapon knocked him from his horse, which reared white-eyed and galloped away.

Under Tolga's direction, MacÀidh's body was trampled under the hooves of the warhorses and the iron-clad wheels of the chariot. As the chariot lifted, Altan leaped from the car, drawing his sword. With a single, savage stroke and a cry of victory, he struck MacÀidh's head from his shoulders. He caught it as it fell and lifted it high, still shouting. Blood dripped heavily from the ruins of the man's neck.

The nearest defenders, seeing what Altan held, now broke entirely, and the battle turned to rout, the Cateni retreating as the war chariots and mounted soldiers cut them down and the infantry pursued them.

There were no Cateni left alive on the field when Altan returned to Tolga and his chariot and rode into Velimese.

The quartet of scouts Altan had sent out from Velimese returned at a gallop to the night's encampment between Velimese and Siran three days later, their horses lathered with foam and nearly dead from a hard ride. The news from Siran was better than Altan had hoped; the Cateni there had also rebelled, but the Voice and his garrison had been able to subdue the insurrection and kill the leaders. Siran was still in Mundoan hands, but Trusa . . . "From what we heard, Trusa has been burned to the ground," the scouts told him. "Everyone is saying that Great-Voice Vadim was killed, that Ceanndraoi Voada executed him."

"And now her forces have turned south," Altan said, anticipating what they would tell him. *The south is undefended and open to their ravages, and the Cateni there are ready to rise with them.*

But the scouts were shaking their heads, dissolving the thought. "No, Commander. They haven't gone south. They're on the march toward Siran. Toward us." All the scouts nodded, their faces pale and serious. "We saw them, Commander. They . . . they fill the land. More of them than can be counted. Far more than we have with us."

After questioning the scouts further, Altan dismissed them. Around him, the camp was bustling as tents were taken down and stored in the dawn light. They were surrounded by low hills and forest draped in tendrils of fog. He might have found the sight idyllic and meditative, coming upon it at some other time. Not now. He turned to Musa, whose scarred face was twisted into a scowl. "Not south?" Altan grunted. "Why? The southern cities were theirs for the taking, unprotected."

Musa shrugged. "The draoi bitch Voada is overconfident. That's

fine with me. So we go and meet them. I'll look forward to that;
we can pay them back for all that they've done. Look at the buffoons we just routed."

The sun was rising above the haze, promising a warm day,
though Altan saw clouds massing behind them in the west—he
suspected it would be raining by the time they stopped again. To
the east, the sky was blue and open, as if nothing troubling
awaited them there.

"You're wrong about that, Musa. The ceanndraoi and ceannàrd,
so many of the àrds of the northern clans, the draoi with them . . .
Those aren't buffoons and rabble; they're true warriors who will
make the battle far more difficult than Velimese."

"We've faced them already. We would have taken Onglse had
we stayed, Commander," Musa answered.

"Would we have?" Altan bit his upper lip, shaking his head.
"Maybe we would have—but our victory would have been because
those two abandoned the Red-Hand. Maol Iosa, Voada: they were
the most powerful foes we faced there, and we didn't make significant progress until they left." He didn't mention to Musa the fact that
Voada had offered them peace, at least in his dream. "Who knows,
maybe that was the Cateni's plan all along—to keep us occupied in
Onglse while those two left, gathered the northern clans, and crossed
the Meadham. If so, that was a masterful tactical stroke, and if I'd
followed Great-Voice's orders, it'd be you or Ilkur facing the ceanndraoi and ceannàrd with only half of the cohorts at your back.
Still . . ." Altan sighed. "If they'd gone south, we could have peti-
tioned the Emperor to send troops across the Barrier Sea and caught
the ceanndraoi in a vise. Now there isn't time. We'll face her and the
ceannàrd, and if we lose, there'll be no stopping them at all."

Tolga approached them, bearing Altan's armor for the day's
journey. "Musa," Altan said, "I want you to choose two fast riders
to send back to Gediz; we need to know where Ilkur is. Tolga, I
need my field desk, parchment, and pen; I have messages to write
that will go with the riders . . ."

31

The Gathering Storm

VOADA'S ARMY RODE THROUGH a land that seemed strangely empty. All the tiny villages they passed through appeared to have been recently abandoned. No one seemed to be watching them, though their ranks continued to swell with Cateni volunteers from the countryside. Voada could hear Maol grumbling about their lack of military skills and discipline, but he had Comhnall Mac Tsagairt and the officers drilling and teaching them as the army made its slow way along the Stormwind Road toward Siran, the next significant city.

And while Maol continued to have Voada ride in his war chariot with Hùisdean driving, he spent more time now riding with Àrd Mac Tsagairt and talking with him. His discontent with Voada's decision to press the battle with Commander Savas was obvious, even as the voices of her anamacha consoled her, telling her that this was the proper strategy and the only way to victory.

<*We must finish this now . . . If we wait, you'll only have more Mundoan troops to face, and both Albann Deas and Albann Bràghad will be lost . . .* >

Those voices felt right. Listening to them eased the fears in her head. She consoled her fears with the thought that they were only saying what she believed herself, that she wasn't the Moonshadow's puppet but was actually following her own heart.

As they passed through yet another empty village, the army flowing around and through it like a swarm of bees, Magaidh came to ride alongside Voada. "It seems that all the Mundoa have fled before us, and many of the Cateni as well. Even the sheep and cows are gone."

"Or they've been hidden away so we don't eat them," Voada answered. Magaidh gave a short laugh that collapsed quickly, and they rode on for a time in silence. Voada could sense that Magaidh wanted to say more but was holding back. She kept looking over toward Voada with her lips pressed tightly together, yet her gaze was sympathetic and open. "What is it you're thinking, Magaidh?" Voada finally asked her over the creaking of the chariot's wheels, the plodding of the warhorses' hooves, and the general clamor of the army's march. The dust they raised coated their cloaks; Voada could taste it, gritty, on her tongue. "Tell me. As a friend."

Magaidh dropped her gaze, then lifted it up again. "You already know, Ceanndraoi."

"Tell me again, then."

"It's the Moonshadow . . ." Her voice trailed off, her gaze dropping once more.

"You think I'm no longer in control?" Voada could feel the chill of her anamacha, invisible against the sun's glare but very close to her. She could almost hear their voices.

"Not that." The answer came hurriedly, with a widening of Magaidh's eyes. "I've told you this before, in Trusa. I worry about you, Ceanndraoi. I worry because I care about you, because you've been a good friend to me and you've given me and shown me so much. I don't want to see you hurt or . . . lost."

Voada gestured toward the road before them. "So you think that none of this is my idea? You think that I'm following the Moonshadow's commands?"

Voada could see Magaidh's reluctance to answer that. The young woman swallowed hard once, then again, looking somewhere past Voada's left shoulder as if the answer might be written in the empty air there. "I can't know that, Ceanndraoi. Only you can answer that. But I thought . . . I know I heard the power of the Moonshadow when you spoke outside Trusa. I heard you speak of 'we,' not 'I.' Ceannàrd Iosa heard that as well, and Comhnall. Others, too, I suspect. We all care for you, we all love you, and we worry."

The anamacha's chilly presence pressed into Voada's spine. She heard their voices, and among them that of the Moonshadow. *<How can you allow her to insult us this way . . . ? She doesn't know us . . . How can she call you 'friend' when she doesn't believe you . . . ?>* An empathetic anger rose up inside Voada as the voices continued to rail, but she forced it back down, pushed the voices away from her and closed off her mind to the otherworld so that the anamacha retreated to only a whisper.

She could see that Magaidh was half anticipating a biting reply, but Voada forced herself to smile, hoping that it appeared at least somewhat genuine. "Magaidh, my friend. Understand this: my decisions, right or wrong, are only my own, and that's the truth. Yes, I called on my anamacha to strengthen my voice, and yes, it was Leagsaidh Moonshadow's ghost that I used. And it's also true that she would have made the same decision I have, were she standing here instead of me. *But I control my anamacha.* I use them, not the reverse. I appreciate your concern as I appreciate your friendship and your support, but you're worrying for nothing." She paused, then made an effort to laugh. "And you may tell your husband to relay that message to the ceannàrd as well. The Moonshadow hasn't yet driven me insane."

Voada held out her hand to Magaidh, who took it, grasping it gently. The corner of Magaidh's lips turned up tentatively. "That's good to hear."

Voada returned the smile as Magaidh's hand fell away, but she found herself reaching for the silver oak leaf that hung around her neck. *If Meir hadn't died, or if Voice Kadir and Voice-wife Dilara had been more understanding when he died and had left Orla, Hakan, and me to live in peace, I wouldn't be here. I only wanted my family; I didn't want to lead an army, I didn't want to tear down the Mundoa or kill the Great-Voice. I would have been content with my lot, content to play with my grandchildren when they came. But they wouldn't let that happen.*

With those thoughts, she felt the touch of her anamacha again. <*If, if, if . . . We almost chose differently . . .* >

What do you mean? Voada asked the voices. *Who would you have chosen?*

Cold laughter answered her. <*It's too late now . . . And if we had not come to you, you would be dead and rotting in the earth . . . The past is unchangeable; only the future can be shaped . . . We want the same future . . . We are your future . . . We are one . . . One . . .* >

"No." Voada only realized she'd spoken aloud when Magaidh glanced sharply at her. She might have responded, but her anamacha was still with her, Magh da Chèo overlaying her own world. The bleak, sterile landscape was full of images of past draoi who crowded around her, reaching out for her, grasping her. She tried to push them away, but they held her more tightly than before, and the chorus supporting the Moonshadow's voice roared in her head. <*We have given you the power . . . You are our instrument; we are not yours . . . The Cateni may shout your name afterward, but it is we who will make your victory possible . . .* >

"No," Voada said again, more forcefully. "I made the decision. It was mine, and it was right. And I wield the power. You have no choice in the matter."

More amusement roared in her head, echoing in the stormy air of the otherworld. Voada tried to shove her anamacha away again, and this time it retreated, the laughter slowly fading and the real world snapping back into focus around her.

Magaidh was staring at her, fear and sympathy in her eyes. On the harness of the chariot, Hùisdean was also looking back over his shoulder at her, his dark eyes narrowed. Magaidh, Voada knew, had sensed the anamacha's presence within her, would have felt it moving even if she couldn't see it in the daylight. Voada held Magaidh's stare.

"I'm fine," she told her. "You see, I cast out the anamacha. I didn't let them hold me. They obey me, those within. With Elia's help—and yours, Magaidh—we'll have a victory, and all of Albann will be ours again, as it should be."

"Yes, Ceanndraoi," Magaidh answered, her voice careful. "With Elia's help. And should you need mine for any reason, know that I'll be there for you. Always."

Voada smiled at her and touched her face with her hand. "You're worrying about nothing," Voada told her. "We're fine."

<We're fine . . . We're fine . . . > The words seemed to echo, frigid and isolated.

Altan rode into Siran to huzzahs from the Mundoan populace and sullen, resentful glances from the Cateni. Armed and mail-clad guards were prominent on the streets, patrolling in groups of three or four. The town appeared to be ready for a siege, with earthen ramparts raised in a broken circle around the central town structures.

The Voice of Siran was a nervous, slight man of middle age with a much younger wife and a gaggle of children. Altan spent a quick luncheon assuring the Voice that he didn't need to send his family out into the country just yet, nor did he need to imprison or execute the Hand of Siran for the fact that he was Cateni (". . . but he is a distant cousin of this Ceanndraoi Voada"). He informed the man that the army would encamp well outside Siran as long as the Voice could promise that sufficient provisions would be sent to the troops who were protecting him, and afterward Altan rode out with Musa and a small company of soldiers to survey the land just east of the village.

"Here," Altan said a few turns of the glass later, raising his hand to halt the others. They had come down the main road through a wood, entering a narrow defile between two steep-sided and wooded hills. Ahead of them were two large, long meadows flanking the road, rising and spreading out well to either side as they climbed the next rise toward another forest a good two turns of the glass away on foot. "This is where we'll wait for them."

Musa made a grumbling dissent. "We don't have the heights here, Commander," he said. "The Cateni will be above us."

"Which will make them feel comfortable and overconfident," Altan told him. His hand swept across the landscape, already seeing the ghostly shape of the coming battle in his head. "They have the advantage of numbers. The rise to either side will funnel them down before they can reach us—that will take away their advantage in numbers. With the woods and the defile at our backs, they can't swing around to outflank us and attack from the rear, and in a frontal attack, they can't bring more warriors to us than we can bring to them at the same time."

Musa scowled and squinted outward, as if trying to see what Altan was seeing. "Commander, they don't have the discipline of our troops. This witch-woman doesn't have your experience or your knowledge, and Ceannàrd Iosa might be brave, but he's only one man. The Cateni who have come to them here aren't properly trained or equipped. These numbers that worry you aren't—"

Altan cut him off with a raised finger. "The mistake we've all made too often is thinking of the Cateni as an undisciplined mob. I made the same mistake the first time I met them in battle, back when I first came here."

The memories of that battle three hands of years ago—the first time, as a young cohort officer, he'd been asked to lead his cohort on a mission—were seared into Altan's memory. Ordered to lead his troops across the River Meadham to punish a clan that had raided a Mundoan-controlled town, he'd expected an easy victory—he had a group of disciplined soldiers, and the clan's tactics seemed chaotic. Instead, he'd found that men in formal ranks on foot could do little against the furious charge of Cateni war chariots or against an enemy fighting on ground it knew far better than he. The chariots had torn his initial formation to shreds, and the àrd against whom he was fighting retreated into a tight valley between high hills. When Altan pursued, hidden archers suddenly poured arrow fire down on them. Altan had won the battle through luck and his grudging decision to abandon the normal Mundoan battle tactics, but even so, half the cohort hadn't returned across the Meadham with him. Since that experience, Altan had adapted many of the clans' tactics for his own use: their chariots—faster and more maneuverable than those the Mundoa used at the time; their use of the land itself to shape the battle; being willing to attack from hidden positions . . .

"My failure to think of the Cateni as worthy opponents was a mistake that cost far too many Mundoan lives, and it's not something I intend to repeat. Yes, many of the people with the ceanndraoi and ceannàrd are untrained and poorly armed and armored—just farmers and servants and slaves. But they also have a large core of trained and seasoned warriors from the northern clans and draoi trained at Onglse, and those . . ." Altan shook his head. "We can't take them lightly, Musa, not if we want to win this battle. We need to hear from Ilkur. He should have received my orders and marched out from Gediz by now. We need to know how far away he is—I want you to send riders out in search of him as soon as we get back to Siran. And as for meeting the ceanndraoi's army . . ." He paused, looking around the landscape once more, seeing it overlaid with cavalry, chariots, and infantry as well as the smoke and fire from the spells of the draoi. He could hear it, hear the screams of soldiers dying and the clash of weapons, and too many of the dead and wounded he saw on the ground in his vision wore the krug of the Mundoa.

He closed his eyes to banish the scene.

"It must be here," he said. "Here or nowhere. We'll ride back to Sivas and draw up our plans with the officers of the cohorts. This is where we'll meet them, and this is where we'll either defeat them or fall ourselves."

32

The Battle of Síran

THE TWO HANDS OF outriders came hurrying back to the vanguard of the army, pulling their horses to a halt at the banner of the ceanndraoi and the ceannàrd and giving both Voada and Maol Iosa a salute. "Savas is waiting just over that ridge," one of them said, pointing to the summit of the green-cloaked hill that the road ascended. "We lost two of our own to Mundoan arrows when we came across a group of their scouts in the woods along the ridge, though we killed several of them as well. Still, we saw the entire Mundoan army in the valley beyond, encamped just before a forest. They haven't even taken the high ground of the ridge. We'll be able to sweep down on them from above, and our archers will have the greater range."

"They have far fewer soldiers than we do ceanndraoi, Ceannàrd," another proclaimed. "I think we may be nearly two to every one of them." The others nodded agreement. Voada smiled at the news, glancing at Maol, who was nodding.

"Go to the cook wagons and refresh yourselves," Maol told the outriders. "Then go out to either side of the ridge—I want to know if they have cohorts out on their flanks waiting for our approach. Be more careful this time. Don't make contact with them if you can avoid it—just find out where they are. I don't want any more of you lost. Report back to me by nightfall. Now go . . ."

He waved; the outriders saluted again and galloped off to the rear, where the wagons rumbled slowly forward.

"If this is true . . ." Voada began.

"Then we may prevail here," Maol interjected. "And I'll have to admit that you chose the right path for us." His scarred face slowly slipped into a grin. "Will you expect a formal apology from me, Ceanndraoi?"

Voada laughed. "Hardly. I could have done none of this without you, Maol. We'd both still be in Onglse with the Red-Hand and a much smaller number of warriors fighting with us while we try to keep this same army from taking Bàn Cill. That would have been a hopeless task, and I think we would have failed."

Maol gave a quick laugh, then his face went serious once more as he stared at the ridge. "No matter what, this won't be a simple battle. I know Savas too well. If he's encamped, then he's comfortable and satisfied with the field he's chosen, and he'll have set everything up to his advantage. The scouts our outriders say they met will have already informed him of where we are, how we're arrayed, and how many we are, just as we know their numbers. The man's not a fool, and he's deft with strategy."

"And you're no fool either, and the better tactician when the battle actually starts."

He nodded again. "We'll soon find out whether that's the truth, won't we? When the riders come back this evening, we'll make our final plans. We'll camp on the ridge summit this evening, and if all goes well, we'll attack in the morning."

"Sir," Musa said, entering the open flap of Altan's tent and giving a brief tap of his fist to his krug as the guards there stepped aside. "The scouts have returned. They met a small group of Cateni scouts in the woods along the ridge; they lost a man but claim they killed at least a hand of the Cateni riders in the melee and sent the rest fleeing back down the far side of the rise. They tell me that the Cateni main force is approaching quickly. They'll be here before nightfall at their current pace. I expect they'll camp on the ridge, taking the high ground as you anticipated."

Altan was seated at a camp table with Tolga across from him. Tolga had brought him a flagon of wine from the cook, and Altan had opened it, pouring them both a measure. Altan lifted the flagon toward Musa in invitation. "No thank you, Commander." Altan saw Musa's gaze flick over toward the driver, then back to Altan. Musa kept his face carefully neutral; he had known of Altan and Lucian's relationship, and it was obvious that he suspected Altan had taken Tolga to his bed, but this wasn't the time to tell the man how badly he was mistaken.

"Is there any news of Ilkur?" Altan asked.

Musa silently shook his head, and Altan sighed.

"Then we'll hope to hear of him tonight yet," he said. "And I'll hope he understood the message I left him. Tomorrow, then, will bring the battle. Are you ready, my friend?"

Musa sniffed. "I'm eager for it, Commander, and so are the troops after what they've heard of Trusa."

"Have you heard from your family there, Musa?"

Musa shook his head. His complexion darkened further. "No, Commander. Nothing. I can only hope they fled the city before the Cateni arrived. And your parents, your cousins?"

Altan shrugged. "As with you, I've had no news of them, but given the upheaval in Albann Deas, that's only to be expected. In the silence, at least we can still have hope."

Musa sniffed. "So many lost or made homeless, and the barbaric insult of what they did to the Great-Voice . . . It's time we deal with these upstarts and show them the points of our spears and the edges of our swords. It's time we began to pay them back."

"Likely you'll have that chance with the sun tomorrow. In the meantime, go and get what rest you can. Tomorrow there'll be no chance."

Musa nodded, saluted, and left. The guards outside closed the tent flaps after him. Altan glanced over to Tolga.

"You told Musa to rest," Tolga said with a smile. "Are you intending to follow your own advice, Commander?"

"Eventually," Altan told the man. "After I've decided the battle formations for tomorrow. But you should retire. I'll expect to see you at first light to help with my armor."

"Sir, if you want me to stay . . ." Tolga managed a small smile with the unsubtle invitation. Altan didn't return the gesture. It was difficult to resist the temptation to respond angrily. *Do you think that my feelings for Lucian were nothing more than base lust? That all I need is a body to fill the void his loss has left in me? Are you that shallow and foolish?*

But he said none of it. He only looked away from his driver. "You'll help me with my armor at first light, Tolga," he repeated. "And please make certain the horses have been properly fed and groomed before you retire."

Altan watched impassively as Tolga drained his wine chalice and rose, disappointment on his face. "As you wish, Commander," he said.

Voada, Maol Iosa, Magaidh, and Comhnall Mac Tsagairt walked in the bright moonlight to where the Stormwind Road emerged from the forest and crested the ridge. They looked down the long open meadow of the slope to the valley still a long march away, where myriad yellow stars marked the Mundoan camp. Voada glanced back through the trees and down the eastern slope to their own encampment, where an entirely different and larger collection of stars gleamed at the point where the road began its climb. Maol evidently noticed her glance, for he cleared his throat, his voice low and husky in the night. "Numbers don't always matter. Look at how he's placed his troops in that cut. What do you think, Comhnall?"

"If he met us on open ground, his line would be too short and thin; we'd be able to flank him and get behind the lines. See how the woods close in and the land rises on either side as we'd approach their front? He's using that to shorten our line so we can't all get to him at once or outflank him. Clever."

Maol nodded. "Exactly. You have to admire a military mind like that."

"Can we send some of our troops to circle around him and attack from the rear?" Magaidh asked. "Or could we bypass Savas entirely and take the town of Siran while he's waiting for us here?"

"Either of those choices would cost us days," Comhnall answered. "The hills become higher and steeper as we go west. The ridgeline's long here, and Stormwind Road crosses at its lowest point. We couldn't get our chariots or wagons over the slopes and through these woods; we'd be strung out and easy for archers to pick off. There's no element of surprise in that, and there's no advantage in taking the town just to delay this battle. No."

"Your husband's right," Maol told Magaidh. "Savas has picked his spot, and he'll wait for us there, knowing we must meet him, try to go around, or retreat."

"So you're saying we shouldn't attack?" Voada asked. "We should turn tail and go south, as you suggested back in Trusa?" She couldn't entirely keep the irritation from her voice. She saw her anamacha stir and move closer to her. This wasn't what she wanted; it wasn't what *they* wanted. To come so far and stop just when a final victory was so close . . . The touch of the anamacha was cold. She could hear their voices echoing her own thoughts. <No . . . We will not accept that . . . We cannot . . . >

"No," she heard Maol say through her rising anger, through the storming of the otherworld and the massed protest of the dead draoi there. "A funnel can be a trap for both sides. It restricts the Mundoa's movements as much as it does ours. Think of what you draoi can do; Savas won't be easily able to escape what you rain down on him." Maol grinned. "I think we have them exactly where we want them, Voada."

The ceannàrd looked over the valley, nodding as if enjoying what he saw. Voada heard him sniff the air. "This night will bring mist, and we should have the draoi send rain and storms with it to remind Savas who he faces. Ceanndraoi, why not bring some of them forward to start their spells now? Make their night a misery and their camp a muddy swamp. Burn their tents with lightning. And with the morning, we'll show them what the Cateni do to those who would steal our land, our towns, and our people. Does that sound satisfactory to you, Ceanndraoi?"

Voada could feel the surge of exultation from her anamacha. "Aye," she told them, all of them. "That's exactly what we'll do."

"Damn the draoi," Altan cursed. "And may our sihirki boil forever in the caves of Pamukkale for being unable to end the draoi's spells."

It had been a long, awful, and miserable night. Altan doubted that anyone had slept much at all. The draoi sent rain and storms down upon them, with lightning that ripped open tents and killed and injured men in their bedrolls. According to the reports the officers had sent him, at least half a full cohort of soldiers had been killed, and twice that many had been injured, most of them badly enough that they were unfit to fight and had been sent to the rear of the lines. Morale among the soldiers in the wake of the uproar and casualties had sunk, and that worried Altan more than the loss of soldiers.

The newly risen sun struggled to illuminate the battleground through the clouds and mist. Altan's boots were already heavy with caked mud, and the draoi-caused downpour quickly soaked his cloak and ran in an unending stream down his polished krug. The rain beat its uneven rhythm on his helmet and the floor of his chariot as the torrent continued to sluice down from low, dark clouds that hid the ridgeline ahead entirely. The air smelled of burning oilcloth. Altan knew that up where the Cateni troops were already gathering, there was no storm at all, according to what the men he'd sent forward had told him.

"News, Musa?" he asked as Musa's chariot came forward to where Altan waited, spewing clods of mud from its wheels and from the hooves of his warhorses.

Musa shook his head. "Nothing yet, Commander," he said.

Altan grimaced but remained silent. Ahead on the chariot's yoke, Tolga tightened his grip on the reins of their steeds, who were restless in the hammering rain. Altan had ordered that long sharpened stakes be set in the ground facing the hill to slow the charge of chariots and mounted warriors; that artificial, leafless forest bristled in front of them at the narrowest part of the valley. Behind the stakes, the cohorts were arrayed with archers placed among them, their own cavalry and war chariots set to either wing. The army filled the defile; the Cateni wouldn't be able to bring their full lines to bear on them, and reinforcements could be brought up quickly from the rear if they threatened to break through.

Altan's army was as ready as it could be, and if the damned rain would stop . . . he scowled upward, narrowing his eyes against the sheeting downpour. He thought the clouds were breaking apart, but that may have been only wishful thinking.

They all heard a shout from within the mist, and the distant chanting of the draoi halted at the same time. From the murk, a Cateni war chariot appeared, dim and gray through the foul weather. "Altan Savas!" someone roared in challenge from the Cateni chariot, which was still well up the slope at the edge of arrow range. "Come meet me! Let us see who's the better! Or send out your champion! Let's finally meet like true warriors!"

Altan knew the voice, even if he couldn't see the face because of the distance, the rain, and the general gloom. "Maol Iosa . . ." He sighed.

"The Cateni are nothing if not predictable," Musa grunted. "And rather tiresome. Should I have the archers send him away as we did on Onglse?"

"If they think they can hit the man. But I don't want you going out there to meet him; I know you're tempted, Musa, but I need you here."

Musa sniffed, saluted, and wheeled away. Altan stared outward as Iosa continued to shout his mocking challenge toward the Mundoan line: "What, are you all cowards? Are none of you brave enough to come out and fight me? Are you all afraid? Are you all like Great-Voice Vadim, cowering like frightened children? Then we'll do to you what we did to your precious great-voice. Commander Savas, the crow-plucked eye sockets of your head will end up on a spear, staring blindly at the ruin of your army. Come out if you think you can defeat me!"

The ceannàrd wheeled closer, near enough that Altan could see the gleam of the torc around his neck. The rain was now only a drizzle, and the clouds were slowly clearing in the steady wind. Altan could see that the ceannàrd was alone in his chariot except for the driver, so Ceanndraoi Voada was probably still with the rest of the draoi on the ridge. Iosa's war chariot hurtled across the front of the Mundoan line, the ceannàrd pounding on his blue-streaked, unarmored chest as he screamed his challenge, standing spread-legged and balanced in the chariot's car without holding onto the rails even as the vehicle bounced over the uneven ground. Altan had to shake his head in admiration; he certainly couldn't deny the bravery and ferocity of the Cateni, even if he found their tactics undisciplined. Part of him—like Musa—yearned to respond to the challenge, to ride out in his own chariot and meet the man directly, warrior to warrior, and see which of them would emerge as victor.

He understood the lure of testing one's bravery one-on-one against a worthy opponent.

But he couldn't do that, as much as he wanted it, as much as his own blood boiled at the taunts this man hurled at him.

As Iosa reached the center of the line once more, the bow-strings of the Mundoan archers sang percussively as a flock of arrows rose. Iosa's driver raised his shield, and Iosa took up his own as the barrage fell. The majority of them fell just short of or behind the moving chariot, but many struck the shields, the wooden rails, and the chariot's floor.

Iosa howled with derisive laughter, flinging down his shield. "Then cower away, Savas! Stay behind your men and let them die uselessly for you. We'll force you to fight in the end! We are coming for you! Your doom is already set." With that, his driver turned

the chariot hard, and the horses galloped away up the hill toward
the misty ridge. The wan sun shone on the ceannàrd's arrow-
feathered shield sitting mockingly near the line of stakes atop the
trampled, rain-slick grass.

Altan knew that the grass would soon become a field of blood-
stained mud, littered with bodies and fallen weapons.

He hoped that most of those bodies would be Cateni, but he
feared that wouldn't be the case.

Maol was grinning when he arrived back at the ridge. "They're
soaked and miserable and as cowardly as ever," he told Voada and
the others gathered there. "You should have seen the terror in the
eyes of their front line as I rode up and down in front of them. It's
time. Ceanndraoi, will you ride with me again?"

Voada nodded. She went to his chariot, and he extended his
hand to pull her up. "And our attack formation?" Àrd Mac Tsagairt
asked Maol. Magaidh was already in her husband's chariot, lashing herself to the rails.

"Let the draoi who wish to do so ride with the chariots and
prepare their spells as we ride down," Maol answered. "We'll need
spells to clear the stakes they've placed against our chariots and
mounted warriors. Once those are gone, we'll have the archers
send in a volley, and we'll follow behind to charge frontally: first
the chariots and cavalry, then those on foot. Their line will break
quickly," he said confidently, "and we need to be prepared to face
their own chariots and cavalry. Savas has set them to either side,
waiting. This battle will be over by the time the sun is overhead."

"Let me first talk to our people," Voada told Maol. "Hùisdean,"
she said to the driver, "hold here a moment."

Voada turned and faced the Cateni troops gathered on the ridgeline. She let her gaze travel over them: men and women alike, all
clutching their weapons, clad in whatever armor they had or had
recovered from the fallen. At the very summit of the ridge, just
beyond the massed warriors, the wagons had been set with wheels

chocked, the horses unhooked from their yokes so that the Cateni could ride them into battle. The faces of children and the elderly peered out from the wagons.

Voada let her anamacha slip into her. The Moonshadow remained silent and hidden; she found Iomhar easily and took the energy he offered, using it to carry her voice to the gathered warriors.

"This," she said, her voice echoing, "is not the first time that the Cateni have been led into battle by a woman. But I didn't come to boast of a long line of ancestry, nor to recover a kingdom or the plundered wealth of my family. I take to the field like the least among you: to press the cause of liberty, to avenge the fact that our freedom was taken from us, and to avenge my own scourged and lost family. Pride and arrogance are all that are sacred to the Mundoa. In their minds, all Cateni are subject to violation; old and young alike endure the lash of slavery, and our virgins are deflowered. But Elia's day—and that of all Her children—is now at hand.

"A Mundoan army *dares* to await us just below." Voada pointed down the slope to where they could just make out the line of the Mundoan army in the fading mist, in the growing sunlight. "They will pay for their rashness with their lives. Those few of them who will survive the carnage of this day, who are now cowering, poorly hidden behind their entrenchments, are thinking of nothing but how to save themselves with ignominious, cowardly flight. From the din of our preparations and the shouts that you will send toward them in just a few breaths, the Mundoa will shrink back with terror. Look around you and view our numbers. Behold our proud display of warlike spirit. Consider why each of you has come here to draw your avenging sword. On this spot, here and now, we must either conquer or die with glory. There is no alternative. My resolution is fixed: I will go down now to meet them. The rest of you, if you please, may leave now and live in bondage, or you can ride with me for Elia and Cateni. What do you say?"

A great shout erupted from the massed throats of the army. Maol answered as well, his voice sounding thin next to the memory of Voada's. "We fight for Elia and the Cateni," he cried, and they echoed the line back to him, so loudly that Voada felt the impact in her chest.

"For Elia and the Cateni!"

Even the souls captured in her anamacha echoed the shout. Even the Moonshadow. *Especially* the Moonshadow.

"Now!" Voada roared. And with that, the army surged down the ridge toward the waiting Mundoa.

The Mundoa heard them coming before they saw them: a cacophony louder than the fierce thunderstorms of the night before. A shrieking, howling monster was descending from the ridge, dark and huge and multi-armed, resolving slowly into a many-bodied creature spreading out over the fields to either side of Stormwind Road. Altan, in his chariot atop a small hill behind the front lines, could see the Mundoan ranks visibly shudder in response to seeing the onrushing, clamorous wave of the assault. "Hold!" he cried to them. "Hold! Bannermen, alert the archers!"

Flags began to wave around Altan in response, but well before the Cateni line reached the range of the archers, the draoi launched their initial spells. From the lead chariot rushing down the Stormwind Road in the middle of their formation—Ceannàrd Iosa's chariot, Altan was fairly certain, with Ceanndraoi Voada riding with him—a huge gout of fire went hurtling ahead, slamming first into the field of stakes so that the wood erupted and turned to ash, then tumbling forward into the lines of infantry beyond. Screams and cries filled the air from those burned and injured; the dead simply fell. Altan saw a terrible, huge hole open in the first phalanx. Officers shouted for reinforcements to move forward into the gap, but the soldiers had to climb over the smoking dead and wounded to replace the line, and they were slow to move.

Other spells followed: at least a hand more, though none as powerful or as destructive as the ceanndraoi's. The Mundoan lines were shifting uneasily, their discipline falling away, and Altan shouted at them even as he heard Musa's roar ordering them to reform their ranks. Another spell erupted from Iosa's chariot as it approached the range of the archers. A swarm of arrows filled the air, but an unnatural wind hurled them back, and Mundoan shields snapped up as the deadly rain from their own weapons turned against them.

With a gut-wrenching sound of horses, swords, javelins, and armor all crashing together, the Cateni line slammed into the Mundoan phalanxes with a shock that rippled all the way back to Altan, the horses of his chariot rearing up even as Tolga tried desperately to regain control of them. "Cavalry!" Altan shouted to his bannermen, and they waved their flags to signal the chariots and mounted warriors on either side of the formation to begin their own attacks, closing in like a pincer on the crowded, narrowing field of battle.

In descriptions of war that Altan had heard from the poets and orators, the great battles between large armies always seemed clean and ordered. It sounded as if the commanders moved their phalanxes and cohorts like pieces in the Cateni game called *fidh-cheall*, in which the figures of warriors, druids, forts, and chariots slid about on a checkered board, trying to surround and capture the enemy emperor.

That description was entirely unlike any battle Altan had ever experienced. Battles—no matter how carefully the commander had choreographed the expected movements, feints, and charges beforehand—were noisy, chaotic, and messy affairs, and even the commander on a hill behind his army couldn't see the overall picture, only small flashes of it. The view became worse when one was an active part of the battle; the world constricted to the soldiers in front of you, who were doing their best to kill you as you attempted to kill them. There was no overall sense of whether the battle was going well or ill. Everything came down to simple individual survival, not a grand victory or inglorious defeat.

The song of victory or defeat was left to the poets to compose afterward.

From the hill, Altan could only glimpse tiny figures struggling against each other, his view increasingly obscured by the smoky remnants of draoi and sihirki spells that drifted over the field. He could hear the faint clash of metal and the shouts and screams of Mundoan soldiers and Cateni warriors. On one side of the field, Musa's banner flew, but Altan could see that the sub-commander was surrounded by the enemy and fighting for his very life.

Runners came hurrying up the field toward him, bearing snippets of news. Altan found himself increasingly restless. Below him, the hole that the Cateni had torn into the center of his forces widened into a gaping chasm as the enemy continued to push forward. The cavalry advance from the sides of the field was being held back by the crush of Cateni warriors on foot, wielding lances and pikes to tear the riders from their mounts or chariots and to impale onrushing warhorses. The sihirki, for all their clamoring, were useless against the far more effective and quicker spells of the Cateni draoi.

Altan didn't like what he saw, and the reports continued to become more dire and urgent.

"Commander?" Tolga asked, looking back over his shoulder, the muscles in his arms standing out from the effort of holding the warhorses. Altan wanted to tell him to charge into the fray, to take him down to meet Ceannàrd Maol Iosa and Ceanndraoi Voada, to cleanse his unease with blood and fury. But he shook his head. He wondered how much longer he could allow this to go on before he must have the bannermen signal retreat, have those who still lived fall back to Siran and let the Cateni claim the field.

We can't stay here much longer. This is already too costly. We've lost . . .

"Hold," Altan told Tolga. "Not yet. Wait . . ."

Wait . . . Altan hated the word even as he spoke it. He gripped the hilt of his sword, half pulling it from the scabbard.

Maol and Hùisdean drove Voada into the midst of the battle as she tried to cling to her outer vision against the wild storm of the anamacha's world. <*Now! We must be one!*>, the Moonshadow had roared as they rushed downslope toward the Mundoa, and nothing, nothing Voada did could hold back that presence. She tried to hold on to Iomhar, but his shade went falling back into the storms of Magh da Chèo, and there was only the Moonshadow before her, her wild presence wrapped in lightning and cloud, all the other souls trapped in her anamacha no more than faint shadows spiraling around her.

<*Join with me!*> she roared, and Voada had no choice. She opened her arms. She let the Moonshadow fill her.

The Moonshadow's massed voice shrieked in her ears, and her energy burned Voada as if she had swallowed the very sun. She made desperate patterns in the air to contain the power, her voice torn and hoarse as she chanted the words of the spells the Moonshadow fed her. She had to release the power quickly lest it consume her.

Voada was a bright, fiery, giant's sword, laying waste to the Mundoan soldiers around them, their dying cries faint against the tempest raging inside her. Even Maol had paused, lance in his hand, glancing back at her with awe as his chariot bucked and lurched over the ground, hooves and wheels pounding Mundoan dead into the earth. Her spells were weapons that scythed through the enemy, clearing a path before them, leading them ever deeper into the Mundoan ranks. They were past the first phalanx already, tearing into the reserves behind them, and through the bloody vision overlaying her eyes, Voada could see the hill where Savas waited with his banners.

This was unlike the few other times she'd been in battle as a draoi. Then she'd been in control; she'd taken time with each spell and crafted it as needed. Not now. What flooded into her from her anamacha was unfettered madness and fury and rage as Leagsaidh Moonshadow stepped fully from the shadows. The Moonshadow controlled her now, and Voada was simply a vessel through which that vast power flowed.

A vessel that was cracking and failing under the intense pressure of containing that force.

She couldn't do this much longer. The toll on her body was too great, and exhaustion threatened to send her pinwheeling, lost and terrified, entirely into the world of the anamacha. "Maol!" she called even as she felt the urge to release another spell, as demanding as the urge to push during childbirth. "I can't keep this up . . . I have to . . ."

From her hands, she disgorged another fireball that went careening over Hùisdean and the flattened ears of their horses, erupting as it reached the soldiers who were scrambling and fleeing away from them. Voada hung limply from the ropes holding her upright. She fought to stay conscious, fought to thrust the anamacha of the Moonshadow out of her, but she couldn't push the specter from her.

<No . . . You can't stop . . . We did that, and they killed us . . . >

"Rest, Voada," Maol Iosa shouted, his voice nearly lost against the interior din. "You've done enough."

<Not enough . . . Never enough . . . You'll die . . . You'll die . . . >

"Leave me!" she shouted to the Moonshadow's voice. She was sweating, her hair damp and darkened with it, and a fever burned within her. Her eyes wanted to roll back in her head. She clutched at the silver oak leaf around her neck as if it alone could hold her sanity. The real world was growing dim around her, and only Magh da Chèo seemed real to her; she could barely hear the screams of the wounded, the shouts of the warriors as they hewed down the Mundoa.

<You'll die . . . You'll die . . . You'll become part of us . . . One of us . . . > the other draoi in her anamacha shouted at her. There was almost an eagerness to the voices.

"No!" she shouted at that, and Maol jerked around to look at her.

"Ceanndraoi?" His voice was alarmed, but she couldn't find his face in her vision. Instead, the shapes of long-dead draoi were huddled around her, crowding her. She pushed them aside, but it was like swimming in mud. There was a glimpse of sunlight ahead of her, and in it were the sounds of battle. She lunged toward it desperately in her mind and found herself back in the living world again with the anamacha outside her for the moment. She gasped for air, her body wracked. She knew she shouldn't take them into her again, but she also knew that she must.

She must.

"I'll take you back to the wagons," Maol was saying, as if he heard her desperation, but she shook her head.

"No. You can't. We stay." The short bursts of words were all she could manage. "Win this," she told him. "Finish it."

Maol stared at her, then nodded. He plucked another spear from the rail and bellowed a challenge, shaking the spear toward the hill where they could see Savas' banner. "We're coming for you, Commander!" Maol Iosa bellowed. "You can't escape me! Hùisdean, forward!"

The chariot bucked as Hùisdean shouted commands to the horses from the traces. Àrd Mac Tsagairt's chariot carrying Magaidh turned to follow them, as did several mounted warriors and those on foot. They plunged into the opening Voada had created even as it threatened to close, pushing deep into the Mundoan lines. Soldiers before them either fled or were run down.

"They're ours!" Maol crowed. "Look at them running!"

At Voada and Maol Iosa's backs, they could hear horns blowing.

The lines were broken, and the Cateni kept coming: an endless, shrieking horde. Altan saw the phalanxes shiver and break, and heard the officers shouting at the men to "Hold! Hold!" Tolga was craning his head back over his shoulder, expecting Altan to enter the fray himself.

Retreat. We must retreat. This battle is lost.

Below him, Altan could see Iosa's chariot carrying the ceann-draoi, and he witnessed the terrible toll that the woman was taking with her spells. Nothing and no one was able to touch her. Iosa's war chariot moved in an untouchable bubble rimmed with fire and carpeted with Mundoan bodies and blood. More Cateni flowed into the gap the woman had made, all the way through the phalanxes and nearly to the bottom of the hill on which Altan stood watching. As the witch-woman sagged in exhaustion from her efforts, Iosa ripped a spear from the chariot and brandished it toward Altan. He shouted; Altan couldn't make out the words, but the challenge was obvious. Tolga recognized it as well, and again he glanced back at Altan.

It was what Altan wanted as well; it wasn't his preference to lead from behind. But he had another duty as commander: to tell his men to fall back, to save as many of them as he could so that they could fight another day.

As he opened his mouth to give the command, though, there was a blaring of horns from well up the slope and from the woods to the south, and the banners of Ilkur's cohorts emerged from the cover of the trees. Ilkur's cavalry came flowing out, lances held low, and slammed into the rear flank of the Cateni. These were the least trained of the Cateni, mostly young men and a few women who had left home to be with Voada's army, and Ilkur's soldiers sliced into them like a well-honed axe into a decaying tree trunk. Altan could see the immediate response from his troops as they noticed Ilkur's arrival. The Mundoan phalanxes rallied; the lines stiffened, the soldiers shouted with a new defiance and energy, and Altan's horns answered those of Ilkur. As for the Cateni, the spells of the draoi, whose deadly power had won the initial skirmishes, faltered as the spellcasters looked behind them. The Cateni war chariots, which had been about to storm the hill where Altan stood, halted to look behind.

Altan could sense the shift in the battle. *"Now!"* he shouted to Tolga, to the bannermen. "Send everyone forward. Now!" He pulled a spear from the railing of his chariot, holding it aloft. "Tolga, to Maol Iosa!" he roared.

He could hear the blood singing in his ears. He could taste change in the air. As the banners waved from the hilltop, Tolga leaped forward on the yoke, slapping the reins on the backs of the warhorses, and Altan's chariot rushed forward down the hill and into the center of the battle.

Suddenly, Elia turned away from them, and the landscape shifted. Voada could barely hold her head up by the time the chariot whipped around at the sound of the new threat behind them. All was confusion, and people were dying around her, Cateni and Mundoa alike. The warhorses were trampling foot soldiers who pressed hard around them—dark faces under armored helms with open mouths—and she saw a spear glance away from Maol's upraised shield, narrowly missing her.

Her eyelids were heavy, and every muscle of her body felt as if it had been pummeled. She could feel her anamacha nearby, and the thought of the Moonshadow entering her again made her sick and nauseated. She was weeping and didn't know why, the tears cold against her fevered skin.

"Voada!" Maol was shouting, loudly enough that she lifted her head and tried to focus on his face. "We need you! A spell . . ."

"I can't . . ." she said. Her voice seemed a whisper against the uproar of the battle. She shook her head. *I can't do any more. All I wanted was to have my children back, and all the lives I've taken in revenge for what was done to us have given me nothing. Nothing. I can't do this anymore. It's not what I want any longer. Fight if you must, but do it without me. Just let me sleep . . .*

She wondered whether she'd said the words or only thought them.

<Give yourself to us . . . >

She felt the cold press against her spine as her anamacha entered her without invitation, invading her body. The Moonshadow loomed like a thunderhead before her. "No . . ." she tried to say, trying to refuse them, but they slid inward, the black curtains of their storm-wracked world flowing into in her mind and over-shadowing her vision of the battle.

<You're lost if you don't give yourself to us . . . To me . . . >

"No," she said again, but the word was weak and powerless, and she felt the Moonshadow driving deep into her. Lightning crackled, and she saw herself *as* the Moonshadow, cloaked in energy and power. Voada's mouth opened, her hands began to move of their own volition in the pattern of a spell, and the channeling words spilled out of her, but someone else had taken control of her voice. She could feel the fire flowing through her veins once more, burning her from the inside but bringing her head up and forcing her to stand tall in the chariot. She was a puppet, part of her simply watching as her hands cupped the spell and the chant ended. She released the spell, heard it hiss and flare outward to rip into the Mundoan troops in front of her. Maol shouted, lifting his bloodied spear in response. Their chariot sped forward into the hole with Àrd Mac Tsagairt and Magaidh's chariot behind it, now heading back up the slope toward the new threat to their flank.

<We will do this . . . We will do this together . . . >

Voada couldn't even protest. She had no voice, had no control of her own body. Her hands began to weave the air once more; her voice spoke words she didn't understand. The world of the anamacha was all she saw, and she lived in the center of that storm. Her body was a rag torn and shredded by a hurricane, holding desperately to life. Again, the Moonshadow and the other draoi around her filled Voada. It was as if she were alight with their power, their energy glaring through her skin as if it were paper, her bones casting long shadows into the anamacha's world. She could not hold a spell so potent, couldn't bear the pain as it ripped outward in fire and wind, indiscriminate and uncontrolled, destroying Cateni and Mundoa alike who stood before them.

"Voada, what are you doing?" Maol shouted at her, his face a rictus of battle-fury. She couldn't answer. Her vision was dark, her body sagging and failing even as the anamacha started to fill her once again.

<We will do this . . . >

She could hear someone shouting from behind them, and in the confusion that was her vision she saw Maol looking back over his shoulder and pointing. Hùisdean turned the chariot hard, sending Voada slamming into the rail even in her bonds. The Moonshadow shrieked in response, and again Voada found herself helplessly taking in the energy. The chariot shuddered around her; she saw Maol grab a new spear and cast it, then grab for another.

Time seemed to have slowed. Voada managed to turn her head even as she desperately tried to weave the spell. She saw Savas in his chariot behind them, saw him deflect with his shield the spear Maol had flung and throw his own. She saw the weapon hurtling through the air—not toward Maol, but toward her. Maol saw it as well; he lunged toward Voada with this shield out, but the spear had already struck.

Voada felt a searing, jarring pain in her abdomen that sent the half woven spell spilling uselessly into the sky, a fountain that rained sparks and flame. She grunted, tasting salt in her mouth, the end of the spear jutting from her body. The voices of the ana-macha wailed; she felt their world slip away from her even as she heard Maol cry out when a second spear from Savas sent him sprawling onto the floor of the chariot. Hùisdean screamed at the warhorses, and the chariot swerved sharply once more as Voada's eyesight narrowed and closed in. Everything went black and silent around her as the world faded.

33

A Shattered Moon

MAGAIDH STROKED VOADA'S FOREHEAD with a cool cloth. She half expected the cloth to steam, considering the heat that radiated from Voada's fevered body. The archiater her husband Comhnall had sent was seated on the other side of Voada, shaking her head, and an elderly menach muttered prayers to Elia. Comhnall stood behind Magaidh, silent and still attired in his bloody, dented armor, his face grim and solemn. Voada stirred, her eyes fluttering open to stare up at the night sky. "Magaidh . . ." she breathed. Her eyes rolled back, showing white, and Magaidh thought she'd lost Voada, but then the ceanndraoi blinked and her gaze returned. "Where . . . ?"

"We're in the woods to the north of the road, Ceanndraoi. Comhnall has taken charge of the clans and those warriors we have left. We're safe for now."

"Ceannàrd Maol?"

"Dead," Magaidh said flatly. She glanced up at Comhnall. "Hùisdean drove your chariot from the field, but the ceannàrd was already dead by the time we were able to stop our retreat. We left many of the people of the clans on the field, Ceanndraoi. Too many."

"I'm sorry . . ." Voada breathed. "It's my fault . . . I couldn't hold her . . . I'm so sorry . . ."

Magaidh could hear the rattle in her breath, could see how the thick cloth bandage around the woman's waist, changed not half a stripe ago, was again soaked with blood despite the ministrations of the archiater. Voada's anamacha stood near them, watching, though neither the healer nor Comhnall noticed or felt its presence. Magaidh's own anamacha watched as well from her side. Her anamacha had been no help; Magaidh had called it to her when they'd stopped to tend to Voada, and she'd pleaded for those draoi inside to give her a spell that could heal Voada's terrible wound, but they had only laughed sadly at her.

<There are no spells for that . . . Healing is not a gift any draoi has . . . None of us can help you with this . . . >

"You've nothing to be sorry about, Ceanndraoi." Magaidh glanced at the fires in the woods behind Comhnall: nowhere near as numerous as they should be, though at least Savas hadn't pursued them far after their retreat from the battle. The Mundoa had suffered tremendous losses as well and had drawn back to lick their own wounds.

The battle had not been a victory for either side.

"Àrd Comhnall is leading us back across the Meadham into the Albann Bràghad, where we'll be safe and can recover," she said to Voada. The cloth on Voada's head already felt hot, and she dipped it again in the basin of spring water the healer had brought, dabbing at the sweat on Voada's pain-wracked face. "You accomplished so much, Ceanndraoi, and I'll always be grateful to you for what you taught me."

Voada coughed, her spittle leaving her mouth flecked with blood, and Magaidh wiped the woman's dry, cracked lips. "It wasn't me, not at the end. The Moonshadow . . ."

"I know," Magaidh told her. "I know. I felt that. I've felt her closeness to you ever since Pencraig."

"Pencraig . . ." The word was a sigh. "I failed, Magaidh. I failed Meir. I failed Orla and Hakan. I failed you and Comhnall and

Maol. I failed everyone. I failed Elia most of all. I thought I knew what She wanted of me . . ."

"You failed no one," Magaidh crooned to her. "That's not true, Ceanndraoi. You did so much."

"This wasn't failure, Ceanndraoi," Comhnall added, his voice low and graveled. "You've brought glory and honor to all the clans. The bards will sing songs about you forever."

Voada's hand lifted and clutched at Magaidh's, her skin nearly as hot as the fire crackling nearby. Voada's eyes pleaded as she lifted her head from the ground, as her desperate voice grated out the words. "Magaidh, you have to find her for me. Find Orla. Tell her what happened. Tell her I tried to find her . . . that I loved her . . . that . . ." Voada sank back, her hand loosening around Magaidh's and going to her own throat. She plucked at the leather thong there, lifting it so that the silver oak leaf at the end glittered in the firelight. The rattle in her throat grew louder as she spoke again, and blood stained her lips. "Give Orla this . . . Tell her for me . . ."

Voada's eyes fluttered closed, though she still held the pendant loosely in her hand. Magaidh bent over her, closing Voada's hand around the pendant with her fingers. The menach's prayers grew louder. "I'll find her," she promised Voada, glancing up at Comhnall and wondering even as she spoke the words how she would keep that oath. "I'll find her, and I'll give her the oak leaf, and I'll tell her how her mother inspired all Cateni to rise up with her and how she very nearly drove the Mundoa out of our land. I'll tell her everything so she knows you and knows how you came back for her and how you loved her. She will never forget you, Ceanndraoi. Never. None of us will forget you . . ."

In the midst of Magaidh's oath, Voada's anamacha had glided closer to Voada's prone body. Now it stood directly beside her, the faces of the draoi within flitting over its visage. Magaidh realized that Voada hadn't taken another breath, that her chest was still and the hand Magaidh held was limp. The menach began the prayer for the dead, the archiater sighed, and Comhnall threw his head back and roared his grief to the night.

Around them, the other Cateni in the encampment took up the cry of mourning.

Magaidh saw Voada's taibhse rise from her body as the Moonshadow's anamacha spread its arms, the same gesture that Magaidh herself made when bringing her anamacha into her. Voada's taibhse ignored everything around it except for the anamacha, flying swiftly toward its embrace. The anamacha enfolded the taibhse in its arms, and for a breath, Magaidh saw Voada's features on the anamacha's face. Then they were gone, and the anamacha turned and swiftly began to move away. Magaidh watched them go, vanishing into the darkness and moving northward with some purpose of their own. She wondered where they were going and whether she would ever encounter them again.

Magaidh lowered Voada's hand softly to her body, then gently lifted the ceanndraoi's head to slip the necklace from her neck. The silver oak leaf shone in the palm of Magaidh's hand, and she placed it in the pouch on her belt. "I'll find her," she whispered to the empty body, then rose to her feet.

"Wrap the ceanndraoi's body carefully," she told the archiater and the menach. "We will bring her with us until we cross the Meadham, then we'll give the body to the cleansing fire. We'll remember her as we watch the flames take her. She hasn't left us, for her taibhse has gone with the Moonshadow's anamacha."

Magaidh looked down at Voada's face, serene and still. "She will return to us," Magaidh said. "She will always be here for us."

THE GHOST'S CLOSING SOLILOQUY

WE ARE HAND AFTER hand of souls, not merely one. We are Iomhar of the Marsh. We are Leagsaidh Moonshadow. We are Voada the Avenger. We are many, and in time we will be many more.

We recall our names again, lost for so long . . . We remember the oath we took so long ago.

We are the fiery spear of the Cateni, and our task is not yet done.

Perhaps we chose wrongly when we awoke from our slumber . . . Perhaps we should have taken the daughter, not the mother, as the stronger of the two. Almost, we did that.

Orla . . . yes, that is the new name that calls to us . . .

Orla. . . .

We will search, and we will find her, and we—all of us—will make her what she can be . . . what she *must* be.

We are coming to her. We are coming . . .

CHARACTERS
(in order of appearance)

PART ONE:

Voada Paorach (Voh-AH-dah POO-rahk)	Protagonist of the novel. Wife of Meir and Hand-wife of Pencraig.
Pashtuk (PASH-took)	Emperor of the Mundoa
Elia (Eh-LEE-ah)	The sun goddess of the Cateni
Ailis (AY-less)	Voada's seanmhair (grandmother)
Meir Paorach (MEER POO-rahk)	Husband of Voada and Hand of Pencraig
Orla (OAR-lah)	Voada and Meir's daughter
Dilara (Deh-LAR-ah)	Voice-wife of Pencraig, wife of Kadir
Maki Kadir (Mah-KEE Kah-DEER)	Voice of the village Pencraig, husband of Dilara
Hakan (Hah-KHAN)	Voada and Meir's son
Bakir (Bah-KEER)	Head of Pencraig's military garrison
Una (OO-nah)	Voada and Meir's house servant, in charge of the children

Fermac (FERR-mack)	Meir and Voada's dog
Boann (BOO-ahn)	The Voice's archiater (physician), an elder Cateni woman
Ina (EE-na)	Voada's mother, Orla and Hakan's grandmother
Doruk (DOHR-Uk)	Son of a local merchant who admires Orla
Altan Savas (ALL-tan SAH-vahs)	Mundoan commander in charge of the war against the northern tribes
Tamar (Tah-MAHR)	The "One-Eye." Leader of a failed rebellion by the northern Cateni tribes.
Lucian (LOO-shin)	Commander Savas' chariot driver
Ceiteag (Kay-tig)	A female draoi and menach in the village
Seor (SOAR)	A man in the village
Anabia (Ah-NAH-bia)	A woman in the village
Isbeil (ISS-beal)	A woman in the village

PART TWO:

Vadim III (Vah-DEEM)	The Great-Voice of Trusa
Beris	Emperor of Mundoa when its armies conquered the Cateni tribes south of the River Meadham. His reign was followed by that of his son, Emperor Hayat, then by the brief reign of Hayat's daughter, Empress Damla, who was deposed and executed by the current Emperor Pashtuk.

Greum (GRAY-umm)	The ceanndraoi, or head mage, of Onglse. Known as "Red-Hand."
Bella (BELL-ah)	One of Lucian's warhorses
Ardis (AHR-diss)	One of Lucian's warhorses
Bora (BORE-ah)	One of Lucian's warhorses
Jika (JEE-kah)	One of Lucian's warhorses
Ilkur (ILL-curr)	An officer in the Mundoan army, one of Altan Savas' sub-commanders
Musa (MOO-sah)	An officer in the Mundoan army, one of Altan Savas' sub-commanders
Conn (KAHN)	A male draoi
Leagsaidh (LEGK-see)	
Moonshadow	A long-dead draoi famous in Cateni history
Marta (MARR-tah)	A female draoi
Daibhidh (DYE-vee)	A draoi on Onglse
Iomhar (EYE-oh-var)	Also known as Iomhar of the Marsh, the ceanndraoi of the Cateni at the time of the initial invasion of the Mundoa, killed in the battle of Íseal Head.
Maol Iosa (MAHL EE-sah)	A warrior of the Cateni in Onglse
Haidar (HAY-durr)	An officer in the Mundoan army, one of Altan Savas' sub-commanders
Cumhur (COOM-harr)	An officer in the Mundoan army, one of Altan Savas' sub-commanders
Volkan (VOLL-kahn)	An officer in the Mundoan army, one of Altan Savas' sub-commanders

Tolga (TOLL-gah)	Driver for Altan Savas, replacing Lucian after his death
Tadgh (TAHD)	Driver for Maol Iosa
Comhnall Mac Tsagairt (CAHN-ull Mack TAG-gert)	Àrd (head) of Clan Mac Tsagairt
Magaidh Mac Tsagairt (MAH-ghee Mack TAG-gert)	Wife of Comhnall Mac Tsagairt

PART THREE:

Tormod (TORR-mahd)	A young draoi of the clans
Hùisdean (OOS-den)	Eldest son of Comhnall Mac Tsagairt, stepson of Magaidh Mac Tsagairt
Adem Nabi (A-DEM NAH-bee)	First officer of the Mundoan garrison at Pencraig
Cemal (Keh-MAHL)	Sub-commander of the Trusa garrison
Labhrann MacÀidh (LAW-renn MacKAY)	A farmer in Albann Deas, leader of a rebellious group

TERMS AND PLACE NAMES (in alphabetical order)

Albann Bràghad (AHL-pahn BRAWK-ahd)	The Cateni name for the region north of the River Meadham. The "r" must be rolled.
Albann Deas (AHL-pahn Deesh)	The southern portion of Bhreatain, below the River Meadham
Anamacha (Ah-nah-MAHK-ah)	Literally a collection of souls—the manifested ghosts of dead draoi who

are the channels through which the living draoi gain their power.

Anail (AH-nahl)

Gust or gale

Archiater (ARK-ee-ate-err)

The title for the physician responsible for treating the head of a village or town

Àrd (ARHD)

"Head"—the leader of a clan, group, or place among the Cateni

Bàn Cill (Bahn Keel)

The sacred temple of the Cateni on Onglse. This is where the draoi are trained and where they gather.

Barrier Sea

The channel between the island of the Cateni and the mainland

Beinn (BANE) Head

A headland on the west coast of Al-bann Brághad, north of Onglse

Buharkent (Boo-ARK-ent)

A Mundoan city in Rumeli

Carnyx (KAR-nix)

A bronze trumpet often shaped like the head and elongated neck of a horse or snake, held upright and blown in battle. Creates a raucous and loud sound. Used by the Cateni.

Cateni (Kaw-TEHN-ee)

The collective name for the natives of the island, such as Voada, though there are innumerable sub-tribes or clans.

Ceannàrd (KEY-ohn-ard)

Literally "high chief"—the title for a clan leader or military commander among the Cateni.

Ceanndraoi (KEY-ohn-dree)

The head draoi of the tribes, usually based in Onglse, where the draoi are largely trained.

Clan Mac Tsagairt (Klahn Mack TAG-gert)	One of the northern clans in Albann Bràghad
Cohort	A small subdivision of the Mundoan army, usually consisting of five hundred soldiers or fewer.
Darende (DAHR-ren-dah)	A town on the southwest coast of Albann Deas
Doineann (DEN-yunn)	Hurricane
Draoi (Dree)	The Cateni term for those who are able to use magic
Elia's lamp	The sun
Fidhcheall (Fee-kyuhl)	An ancient form of chess
Great North Road	The road leading north out of Trusa toward Muras and the River Meadham
Gray Wraith	A howling, shrieking ghost in Cateni mythology who sometimes visits people to announce their impending deaths.
Gediz (Geh-DIZZ)	A town on the west coast of Albann Deas
Great-Voice	The Voice over all Voices on the island. He lives in Trusa, the Mundoan capital city.
Great North Road	The road that runs roughly north from Ìseal in the south, through the capital of Trusa, and to Muras on the River Meadham. It crosses the Meadham but ends not far into Albann Bràghad.

Hand	The person responsible for collecting taxes for Mundoa in a town or city. His spouse is called the Hand-wife. Often both are local Cateni.
Ìseal (Eh-SEAL)	A harbor town on Ìseal Head
Ìseal Head	Location of the first battle with the Mundoa at the Barrier Sea
Ismil (ISS-meel)	A town in Albann Deas
R. Iska (ISS-Kah)	The long and wide river on the banks of which sits the capital city, Trusa (Iskameath)
Kavak (Kah-VAK)	A major coastal city in Rumeli
Koruk (KOHR-uck)	A major city in Rumeli
Krug (Kroog)	The "mirror armor" of the Mundoan army officers
Lack-breath	Asthma or shortness of breath
Ladik (Lah-DEEK)	A town in Albann Deas
Léine (LANE-ah)	A long close-fitting smock worn by the northern clans
Magh da Chèo (Mah dah KEE-oh)	The Otherworld of the anamacha—literally, Plain of Mists
Menach (MEHN-Ock)	Title for a cleric of Elia
R. Meadham (MEER-ahn)	For pronunciation, the consonant "dh" sounds like a rolled "r" that is almost a guttural "g." The River Meadham is the central river of the island, roughly dividing the more mountainous north (Bràghad Albann) from the more gently rolling southern landscape (Deas Albann).

Moon-time	Menstrual period. The herbs rue and shepherd's purse are used to ease the cramping and bleeding.
Mundoa (Muhn-DOH-ah)	The empire of the southern mainland or the people thereof
Mundoci (Muhn-DOH-kee)	The capital city of the empire
Muras (Murh-ahs)	A town on the River Meadham where the river is bridged
Onglse (ON-gul-see)	The island fastness of the draoi
One-God, the	The official deity of the Mundoan Empire; the emperor is the One-God's representative in this world.
Pamukkale (PAH-moo-kale)	The Mundoan mythological hell
Pencraig (PENN-craygh)	The town where Voada and Meir live
Rumeli (Roo-MELL-ee)	The continent; the land of the Mundoa, where they have established their empire.
Sarilar (SAHR-eh-larr)	A coastal city in Rumeli
Savur (SAH-voor)	A town on the east coast of Albann Deas
Sea of Serpents	The sea to the east of Bhreatain—it extends well west until it meets the main continent again.
Seanmhair (SHUNN-eh-vah)	Grandmother
Sihirki (Suh-HERE-kee)	The Mundoan term for those who are able to use magic
Siran (SEER-ehn)	A town in Albann Deas

R. Slaodach (SLAHL-dack)	A river that flows into Gediz Bay
Storm Sea	The ocean to the west of Bhreatain—an endless ocean, as far as the Cateni or Mundoa know.
Stormwind Road	The road from Gediz on the west coast to Pencraig in the east
Sun-path	The line described by the dawn of the summer solstice and the sunset of the winter solstice or the dawn of the winter solstice and the sunset of the summer solstice. It is believed that the Cateni dead must walk one of those two paths in order to ascend to the next plane of existence.
Taibhse (TIE-sha)	Cateni word for spirit or ghost (plural: taibhsean (TIE-chan)).
Teine (TCHEE-na)	Fire
Tirnanog (TIR-nah-nog)	The Otherworld of the Cateni—the land of the gods and the spirits
Trusa (TROO-SAH)	Capital city of the Mundoa (Cateni name: Iskameath).
Uisge (OOSH-kah)	Water
Velimese (VELL-eh-mees)	A town in Albann Deas
Voice	The person representing the Emperor/Mundoan authorities in a town or city. His spouse is called the Voice-wife. The Voice is universally someone of Mundoan origin.

R. Yarrow (YAH-roh)

The river that runs past Pencraig. The River Yarrow's source is Loch Yarrow, and it feeds into the greater River Meadham.

Var (VARH)

A town on the southern coast of Albann Deas

Zar atmak (Zahr AT-mack)

A Mundoan game of chance that uses six-sided dice

Acknowledgments & Notes

Special thanks to . . .

- Denise Parsley Leigh, the only person upon whom I inflict my first drafts, for her insightful (and gently blunt) comments. Denise, you shape every story I write as you've also helped to shape my life. I love you.
- Sheila Gilbert, who brought me into the DAW family and whose editorship of my last several novels and friendship in general have been true gifts. Sheila (as I've said before) relentlessly makes certain that each of my books has been as good as I could possibly make it at the time, and for that she has my endless gratitude. Sheila is more than just an editor; she is also a mentor and friend. And hey, she's now a Hugo Award-winning editor, too—a well-deserved accomplishment!
- My beta readers, who have given me invaluable input. You've all made your mark on this novel: Hania Wojtowicz, Alex Duvall, Don Wenzel, Anne Evans, and a very special shout-out to David Perry, who gave me his usual detailed and insightful critique of the second draft of this book.

Notes:

- **This book is fiction, not history.** Yes, as I'm sure the vast majority of readers figured out during the first few chapters, the world of *A Fading Sun* is loosely based on Roman Britain of the first century C.E. and the rebellion of Boudica. Very—no, *extremely*—loosely based. The landscape is imaginary, the Mundoan culture is emphatically (and deliberately) *not* Roman—it's more Ottoman than anything else—and I've not allowed historical facts to stand in the way of how I've portrayed the Cateni/Celtic culture and Voada/Boudica. And of course, there's genuine magic in this world as well. In no way was this novel an attempt at writing a genuine historical novel or alternate history. I simply plucked a few details from history in order to set up what I wanted to examine and wrapped an imagined world around that framework.

Books read as research for this novel:

- Tacitus. *Annals* (Loeb Classical Library). Translated by John Jackson. New York: Harvard University Press, 1937. I was especially interested in book XIV, chapters 29–39, which cover Boudica's revolt in Britain. The speech that Voada gives to the Cateni just before the final battle is a paraphrase of the words that Tacitus puts in Boudica's mouth in *Annals, book XIV, chapter 35*, but given that Tacitus wrote *Annals* half a century after the actual event, it's highly unlikely that Boudica actually said any of those words.
- Hingley, Richard and Christina Unwin. *Boudica: Iron Age Warrior Queen*. London: Bloomsbury, 2005. This is an interesting study of Boudica that examines the various ways she's been imagined, presented, and used symbolically from the time of the Romans through to the present day. The historical Boudica has been forced to represent many agendas throughout history, not all of them complimentary and certainly few of them accurate. In *A Fading Sun*, she wears a mask of my own making, and it's as false as any of the others.

- Robb, Graham. *The Discovery of Middle Earth: Mapping the Lost World of the Celts.* New York: W. W. Norton & Company, Inc., 2013. The author's contention is that the Celts deliberately and knowingly mapped out their kingdoms in now-lost precise straight lines aligned to the solstices and compass points and that important locations were often found at the intersections of those lines. Frankly, I felt Mr. Robb's arguments were hazy, tenuous, and ultimately unconvincing; take any sufficient collection of random dots on a page, and you'll be able to connect several dots with a straight line. But that didn't stop me from borrowing a few concepts . . .
- Curriculum Development Unit. *Celtic Way of Life.* Dublin: O'Brien Press, 2000. This slim volume concentrates (unsurprisingly, given the publisher) on Celtic tribes in Ireland. Rather scant on details or references to source material, but still a decent overview.
- As usual, I also prowled the Internet for articles and information as needed during the writing of this book, far too many sites to list or even to remember at this point. The Web is a wonderful resource and tool. I'm old enough to have written stories and novels before the answers to questions could be found with a quick googling, and I am grateful that the Web is there for all writers.